Maybe This Time
Stand By You

Getting It Right
Finding Their Way
Taking a Chance

Come What May
Say It Right
As I Am

Wild Trail
Roped In
Saddle Up
Lucky Break
Hard Ride
Right Move

Also available from A.M. Arthur

Cost of Repairs
Color of Grace
Weight of Silence
Acts of Faith
Foundation of Trust

The Truth As He Knows It
The World As He Sees It
The Heart As He Hears It
Their Life As They Live It
His Faith As He Finds It

Here For Us
Sound of Us
Uniquely Us
Heart of Us

Body Rocks
Steady Stroke
Hot Licks

Unearthing Cole
Understanding Jeremy
Uniting Hearts

Fractured Hymns
What You Own
What You Make It

Melting For You
Burning For You
Waiting For You
Believing In You

Saved
Seen
Heard
Stronger
Found
Whole
Feel
Claimed
Loved

Save Me
See Me
Hear Me
Find Me
Hold Me
Feel Me

Prodigal
Frozen
Chosen

HIS FRESH START COWBOY

A.M. ARTHUR

carina
press

carina
press®

Recycling programs
for this product may
not exist in your area.

ISBN-13: 978-1-335-44867-5

His Fresh Start Cowboy

Copyright © 2022 by A.M. Arthur

For questions and comments about the quality of this book,
please contact us at CustomerService@Harlequin.com.

Carina Press
22 Adelaide St. West, 41st Floor
Toronto, Ontario M5H 4E3, Canada
www.CarinaPress.com

Printed in U.S.A.

HIS FRESH START COWBOY

Chapter One

"That really sucks, man, I'm sorry to hear that."

Hugo Turner had just sat down at the long kitchen table with his dinner when that particular comment rose from the din of general conversation in the room. He'd chosen a spot in the middle so he could chat with his fellow Clean Slate Ranch horsemen, but now he looked up from his plate of meat loaf and mashed potatoes. The statement had come from Ernie and been said to Colt, both men older and more experienced than Hugo in, well, pretty much everything.

Except horses. Hugo had been around horses most of his life, and he loved working with them every day here at the ranch.

"What sucks?" Hugo asked, unable to help himself. He was the youngest horseman on the ranch, despite having just turned twenty-seven, and sometimes he struggled to really connect with his coworkers. Showing genuine interest in their lives was always a great in, right?

Colt sighed and poked at his own meat loaf. He was a handyman on the dude ranch/vacation spot, rather than a horseman. "Talked to my parents this afternoon. My father's having trouble getting new hands, and Brand is worried that their shift to organic, grass-fed beef is going to fail because they don't have enough people to run the operation."

"Oh, wow, that sucks." While Hugo had left the cattle ranching life a long time ago, he'd grown up on a ranch that failed when Hugo was ten. During his parents' messy divorce, they'd sold the last of their herd and some equipment to Wayne Woods. Small- and medium-sized ranchers were suffering all over the country because of corporate operations, and he was honestly impressed Woods Cattle Ranch was still in business. Especially with the neighboring towns of Weston and Daisy offering few prospects for new families moving to the area.

Families like the one Hugo hadn't gone home to see in years; friends he hadn't seen in years; teenage crushes he hadn't seen in years, except from a careful distance. When the entire Woods family came up to the ranch for Colt's wedding two years ago, avoiding them had turned into an art form for Hugo, helped along by his cowboy hat and allowing a bit of a beard to grow out. A beard he'd shaved off the day they left. He simply hadn't wanted to mix his new life up with his past in Texas. A past Colt didn't know about yet.

"Yeah," Colt said. "Dad and Brand are putting their heads together, but it's not an easy lifestyle, especially if you aren't born into it."

"I know." Off Colt's curious eyebrow quirk, Hugo scrambled to correct his comment. "I mean, I can imagine. I've, ah, heard stories."

After being hired at Clean Slate two and a half years ago, it had taken Hugo a few days to realize Colt Woods was the older brother of his high school best friend,

Remington "Rem" Woods. Colt had run away from home at eighteen, years before Rem and Hugo became friends, so Hugo hadn't had any clear memories of him. And when Hugo realized he and Colt had grown up in neighboring towns, he'd kept it to himself, not wanting to trot down that particular stretch of memory lane.

He'd left Texas for a reason, damn it.

"Your family thinking of selling out?" Ernie asked, then shoveled a fork of steamed green beans into his mouth.

"I hope not but it's a possibility," Colt replied. "Our family has worked that land for generations, and I'd hate to see them sell. It's why Brand is making some changes to their operations, hoping to hang on a while longer. Seems to be having good luck with the wind farm in the south pasture, but he's banking on the organic beef."

"It's a big thing in the larger cities. Not that I can taste the difference. A steak is a steak to me."

Several other guys at the table who were listening "hear, hear-ed" the comment. Hugo smiled and ate his food. This was very much a beef-consuming lot of horsemen, as were their weekly groups of guests. Every Sunday night, they held a welcome barbecue, and most dinners (for hands and guests) featured some sort of red meat.

As he ate, Hugo's mind whirred with all kinds of thoughts about the small Texas county he'd abandoned years ago, heading out on his own to seek…something. A different path, something that excited him more than a part-time job at the local grocery store. And that took him away from the humiliation that had been his first attempted kiss with another boy.

Far, far away from the walking wet dream that had been Brand Woods.

Hugo wasn't ashamed to admit—to himself but not out loud—that after realizing who Colt was, he'd done a social media search on Brand. Hugo had once fallen head over heels for Brand, a tall, well-built blond who was eight years older than him and about to leave for college the first time they'd met. The latest pictures of Brand showed him to be a near carbon copy of Colt, but while Hugo could admire Colt's aesthetic, he didn't excite Hugo the way Brand always had.

Only Brand had ever made Hugo want to roll over and beg. And only Brand had ever broken Hugo's heart.

He finished his dinner in a slight daze, born of old memories and hurts, and he put his plate and glass in the bus bin by rote. Headed out into the dark, late winter night on a familiar trek back to his cabin. Most of the hands lived in small, two-man cabins behind the ranch's main house, and a well-trodden path led him forward. Hugo's roommate, Winston, wasn't there, which was fine, because he wasn't in a chatty mood for a change. His first roommate, Slater, had been quiet to the extreme, avoiding all of Hugo's attempts at communication and friendship for months. But Slater had moved on from Clean Slate, and Winston had been his replacement, both as a horseman on the ranch and Hugo's roomie.

Normally, he adored Winston's ability to chat about anything. Tonight, he was grateful for the chance to sit on his bunk and think. Think about the people he missed and the potential next stop on his wanderlust journey to find what his heart truly desired. Because as much as he enjoyed his work here with the horses and guests, this wasn't his final destination. It was a way station on the path to where he was meant to be.

What if I'm meant to be back home?

It wasn't the first time in the last few years that he'd wondered such a thing. He loved discovering the States and learning new things, but so much of his heart was at home in Daisy, Texas, a one-stoplight town ten miles from Weston. He missed his mom and her comforting, if infrequent, hugs. Leaving her behind was one of his biggest regrets. They didn't speak often, but when they did she sounded happy. Seemed happy that he was far, far away from what had happened with Buck.

But Buck was cooling his heels in state prison for felony assault charges. His temper had finally gotten the better of him and landed him in a locked cage where he belonged. Hugo had contemplated going home this past Christmas, because he knew he'd be safe, but in the end had remained here as part of the ranch's skeleton crew.

He'd stayed away for years, and now he was actually contemplating going back to work and live there. He could catch up with Rem again. Hug his mother. Maybe give Woods Ranch the boost it sounded like it needed. Hugo knew ranching, and he was great on a horse. Maybe he could do something bigger than oversee camping trips and teaching city folk how to ride a horse.

Hugo had his phone out before he really thought about it, and he found the website for Woods Ranch. The background image was a picture of Brand, Rem and their father, all posing next to an impressively large steer. He studied Brand's face, still able to feel the pressure of Brand's lips on his the first and only time they'd kissed. Brand was still gorgeous after all these years—

and according to Colt, single and seemingly uninterested in dating.

No, he couldn't let himself think too hard about that. He found the *Join Our Family* link and uploaded his résumé before he could stop himself. Brand would probably see his name and delete it, but Hugo had done it. No going back now. And it wasn't as if he had to accept the job on the off chance one was even offered.

Nah, he'd done it as a lark. He had friends here at Clean Slate—sort of, since the guys closest to his age all worked at the neighboring ghost town attraction—and a life he liked. Going back to Texas was idiotic.

Except the next day, Hugo checked his cell phone at lunchtime and found a message from Wayne Woods requesting a phone interview. Not from Brand but from his father. Hugo returned the man's call. Wayne actually remembered him as one of Rem's best friends in high school, and when Hugo talked about working with Colt and his own duties at the ranch, Wayne offered him a job on the spot. As soon as he could give notice and move back to Texas. Wayne even had a lead on a trailer Hugo could rent that neighbored the Woods property.

The entire thing happened so fast Hugo spent the rest of his lunch hour staring at the side of the guesthouse, unable to form a proper thought. His cheeks were half-frozen from the February chill but he didn't care. Had he really just accepted a job back in his home state? Had he committed to leaving a job he enjoyed and coworkers he liked for grueling long days under the hot Texas sun?

Would he really be around Brand again?

He was still staring blankly at the guesthouse wall when Colt approached, his brow creased. "Hey, dude, uh, can I ask you something?"

Hugo saw it coming but still nodded. "Sure."

"Were you ever gonna tell me you knew Rem? And me?"

Heat crept across Hugo's neck and cheeks, and he turned to face the older, taller man. "I never really saw the point in mentioning the past. I mean, we didn't really know each other at all. I did know Rem, though. And Brand and your sisters. But all that happened after you left."

Colt frowned at him while his left thumb twirled the gold band on his wedding finger. He'd married the love of his life not quite two years ago, and the pair somehow managed to make a long-distance relationship work, with Colt living here and his husband living an hour away in San Francisco. "You still could have said something when you realized who I was. Can't say as I remember a family named Turner from back then, though."

"Turner is my mom's maiden name. When my parents divorced, we both took it back, and even after she remarried, I kept it. Never did like my stepfather's name. Plus, we lived in Daisy."

"I vaguely recall my father buying cattle from a failing ranch in Daisy not long before I left. Was that you?"

"Yeah. Well, my parents. My mother inherited the ranch, but they went through a bad patch of hoof rot. Didn't treat it right. Money went south and so did their relationship. Everything got divvied up in the divorce."

"Sorry to hear that. It's a big kick in the head that we both ended up here, though, huh? What are the odds?"

"Pretty slim. But I've heard some of the other guys say there's something magical about Clean Slate. It brings people here when they're meant to be, for whatever reason. I, uh…" Hugo took a deep breath, held it, then released. "I applied to work at your family's ranch. Your father offered me a job."

Colt's eyes went comically wide. "You're shitting me. Really? I mean, he called me this morning and mentioned he'd gotten an application from a guy named Hugo Turner who worked here, and he asked me for a personal reference on your working habits. But he didn't mention he'd offered you the job."

"That's because it just happened. I honestly didn't expect anything to come out of it. I love it here. Arthur and Judson have been great, and I've learned a lot since I've worked here, but now I feel as if I have unfinished business back in Texas." No way was he going to admit part of that business included a never-ending crush on one of Colt's younger brothers. "I didn't leave on good terms with a lot of people. I kind of want to fix that."

"You don't have to leave the ranch to fix old hurts. When's your next week off?"

Hugo shook his head. All the hands got a week's vacation on a rotating basis throughout the year, but he'd never used his to go home. He rarely went much of anywhere, because everything he needed was at the ranch. Or so he'd thought. "I like this job a lot, Colt, but this isn't the end of the road for me. I'm only twenty-seven. I've got a lot of miles left to travel, and if those miles take me back home for a bit, I'm okay with that."

More than any other time since he'd left home, Hugo truly was okay with going back. With facing his past and all the ugly parts he'd tried to leave behind.

"Well, I can't say I won't miss you," Colt said. "You always were an easy mark on poker night."

Hugo laughed. Genuine laughter, because he did kind

of suck at cards, and because Colt was just teasing him. The big, blond cowboy didn't have a mean bone in his body—much like his younger brother Brand. "You aren't wrong about that. I'll miss poker nights. And I'll miss our group visits in San Francisco to hang out with Slater and Derrick. I'll miss a lot of things, but the more I sit with it, the more this move feels right."

"Then go with your gut, pal. And hey, I'll see you next time Avery and I go home to visit my family. I'll bring you all the juiciest gossip."

"I'll hold you to that." Hugo wasn't much of a gossip himself, but he definitely wanted to know what was up with the friends he was leaving behind. "I guess I should find my courage and go tell Judson I'm resigning. Give him time to hire a replacement."

"I imagine it's easier for Judson to find new hires than it is for my father. Ranching is a bit more complicated than leading trail rides and camping trips for tourists. You sure you're up for that life?"

"Yes." Hugo stood a bit straighter. "I grew up on a ranch, and my stepfather still works for a local CSA. I got my first paid job there when I was fifteen, so I know hard work. I know cattle and horses. I've got a lot of metaphorical fences that need tending back in Texas, and I know I can't mend them in a week."

I can't mend myself in a week.

"I hear that," Colt said, his familiar, affable smile firmly in place. "I also won't spread your news all over the ranch. Promise."

"Thanks. I'll probably tell Shawn and Miles tonight. Might as well rip the bandage off, right?" Hugo considered the pair of cooks to be his two best friends on the ranch. They were the closest people to his age, and he'd definitely miss seeing them in person. But the power of smartphones and the internet meant they could easily keep in touch.

"Yeah, putting it off never seems to accomplish much except hurt feelings." Colt checked his phone. "I gotta get back to work. Some of the south fencing needs repairs, and that'll probably take up the rest of my afternoon."

"I need to get back, too. I'm on this afternoon's trail ride with the guests. Thanks for the chat, Colt, I appreciate it."

"Not a problem. See you around."

Hugo watched Colt amble toward the big red barn to collect whatever tools he'd need for his fence mending, then walked around the back of the guesthouse to face the main house. Arthur Garrett, the owner of the ranch and adjacent horse rescue, lived there with Judson and Patrice, the woman who cooked for their guests and the hands. Judson was likely in his office, and there was no reason to put off giving his two weeks' notice.

He steeled his spine and strode toward the house.

"Good news, son."

Brand Woods looked up from the paperwork on his desk, startled by the sound of his father's voice coming from his office doorway. Usually, the old Woods family home's floors creaked loudly enough that you heard most anyone coming, going, or moving about above your head, but somehow Dad had gotten the drop on him.

Then again, they were close to the end of the month, and Brand was desperately trying to balance the books before sending things off to their accountant for tax season. He hated February with an unbridled passion, but he'd gotten a business degree for a reason and this was it. To help keep Woods Ranch in the black and running. They employed a lot of people in their county, not only as ranch hands, but also the grocery store, and their feed and hay suppliers. Only half of their current head of cattle were free-range, grass-fed, so the other half needed to eat just like the humans who raised them.

While the demand for organic, grass-fed beef had risen dramatically in recent years, the transition was still a gamble for a family who'd done things a certain way for multiple generations. But Brand was determined to make this transition work.

"What's the good news?" Brand asked, desperate for anything to make him smile today.

"I got us a new hire, and he's got experience with horses and cattle." Dad grinned in a weird way. "And he's someone you and Rem know."

"Oh?" Brand couldn't think of a single person in Weston or Daisy who didn't already work for them, or who'd tried and failed to make the cut. "Who?"

"Hugo Turner." Dad sat in the chair opposite Brand's desk. "Remember him? One of Rem's best friends from high school."

An uncomfortable ball of ice dropped into the middle of Brand's stomach, and he worked to keep his face as neutral as possible. He hadn't heard that name spoken out loud in years. His mind flashed with a memory of the jumpy, hyperaware, brown-haired teenager who'd seemed to be there whenever Brand turned around after Brand returned home from college. And flirting every chance he got—which was crazy distracting from someone Brand considered a kid but who was also cute in all the right (and wrong) ways.

He'd put up with it for two years, until the night things went sideways. The night Hugo kissed him and everything Brand thought he believed about himself changed in irreversible ways.

Brand coughed. "I didn't realize Hugo was back in town."

"He's technically not back yet. As fate would have it, he's been working with Colt out at Clean Slate these last few years. Heard through Colt we'd been having trouble finding qualified help, so he applied. When I saw the application, I called Colt for a reference, and it sounds like Hugo will be a good fit for our staff. Plus, he's familiar with the area and practically family."

"That's…wow." What were the odds Hugo would end up working the same dude ranch as Brand's big brother? Astronomical. What were the odds he'd end up working here alongside Brand, who'd spent years trying to hide the guy side of his bisexuality? Even more astronomical. And how on earth had Hugo hidden himself when their family was in California for Colt's wedding? Hugo hadn't said a word to any of them.

"So, um, when's he coming?" Brand asked.

"I don't have a specific date, but if his momma raised him right, he'll give at least two weeks to his current boss. I also gave him Elmer Pearce's number about that trailer he's always looking to rent. Should be a good fit."

Brand bit his tongue. Elmer Pearce was, well, eccentric, to say the least. The man owned several acres of property next to their ranch, and he'd filled the land with… Elmer called it art, but Brand called it mostly junk. He'd accumulated piles of metal, usually from properties that had been torn down in their county and neighboring ones, and while Elmer did make folk art out of some of it, a lot of it just sat in rusty piles. Pickers constantly tried to buy from Elmer, but the man rarely sold anything.

But the property did have a single-wide trailer not too far from Elmer's house, and more than one Woods Ranch employee had rented from Elmer over the last thirty years or so. Elmer always said the extra income gave him money to keep buying more stuff. Brand wasn't keen on continuing to feed the man's semi-hoarder habits, but their ranch needed hands, and Hugo would need a place to live.

"Sounds like it's all worked out, then," Brand said, a little annoyed that he'd been left out of the decision. Despite being named foreman about five years ago, sometimes he still felt like Dad was looking over his shoulder. Not quite trusting Brand to run the ranch as they'd agreed. "Wouldn't have minded a little heads-up about the new hire."

Dad waved a hand in the air. "You've got so much going on right now that I don't want to bother you with every little detail. I may have stepped back a bit but I can handle new hires no problem. You focus on keeping us afloat."

"I'm doing that, sir."

"Good man. Sage and her family are coming over for supper at six. Your mother's making pork chops."

"I'll have this finished up and be at the table on time."

"All right. See you in a few hours, then."

After Dad left the office, Brand leaned back in his chair and let out a long, frustrated breath. He loved his family, this ranch, and his job, but some days he wasn't sure his father completely trusted him to run the business. As if he was always looking over Brand's shoulder, because Brand had been the second son. Not the first choice.

His big brother, Colt, had run away from home when Brand was sixteen, and the job of taking over from their father had defaulted to Brand. At first, Brand had been furious, because he'd wanted to be a teacher, not a cattle rancher. He'd grown up expecting that task to fall to Colt. But Brand had enjoyed getting his business degree, and so far, it had helped keep their small-to-medium-sized cattle operation going in a time when small ranches were going out of business all over the Southwest.

Still, he couldn't help wonder if Dad would have been as hands-on if Colt was the foreman now, instead of Brand. Would Brand always be second best?

Only time would tell.

Brand tried to push those self-doubts out of his head and got back to work.

Chapter Two

After giving his notice, Hugo spent every single second he had left at Clean Slate enjoying himself, interacting with guests, and spending time with his friends Miles and Shawn, who worked at the neighboring ghost town. He tried to have one personal goodbye conversation with each of his fellow horsemen; some were heartfelt while others were downright awkward. Hugo even went into San Francisco that Saturday night to hang out with his former roommate Slater and his friends. For old times' sake.

Saying goodbye to Slater was bittersweet. They hadn't been too friendly while they shared a cabin, but had gotten closer—ironically—after Slater broke his ankle and moved away. Hugo liked the older man and had no idea if their paths would cross again. His mental Magic Eight Ball said chances were good, especially if a wedding was in Slater and Derrick's future. Hugo hoped he'd get an invitation.

He was somewhat surprised when, on the evening of his last day as a ranch hand, Judson and Patrice hosted a small going-away party for him in the guesthouse kitchen. He would truly miss this place where he'd worked for roughly two-and-a-half years but felt con-

fident in his decision to go back to Texas. To try and
fix things he'd left unattended for too damned long.

To try and finally make the nightmares stop by facing his bogeyman.

His now-former roommate Winston had volunteered
to drive Hugo and his two small suitcases to the airport in San Jose the next morning, and they spent most
of the hour-long drive in silence, only the radio playing for background noise. They weren't close friends,
but both Miles and Shawn had to work in the ghost
town saloon that morning. They'd already said goodbye, anyway. Hugo's stomach was a ball of acid, and he
kept giving himself pep talks in his head. He'd never
actually been on an airplane before, having made his
journey from northern Texas to California via various
buses and over several years. He didn't know what to
expect, other than being inside a pressurized metal tube
at thirty-five thousand feet in the air, hurtling forward
at five-hundred-fifty miles an hour.

Maybe he'd be early enough at the airport to grab a
drink before he boarded.

The drink didn't happen. He barely had enough time
to check his bags, go through security, and get to his
gate before boarding numbers were called. But he'd had
a few minutes to text Shawn that he'd arrived at the airport safely. He'd miss the guy, who'd taught Hugo how
to play chess. Hell, he'd miss everyone he'd worked
with at Clean Slate, even if he wasn't sure they'd all
miss him. For all the odd jobs he'd had since leaving
his hometown of Daisy, Texas, Hugo had truly felt at
home there. Accepted and safe.

But he'd also grown up quite a lot around his Clean
Slate family, and those men and women had given him

the courage he needed to do this. To take this new step forward and go home, instead of constantly running.

He did indulge in one alcoholic drink on the flight, mostly because the takeoff left him an armrest-gripping fool who couldn't relax until the airplane leveled out. He had purposely booked an aisle seat so he didn't have to be near a window, and his row-mate gave him funny looks. Whatever. No way was Hugo going to admit to anyone his first flight on a plane was at twenty-seven. And it wasn't as if he'd ever see the stranger again.

Since he was prone to motion sickness while reading in a moving vehicle of any sort, Hugo listened to podcasts on his phone and tried to keep himself calm. His last email with Wayne Woods had promised someone would be at the airport in Amarillo to pick him up but not specifically who. Part of Hugo hoped it would be Brand, but he doubted it. As foreman of the ranch, Brand had way too many duties to be bothered with such a mundane task as picking up a new employee.

Especially not a new employee he'd kissed once upon a time.

Brand wasn't much on social media, beyond the few pages for the ranch and their rollout of organic, grass-fed beef, so Hugo had no idea if the guy was married, single, or whatever. And he'd never drummed up the courage to ask Colt these last two weeks. Colt had been kind and encouraging and had wished him well at the party last night. As far as anyone knew, this was just Hugo trying something new.

Only a handful of people knew about Buck.

The landing was almost as anxiety-inducing as the takeoff, but the plane finally taxied over to its terminal, and Hugo was free. If he did receive an invitation to an eventual wedding between Slater and Derrick, he'd just take a lot of vacation time and drive to California and back. Flying was just…nah.

It seemed to take forever for their bags to finally start cycling around the belt, and Hugo nearly missed grabbing his second case. Once he had his luggage, he followed foot traffic toward an exit and found himself in bright, if slightly cool, sunshine. He gazed around, curious who was supposed to be picking him up, expecting a cardboard sign with his name on it or something. Instead, a tall, broad body inserted itself in his path, and Hugo took a frightened step backward.

Remington "Rem" Woods grinned at him from beneath his Stetson, a strong mix of both his parents with a broad grin and blue eyes. "You son of a bitch," Rem said cheerfully. "How the hell did I not notice you at Colt's wedding? You were there, right?"

"I was there." Hugo relaxed a fraction, because Rem seemed more amused than angry. "Back then I didn't want my past to clash with my new start, so I did my best to avoid your whole family that weekend. I needed to be anonymous."

"I get that. Might be still mad at you a little for working with my brother all this time and us not knowing, but I get it. You needed to stay safe."

"Yeah." Maybe Hugo had never told Rem about his huge crush on Rem's big brother Brand, but Rem knew what had happened with Buck. Rem had been his metaphorical shoulder to cry on while Hugo made the difficult decision to leave his mother behind and find a safer place to live. To exist as a whole human being, rather than his stepbrother's punching bag.

"And now you're back. Talk about a crazy cosmic

irony." Rem took the handle of one of Hugo's suitcases and led him toward the pickup area. "That you and Colt would end up working on the same ranch."

"Yeah, it's a kick in the head. But I've heard more than one person talk about the magic of the land back at Clean Slate. She puts people where they're supposed to be at the right time. Judson can find someone to replace me, but it sounded like your dad was having problems with help."

"It's been hard, for sure, so even Dad's been back in the saddle a lot, helping out with the herds." Rem hefted his suitcase into the back of a pickup; Hugo did the same. "It's not easy work, and ever since they opened up that new gristmill, it's even harder to find folk for what we can afford to pay. But we've had some good turns."

Rem didn't elaborate on that until they were both in the cab of the truck, because other drivers needed their spot. "We're doing pretty well with the wind farm Brand set up on the south pasture. And Weston is hosting this year's county carnival, so that'll bring folks into town. Mom's already practicing her recipe for the chili cook-off."

Hugo fondly remembered Rose Woods's chili recipe. The perfect blend of savory, tender meat and spices, served over a bowl of white rice. He'd eaten a lot of dinners at the Woods kitchen while avoiding his home. And Buck. "And I'm sure Rose will win the blue ribbon," Hugo said. "Never had a bad thing from her kitchen."

"Mom is a fantastic cook." Rem navigated his way out into traffic, and Hugo marveled at how easy it was to talk to his former best friend again. "I expect you'll be eating with us quite a lot, unless you taught yourself how to cook. Elmer's trailer is really basic."

Hugo snorted. "I can cook enough not to starve, but yeah, I got the photos of the trailer. I appreciate the lead on a place to live close to work, but once in a while I'll want more than a simple PBJ for dinner." The trailer was actually a fifth wheel that had one bedroom, a tiny bathroom, and a kitchen that consisted of a two-burner stove, mini-microwave, and a dorm-sized refrigerator. Perfect for a single person but not exactly equipped for gourmet cooking.

Not unless he spent a lot of time on YouTube looking for tutorials on cooking with next to nothing.

"Cool, well, I'm sure Mom won't mind." Rem showed off the gold band on his left hand. "You ain't gonna ask?"

Hugo chuckled, then coughed and kind of wished he'd asked to stop for a soda or something. They had about an hour's drive to Weston and few places to get food along the way. "Tell me all about her, player."

He vaguely remembered Shelby Waterson as an upperclassman. Hugo and Rem were two years apart, so Rem had known a lot of people Hugo didn't normally hang out with, despite them all attending a fairly small county high school. She'd been the classic buxom blonde with a smile for everyone, and they'd apparently gotten married not quite nine months before their daughter, Susie, was born. Rem handed over his phone, and Hugo thumbed through a bunch of pictures of the small family. Susie was adorable with a strong resemblance to her mom.

"Congrats, man, I mean it," Hugo said.

"Thanks. Susie is the best, and we've been trying for a second kid but no luck so far. Which is okay, with the ranch struggling like it is. Shelby is a waitress and survives on tips, so money can be tight sometimes."

"I'm sorry things are hard, money-wise." Hugo had been very lucky in that free rent on the Clean Slate cabin and meals had been part of his pay arrangement, so he'd been able to tuck some cash away for a rainy day. Not everyone was so lucky, and he would never rub that in Rem's face. Hugo knew what it was like to struggle to pay his bills, like most people his age.

"Tale of most farmers these days. Big corporations keep taking over, so the little guy gets shafted. But Brand...he's doing a good job. Dad believes in him and so do I. He'll keep us going for at least another generation."

Hugo fought back a flinch, unable to stop a flash of his mother's face the day they sold their herd and land. The devastation and loss of her grandparents' legacy. While part of his heart was okay with the herd being sold to Wayne Woods, the other part ached knowing her land had been turned into a housing subdivision.

"Shit, dude, I'm sorry," Rem said. "I forgot what happened to your mom's ranch."

"It was half a lifetime ago, don't worry about it." More than half. Almost two-thirds, but whatever. And it was a good time for a conversation switch. "So how is Brand?"

"The perfect workaholic. His entire life is about the ranch, except for the occasional night he goes to the Roost for booze and to flirt with Ramie."

Hugo knew the bar but he tried to place the other name and failed. "Ramie?"

"Yeah, Rachel Marie Edwards. She was a year ahead

of Brand in school, I think. She bartends there, and they've been spending a lot of time together lately."

He tamped down on a well of cold jealousy. "They a thing?"

"Not sure." Rem turned left onto the state road that would eventually take them to Weston. "He never brings her around so it's hard to know what they're up to, but he's way overdue for a nice girl in his life. Can't remember Brand ever really dating, other than Ginny Something-or-other his junior year. And he took SueEllen Hurley to his senior prom, but that didn't last long, either."

Rem changed subjects faster than greased lightning, and he nattered on for a while about his two younger sisters, Sage and Leanne, and their husbands and kids. Hugo got quite the history lesson of the extended Woods clan on the long drive, which was fine, because he'd be up to speed with folks he hadn't seen in nearly a decade.

He'd already spoken to Elmer over the phone about the fifth-wheel, but it didn't occur to Hugo until right then that he needed a way to get from Elmer's property to the ranch every work day. He'd never owned a car. Hell, he hadn't learned how to drive until he was twenty, because he'd been desperate for the independence.

"We're going to your house?" Hugo asked dumbly.

"Sure. I mean, it's almost dinnertime, so I figured you'd want to hang for Sunday supper and get to know the family again. It'll probably just be me, my parents and Brand, but still."

"Okay, sure." He'd have to face Brand again eventually, and maybe it would be less awkward with his family around. They wouldn't have to talk about the past and that kiss. "You know, I just realized I have no idea how to get from Elmer's trailer to the ranch for work. It's not like I could pack a car in my luggage."

Rem laughed. "No worries, dude. I've got a scooter you can use until you get yourself a car or whatever."

"A scooter?"

"Yeah. It's not the fastest thing ever, but it's better than a bicycle. I picked it up cheap at an auction, fixed it up, and it runs great. Unless you wanna walk."

"No, thanks, the scooter sounds great, thank you."

Rem shot him a familiar shit-eating grin. "It really does feel like old times, having you back. Your parents know you're here?"

Hugo swallowed back the urge to say that Frank was his stepfather, not his parent, but Rem was likely referring mostly to Hugo's mother, Joanne. "Not yet. I want to get settled in first. Not just the trailer but with my new job. Going back to rustling cattle is a far cry from wrangling tourists on a dude ranch."

"I know. Brand and I actually spent a week's vacation out at Clean Slate once, but that must have been before you signed on."

"It was. Honestly, it took me a while to figure out who Colt was, and when I did I couldn't make myself say anything."

"Dude, I get it." Rem knuckled him lightly on the shoulder. "But as one former best friend to another, I'm proud of you for coming back. Dunno if I'd have been so brave."

"Yeah, you would. But you also wouldn't have had to because you have a pretty amazing family. Two parents who love you and four siblings who protect you, instead of pounding on you every chance they get."

Rem passed the car in front of them, then set the

cruise control and relaxed a bit into his seat. They still had a bit of a drive ahead. "Do you know about Buck now?"

Hugo went rigid. "What about him?" Had something changed?

"He's been up the river these last few years, serving time in state prison for assaulting a law officer."

"Wow." He'd known Buck was in prison, but he'd never asked anyone for the exact details of the assault. Buck had hit a cop? "What happened?"

"He beat up his girlfriend so bad that her parents called the county sheriff, and when a deputy went to arrest Buck, the asshole was so drunk he attacked the deputy." Rem grunted unhappily. "Assault charges for the girlfriend didn't go far, because she was too scared to stand up to him with a statement, but the new sheriff? Seamus McBride? He refused to back down on pressing charges for assaulting his deputy. Judge gave Buck three years."

A ripple of worry unsettled Hugo's gut. "How long ago?"

"About two years or so now. Rumor is he's had parole hearings but he gets into a lot of fights, so it's not been granted yet."

That made sense. Buck was…unstable. Ever since they first met when Mom started dating Frank, Hugo had seen something mean in Buck's eyes. Something that scared him. But Mom had fallen for Frank, and Buck had been fine for a few months after the incident at the wedding. Then his true nature had started showing its ugly face—that of a cruel man who loved to bully his younger stepbrother every chance he got.

"Good," Hugo snapped. "He belongs in prison." But

the idea that he could be paroled in a year made his gut knot.

"Yeah. Let's hope that when he gets out, he stays far away from Weston."

"Yeah." Far, far away from Weston, or Hugo wouldn't be held responsible if he saw the man again. On the outside, he was still an average guy, but on the inside, he was no one's pushover anymore. No one's victim. "Away from here and Daisy. But I can't help wondering if Mom and my stepdad will take Buck back if he ever gets out."

"Hard to know. If not, he'll probably go to a halfway house somewhere in the county. Not great for those residents but probably better for us."

"Right." Hugo sank deeper into the passenger seat and watched the boring scenery go by. They didn't chat much more after that, other than a few vague questions from Hugo about the ranch, and from Rem about his adventures since Hugo left Texas. Hugo stayed vague on the details, only mentioning various odd jobs that took him west, until he landed at Clean Slate Ranch. Rooming with Slater and learning the ropes of a tourist-focused dude ranch. How much he loved the overnight trips spent under a bazillion glimmering stars.

Eventually, Rem took the exit to Weston, and Hugo's stomach rolled again. His hometown of Daisy was only ten miles farther east, but the towns weren't all that different. Weston itself had a single stoplight at the intersection of Main Street and Weston Avenue—named after the founding family of their small town back in the eighteen-nineties—one grocery store, three bars, and five churches. The only change was that one of the bars had a For Sale sign on it.

"Everything looks the same as I remember," Hugo said.

"Yeah, not much has changed." Rem paused at the red light and glanced around. "Pretty much the same my entire life. Wish those would go away, though." He pointed at a house that had a Confederate flag hanging from the porch.

Hugo's heart swelled a tiny bit. "Me, too, brother. Me, too."

Brand spent as much time as humanly possible in his office that day—not only because he was reading a proposal on expanding their wind turbine farm by another few dozen acres, but also because of the new hire arriving today.

Hugo Turner.

His résumé was beyond reproach, and Dad had already offered him the job based on a remote interview, but Brand was still leery. The kid—okay, he was twenty-seven now, so not a kid—had plenty of experience, but he'd left so suddenly not long after turning eighteen. And he'd never been back. Why take a job at Woods Ranch now? Why come back after all these years? Not simply to fuck with Brand's head. Unless Hugo had changed completely, this wasn't some sort of revenge for their single encounter so many years ago.

Right?

His phone chimed with a text from Dad: They're here, come down.

Brand heaved a sigh no one but himself heard, then pushed away from his desk. He'd spent so much time up here lately, plotting how to keep the ranch going, and he missed being in the saddle. Following the grazing herds and making sure none of the steer wandered off. But this was the lot he'd been dealt and by God and heaven, he'd do his best.

He thumped downstairs and into the home's small foyer right as Rem opened the front door, grinning to beat the devil. His little brother had always been a spirited guy with a friendly smile for everyone, and he loved picking on Brand for still being single at thirty-five. And right behind Rem was the guy who'd starred in more than one jerk-off fantasy over the years.

Hugo was all grown up. Taller, with more muscles on his lean frame, and a healthy tan to his skin. He stood with his back straight, head up, confident in himself. So different from the skittish teenager Brand remembered clearly. But still as good-looking as ever in the perfect boy-next-door way.

Get it together, Woods, he's an employee not a fantasy come true.

"Hey, dude," Rem said to him as he draped one arm across Hugo's shoulders. "Look what the cat dragged in all the way from California."

"Good to see you again, Hugo," Brand said, reaching for politeness because part of him wanted to remove his brother's arm from Hugo's body. Not an impulse he was allowed to act on. Ever.

"You, too, man," Hugo replied, offering an affable smile that broadened when Mom and Dad came into the foyer from the hall leading back to the kitchen. "Mr. and Mrs. Woods, it's amazing to see you both again."

"Welcome home, hon," Mom said. She walked right up to Hugo and hugged him. "We've missed you. You spent so much time here when you and Rem were in high school, it felt like we'd adopted a new boy."

"I always felt very welcome here, ma'am, thank you." Hugo shook Dad's hand. "I really appreciate the job, sir."

"You've got the experience we're looking for, son," Dad replied. "Outsiders think everyone from Texas is born knowing how to ride a horse and rope cattle but that just isn't true. Plus, we've got some heifers due to calve this spring, so we need the help."

"I get it, believe me. And your family always treated me well, so it felt like the right time to give back. And to make a change for myself." His eyes flickered briefly at Brand.

Brand kept his face perfectly neutral—he hoped.

"Do your parents know you're back?" Mom asked. "I almost called and invited them for supper tonight, but I didn't want to overstep."

"They don't know yet, ma'am," Hugo replied, his expression pinching briefly. "Like I told Rem, I want to settle in first. Not just at the trailer but with my new job here. Then I'll call Mom and let her know I'm back in the county."

"Good, good. You do what's best for you, hon. Now, if you men are hungry, supper should be ready to go on the table."

Their spacious kitchen had a built-in breakfast nook where they took most of their meals nowadays, since it was usually just Mom, Dad, and Brand. But Brand wasn't surprised to see Mom had set the formal dining room for the meal with five places out. Brand offered to help bring food to the table, mostly to keep his distance from Hugo for as long as possible. He was far too aware of how the younger man's ass fit in his faded jeans.

Mom had cooked up a pot of short ribs, along with

mashed potatoes, glazed carrots, and dinner rolls. A fairly typical Sunday evening supper. She had been raised in a very conservative household with the expectation of becoming a wife, mother, and homemaker, and while that irked Brand on occasion, she was an amazing mom and cook. And especially now that Colt was back in their lives, she was happy in her role here, spoiling her grandkids and keeping their bellies full.

"This all looks amazing, ma'am," Hugo said as the bowls went around the table. "After so many years of eating Patrice's home-cooked meals, eating with your family once in a while is gonna be a huge treat for me. The trailer I'm renting doesn't have much of a kitchen for me to use."

"Colt's mentioned a lady named Patrice," Mom replied. "She's the Clean Slate cook, right?"

"Yep. She's a sweet lady who's been there a long time. Does a great job looking after the hands and guests."

"Not that I'm complaining, because we can definitely use the help," Brand said without thinking, "but I'm really surprised you left. Sounds like you had a sweet setup there with room and board built into your pay."

Hugo looked right into Brand's eyes, and a kind of challenge seemed to linger there. As if daring Brand to mention their shared history.

"Boys, a moment, please," Mom said. "Let's say the blessing first so we can eat."

Brand lowered his head and stared at his plate while Dad said Grace, all familiar words and phrases that Brand rarely felt deep inside. He only occasionally attended church with his folks, mostly holidays or if Mom guilted him into it. It just…wasn't his thing anymore. Youth group trips had been fun when he was a kid, but so much of what their local churches preached on made his skin itch in a bad way. Maybe he wasn't entirely sure of his sexual orientation—although Jackson might argue about that—but he knew he wasn't destined for eternal hellfire just for liking dick on occasion.

His mind must have wandered deeply during the blessing, because Mom nudged him in the ribs to start eating, while everyone else already had.

"To answer your earlier question," Hugo said after a moment, "I left for a lot of reasons. To be honest, since I was eighteen, I haven't stayed at any single job longer than a year, so Clean Slate was a bit of a record for me. I can't promise I'll still be working here five years from now, but I can promise to do my very best every single day and help this ranch continue on the way your family wants."

Brand held Hugo's firm gaze, kind of liking the subtle challenge there. The way Hugo looked him right in the eye now when he rarely had before. Brand nodded. "Fair enough. You start tomorrow, eight o'clock."

"I'll be here. Boss."

He squinted, liking that nickname a little too much. Liking the way Hugo's pink lips closed around the tines of his fork a little too much. "I'll have Jackson show you around, introduce you to the horses, get the lay of the land again. He's been here a few years and knows his stuff."

"Okay." If Hugo was the slightest bit disappointed that Brand wasn't showing him around personally, he didn't show it. Instead, he kept eating.

Brand shoveled mashed potatoes into his mouth and tried to ignore the cute guy across the table from him. And to ignore how complicated his personal life had just gotten.

I need to talk to Ramie. Soon.

Chapter Three

The entire hour-long dinner with the Woods family was a unique exercise in patience for Hugo, and it had everything to do with the tall, broad man sitting across the table from him. Brand was a younger version of Colt, with slightly lighter blond hair and less of the sassy flirtatious nature Hugo associated with Colt. Brand was serious in an oddly joyful way, as if the burden of keeping Woods Ranch afloat hadn't completely squashed his zest for life.

Brand was almost exactly the guy Hugo remembered, right down to him seeming to have no clear idea why Hugo had left the state nearly a decade ago. Apparently, Rem had kept all of Hugo's secrets, and he adored his former best friend for that. If the other adults in Hugo's life hadn't seen fit to do something about it, why would Brand have?

Except…maybe he would have? All kinds of murky water under the bridge now, though, so whatever. Hugo ate his supper and praised the cook more than once. Bringing groceries back to his new trailer on a borrowed scooter would probably be a time-suck and pain in the ass. Maybe he could bum a ride off Rem again so he'd have basic supplies for a couple of days. Protein bars for breakfast were easy, but he had no idea how lunch worked around here nowadays.

"Mr. Woods," Hugo said, "I hate to bring business into such a lovely meal, but I'm curious how lunch, um, happens."

"No worries, son," Mr. Woods replied. "We've got a small break room of sorts in the barn for staff to keep snacks and food, and it's got a refrigerator, so if you're working close to the house, feel free to bring what you like. If you're out in the pastures, I'd pack something that will keep in a saddle bag. But I dare say we'll have you close to the house and barn for the first week or so, until you get acclimated."

"I see. Thank you."

"We've got two different herds right now," Brand said. "Our grass-fed, organic steer get a lot more pasture time so they can eat as much natural grass as possible and keep their certification. The regular beef stay closer and still get feed and hay."

"Got it. Rem mentioned the change to organic beef. I mean, it's popular right now so it's gotta be worth the extra effort."

"So far, so good. We've only had one slaughter so far and we did okay. This new herd will set the tone going forward."

"And it'll be a great tone," Mr. Woods said with a broad smile. "Brand's been putting that business degree of his to good use, and I have every confidence in him."

The way Brand's smile wobbled made Hugo wonder if Brand had that same confidence in himself. "Thank you, sir," Brand said.

"No more work talk tonight, gentlemen," Mrs. Woods said. "I have a pecan pie cooling in the kitchen,

if you men have any room for dessert." She rose from
the table without waiting for answers and disappeared
into the kitchen.

. Hugo was stuffed from dinner, but he did agree to
take a slice of pie home for later. Home being a glori-
fied camper he'd yet to see. The sun was setting low on
the horizon by the time Rem agreed to drive him—with
his scooter in the bed of Rem's truck—into town for a
quick trip to the grocery store. The protein bar selection
was sad, so Hugo made a mental note to check online,
and bought what he could, along with fixings for basic
sandwiches, and a few frozen dinners to tide him over
for a couple of days.

With his supplies set, Rem drove him to Elmer
Pearce's property. Hugo remembered the eccentric old
artist, mostly because the entire roadside fence of his
property was lined with metal sculptures of all sorts,
including several different renditions of Elmer Fudd.
He was a folk artist of sorts, and from the gossip Hugo
had gleaned, had a grown son who never visited, but
that was about all Hugo knew.

The gloomy yard was somewhat lit by the occasional
floodlight, and Rem pulled up past some sort of T-Rex
built out of car parts to the fifth wheel. By the time they
had the scooter parked and Hugo's meager groceries put
away in the tiny kitchen area, someone knocked on the
front door. Elmer came inside without an acknowledg-
ment. The man was in his late sixties or early seven-
ties, Hugo wasn't sure. But he stood with assurance and
gave Hugo a long look up and down.

"So, you're the new tenant," Elmer said. "Elmer
Pearce. Good to meet you, son."

"Hugo Turner, sir," Hugo replied. He shook the man's

gnarled, burn-scarred hand. "I appreciate the place to stay. I promise no late-night parties."

"Shit, you want to have a party, I better be invited. Threw plenty of 'em back in my day. And if you ever need weed, I got you covered."

Hugo glanced at Rem, who just grinned. "I'll keep that in mind, I guess. But I'm here to work."

"Sure, sure, you youngins. Trailer is hooked up to gas and water, but don't go crazy using either. But being one man, I can't see you doing too much of that."

"No, sir, I won't. I'm a very basic cook, and I've lived with a lot of roommates, so I'm used to quick showers."

"Good, good." He looked from Hugo to Rem, then back to Hugo. "You two rascals used to run around and get into trouble when you were teenagers, didn't you? I don't recall the name Turner, but I never forget a face."

"We sure did get around," Rem replied with a grin. "But Hugo's family lived out in Daisy. And Turner is his mother's maiden name. They both changed it back after her divorce." He snapped his mouth shut, as if realizing he was telling a lot of personal things about Hugo to a near-stranger. Hugo wasn't mad, though; Rem always did have a motormouth, and that apparently hadn't changed.

"We definitely got into our fair share of trouble," Hugo said. "But what teenage boy doesn't, right? I'm sure you've got your own stories to tell, Mr. Pearce."

Elmer laughed. "Don't Mr. Pearce me, son, just call me Elmer. And if you ever want to sit on my porch one evening and share a joint, I'll probably tell you some. Don't worry, it's medicinal." The wink he flashed at Hugo suggested otherwise.

Hugo hadn't smoked weed in years, but he had a

feeling a visit with Elmer would be worth it just for the stories. He was so curious about the various sculptures decorating his yard, and the man's actual work history. Couldn't remember anyone ever mentioning what he'd once done for a living. Considering the acreage he seemed to own, he might have been a rancher once upon a time. Hugo actually looked forward to getting to know his landlord.

"Well, I gotta get home," Rem said. "Need to kiss Susie goodnight before she goes to bed."

"Of course." Hugo shook his hand, then gave Rem a friendly bro-style hug. "It was great seeing you, and I'll see you bright and early tomorrow. First day actually working your ranch, instead of just pissing around and getting into trouble."

"See you in the morning. Hey, you drink coffee? I can bring a thermos from the house."

He'd grabbed a jar of instant coffee at the store, but that would taste like bitter water compared to what he was used to Patrice making for the staff. "That would be great, actually, until I can buy a coffeepot of my own." He actually needed to take a quick inventory of the place and see what else he might need, in terms of plates, pots and pans, and such.

At least he'd thought to buy a package of toilet paper.

"I won't keep you, either," Elmer said. "I'm sure you want to settle in. Sorry there's no TV, but there's a card in that drawer there with the Wi-Fi password, so feel free to use that for your phone or whatever gadget you've got."

"Thank you, sir," Hugo replied. He hadn't really thought ahead about how to entertain himself in the evenings, so now he'd be able to stream things on his phone. And use his reading app.

"Sure, sure. You need anything, feel free to knock on my door."

Once both his guests left, Hugo glanced around his new digs for, well, however long he stayed. It had about as much square footage as the cabin he'd once shared with Winston, but now all this space was his. No roommate for the first time in years, and the rent was really reasonable. Might only have to touch his savings once until his first paycheck from Woods Ranch came through.

He'd actually done this. Made the move back to Texas. Had dinner with his old crush at their family home. Moved into a fifth wheel with a plan to start a brand-new job tomorrow. He wasn't sure how things would turn out with the ranch or Brand, but he'd abide by his promise to work hard and do his very best to make Woods Ranch a success.

Smiling to himself, Hugo hauled his suitcases into the tiny bedroom area and started to unpack.

Instead of waiting for her to call him back whenever she got a break, Brand drove into town to the Roost, the bar he preferred drinking at the most, because it was cleaner and had better music. Also, Ramie worked there, and he really needed to talk. Seeing Hugo again was fucking with his head worse than Brand imagined it might in the two weeks since Dad announced Hugo had been hired.

The little shit was under his skin already, and they'd only spent an hour together today. Spending multiple hours with him daily going forward? Not good, which

was why he was having Jackson show Hugo around
tomorrow.

The Roost was an unassuming building on the outskirts of town with a gravel parking lot and only a handful of neon beer signs in the windows. Less flashy than
the other two bars in town, which tended to attract the
older, grumpier clientele who loved to down pitchers
of beer and loudly complain about liberals ruining the
country. He parked his pickup next to half-a-dozen others and climbed out. Despite being close to town, thou-
sands of stars still twinkled brightly overhead, and he
took a moment to admire them. To wonder if his big
brother, Colt, was seeing similar stars as the sun set
over California.

Brand had been sixteen when Colt ran away from
home and disappeared from their lives, and it had hurt.
A lot. And then sixteen more years passed before Colt
drove back home with his boyfriend in tow, and Brand
finally began to understand Colt's reasons for leaving.
He'd left to be his true, gay self, while Brand…hid. And
worked. And denied himself anything except the most
basic physical pleasures.

But Hugo had stirred things back up, and Brand
needed to talk to his best friend.

He stepped into a familiar space that was mostly a
long, oval bar, with a few tables and chairs off to the
left, and a meager dancing area in the back. The place
served basic bar food like nachos and potato skins,
which allowed them to open at ten on Sunday and ap-
pease old liquor laws. It smelled like cigarettes, booze
and sweat, and the dim lighting made it look sleazier
than it actually was, because the owners were good

people. Took care of their guests and made sure single women got to their cars safe at night.

Brand plopped himself on a free stool at the bar and waited for Ramie to notice him. She was pouring something out of a shaker into two martini glasses, which she eventually delivered to a pair of women. When she noticed him, she winked, then took the order of someone who'd been there before Brand.

He took a moment to admire his friend. Ramie was his age, with thick black hair and a very curvy figure she showed off with tight blouses and even tighter jeans. "It helps me get better tips," was her excuse for the clothes, and he didn't blame her. Bartending was a hard gig sometimes, and despite her petite frame, she took no bullshit from her customers, snapping right back with on-point sarcasm or dry wit.

Brand didn't have that same sort of self-confidence; no wonder he liked her so much.

She finally came over with his standard longneck and a bowl of peanuts. "He got in today, didn't he?" she asked.

"Yeah." Brand took a long, hard pull on the beer, savoring its yeasty goodness. No one sat on either side of him, so Brand leaned in. "I knew I'd feel something when I saw him again, but this is more confusing than I imagined. And I'm his fucking boss now, so I can't do anything about it."

"So what are you going to do? Avoid him at all costs? Spend every night either banging me or Jackson, so you don't have to think about him?"

Brand grunted and drank more beer, nearly emptying the bottle this time. "Maybe. I don't know. Can't see that working anyway, since we've always been a once-every-few-weeks sort of thing."

"Well, you *are* good enough to scratch the occasional itch. Be back." She moved off to serve another customer. Eight o'clock on a Sunday didn't mean booming business, but tips were always better if customers didn't have to wait for service.

If Brand wasn't still full from supper, he might have ordered a plate of their spicy wings just for something to do with his hands while Ramie handled customers. She moved fluidly around the bar area, filling drinks and delivering food from the window to the small kitchen. They'd first met here, not long after Brand came home from college, and they'd hit it off right away. A strong connection that didn't turn into a sexual relationship until a few months later.

The sex had been good, and it still was, but they didn't have that deeper emotional attraction to make this anything more between them than the need for the occasional one-off. They had, however, become great friends, always there to lean on the other in times of drama or personal crisis. Like now.

He ate a few peanuts, then nursed the second beer Ramie left in front of him. They both knew his drinking limits. By nine, two people were dancing to a Kenny Rogers song, but a lot of the bar had thinned out, so Ramie parked herself near Brand's spot.

"So do you still have feelings for this kid?" she asked as she wiped a glass dry.

"Fuck if I know." Brand poked at the paper label on his bottle. "And he's hardly a kid anymore. He's very much grown and has gone through stuff, I can tell, and I'm curious but…ugh."

"You don't want him to read too much into your curiosity and make a pass that you might not be able to resist?"

He glared at her. "Maybe. It was just so odd the way he left without a damned word after we...you know." He couldn't make himself say the word *kissed* even though he'd admitted it to her years ago. And maybe a year stood between that kiss and Hugo leaving, but it had still hurt in its own way. "Just left the whole state without a word." More than once, he'd considered asking Rem if he knew what had happened, but Brand had been too scared that Rem would say he knew what Brand and Hugo had done that day in the barn.

Then years passed, Hugo stayed away, and Rem never said a word. Not even after Colt came home and announced he was gay. So Brand had left it alone. But what if his little brother knew more than he was saying?

Tonight was not the night to ask.

Ramie glanced around the almost empty bar, then ducked her head low. "If you still have questions about that night, then ask Hugo. Be an adult and talk to him. At least get it off your chest so working with him won't be so weird for you. You owe yourself that much, especially with all the other stress you've got going on right now."

"You're right." As much as Brand dreaded it, he did need to talk to Hugo. To clear the air between them so they could work together well as boss and employee for the next, well, however long. "Shouldn't I give it a few days, though? Let Hugo get comfortable at the ranch and his new job?"

"That's up to you. I'd think about being honest sooner than later, considering you're his boss now, but that's just me. I don't know Hugo at all, but I do know you, Brand. You're a good guy, and you deserve to find someone who'll make you happy for a long time. Not just for an hour of fun."

"Thanks, Ramie. You do, too, you know."

She grinned. "Maybe. But I don't want anyone long term. I'll scratch my itch and then go about my life. And I promise if you find someone who'll keep you for the long run, I won't be jealous. I'll be first in line to cheer you on."

He held up his hand, knuckles out. "You're a good woman, Rachel Marie."

"Don't you tell anybody." She fist-bumped him, then went off to take a drink order.

Brand watched his friend work her magic, whether expertly snapping a cap off a beer bottle so it flew straight in the trash or pouring a mixed drink for the occasional high-end patron. They got along great, had decent chemistry in bed, and they both listened really well. Until Brand got his Hugo problem figured out, he'd need someone to listen.

Probably for a while.

Ugh. Why couldn't life have stayed as simple as it had been before Hugo Turner marched back into his family's ranch?

Chapter Four

It took Hugo a few minutes to figure out the scooter the next morning—mostly because the mug of instant coffee he'd made wasn't doing him any favors with his slight jet lag—and then he was puttering down the state road toward Woods Ranch. His stomach roiled with nerves like it always did on his first day at a new job, but at least he knew people here and had support. Rem had his back. He had no idea what Brand thought about this whole thing, because he'd been cagey as hell during dinner last night.

Hopefully, he'd get at least one private conversation with his new foreman today.

He admired the wide-open skies on his drive up the dirt lane to the ranch. Ever since he was a kid, he'd loved being outdoors, free to run around and experience nature. Maybe that was why he'd never landed in a big city, preferring small towns and small jobs as he wandered from state to state. Trying to leave his past behind in another small town not too far from here.

A few other vehicles were parked near the barn, so Hugo left the scooter there. Woods Ranch was a small, family-run operation with only a handful of employees, so the hands didn't live on-site anymore. The structure of the former bunkhouse stood behind the barn and was mostly used for storage, Rem had told him. No one had lived in it in all the years Hugo had known Rem.

A tall, well-muscled, tanned man stepped out from the open doors of the barn, hands on his hips. He wore a typical arrangement of boots, jeans, a light jacket, and Stetson, and his pointed look settled directly on Hugo. "You the new guy?"

Hugo nodded. "Yes, sir. Hugo Turner. I was told to be here by eight."

The man glanced at his wristwatch—something Hugo wasn't used to seeing much anymore since most people had cell phones. "You're two minutes late."

Oh good grief, really? "I apologize. I've never ridden Rem's scooter before and wasn't sure how long the drive from Elmer's place would take me."

"Do better tomorrow. Name's Jackson Sumner. Brand told me to show you the ropes today."

"Nice to meet you." Hugo shook his hand, unsurprised by the tight, calloused grip. Jackson definitely had "career ranch hand" written all over him. A few of the guys he'd worked with in California had had a similar look and feel to them, and Hugo definitely wanted to stay on Jackson's good side. "I'm somewhat familiar with the barn and land, since I was here a lot as a teenager."

"That's fine, but I imagine a few things have changed, including our gradual switch to organic, grass-fed beef. Today is easing you into our routines, learning where everything is kept, meeting the horses you'll be riding, and the lay of the land. The grass-fed have a lot larger grazing pasture than the other beef, so we gotta keep a special eye on wanderers."

"Understood." Hugo glanced around but didn't see Brand or Rem anywhere in sight yet. "Is it just us?"

"Nah, Rem and Brand will be out soon enough, I reckon. Other guy we had broke his hand a few weeks ago and is on leave, so things are a little tight with the workload around here. You're in for long days, kid."

The "kid" comment irritated him a bit, because Jackson didn't look that much older than him, but appearances were often deceiving. Especially when you met someone for the first time. "I'm no stranger to hard work. I came here to work and I'll do my part."

"Good man. I'll show you around."

They went into the barn's small break room first, which was basically a converted horse stall with a half-sized fridge, microwave, and three-seat table. But it was clean, and Hugo put his sandwich in the fridge to eat later. The barn was mostly what he remembered, from the horse stalls to the tack room full of equipment, to the area where the horses were regularly cleaned and/or tacked for riding.

"We've got a fair mix of mares and geldings," Jackson said as they peeked into various stalls. "Good mounts, and they know how to act around the cattle."

Hugo didn't see nameplates on the stalls, and he glanced in at a beautiful palomino. The horse approached and let Hugo stroke her velvety-soft nose. "What's this one's name?"

"No name."

"The horse doesn't have a name?"

Jackson tilted his head to the side, one eyebrow quirked. "No name."

"Why haven't you named the horse yet?"

"I said No Name."

Then it clicked. "Wait, the horse's name is No Name?"

"That's what I just said."

Hugo felt like he was in the middle of an Abbott and Costello skit, and he very nearly asked "Who's on first?" but refrained. Jackson didn't seem like the kind of guy who'd take well to the joke. "That's, um, an interesting name."

"Mr. Woods chose the name when the horse was born two years ago. Based on the lyrics of a song he loved."

Unsure if Mr. Woods was Brand or Wayne, Hugo erred on the side of it being Wayne, since Brand had always been fond of more modern rock music. At least as far as Hugo knew, but Brand could have changed. "It's definitely unique. Hello there, No Name."

The horse nickered.

Hugo met the other mounts, doing his best to remember everyone's name. Learned where the feed and hay for the nonorganic herd was stored, and where all the equipment was stored around the large barn. Deeper in the barn were all the cows currently pregnant after the last visit from the local AI technician, and who were scheduled to calf in the near future.

"All the new calves will go into the grass-fed pasture," Jackson explained. "The plan is to transition over the next year into all organic, grass-fed beef. Brand says it hits an eager niche market, so that's what we'll do. Just means a bit more attention on the cattle in the west pasture as the herd grows. He wants the herd to have room to wander, but not to separate too far."

"Makes good sense." Hugo gazed around at the cows, who were confined because they looked ready to burst soon, but who still had plenty of room to move around.

The Woods family kept a humane ranch. Or as humane as it could be when the intent was for all the steer to eventually end up on someone's dinner table.

It made him think of Levi, a man whose unique brand of inner peace and "one with the earth" mentality always gave thanks to Mother Nature for what she provided. If an animal's short life was going to be sacrificed so a longer-living mammal like humans could thrive, they should allow that creature to live the kindest short life possible.

"Are the cows who birth allowed to nurse the calf?" Hugo asked.

"Definitely," Jackson replied. "We're not a dairy farm, so the calves nurse until weaned, and then they join the regular herd. Should have at least ten new calves by summer. The heifers who can still breed will go back to the regular herd, and the ones who can't will go to slaughter."

"Of course." Such was the circle of life in the cattle industry. They weren't pets; they were food and profit.

"We'll go out to the west pasture in a bit and do a head count, make sure no one's wandered too far from the herd. We've also got—"

As if sensing the introduction, a pair of dogs raced down the length of the barn and came up to sniff Hugo. One was clearly a German shepherd and the other some sort of mutt that might have had a bit of Australian shepherd in it. Hugo had never been a huge fan of dogs, even though they'd always been around the Woods Ranch, but they both seemed friendly enough.

"That's Brutus," Jackson said, pointing to the German. "He's Brand's dog. The other one is mine, I guess, and she's just Dog."

Hugo stared a beat. "You named your dog Dog?"

He shrugged one shoulder. "She wandered into my yard one day and then started following me everywhere after I fed her. No one in town responded to the posters I put up, so now she just…hangs out."

A horse called No Name and a dog named Dog. What the hell kind of alternate universe had Hugo landed in?

Jackson patted his own chest. "Come here, Dog." Dog obediently jumped up and put two furry paws on Jackson's stomach. The dog seemed small for the big man, but Jackson rubbed her ears affectionately. "Good girl."

"They any good at rustling cattle?" Hugo asked.

"Brutus is trained. Dog goes out with us but I found her too old to really train her to herd the cattle, so she just sort of chills with me. I'm just grateful the Woods family loves dogs, because she's a loyal beast. Can't imagine having to leave her locked up while I'm working."

"Gotcha."

They continued touring the main area around the barn, from the big corral to the cattle chutes. Hugo spotted the regular herd in the east pasture, hanging out close to the fence line where he imagined they'd eventually lay out hay for them to munch on. When they circled back to the barn, Rem and Brand were both inside tacking horses.

"You gettin' the lay of the land?" Rem asked as he tightened a saddle strap.

"I'm getting a first-class tour, for sure," Hugo replied. "You heading out?"

"Yep, we gotta do a fence check today. Make sure the perimeters are secure. You've probably got a fun day of mucking stalls, feeding cattle, and cleaning horse hooves ahead of you."

"It's what you get when you're the new guy."

Brand didn't look his way once during the entire exchange, and it annoyed the hell out of Hugo. But for now, he'd keep his head down, do his job, and prove it hadn't been a mistake for Wayne to hire him.

Only by lunch, Hugo was exhausted. Sure, he was no stranger to mucking a horse stall, but he was also used to sharing the job with half-a-dozen other people. While Rem and Brand tended to the fencing and the grass-fed herd, Hugo and Jackson had fed the other herd, mucked six horse stalls, tended to the pregnant heifers, and cleaned mud and gunk out of the hooves of several horses, including No Name.

Hugo rewarded No Name's good behavior with a sugar cube from the box he'd found in the tack room.

Rem and Brand were back from their fence check around noon when Jackson called for lunch. The brothers went inside the main house, and Hugo and Jackson headed for the break room. A little disappointed in not seeing more of Brand, Hugo ate his sandwich quietly, while Jackson heated up a cup of instant noodles. Dog sat quietly at Jackson's feet the entire time, observant of the food without begging.

"So what's your story, kid?" Jackson asked near the end of their thirty-minute break. "You leave Texas, end up in California, and then come back again?"

He seemed genuinely curious, rather than obnoxiously rude, so Hugo went with honesty. "No big story, really. I wanted to leave, so I left. Had some interesting experiences. Now I'm back to... I don't know, fix some stuff that was broken when I left. Rem was my best friend in high school. My mom still lives out in Daisy. Felt like the right time to come back. Maybe it's not forever, but it's a good place to be for now." Hugo quirked an eyebrow. "What's your story?"

Jackson snorted, then sipped at his leftover noodle broth. "Not much to say, really. I was born into this life and don't know much else. Failed out of high school, so I never bothered with college. I learn better on the job than with books anyhow. I drifted for a while until the Woods family gave me a chance. Now I've got a stable job and my place, such as it is. I'm not unhappy. I've got Dog. Can't ask for too much more."

The man hadn't mentioned a wife or kids, but Hugo and Jackson had also known each other for a grand total of four hours. Not really long enough to delve into more personal questions, and the last thing Hugo needed was to be asked why he was still single.

Because I've hidden being gay and pined for our boss for years.

"Fair enough," Hugo said. "So when do we do something besides grunt work?"

Jackson snickered. "After lunch, we'll go out and I'll show you the pasture borders. We've got a lotta acres, and there are a few spots the steer get stuck in on occasion, so you gotta know where to look if someone's missing." He told Hugo the head count for each herd; not an unmanageable amount, but enough to keep the workers on their toes while the herds were grazing.

And they did exactly that. Hugo saddled up No Name, while Jackson went out on Juno, a pretty paint mare with a lot of spirit. She kind of reminded Hugo of Tude, a horse from his old life back at Clean Slate.

No thinking about that, though. It was time to look forward, not keep wandering back into the past.

Even if he did miss his old friends after less than a day.

The land was as open and beautiful as he remembered, in a far different way than California. Where Garrett land had mountains rising in the distance, Woods land was flatter, a bit dustier, with the occasional dry gulch or outcropping of rocks. Plenty of scrub trees and shrubs, the occasional cactus, and while it was chilly, there was none of the snow dusting they sometimes saw in winter. But it was also nearly March and the area was warming up for the season.

Hugo took care to remember the blind spots and dangerous spots where a steer sometimes got caught. They were pretty far out to the west, though, and Jackson said they only drove the herd that far out every other week or so for fresh grass, so the field closer to home had time to regrow. Hugo liked Brand's idea to switch over to organic beef. With as much land as they had for the herd to graze, it would save them a lot of money on hay and feed—which they'd still have to buy for the barned heifers, but in smaller quantities than right now.

He spotted the wind farm turbines, too, and even though a lot of people objected to wind energy because it "looked ugly," it didn't mar the beauty of the land for him. They added to it, because Brand was trying to save the land by relying less on fossil fuels for electricity.

After returning to the barn and untacking their horses, they did a few more odd jobs around the property. Similar to work Hugo had done in California, just without the added bother of tourists around. He'd miss the overnight camping trips, but such was life. Things

changed. Maybe he'd ask Elmer permission to camp out
in one of his fields some night. Sleep under the stars.

The only other time he saw Brand was when he and
Rem brought their horses back after a long afternoon
out on the land. It was only four o'clock, but Brand excused himself quickly to his office, citing paperwork.
Hugo tried not to let that sting as much as it did.

"So is he up to muster?" Rem asked Jackson as their
trio headed to the break room for some water.

"He's capable," Jackson replied, Dog trotting at his
heels. "He lasts his first week I think he'll work out
just fine."

"Gee, right here," Hugo said with feigned annoyance.

Rem snorted. "You'll do fine. At least you know what
you're doing. The last new guy we hired could barely
ride a horse, push a wheelbarrow, or muck a stall. I think
he lasted three days and then never showed up again."

"It's a hard life, which is why when I heard Colt
talking about your hiring problems, I decided to apply.
I've got the skills, and I was ready for a change." He
accepted a small bottle of water from the break room's
fridge and drank greedily, parched from breathing in
all the dust and hay bits. Hugo made a mental note to
order a good canteen online so he could keep water on
him while out in the pastures.

"Well, your need for change is our good luck. You
wanna go get a beer when we're done? Shelby works
until eight, and Susie's with her other grandparents tonight, so I've got some free time."

"Sounds good to me."

"Jackson?"

Jackson shook his head. "Nah, you two catch up.
I'd just be a third wheel in this re-budding bromance."

Rem laughed and took a good-natured swipe at Jackson's head. "Fuck off."

"If you insist." Jackson left the break room with his bottle of water.

"He seems like a decent guy," Hugo said. "A little quiet, but he showed me a lot today. Got me back into the ranching groove."

"Yeah, Jackson is solid. Been here a few years now. Doesn't like to talk about himself much, but he gets the job done so what's to complain about? I'm just glad Brutus and Dog get alone great, because Brutus is a protective dog. When Dad's dog Chance died last year, Dad tried getting another puppy but Brutus wasn't having it, so we had to rehome her."

"Bummer. But Brutus likes Dog okay?"

"Seems to. The first time Jackson brought her around, they sniffed and postured a bit, and now they're friends. Sometimes it just takes a minute to figure someone out."

If Hugo didn't know better, he'd think Rem was referring to Hugo more than the pair of dogs. "Guess so. So what, no barn cats for mice?"

"Actually, we've got two, but they're pretty shy during the day. Come out more at night when things are quiet and they can hunt better. Mom saves up all the meat table scraps for them so when she calls at night, they come running from wherever they've holed up."

He could totally see Rose Woods feeding meat scraps to a pair of shy barn cats every night. "Makes sense. So should I meet you somewhere after work?"

"Nah, I'll just toss the scooter in my truck bed, and we can drive out together. The Roost serves burgers until seven, so we can get dinner and a few beers at the same time."

"Sounds good."

And at five-thirty, they did exactly that. Hugo was tired, sore, and he smelled like horse and dung, but they were heading to a small-town bar in a small town surrounded by cattle ranchers and farmland. No one was going to care what they smelled like. Hugo had left the county before he was legally able to drink so he'd never been inside the Roost, only driven past it. The place was clean and less smoky than other bars he'd patronized, and they had to wait about ten minutes for a table.

"It's nice to have a few hours to myself," Rem said once they'd been seated and handed very brief menus. Mostly burgers and typical bar snacks. "I love my wife and kid, but sometimes you just need a night off, you know?"

Hugo did not know, not really, but he nodded for his friend's sake anyway. "Sure. Still can't figure on you being a dad. So much has changed."

"Yeah. We've been trying for another kid but so far no luck. If nothing happens in another year or so, Shelby wants to try one of those fertility doctors. See what's what." Rem scowled. "Hate to think it's my plumbing, but Shelby wants more kids so we'll do what it takes to give her some."

"Good man." Hugo had never pictured himself as a dad. To be honest, he'd never pictured himself as much of anything, other than an odd-job-working drifter. Someone simply trying to blend in and survive, and to forget the giant crush he'd left behind here in Weston.

Their waitress came by and Rem ordered them a pitcher of beer. "So you're obviously still single. You and Brand should compare notes. I swear, that man is never gonna get married. You see that dark-haired gal behind the bar?" He pointed, and Hugo spotted the petite woman pouring something into a shaker. "That's Ramie. Rachel Marie. They've been close lately, but he never brings her around like as a date, so I don't know what's up for sure. She's pretty, though, and single. He needs to snatch her up before someone else does."

"Maybe she's the one not interested in dating." He couldn't stop the statement, because the hint of misogyny in Rem's comment annoyed him, as if Ramie was pining away for some hot dude to come along, flash his dimples, and marry her. He didn't know the woman at all, but it was the fucking twenty-first century. Not everyone wanted or needed marriage and kids.

"Well, Brand's running out of options."

Maybe Brand isn't interested in her either, because he wants something else. Someone else.

Instead of voicing that, Hugo skimmed the meager meal offerings and decided on a simple bacon cheeseburger. They both ordered when their waitress dropped off the beer and two chilled glasses. Rem poured them each a glass, then held up his. "To old friends coming home, dude."

"Cheers." Hugo tapped the rim of his glass to Rem's and smiled. "To being home and facing old ghosts."

The burgers were great and the company even better. He and Rem bullshitted about high school for a while, until a pair of girls from Rem's class joined them with a platter of nachos everyone shared. Hugo vaguely recalled them both, but they'd been older, and he spent a bit of time explaining his whereabouts of the last ten or so years. They were interested in the ghost town, and

Hugo kind of wished he'd brought along some business cards, but Texas had enough of its own similar attractions that didn't require airplanes and out-of-state travel.

Around seven, the music cranked up a bit and people started dancing. Rem went out with the girls, but Hugo begged off, citing zero rhythm, which was mostly true. He could dance in a pinch, but tonight he wanted to people watch for a while. He watched them all dance and sipped his beer, content to simply exist in that space. No responsibilities, no tasks to complete. No new roommate to show around. Just beer, chips, country music, and a free evening to…be.

What he really wanted to be was with Brand, but Brand had made it very clear today he didn't want the same thing. Which sucked. But Hugo was an adult, and he could handle being ignored. Except around eight that night, just as a second pitcher of beer arrived for him, Rem, and their lady friends, Brand strode into the bar in his boots and hat, and Hugo's heart swelled with appreciation for the perfect cowboy package he made.

"Hey, dude, join us!" Rem said over the din of conversation and Dolly Parton belting out "Jolene."

Brand's gaze flickered toward Hugo once, uncertain, before approaching their table. "Didn't know you guys would be here tonight."

"Getting Hugo used to the life again. Dana, another glass!"

Their waitress flashed them a thumbs-up. Hugo tried not to stare at Brand, who looked as comfortable as a long-tailed cat in a room full of rocking chairs, and he avoided all of Hugo's curious glances. Was he here to see Ramie? To simply have a drink and relax? None of the above?

Dana delivered the glass, and Rem poured one for Brand. They all stood around drinking until "Achy Breaky Heart" came on. The brunette in the group grabbed Rem and dragged him onto the dance floor, while the blonde set her sights on Hugo. Hugo immediately sat and nursed his beer, not interested in fucking up a dance number he didn't know. When Brand did the same, she wandered off to find another partner.

And now that Hugo was finally alone—well, as alone as he could be in a noisy bar on a Monday night—with his old crush, he couldn't think of a single thing to say to the man. Then he blurted out the most trite thing possible: "You look good."

Brand stared at him over the rim of his beer glass, blue eyes cold as ice. He took a sip of beer and said nothing.

Great, we're right beside each other and he still won't talk to me.

Maybe taking a job at Woods Ranch had been a mistake after all.

Chapter Five

Brand had come back out tonight for a beer, some music, and to think. Sure, he'd used paperwork as the perfect excuse to avoid showing Hugo around the ranch, but Brand hadn't been lying. As foreman, he had better things to do than break in a newbie, and Jackson was fully capable. Brand had managed to avoid Hugo for the rest of the day, and he'd never admit to having watched Hugo a few times from his office window. Nope.

Except he had. Hugo moved like a dream on his horse, even better than when he was a teenager. He was more confident now, walked with his spine straight instead of scuffling around like he didn't want to be noticed. Until teenage Hugo had made it his mission to make Brand notice him. And he had.

Now, Brand was stuck at a table with Hugo, drinking beer, because he had two left feet and knew better than to get out on the dance floor. Ramie once told him he had legs like tree trunks, quoting from a TV show they both loved and had binged together more than once when they both simply wanted companionship for a night.

Brand glared at Hugo's compliment. Not because he didn't appreciate it but because he did. Hugo seemed equally uncomfortable with the situation, as if he had things to say but those things required privacy. And Brand wasn't sure he trusted himself in private with the younger man. Seven years wasn't a lot for some folks, but Brand remembered Hugo as the gangly, unsure teenager he'd first met during summer break from college. By the time Brand graduated and returned home, Hugo had filled out and grown a few inches, and he'd been insanely cute.

He still was. And he was here. Now. Within touching distance.

Brand put his glass down with a too-hard clank and topped it off from the pitcher. "Um, thanks. You grew up."

Hugo didn't hide a flinch. "Yeah, that happens over time. Life experience helps you grow up real fast, especially when you're on your own. But I bet Colt has told you stories about his time after leaving home."

"Some stories, but he prefers sticking to the present. Living in the now. Guess that's a Woods thing." Maybe Hugo would get the subtle hint and drop the topic for now. The middle of a crowded bar wasn't the time or place to follow Ramie's advice about clearing the air.

Instead of backing off, Hugo looked more determined. "Colt didn't leave the past in the past, and you got your big brother back. Colt got Avery back and married the man."

"I don't know what you think we'll get back if we talk about our past."

His face hardened, as if he'd just accepted some kind of silent challenge Brand hadn't meant to throw down. "So are you and Ramie dating?"

Brand opened his mouth to ask how the hell? Then it hit. "I see Rem's been running his mouth."

"Like a motorboat. So?"

"Ramie and I are good friends who occasionally fuck." He hadn't meant to let that slip, because he never confirmed or denied what he and Ramie were to each other to other people. It was easier to let folks speculate. But for some reason, Hugo's nearness fucked with his brain-to-mouth censor.

"Hey, at least you're getting laid," Hugo said in a nonchalant tone Brand didn't buy for a second.

"There's tail in this town if you know where to chase it." He watched Hugo's face, curious if Hugo would rise to the bait and ask where to find it, or swat it away because he had his sights set on Brand.

Hugo's eyes narrowed. "Trust me, I know where to chase it."

Thought so.

They held eye contact for a long moment, neither of them blinking. Hugo's eyes offered a subtle challenge of their own, but as much as that challenge appealed to Brand, he wasn't biting. Not tonight. Despite finding the kid attractive, and liking this new pushy side of Hugo, Brand was his boss. To everyone except Jackson and Ramie, Brand was also straight, and he was going to keep it that way. Maybe Brand did need to clear the air with Hugo, but not tonight.

Right now, the ranch was his first priority, and he couldn't risk their conversation scaring Hugo off.

"Well, then maybe you better go chasin' it and stop botherin' me," Brand said with a thicker drawl that usual. "Tell Rem thanks for the beer." Spots had opened up at the bar, so Brand grabbed his glass and headed that way.

Ramie shot him a few curious looks while she made drinks, then sidled her way over to his corner, which was about three empty stools away from other people.

"So did that look as awkward as it felt?" Brand asked as softly as he could over the music. Part of him regretted how rude he'd been but it couldn't be helped now.

"Nope." She gave him a bowl of peanuts to munch on. "You looked like a pair of alpha wolves circling each other, unsure if you're about to start a brawl or go out back and fuck each other."

He dropped his forehead into his palm. "Think anyone else noticed?"

"Hard to say, but no one else had a reason to watch you guys like I did, so probably not. I hate to say it, but it looks like there's chemistry there, Brand."

"There is, which is why I need to stay the hell away from him. Fucking an employee is not a good look."

"You fuck Jackson."

He glanced around, slightly alarmed, but no one was paying them any attention. "That's different. We started fucking around before Dad hired him."

She picked up his beer glass and put a napkin under it. "So it's different with Hugo because all you ever did was kiss?"

It was one doozy of a kiss, though.

"Yes, it's different. Ugh. All I wanted was to come out for a beer and relax, and now he's got me all twisted up. Mouthy brat."

"You wouldn't be twisted up if you didn't like him. Be back." She hustled off to take an order.

Brand wanted to bang his forehead off the bar rail,

because she wasn't wrong. He'd never forgotten Hugo—which was hard to do with Rem around all the time working the ranch. He wanted to know more about the journey that had turned a watchful teenager into the challenging man Hugo was now.

He wanted it but he couldn't have it. So he nursed his beer and tried to ignore the sense of being watched from behind.

Hugo tried not to stare while Brand and Ramie spoke, unsure exactly what they were discussing but he had a good feeling it was him. Hugo was generally an easygoing person who got along with most people, and he'd been friendly with everyone at Clean Slate Ranch. He was friendly with everyone at Woods Ranch, too—except Brand.

Brand was keeping a deliberate distance, and that not only intrigued Hugo, it also woke up the part of himself who'd pined for Brand for a long time. The part of himself that knew Brand had enjoyed and responded to their first and only kiss. And it made him want to fight. Fight for exactly what, he wasn't sure, only that he wasn't letting this go.

They would have their damned conversation about that kiss.

Rem and his dancing partner came back to the table and downed some beer. "Hey, where'd Brand go?" Rem asked.

"Over to the bar," Hugo replied, pasting on an affable smile. "Guess I smell."

"You kinda do, pal."

He took a swipe at Rem's side. "Asshole. If I smell, you smell."

"Hey, I'm not the one who spent all day mucking stalls."

"True." They had a boot scraper outside the barn doors but some odors stuck to your skin, too. Oh well, it wasn't as if Hugo had come out to meet a girl. He just wanted to spend time with his friend and celebrate a successful first day. Running into Brand here had been an intriguing bonus.

It was getting late, and Hugo had a bit of a drive out to Elmer's place on his scooter, so he thanked Rem for the beer and headed out. Wasn't too hard getting the scooter out of the truck bed himself. It was sturdy like a Vespa but not as heavy as a proper motorcycle. He put on the helmet, stuck the keys Rem had given him earlier into the ignition and she roared to life.

He took one last glance at the Roost's front door, just in time to see Brand step outside. Their eyes met, and even from the distance, he could tell Brand's narrowed. Brand turned and walked toward the other end of the parking lot.

Interesting.

It took Hugo about ten minutes longer to get to Elmer's house on the scooter, because his property was farther from town than the entrance to Woods Ranch. Only a few lights were on in Elmer's house when he parked by the trailer, but more lights and a commotion were coming from the barn out back. Curious, Hugo hung the helmet on the scooter and ambled toward the barn.

Both big doors stood open, and just inside a sea of sparks colored the air. Elmer was bent over a workbench of some kind, a welder's mask on, working on a project. Hugo had admired all of the iron and metal artwork littering both the front fence and Elmer's yard. Apparently, he'd begun the hobby not long after marrying and buying the property. He was retired now, and a widower, but that was really all Hugo knew about the man.

He watched from the barn's entrance, one shoulder leaning against the frame, as the elderly man worked. After a few minutes of careful welding, Elmer turned off his torch, put it down, then snapped up his mask. He finally seemed to notice Hugo watching him and smiled. "How'd your first day of work go, lad?"

"Pretty basic, but it went fine. Jackson showed me the ropes." He took another step into the barn, now better able to see the piles of metal objects strewn all around the place. Bike frames, old tools, appliance parts, a rusty woodstove. It was a picker's paradise. "Went down to the Roost with Rem for a beer. It was a good day. You?"

"Can't complain too much, can I? Got a roof, food, and a hobby that keeps me busy most days. Could be a lot worse."

"Yes, sir. I never was very artistic. Always had a good head for math and science, though. I like puzzles." He chuckled over the memory of seeing his very first Rubik's cube when Hugo watched his ex-roommate Slater sit there and solve the damned thing. Hugo had looked it up on his phone later, and it was apparently pretty hard to master. So he'd bought himself one, which was tucked away in his dresser drawer. He was so close to solving it...

"Jigsaw puzzles? Because I've got a two-thousand piece going on my dining room table and can't seem to manage it. You should come inside one night after work and help me."

Jigsaws weren't his favorite, but how could he tell his landlord no? "I'd like that, thank you. I also like those logic problem books, and I was really into Sudoku for a while."

"Bah, that numbers stuff bores me. I need to do stuff with my hands."

Hugo grinned. "I completely understand. I can only sit still for so long." A wide, unexpected yawn made his eyes water. "Gosh, I should be getting settled in for the night. Another early day tomorrow. Good night, Mr. Pearce."

"I told you to call me Elmer."

"Elmer."

He turned and headed for his trailer, eager for the privacy after being around other people all day. His interaction with Brand tonight still stuck in his craw. He got the sense that Brand did want to talk to him, but something was holding him back. Something big. Maybe scary. Maybe potentially amazing.

He walked inside and smiled at the latch hook rug Slater had made for him as a going-away present. After the gruff cowboy busted his ankle almost two years ago, he'd taught himself craft projects as a hobby, and he'd made profane pieces for all his friends. Hugo's rug said "Live, Laugh, Fuck Off." He loved it.

As he shucked his boots and jeans, Hugo reminded himself he wasn't here to find a boyfriend. He was here for a job, first and foremost. Then he was here to try and patch old hurts, and while that included talking to Brand about their toe-curling kiss, it also included reuniting with his mother. He wasn't ready for his mother yet. Maybe after he'd settled in a while longer. Gotten more comfortable being back in Texas. He did miss her, but he also hadn't forgotten the way she'd brushed off his concerns about how Buck treated Hugo.

"Boys will be boys," she'd often said.

He despised that phrase down to his bones.

After a quick shower to wash the day off him, Hugo stretched out in bed, closed his eyes, and remembered how handsome Brand had looked tonight. Leaning back in his chair with a beer in his hand, doing his best to ignore Hugo and kind of failing at it. Hugo had squashed back a slight pang of jealousy when Brand retreated to the bar to speak with Ramie, but he believed Brand when he said they weren't an item. Still, good friends who occasionally fuck could still become a couple.

Nah, Brand was into him but he was scared of something. Weston was a pretty small town, even for this part of Texas, and Hugo had no idea if any other gay folks lived here openly. Brand's family wouldn't give him a hard time, considering Colt and his husband. Maybe Brand had had a bad experience with a guy that left him gun-shy? Hugo hated to think that anyone could have hurt him, especially given Hugo's history with Buck.

One of these days, Hugo would finagle a real conversation out of Brand. A private one. He drifted off to sleep hoping it happened soon.

Because of their current small staff, Hugo and Jackson rotated their days off, with the Woods men filling in and often going up to a week without real time off. Brand spent about half his time in the office, and the other half out in the pastures checking on the herds. Hugo was still mostly on barn duty, which he didn't mind. He was used to that sort of work, and his first week at Woods Ranch passed pretty fast.

Hugo's first day off was Friday, and he wasn't sure what to do with himself. He should drive out to Daisy and see his mother, but he wasn't ready for that conversation yet. So he drove the scooter around Weston for a while, re-familiarizing himself with the place. Not much had changed, other than an empty storefront that he swore had once been an antique shop. Now it had a For Rent sign in the window.

He had lunch at Weston Diner and spent some time emailing his friends while he chowed down on a chicken fried steak and fries. Shawn and Miles kept in frequent contact with texts, and Hugo had sent them photos of not only his trailer, but also some of Elmer's amazing artwork. Neither of them knew a thing about his history with Brand, though, and he kind of wished they did. He really wanted to talk to someone about this, but the only real friend he had here was Rem, and Hugo was so not going there with him.

He was friendly with Jackson, but the last thing he needed was for Jackson to blab something to other people. Not that he seemed the gossipy sort.

A short body plunked down in the booth across from him and folded her hands on the table. Hugo blinked hard at Ramie, who'd invited herself to join him, apparently. "Uh, hi?"

"I saw you with Rem and Brand at the Roost the other night," she said in a pleasant, somewhat deep voice. "You're the new guy at the ranch. Bruno?"

"Hugo. Hugo Turner." But why did he have a feeling she knew that and had misnamed him on purpose?

"Nice to meet you. I hear you and Brand are good friends."

"We are. I think I know him pretty well, and he tells me stuff. Private stuff."

Hugo put his phone down and rested his hands in his lap, caught between annoyed and intrigued. "Okay."

His waitress came over and asked if Ramie wanted anything; Ramie said no. When the waitress left, Ramie continued. "Brand is a very guarded person, because he thinks he carries the weight of the entire ranch on his shoulders. He puts the ranch and his family over himself, instead of going for what he might want."

"So what is this? You telling me to leave Brand alone?"

"Nope." She leaned forward and lowered her voice. "I know a bit about your history, and he's conflicted about things. He also deserves a good person who can love him the way he deserves to be loved. I don't know if that person's you, or if they're still out there, but if you do have feelings for him? Don't be subtle about it. Sometimes you have to knock the Woods men upside the head with a boot to get their attention."

Hugo studied her, surprised she seemed to be nudging him toward pursuing Brand, rather than trying to turn him off the idea. Goading Brand would be easy enough, but now that he'd met Ramie, he didn't want to get in between something. She was pretty in a country girl way, with a round face and dark brown, almost-black hair that hung low around the middle of her back. "Why aren't you and Brand a couple?"

"Can you keep a secret?"

"Definitely."

"Good. So can I." She flashed him a charming smile. "Maybe when I know you better."

"Fair. I appreciate the advice, and I really do wanna talk to Brand, but he's harder to pin down than a bucking bronco on an eight-second ride."

"See? You know him better than you think. He's avoiding you because he wants to avoid facing something about himself. But he's thirty-five years old and needs to face it."

As much as Hugo agreed with her, he asked, "Shouldn't that be his decision?"

"Yes. But as his friends, it might not hurt for us to nudge him that way."

True. Someone as stubborn as Brand didn't always react well to blatant nudging, though. He'd clammed up when Hugo tried to engage him at the Roost on Monday. Maybe backing off and letting Brand stew for a while, until Brand came to him, was a better plan. Hugo got the feeling the stubborn cowboy did not like being ignored.

"You seem like a nice guy, Hugo," she said. "And Brand does like you, even if he won't admit it."

"I've been in love with him since I was sixteen." Now why on earth had that slipped out? "Um."

She just smiled. "Then don't give up. I love Brand. He's one of my very best friends, and I want him to be happy."

"Thank you, Ramie."

"Anytime. I gotta get to work. Good luck, Hugo." She slid out of the booth.

Hugo stared at her empty seat, the last of his lunch forgotten, unexpectedly buoyed by her words. As one of Brand's best friends, she had a vested interest in his happiness, so she wouldn't say those things if she didn't mean them. And she didn't strike him as the type of person who'd say something untrue just to see Hugo crash and burn with Brand.

Maybe he had a true ally in this push-pull he was playing with Brand.

Time would tell.

Chapter Six

The next two weeks passed, easing February into March, and Brand couldn't figure out what game Hugo was playing. After being pushy and challenging during his first week at the ranch, now he was keeping his distance. Being as professional as possible at all times. He turned down Mom's invitations to Sunday dinners, avoided Brand whenever he came out to the barn, and kept his answers to questions clipped and unemotional.

What the fuck is he playing at?

Brand didn't know but the little shit was irritating the hell out of him. After lunch on Monday, he found Hugo alone in the barn, mucking Mercutio's stall—Rem had apparently been in a big Shakespeare kick when they bought and named him. It was Rem's day off, and Jackson was out in the pastures checking the herds. They really needed to hire another temporary employee until Alan's hand healed, which wouldn't be for another few weeks. But calving season was coming up, and they already had three temps lined up to help with that work. They could stick it out for a few more weeks.

He watched the way Hugo's entire body got into the motions of shoveling through the shit and hay, and then twisted at the waist to dump it into the wheelbarrow. The way his ass filled out his jeans—nope. "Ahem."

Hugo yelped in an adorable way and spun around, shovel half-raised as if ready to strike. "Christ, Brand, you scared the shit out of me."

"Sorry." Not sorry. "You about done?"

"Yes, sir." He turned back to the stall.

"Really? Then why have you been avoiding me?"

"You made it very clear this is a boss-employee relationship, *sir*. That's how I'm treating it, too. Can I finish my work?"

Brand flinched as his own attitude was tossed back in his face. First, all Hugo wanted to do was talk, and now nothing? "Fine. Have you seen Brutus around? He's usually at the house for lunch, begging for scraps." It didn't worry him none. Brutus might have followed Jackson and Dog out into the fields, but it continued his conversation with Hugo.

"Not since early this morning." Hugo glanced over his shoulder. "I'll keep an eye out for him, though. Probably out there chasing steer with Dog."

"That's what I figure, too. Um, see you later, then."

"Yeah."

Unused to being so bluntly dismissed by his own employee, Brand turned and headed out the main barn doors. He debated going back to his office, versus maybe taking a long walk to clear his head and think, when the sound of galloping hoofbeats turned his head to the west. Jackson was riding in like a bat out of hell, Dog not far behind with her tongue lolling out.

The closer Jackson got, the higher Brand's heartbeat rose. Something furry was draped across the saddle in front of Jackson.

"No," Brand said. "Brutus!" He started running. Behind him, Hugo shouted, asking what was wrong. But Brand only had eyes for his dog, who shouldn't be weak enough to be carried like that. Not unless something was very wrong.

"Get a truck!" Jackson shouted. "He needs to see Dr. Joe stat!"

Brand glanced over his shoulder, grateful to see Hugo changing direction and heading for one of the ranch's work trucks. They kept keys on top of the sun visor so anyone could use one who needed to. Jackson pulled his horse to an ungraceful stop, and Brand saw the blood all over Brutus's coat. "Fucking hell, what happened?"

"I don't know for sure," Jackson replied. "He followed us out first thing, but then I lost track of him. Figured he was off scenting a missing steer and he'd be back to lead us to him. Then Dog took off, and I followed her. Brutus must have gotten into a fight with a coyote or something, because we found him like this. He's alive, man, but he's weak."

Brand fought back furious tears as he eased his dog out of Jackson's saddle and into his own arms. Brutus was heavy, but Brand had raised him from a pup, and he wasn't letting go now. "I've got you, boy, I've got you."

Brutus whined, and the sound nearly broke Brand's heart.

Hugo sped over with the pickup, the back wheels kicking up dirt and dust. He leaned across the bench seat and shoved the passenger door open. With some help from Jackson, Brand got inside with his dog in his lap. One of Brutus's brown eyes blinked at him, seeming to ask what was going to happen. And also ask if he was a good boy.

"You'll be fine, buddy, just fine," Brand said. "Hugo, take the road to town. I'll give you directions to the vet's office."

"Okay." Hugo sped off, face set and determined. "He'll be all right, Brand. Believe that."

"Yeah." He petted Brutus's smooth muzzle, hating all the cuts on his beautiful coat. All the blood soaking into Brand's own clothes. "Fuck."

A strong hand squeezed his shoulder. "Come on, pal, keep it together."

Since Brand wasn't sure if he could speak without crying—this was his dog, damn it!—he only nodded and kept his focus on Brutus. When Hugo reached the end of the ranch road and the state road to town, he found the strength to say, "There's a blanket under the front seat. Can you give it to me?"

"Sure." Hugo shifted into park and rummaged around until he found the cheap wool blanket. He helped Brand situate it around Brutus as best they could to stanch some of the bleeding, and then he was driving again. Way over the speed limit, but Brand didn't care. He'd pay the ticket gladly as long as they got to Dr. Joe's on time.

His house/practice was on Main Street and easy enough to find. Once Hugo parked, he ran around the front of the truck to help Brand get out. Hugo supported Brutus's head with surprising care on the short journey up a sidewalk to the main office door. They burst inside, surprising a small dog in a carrier into yipping at them. Brutus barely twitched.

"Please, I need help," Brand bellowed. "Dr. Joe!"

His receptionist, a young woman named Lucy, took one look at them and indicated they should follow her behind a closed door that led to a few exam rooms. Every single one of Brutus's checkups had been in this office, by this doctor. Now that he was here, Brutus would be okay. He had to be.

Brand gently put Brutus on a shiny metal exam table, hating the way his boy whined in agony. It speared his soul. While they'd always had dogs on the ranch, Brutus's sire, Champ, had been the first dog Brand remembered being just his. Brutus had to be fine.

Dr. Joe rushed in with a vet tech Brand didn't recognize. "Do you know what did this?" Dr. Joe asked.

"No, Jackson found him," Brand replied, not really recognizing his own voice. "He didn't know either, didn't see another animal. Could have been a coyote or a wild dog after the herd."

"All right, well his rabies vaccines are up to date, so we'll see about getting these wounds tended to. You two wait outside."

Lucy shooed Brand and Hugo out. Led them back to the waiting room. The yippy dog and its owner were gone, probably sensing their appointment was going to be postponed for quite some time. Hugo planted Brand into a chair, then went over to speak with Lucy. Brand just stared at the wall, numb all over, until Hugo returned with a wet towel that he used to wipe at Brand's arms and hands. Brand looked down at the blood smears and choked.

"Hey," Hugo said, with an unusual amount of steel in his voice. The voice of the man who'd first showed up to the ranch and challenged him. "He'll be fine. Believe that, okay?"

Brand tried to nod but all he could do was gulp in air.

"Jesus, come here." Hugo stood and pulled Brand up into a hug. Wiry arms wrapped around Brand's shoulders, a pleasant weight that simply held without demanding. Warmth seeped into his skin and he let himself be held. So much of Brand wanted to let go and sob out his fear, but he couldn't do that. Not in front of an employee, and not in front of Lucy. He did let himself hug Hugo back, though, arms around his waist. Hugo's own grip tightened a fraction, and Brand sagged against the strong, capable man, soaking in the comfort, grateful for the support. For holding him so Brand didn't fall apart while his dog's life hung in the balance.

He rested his head on Hugo's shoulder and tried to remember how to breathe.

"He'll be okay, babe," Hugo whispered right into his ear. "He will."

"Please," was all Brand could manage. A prayer to God but for what exactly? For sure, he wanted Brutus to be all right. Forgiveness for how rude he'd been to Hugo his first day at the ranch? Maybe. Another minute in this steady, supportive hug? Definitely.

Once Brand knew he could stand without topping over, he gently untangled himself from Hugo's hug and pulled back, noting the smears of blood now on Hugo's shirt. "Thanks. It's just...he's my best friend."

"I get it." Hugo tugged him down and sat in the chair beside him, his expression all concern and sympathy. "Think positive, man. We got him here fast."

"Yeah." His phone buzzed with a text but Brand couldn't think to answer it. He didn't even flinch when Hugo dug into his jeans pocket to find his phone.

"It's from your father, asking if we know anything."

"We don't but at least we're here, right?"

Hugo's fingers flew across the screen, much faster than Brand could text, and he assumed Hugo was sending along a similar message. "I also added we'll text when we know something."

"Thank you. For all of this."

"I wouldn't be anywhere else while you're hurting."

Brand glanced over, but Hugo had gone bright red and looked down at his lap. Had these last two weeks of professionalism been some sort of act? And for what? Whatever. Lucy was busy at her desk, so Brand risked reaching out and quickly squeezing Hugo's wrist. "That means more than you know, Hugo. I mean it."

Hugo tilted his head, barely meeting Brand's eyes, and something new burned there. Something protective that spoke to Brand deep inside. The part of Brand who'd responded to a kiss all those years ago. The lizard part of Brand's brain wanted him to lean over and kiss Hugo, but his logical side held back. This wasn't the time or place. The comfort meant the world to him, but until Brutus was out of the woods, Brand couldn't divide his attention.

"You're welcome," Hugo said in a raspy voice.

They sat together, side by side, without touching for what felt like an eternity. Brand was silently grateful for Hugo's steady presence, which was the only thing that kept him grounded until Dr. Joe came into the waiting room. His expression was serious, but not grim, which gave Brand a flash of hope that he'd get good news.

"You got Brutus here at just the right time," Dr. Joe said. "He's lost quite a bit of blood, and has some deep lacerations, which I was able to suture. He'll be in some pain and have to be fitted for a cone so he doesn't mess with my handiwork. I administered an antibiotic and I'll send you home with oral painkillers to help him along, but I expect he'll pull through."

Brand nearly doubled over with relief. "Thank you. Thank you so much."

"Of course. He put up a valiant fight against whatever attacked him. I'd like to keep him here overnight in a kennel for observation and to watch for infection."

"Whatever you think, Doc." As much as Brand hated being parted from his beloved pet, he'd do anything to make sure Brutus was okay. He might already be ten years old, which was up there for a shepherd, but Brand wasn't ready to say goodbye to his best friend yet.

"I'll warn you, though, he may not run the way he used to," Dr. Joe said, as if mirroring Brand's thoughts. "He's an elderly dog, even though he doesn't act it, chasing after cattle out in those fields. But he should be around for a few more years, nipping at your heels and stealing food off lunch plates."

Tears stung Brand's eyes, and he wasn't ashamed of wiping them away. "Thank you again. I'm sorry for busting in like this, and I'll pay whatever emergency fee you want to charge me."

Dr. Joe patted Brand's shoulder. "How about we discuss that tomorrow when you pick Brutus up? You look like you could use a change of clothes and a snort or two of whiskey."

Both of those things sounded like very good ideas. "Can I see him first? Just for a minute?"

The tech led him to a small room in the back with six kennels. Two held adult cats, and one of the largest on the bottom had Brutus. He lay under a blanket, his head facing the door, and his ears perked up when

Brand approached, despite his eyes being a bit glassy. He still knew his human.

Brand squatted, biting back more joyful tears. His hand fit through the bars of the kennel, and he lightly dragged one finger down Brutus's black snout. "Hey, buddy. I'm so sorry you got hurt, but you're gonna be okay, I promise. You gotta stay here tonight, though. I know you'd rather sleep by my bed, but we can manage one night apart, right?"

Brutus licked his fingertip.

"Yeah." Before he did turn into a blubbering mess, Brand stood and headed toward the waiting room. With a vague nod at Dr. Joe, he went directly outside into the fresh, cool air, Hugo not far behind. He stood by the truck and took a minute to compose himself, keenly aware of the dried blood all over his flannel shirt and jeans.

Hugo circled to stand in front of him, and Brand saw the streaks of blood on his own clothes, probably from the comforting hug he'd given Brand. The kind of hug that had kept him together when he'd wanted to fall apart. The kind of hug that said "I've got you" and "We'll get through this together."

The kind of hug Brand had craved for a long, long time.

"I'd offer to take you to the Roost for a beer," Hugo said after they stared at each other in tense silence for a long time, "but we're both covered in blood, and I don't want someone to call the sheriff and report a murder."

Brand wheezed laughter. "Good call. Wouldn't mind that whiskey, though. Dad's got a bottle in the kitchen."

Hugo put a hand over his heart and feigned shock.

"In the middle of a workday, Mr. All Work and No Play Makes Brand a Dull Boy?"

"Brat." He rolled his shoulders and neck. "I should call my dad."

"I texted him while you were with Brutus. Told him what we knew. He and Jackson are out taking care of the herd, so we can take our time." Hugo tilted his head in a way that was both curious and boyishly adorable. "I guess your dad knows how much Brutus means to you, huh?"

"Yeah. Some people might think it's silly to get so emotional over a dog but he's my best friend. His sire was our old dog Champ, but his bitch belonged to a neighbor who bred shepherds. Brutus was the runt of the litter and so small that the woman who'd paid us to help sling the pups was gonna put him down, instead of trying to raise him to sell. I couldn't let her, because he was the only boy pup and Champ was getting on in years. Said I'd buy the pup then and there, at only two weeks old, full-price no matter what happened. If he lived to eight weeks and weaned off her teat, I'd take him."

"Wow." Hugo stared at him with something like respect in his dark eyes. "You had a lot of faith in Champ's genes, huh?"

"And in Brutus. He was the tiniest pup I'd ever seen, but man, when he was a year old, he saved my life. Bit the head clean off a rattler before it could bite me. I didn't even see or hear the damned thing coming but Brutus did. He's a loyal dog."

"And that loyal dog will be home tomorrow. Might take some time before he's out there working the cattle again, but he's going to live, Brand. Hang on to that. Faith is the most important part."

"Thanks." Brand's own heart betrayed him and his gaze strayed briefly down. Right to Hugo's lips. But only for a split second, before he cleared his throat and looked at his own feet. "We should get back."

"Yeah." Hugo squeezed his wrist gently, then circled to the driver's side of the truck. Got in and started the engine.

It took Brand a moment to unstick his crank and get into the truck. Some of Brutus's blood stained the seats, and Brand made a mental note to clean that up before it set in too deeply. They didn't speak on the drive back to the ranch, the radio quietly playing a local country station. Without meaning to, something had shifted between him and Hugo today, and Brand didn't know what to do about it. Hugo was loyal, supportive, and kind (not to mention ten kinds of cute), and he'd dropped everything to help Brand save his dog. So much stronger than the scared teen he remembered.

But Brand couldn't be more than friends with Hugo, no matter how much the idea intrigued his mind and warmed his heart. Too much was at stake with the ranch and keeping his family afloat. He'd resented his big brother, Colt, for a lot of years after Colt disappeared and Brand became the default next Woods to run the place. Brand had wanted to be a teacher, to help kids learn and grow. But he'd accepted the responsibility with both hands, and he couldn't risk it all now.

Not for a fling with an employee.

Rose Woods flew out the front doors of the main house as soon as Hugo cut the engine of the truck, hands clasped over her chest as she approached. Brand climbed out, a bit stiff with shock, and he allowed his mother to squeeze both shoulders, and then his cheeks. Hugo had no doubt she would have hugged him if Brand wasn't covered in blood.

Hugo put the keys under the visor, then got out and circled the truck, unsure what to do next. He and Brand had shared a moment. A real, honest-to-God moment back at the vet's office. From the hug to Brand looking at his mouth like he wanted to kiss him. For all Hugo had tried to keep his distance and play it cool, he'd been helpless under the force of Brand's fear and uncertainty. Helpless to do anything except try and fix it for him. But Hugo couldn't fix Brutus. All he could do was be present and give Brand anything he needed.

"Poor Brutus," Rose said. It had taken Hugo a while to start thinking of the elder Woods couple by their first names, but Wayne had encouraged it. "He'll be okay?"

"Dr. Joe thinks so," Brand replied, still a bit hoarse. He looked like he wanted to burst into tears but was keeping it together for appearances, even though he was around family. No one would care if he showed emotion. "He's keeping him overnight, but I should be able to bring him home tomorrow. Probably have to make a bed for him in the living room. Doubt he'll be able to take the stairs with all those stitches."

"Then we'll do just that. Brutus might have four legs but he's still part of the family."

"Thanks, Mom."

Rose kissed his cheek. "Go on upstairs and change out of those clothes. Bring them down so I can get the stains out."

"Okay." Brand headed toward the house.

After giving Hugo a quick once-over, she said, "Brand! Bring a clean shirt down for Hugo. I'll wash his, too."

He gave a thumbs-up without turning around. Hugo glanced down at his own blood-speckled shirt, evidence of his hug with Brand. "Thank you, ma'am," Hugo said. He doubted the horses would mind a bit of blood, but it was a kind gesture. "I don't guess Jackson found what attacked Brutus."

"Wayne called a bit ago and said they found a blood trail heading toward the west fence, but it faded before the property line. Whatever it was is wounded." Her sour expression signaled she hoped it died in a ditch somewhere, but old-fashioned manners kept her from voicing it. "Never had a wild animal attack one of our dogs before. I just hope it wasn't rabid."

"It could have been starving. Desperate." Hungry people did crazy things for food, so why should wild animals be any different?

"True. Why don't you come inside for some lemonade, and then we'll get your shirt changed."

"Thank you, ma'am, I'd like that."

Hugo had avoided going into the Woods house after that first Sunday supper, mostly to avoid Brand, and the place still felt like home. A much warmer home than either he'd grown up in. The first house he'd lived in on his mother's ranch had been…a house. No real warmth or character, but it had also been small and over a hundred years old, with only a single window a/c unit in the living room for summer, and a woodstove for winter. The Turner Ranch had been struggling for two generations by the time Hugo's father decided to sell.

And divorce Hugo's mother, leaving her with no job,

a small pile of cash, and a ten-year-old to raise by herself. Until she met Frank Archer a year later. Frank lived in a dingy double-wide with his son, Buck, who was three years older than Hugo. While Frank was indifferent to Hugo, Buck seemed to resent him right off the bat because he wasn't the only son anymore.

At the time, Hugo had never imagined how bad it would get.

"Hugo?" Rose said.

He realized he'd stopped in the middle of the hallway, staring at nothing in particular. Rose watched him from the kitchen entrance, a curious smile on her age-worn face. "Sorry, I got lost in thought." He got his engine in gear.

"Thank you for being with Brand today." She pulled the pitcher of lemonade from the fridge, then got two tall glasses from a cupboard. Ice from the freezer. Hugo just stood there, watching, unsure if he should sit, stand, or flee so the truth didn't fly out of his mouth like it had with Ramie.

As a teenager, Hugo had been in love with Brand Woods, who'd demonstrated a mix of determination, compassion, and family loyalty Hugo didn't have in his own home life. Brand had been his hero, and even after things went sideways between them, Hugo had loved him. Until time and distance faded the shine of those feelings. Some had lingered, sure, but Brand's snubs since Hugo's return had kept them from redeveloping. Until today.

Until he saw the love and loyalty in Brand again while he grieved and worried over his beloved pet. Hugo no longer saw his childhood crush, but a compassionate adult who was hiding something about himself. Something he hoped Brand admitted to one day, whether with Hugo or someone else.

Nope, definitely not admitting any of that to Rose. "I saw the look on his face when Jackson rode up. I couldn't not help him. I've never had a pet of my own, but I could see how much this was hurting him."

"You're a good man, Hugo." She handed him a glass of lemonade. "Saw it before and I see it now. I imagine your mother would be happy to see the man you've become."

How the hell did she know he hadn't—Rem. Had to be Rem's motormouth. "I'll visit her soon." He took a long drink of the sweet, tangy liquid to buy himself some time.

Rose didn't press the subject, though, simply went back to fixing whatever was for supper. Brand came into the kitchen a few minutes later with a pile of soiled clothes in one hand, and a clean shirt for Hugo.

Even though it was just a shirt and he had an undershirt on, Hugo still excused himself to the downstairs bathroom to change. A tiny bit of blood had seeped through to his undershirt, but it was dry now, and his skin was clean, so he shrugged into the soft cotton and buttoned it up. The weather was almost too warm for his flannels anyway, so Hugo would have to find a store and get some more shirts. He hadn't brought a lot from Clean Slate, because he'd worn the ranch polos seven days a week.

He'd kept his possessions simple and practical for a long time, so he could move whenever necessary and without fuss. Most of the horsemen at Clean Slate had done the same thing. But here in Weston? He had space. He had a chance to settle in and maybe buy a useless trinket or two at a swap meet. To come to terms with his past and figure out who Hugo Turner really was under the bright, innocent mask he'd worn for the last nine years.

He actually did have to pee, so he did his business, washed up, and returned to the kitchen. Rose was alone, chopping something on a butcher's block. She glanced over her shoulder and smiled. "Brand went upstairs to his office. Says he wants to be alone, but I wager he could use a friend right now. Second door on the left."

"Thank you, ma'am." He grabbed his lemonade out of politeness, then headed down the hall to the base of the stairs. He hadn't been up them in ages, not since the last time he'd crashed in Rem's room after a particularly nasty encounter with Buck. The walls were lined with family photos of all sorts, including ones of Colt he'd never seen before. Apparently, after he ran away, all but his baby picture had been exorcised from the walls.

Now he was back and part of the family again.

The second door on the left was shut. Hugo knocked once, a sharp rap of his knuckles. Determined now, he knocked a second time, then went in without permission. Brand stood at the nearest of two windows, back to him, a glass of something amber in his hand. "You don't have to keep it all inside, you know," Hugo said as he shut the door behind him.

Alone in a small room for the first time in nine years.

"You have no idea what I'm keepin' inside. You don't know everything I'm responsible for."

"Then talk to me about it."

"No." Brand turned his head. His eyes were red but his cheeks dry, and his accent had thickened a bit. "Can't stand seein' an animal in pain."

"It's worse when it's an animal you love. Or a person."

He snorted, then looked back out the window. Sipped what was probably whiskey. "I gotta find Jackson and thank him for savin' Brutus."

"I'm sure he knows you're grateful."

"Still. Sometimes you gotta hear the words."

"I can agree with that. About a lot of things."

Brand looked at him again, his brown eyes stormier, full of something Hugo couldn't name. He held Hugo's gaze for several long, charged moments. "I appreciate all your help and support today, Hugo, but I need you to leave."

"Why?"

"I didn't invite you in."

"I'm just trying to be your friend, Brand."

"I'm not interested."

"Liar."

Something seemed to battle in Brand's eyes briefly, as if wanting to amend his own statement. Before Hugo's heart could trill with hope that maybe Brand would open up about today, Brand smashed it into bits by saying, "We need to stay boss/employee."

If today's events had told Hugo anything, it was that Brand was fighting something. Maybe the need to reach out to Hugo, instead of always being the stoic ranch foreman. Why? Hugo could guess, but he wanted Brand to tell him exactly why. That obviously wasn't happening today, because Brand had the same obstinate face Rem got when he was digging in his heels on a subject.

Pressing on the bruise anymore today wouldn't help. If Brand was this determined to keep his distance, even with the sparks Hugo felt bouncing between them, then Hugo wouldn't push. He'd stay away just as he'd done these last few weeks and pretend they hadn't shared that long, comforting hug. Hadn't held eye contact in a way that made Hugo's insides wobble with desire. Hadn't forged a new, intense connection today.

"Fine," Hugo replied, trying to hide his disappointment. "I'll get back to work, Mr. Woods."

Brand frowned and started to speak, but Hugo didn't want to hear it. He pivoted neatly on his boot heel, yanked open the office door, and strode out of the room. He had fucking work to do.

Chapter Seven

Brand hadn't meant to drink more than one glass of whiskey before returning to work, but after his non-argument with Hugo, he'd downed a second. When the third went down a little too smoothly, he realized he was done for the day and face-planted in bed. He'd just drifted off to sleep when Rem's sharp voice belted out, "Dude, why are you asleep in the middle of the day?"

Disoriented from both alcohol and emotional distress, Brand rolled to his side. Too close to the edge, he fell right off the bed and onto the hardwood floor with a pained groan. His mouth was dry, his head hurt, and he really needed to whiz.

"Shit, sorry," Rem said, crouching beside him. "Didn't mean to scare the piss outta you."

"Not quite the piss, but you're close. Fucking ow."

Rem helped him sit up, concern etched all over his face. "I heard about Brutus. That's why I came over. He's okay, though?"

"Doc thinks so." Brand rubbed both hands in his sandy eyes. "Sorry, I just…fell asleep."

"Yeah, you smell like you fell asleep with a bottle of Jack. Come on." He helped Brand up to sit on the bed. Rem sat beside him. "Can't imagine how scared you were today. Brutus is a good dog. He'll be home sniffing our crotches and tryin' to hump Dog before we know it."

Brand smiled at the humorous comment but felt no real mirth. "Hope so. I just...haven't felt that kind of stress in a long damned time." Not since what happened with Ginny their junior year of high school, which had firmly cemented Brand's path to where he was now. Single and in charge of the ranch.

"Well, don't let stress send you into a bottle too much, bro." Rem knuckled him on the shoulder. "Don't wanna lose the operation the way old Elmer did."

Alcoholism was only a rumor as to why Elmer Pearce's only son, Michael, left town a few months after two things happened: Elmer's wife died and Elmer lost the majority of his land to a bank foreclosure. Brand didn't trade in rumors, and he had never once seen Elmer anything except fully sober on the occasion he visited the man's home.

Some of us are really good at hiding secrets, though.

Brand had quite a few of his own he was pretty damned good at hiding. "Don't worry, I'm not about to become an alcoholic. Today was just a shitty day."

"I get that. But maybe gargle some mouthwash before you come down to dinner. One belch could turn a lit match into a blowtorch."

"Ass." He gave Rem a light shove, but he adored his little brother for not giving him a harder time about this. "What the fuck time is it?"

"Almost five."

Dinner was usually at six, which gave Brand some time to collect himself. "All right. You staying?"

"Nah, Shelby had the early shift, so we're eating at home. I promised I'd cook."

"Dude, you can't cook anything more complicated than a grilled cheese. And you used to burn those."

Rem very maturely stuck his tongue out at Brand. "I'll have you know that Susie is very happy her daddy has mastered making boxed mac and cheese with cut-up hot dogs. It ain't Mom's cooking, but Susie loves it."

"Hey, as long as your kid loves your food, that's what counts."

"Like you know what it's like to have a kid."

Even though Rem was joking, something deep inside Brand flinched, and his seventeen-year-old self wanted to snap back. But he refrained, because Rem had been too young to be involved in that drama. It was a lifetime ago, anyway. "You're right, I don't," Brand said with a bit more bite than he'd intended. Rem quirked an eyebrow. "Sorry, bro, it's been a stressful day."

"I know, I'll stop giving you a hard time until Brutus is home. How's that?"

"Sounds like typical Rem. Get out of here. Go home to your family."

Rem flipped him off on his way out of Brand's bedroom. Brand spent a few minutes in the bathroom washing his face and brushing his teeth to get rid of some of the whiskey funk. Despite his fear for Brutus, he was ashamed of himself for getting so drunk in the middle of the afternoon, and then passing out in his room. And he couldn't blame Brutus for all of it; Hugo got his own fair share for being so kind, attentive, and cute. For making Brand want to hug him again until the monkeys in his head quieted and life didn't seem quite so stifling.

For making Brand feel like he could have more than

a single life running this ranch, with the occasional hookup on the side.

Hungry and a tad queasy from the alcohol, Brand descended the stairs and followed the scent of Mom's fried pork chops into the kitchen. Seeing Dad seated at the built-in nook didn't surprise him, but Jackson sitting across from him did and Brand stopped short. Jackson almost never ate at the house, and not because he and Brand secretly hooked up on occasion. Jackson was a self-proclaimed lone wolf who liked his privacy.

"Hey, son," Dad said. "I thought Jackson could use a home-cooked meal for acting so fast with Brutus today. For once, he didn't say no."

Jackson flashed him a somewhat apologetic smile, then busied himself with his lemonade.

"Are you washed up?" Mom asked Brand as she placed a platter of pork chops on the table, next to a bowl of what looked like roasted broccoli. Her home-made applesauce was probably on its way next. She made the best pork chops and applesauce.

"Yes, ma'am," Brand replied. He slid onto the bench seat next to Jackson, because Mom would expect to sit next to Dad. "It looks and smells amazing."

"In forty years, your mother has never made a bad meal," Dad said.

"Not quite forty yet, Wayne." Mom put the apple-sauce down, then took her place by Dad's side. "That isn't until September."

"Near enough. With the calving season coming and the county fair, summer will be over before we know it."

Brand had half a mind to ask if they wanted a party to celebrate, but his parents had never been those people. It had taken everything in Brand and his siblings to convince them to celebrate their twenty-fifth anniversary with a small bash here at the house. They'd invited their extended family, their employees, and friends from town. Dad had spent most of it outside on the porch with a glass of whiskey, avoiding the crowd.

But someone had been missing at that party. This year, Brand could invite Colt and his husband. Their family would be complete. He made a mental note to talk to all his siblings about this later.

Their quartet didn't chat about much during the meal, mostly requests to pass the salt or a comment about the feed supply. Mundane things as ordinary as a peanut butter sandwich, and Brand was grateful. Between Brutus's scare and his interactions with Hugo, he was spent and ready for bed. Even after his impromptu nap, all he wanted to do was sleep again.

Mom offered yesterday's apple pie for dessert, but everyone was full. She did send a slice home with Jackson, though, wrapping it up on a paper plate with tin foil. "We'll see you tomorrow," she said with a grin.

"Thank you, ma'am," Jackson replied. "You do make the best pies. You'll be entering them in the county fair this year, right?"

"Of course I am. I've gotta get Shirley Johnson back for stealing the blue ribbon from me last year for my peach pie. I've even got a lead on some fresh, Southern peaches through the Grove Point CSA." Mom looked at Brand, who'd stood from the table but hadn't really gone anywhere yet. "Doesn't Hugo's stepfather work there?"

"Uh, yeah, I think so," Brand replied. Grove Point was a farming collective that offered both an on-site farmer's market, and also weekly or bimonthly subscription boxes of the produce brought in by local farmers. He was pretty sure Frank Archer had worked there for as long as Brand had known Hugo. "Anyway, Jackson, if you're ready to go, I'll walk out with you. Something I wanted to talk with you about."

Jackson's right eyebrow twitched so subtly Brand almost missed it. "Sure. Thank you for the lovely meal, Rose. It's always a delight to share your table."

"The pleasure is mine," Mom said. "I spent so many years cooking for upwards of seven people that I love having extras for supper."

True story. Growing up with four other siblings, they'd almost never used the kitchen nook, because there hadn't been room for most family dinners. Once everyone began to grow up and move out, the dining room became less of a casual spot and more formal. Used for birthdays, holidays, and special occasions like Colt's homecoming three years ago.

For all that Brand had spent half his life without his big brother in it, right now he really wished Colt was around so Brand could ask him for advice about Hugo. Phone apps were a thing, but it wasn't the same as a face-to-face conversation. Especially when only two people in the world knew he was bi.

He trailed Jackson to the front door, where both men put on their boots. Jackson grabbed his hat from the coat tree and plopped it on his head as soon as they were on the porch. "Follow me to the barn," Brand said. Not a request.

Dog trailed them most of the way there, her tail wagging, probably eager to get home and have her own supper. Jackson made a noise and gesture at her, and she loped off toward his truck. "I think she misses Brutus," Jackson said as he and Brand ambled their way to the barn. The big doors were shut for the night, but the regular-sized door stood open. Dim light was cast from inside, kept low at night so the horses and heifers could rest.

"We both do," Brand replied. A few steps inside the barn, he wasn't even startled when Jackson crowded him against the rough-hewn wall. He did manage to turn his head before Jackson's mouth could land on his. "Not what I meant when I said I wanted to talk to you."

Jackson immediately took a step back, hands in the air in a gesture of surrender. "My bad. Thought you might need a distraction from what happened today."

A few weeks ago, Brand would not have said no to Jackson wrangling him up into the hayloft, bending him over a bale, and fucking Brand senseless. Today? No. "I do need a distraction but not that, and not from you." When Jackson's face flickered with hurt, Brand added, "I really wanted to say thank you for finding and saving Brutus. If Dog means as much to you as Brutus does to me, then you know how much I mean it. Thank you."

"You're welcome. I do know how you feel about your animal, and I'm grateful we found him when we did. He's a special dog."

"Yeah. And you're a special guy, Jackson." Brand slid his gaze toward the open barn door. "But I don't think I can do this anymore."

Jackson gave him a long, slow blink that said nothing to his emotional state. "I see. Should I, ah, say congrats to you and Ramie?"

"No." He had always been honest with both Jackson and Ramie about…well, seeing them both wasn't quite the right way to phrase it, since he wasn't dating anyone. But they knew about the other. Brand and Ramie were officially just best friends; it was beyond time Brand set the same boundary with Jackson, especially with his conflicted feelings for Hugo clouding his judgment. "Ramie and I are friends, the same way I hope we can stay friends. I have no regrets, Jackson, but I don't see this going forward anymore."

Something flickered in Jackson's eyes, and then he nodded. "Understood, and no hard feelings. We both knew this was a temporary thing, and it was fun while it lasted."

"Yeah. See you tomorrow?"

"Bright and early." Jackson tipped his hat and left the barn.

A little sad and a lot annoyed with himself, Brand climbed the ladder to the barn's hayloft. While they mostly moved bales of hay from the loft out the upper doors via a pulley system, Brand loved going up the vertical, somewhat rickety wood stairs that sometimes felt like a ninja warrior challenge to ascend. Or maybe he was just getting older.

He sat on the plank floor strewn with bits of old hay and chaff as so many memories of this loft assaulted him. Not only dozens of memories of being up here with Jackson these last few years—and while the sex had been great, it had also been unsatisfying in its own way—but also that single encounter up here with Hugo a lifetime ago. An earnest sixteen-year-old, eager to please his older crush, ready to give Brand everything when Brand had been shocked as hell simply from a kiss. A long, sensual kiss that had lit a fire inside his belly, made Brand want more, and scared him to death all at the same time.

Hugo had been temptation in tight jeans, boots, and

a sassy smirk, and it had taken everything in Brand to stop after that first kiss. To stop when his entire body longed to shove Hugo down, tear his clothes off, and see exactly what the younger man was down for. But as much as Brand regretted not finding out back then, today he was glad for his own restraint. Glad he hadn't done something they'd both have regretted.

Glad he hadn't taken something he wasn't sure Hugo had been truly ready to give.

On a whim, he texted Colt: You up?

It wasn't super late yet, and California was two hours behind, but Brand didn't want to interrupt his big brother if he was busy. A few minutes later his phone rang. Colt.

"Hey, man, you didn't have to call," Brand said.

"No sweat," Colt replied. "I haven't done much for the last few hours, because I'm the stupid-ass idiot who missed the nail he was trying to hammer and smashed his thumb instead, so Judson made me take the night off."

"Ouch." His entire body flinched because yeah, Brand had done that more than a few times. "Gonna lose the fingernail?"

"Not sure yet. It's bruised but not black. Prolly just be sore for a few days. So what's up? Hugo fitting in okay?"

Too okay, and I don't know how to tell you about it. "He's doing fine. He's smart and great on a horse. He helped me out a lot today." Brand told Colt about Brutus and the attack, leaving out some of the more tender moments he'd shared with Hugo that day. "Got a good head in a crisis, that's for sure."

"Yeah, I didn't know him well but he always struck

me as a pretty levelheaded kid. He and Rem the same hellions I imagine they were back in high school?"

"Nah, they've both grown up a lot. I mean, Rem's got one kid and they've been trying for another." And Hugo wasn't the same earnest, nervous, occasionally wise-assed kid he remembered. Everyone had grown up. "So do you think you and Avery will be able to make it out for the county fair at the end of April? We're showing off our organic steer, and Mom's got all kinds of pies and jams to show, plus the chili cook-off."

Colt chuckled. "I think we can swing it. I swapped my week off with Ernie, and most of Avery's classes will be close to over by then. He's almost all online now anyway. Slater and Derrick are cool with stopping by every day to feed the cat."

Growing up with dogs, it was sometimes hard to picture Colt as a cat person, but he and Avery had a rescue they adored. "Awesome. Well, you know you guys can stay at the house instead of a hotel in Amarillo. Or if you want, we could even clean out the bunkhouse to give you guys some privacy."

"You don't have to go through the extra trouble. A room at the house is just fine. So why'd you really call me?"

"What?" Brand picked up a piece of straw and turned it over between his fingers—a stalling tactic that didn't work when his conversation partner was hundreds of miles away, instead of right in front of him.

"What *what*? You called me, dude."

"Technically, you called me. I texted."

"Pedant. What's going on? Something besides worrying about Brutus?"

"Worrying about the ranch, I guess. Same shit, different day." Close enough to the truth without lying. "Dad's getting older and it's hard to find good ranch hands right now. Working on a skeleton crew isn't good for anyone but at least the herds are in good shape."

"I wish I had some good advice for you, Brand, I mean it. But I left before I got too far into the management side of things."

"I know, and I swear I'm not tryin' to guilt-trip you or nothing. Honestly, I'm not sure why I called."

"I'll go out on a limb and say something's bugging you that has nothing to do with the ranch, and you can't talk to Dad, Rem, or who Rem refers to as that hot piece of ass named Ramie?"

Brand groaned. "You and Rem talk about my personal life?"

"Sometimes. I mean, all of us are married except you, little brother. It's kinda hot gossip."

"I'm too busy with the ranch to try and settle down with anyone." True enough. But it was also a flimsy excuse for someone his age.

"Dad managed the ranch, marrying Mom, and raising five kids, so try again." Growing up, Colt had always been able to sniff out Brand's bullshit, and even over the phone, he wasn't buying what Brand was trying to sell.

"Fine, there is someone I'm kind of interested in. I knew them a long time ago, and we've recently become reacquainted, but it's complicated. I genuinely do not feel like I have time right now to pursue anything, but I also don't want to stand back and risk them walking away before we have a chance to try."

Colt was quiet for several beats, and Brand really

wished he could see his brother's face. "Does this person have feelings for you?"

"I think maybe, but I don't know for sure. I've avoided having any serious conversations with them about it. I am lonely sometimes but I suck at relationships. I dated Ginny back in high school and managed to fuck that up. Dated a few girls in college, too, but I just…got bored. Broke it off."

"You sure you're sniffing up the right gender?"

Brand let out a long, deep breath that did nothing to soothe his unease. "No. Colt, I'm gonna tell you a secret that only two other people know."

"I won't tell a soul, I promise." He sounded as if he knew what Brand was going to tell him, and he was probably half-right if he assumed Brand was going to say he was gay and in the closet. Brand was very definitely in the closet.

"I'm bi. Known it for a long time."

"Thank you for telling me. I appreciate the trust. I'm going to assume the two other people who know aren't in the family."

"Definitely not." When Colt came out to the family three years ago, Brand and Rem hadn't really cared too much. Brand had been a little confused at first, but he'd also been carrying on with Jackson in secret, so he'd made a show of not quite understanding Colt being in love with a man. Their sisters had been a bit more standoffish, and their husbands quietly hostile about the whole thing. Last Christmas had been a little awkward at the Woods house with Colt and Avery there, but no one actively gave the pair shit.

Wayne Woods had laid down the law about that.

But the idea of coming out to his family as bi, not to mention maybe having feelings for his little brother's former best friend, made Brand's insides all kinds of squirrely. Like he'd swallowed a belly full of snakes.

"I do have a friend I've talked to about this a little," Brand continued when Colt didn't speak. "Ramie's a good listener and she doesn't judge, but she's outside the family. I'm terrified of what Dad might think."

"Speaking from experience, Dad doesn't always understand but he loves us no matter what. He still doesn't understand me loving Avery but he accepts that Avery makes me happy. If you've got feelings for a man and that man's got them back, Dad will still love and accept you, even if he doesn't understand it."

"I know, I just…the ranch is in such a tenuous spot right now. With the transition to organic beef, our lack of staff, the wind farm…the last thing we need is a bunch of bigoted assholes boycotting us or worse, because they find out the foreman is queer."

"Listen to you, using your big-boy words."

Brand snorted. "I never did apologize for that, did I? Not really." When Colt returned to the ranch, Brand had tossed the word "fag" at him several times, mostly out of sheer shock at learning the reason Colt left all those years ago was because he was gay. Their parents had never told the younger Woods siblings about Colt getting caught with another boy in the hayloft. Brand had been rude that day, and unnecessarily cruel in his own fear of his affair with Jackson being discovered.

"I forgave that a long time ago," Colt said. "Water under the bridge and miles down the river. I just want you to be happy, man. That's all."

"Thanks. I honestly have no idea what I want or what I'm gonna do, but talking it out helped. Thanks for that."

"Anytime, and I mean that. Even if this guy you're into isn't your forever person, I wish you luck figuring it out. But before we say goodbye, I'm going to ask you a question that I asked my best friend a long time ago when he was hung up on a guy he wasn't sure wanted him back."

"Okay."

"If this person you like were to go out tonight, say hit up a bar and go home with someone else not you? How would you feel about it?"

Brand made a rough noise, not quite a growl, hating the idea of Hugo hooking up with someone else. Not that he had any claim to Hugo, but still. Bad feelings.

"I think that's my answer, brother," Colt said. Brand could hear the smirk in his voice. "Might not be a bad idea to test the waters. If you don't, you'll never know if you're going to sink or swim."

"Yeah, maybe. Thanks for the advice."

"No problem. Take it easy."

"You, too."

Brand ended the call and stared at his dark cell screen for a while, unsure what to do next. He'd ended both of his long-standing personal affairs, and he felt fine about it. Today had been a roller coaster of emotions, not only with Brutus's attack, but also the careful, kind way Hugo had taken care of him. That hug back at the vet's office had been everything Brand had needed in a hug, or from comfort. A kind of hug he really wanted to experience again. And again.

Not tonight. Definitely not tomorrow. So many things were still too uncertain around the ranch for

Brand to risk not only driving away a perfectly capable employee, but also to risk his heart. For now, he had to focus on work. His personal life could wait.

Chapter Eight

A week after Brutus's attack, Hugo decided it was time to see his mother, and the decision left him a nervous wreck.

After coming home full of stitches and wearing a cone around his neck, Brutus spent his days on a blanket on the Woods house porch, rather than running the pastures with the horsemen. Dog paid him a lot of attention when not busy sticking close to Jackson, who seemed a bit more dour than usual. Brand was outside more, probably because Brutus couldn't make the steps inside the house, and he was, well, *attentive* wasn't the right word. Extra polite maybe? Hugo wasn't sure. But he wasn't avoiding Hugo like he had those first few weeks.

So weird.

During their lunch break on Tuesday, Hugo brought it up with Rem while they munched on their sandwiches in the barn's break room. "I think I want to see my folks."

Rem nearly choked on a potato chip. "Finally? How come?"

"Feels like time. I've been back for about a month. Got my legs under me now, no fear of losing the job. I'm honestly surprised Mom hasn't called me yet because someone from Weston let it slip I'm back." Not that he'd been around town all that much, just a few times to grocery shop, and another night at the Roost having beer with Rem. No Brand this time.

"Then you should go, dude. Wasn't part of coming back to Texas making things right with your folks? Can't do that hiding out up here."

His purpose wasn't so much making things right as reconnecting and maybe having an adult conversation with his mother and stepfather. He'd likely never appeal to Frank's better nature, because he'd always had a blind eye to Buck's faults, but Hugo wanted a relationship with his mother again. She'd done her best to raise him, and he owed her so much. "That was a big part of it, yes. I've got the day off tomorrow." Part of their rotating schedule. "You think your scooter will get me to Daisy?"

"Should. Make sure the gas tank is full, though. She burns fuel better in town than long distance."

"Noted." He picked at his roast beef sandwich. "So, uh, Brand's been around more this week, huh?"

"You noticed that, too? I think maybe he and Ramie broke up or something. Haven't seen him around the Roost this week, and he's been all over doing basic chores. Almost like he's trying to fill up his spare time."

"I didn't think him and Ramie were technically a thing."

"Well, no, but what else is there? He's finally got a hot girl on the hook, and what does his dumb ass do? Loses her. I swear, that fool is never gonna get married." The tiny bit of venom in Rem's voice caught Hugo's attention.

"Why's that such a bad thing? Not everyone's the marrying type."

"Because Dad's always talking about needing a grandson to take over and carry on the Woods name. Me and Shelby have been trying a lot with no luck. She even does that thing where she's supposed to lay on her back after with her legs in the air and—"

"Dude, TMI."

"Sorry. Anyway, Brand's the only other brother I have who can spawn a kid."

Hugo bit back a snort. "Colt can technically still have a kid if he and Avery want one."

"I guess, it's just not the same. Having a surrogate do all the work isn't like marrying a good woman and starting a family."

"Why not? A baby is a baby. I don't know Colt and Avery all that well but I think they'd make great parents. And your parents seem like the type to love all their grandkids, no matter where they came from. Family isn't always about blood, Rem."

"I guess." Rem poked at the crust of his sandwich. "I just wish Brand would figure his shit out, find a girl, settle down, and pop out a son so I can quit worrying about it."

"You and Shelby talk any more about that fertility test?"

"Some. I hate to think it's my swimmers, but if the only kid we have is Susie I'll be fine with it. I just... Shelby's always wanted a big family. I promised her that when we got married."

"You can always adopt, my friend. Plenty of kids out there who need loving homes."

"I know." Rem shoved the scraps of his lunch into

the small, covered garbage can. "Anyway, I'm back to work. Good luck with your folks tomorrow."

"Thanks."

After Rem left, Hugo choked down the rest of his lunch, which he followed with a bottle of lukewarm water. He'd need the fuel to finish his day, even though he didn't really want the food itself. A lot of his adult life had been like that—eating because he needed the food, not because it mattered all that much to him. Growing up, food had sometimes been scarce, and when Hugo was on his own, he'd tried to save every dollar he could, because he never knew where he'd end up.

All of the big, filling meals at Clean Slate had been a luxury he'd never taken for granted, and he'd enjoyed the family dinners he'd been invited to here. Maybe one day, if he ever settled down in one place with a solid job, he could stop seeing food as simply fuel for the day and see it as something to really experience and enjoy.

Maybe.

That night, he and Elmer sat in Elmer's dining room and worked on a two-thousand-piece puzzle together. Hugo had come over a few nights a week to do this with Elmer. They snacked on pretzels and crackers with squeeze cheese while they worked on the elaborate puzzle as a team. Elmer liked to tell stories about people from Weston, Daisy, and other nearby towns, but he rarely talked about his own personal past. Just as well, because Elmer didn't ask much about Hugo's past, and he was grateful.

He also enjoyed the companionship with the elderly man, who seemed as lonely as Hugo felt some nights. Elmer occasionally talked about his late wife and his estranged son, Michael, and Hugo absorbed the information, but he also didn't push. He'd learned fast that Elmer shut down when pushed, especially about the past. Hugo completely understood that. He talked a bit about his years traveling from Texas to California, but not so much his life in Daisy.

Hugo liked Elmer. The man was kind, generous, and funny. The sort of person Hugo would have liked as a real grandfather.

The next morning, he woke with the sun, unable to get back to sleep for the hornet's nest of anxiety in his belly. He showered, dressed, ate, and then tried to distract himself with a movie on his laptop. Once it was a decent hour of the morning, he headed into town to fill up the gas tank as per Rem's suggestion. The last thing he wanted was to get stranded on the barren road between Weston and Daisy, hoping for either a cell signal or random driver to pass by.

He drove with the wind in his face and the sun beating down on him, already pretty hot for late March, but not unbearably so. He kind of liked the scooter, because it gave him a similar feeling to being on a horse. No doors, no windows, just him and the open air. The scooter was way less bumpy, though.

Daisy was similar to Weston in its size and various businesses. The Grove Point CSA was about two miles farther south, closer to the larger town of Grove Point, where a lot of Daisy residents worked. Rem's sister Sage and her husband lived in Daisy somewhere, but Hugo had no idea where. Besides, he wasn't there to see them today. Part of him wished he'd called first, but sometimes showing up unannounced worked better. At least he had a great chance that Frank was at work and not at home.

Their house was in a small collection of trailers that didn't technically have a name, but folks referred to it as Daisy Hill anyway. He drove past the mailboxes at the front of the circular road, recalling hundreds of days collecting the mail after the school bus dropped him off there. No individual pickups in Daisy Hill. Sun, rain, or occasionally snow, students waited by the mailboxes for pickup.

He found the trailer without issue, its familiar white and blue exterior clean and shining like new. An old sedan was parked in the driveway, which told him someone might be home but not who. Frank had always driven a pickup truck, though, so hopefully it meant Mom was home. He parked the scooter behind her car, rather than risk taking up the other parking spot, in case Frank came home early.

The exterior hadn't changed much. Same small wooden steps by the front door. Same bushes around the front and sides. Buck's freestanding basketball hoop still lay on its side in the yard, dusty from years of disuse. Clothes sun-drying on the line in the rear of the yard. Hugo had spent eight years of his life here, and yet he felt no real emotion over returning. Maybe a little sadness, but no wistfulness. No fondness for the past.

This was a place he'd survived.

Not completely trusting the helmet would still be on the scooter when he returned, Hugo carried it with him to the door. Knocked. Waited. A long moment passed before the storm door swung inward, and Mom stepped into view. Older, more gray in her dark hair, she was still the woman he remembered patching up skinned knees and putting ointment on bug bites. She stared for several seconds before her eyes widened and her lips parted.

"Hey, Mom," Hugo said.

"Hugo? My word, it's really you." She shoved the screen door outward, and Hugo jumped before it clipped his shin. Then she was hugging the life out of him, making soft sounds not quite sobs but also not quite happy. Just emotional, and why not? It had been nearly ten years.

He hugged her back, missing this sort of maternal, full-body hug, grateful she wasn't instantly mad at him for having been gone so long. "Hey, Mom. It's good to see you."

"I should slap you upside the head with my skillet for being gone so long, but I'm just too happy to see you." She pulled back and gave him a long once-over. "You look amazing, honey. When did you get in town?"

"Technically? I got into Daisy today. But I've been living and working in Weston for about a month. I took a job at the Woods Ranch."

Her eyes widened. "You're back to stay? Heck, come on inside before we air-condition the entire world."

They went inside the aging trailer where a window unit was doing its best to belch cold air out into the room. The interior looked the same, with the faded green linoleum in the kitchen and outdated furniture in the living room. Framed pictures of her, Frank, Buck, and Hugo on the wall above the couch. The same floral curtains on the windows. It was home and yet...not.

"Place looks the same," Hugo said.

"No sense in getting rid of things that work just fine. Are you thirsty? I've got lemonade and fruit punch."

Hugo suppressed a shudder at the idea of fruit punch.

Buck had once made him drink an entire pitcher of it until he threw up, and he hadn't been able to stomach it since. "Lemonade would be great, thanks." It was odd being served, rather than pouring the lemonade himself, but he loved seeing his mother smiling so widely.

"So you're working at the Woods Ranch now," she said, plunking herself on the couch next to him with two frosty glasses of lemonade. "How'd that happen? I thought you were in California."

"I was." He explained the surprise of working with Colt Woods and the Woods family's problem finding qualified help. "It felt like the right time to come back. Try something new, see my family, and maybe put some things in my past to rest."

Her smile drooped briefly before returning full-force. "I'd heard the Woodses had been having some trouble recently. Sounds like things might be picking up for them."

"I think so. Brand has some great ideas for changing things up, keeping with the times. The wind farm is doing really good for them. And they'll be showing off their organic beef at the county fair in April. I'm guessing the CSA will have a showing with their produce?"

"Oh, definitely. Frank and his boss hope to pick up quite a few blue ribbons for their farmers this year."

The sweet, almost lovesick way she spoke about Frank made Hugo's stomach hurt in a not-surprising way. Yes, she loved the man, but Hugo had never forgiven Frank for having such a blind eye toward Buck's cruelty. "That'll be good for the CSA and the farmers," Hugo said, choosing his words carefully. The last thing he wanted was to pick a fight with his mother. Not on their first day seeing each other in person in nine years.

"I think so." She sipped her lemonade. "I've missed you so much, but it seems like you've done good for yourself. Had some adventures, seen part of the country. You think you're maybe ready to settle down soon? Put down some roots?"

"Maybe." True enough. Even though the object of his affection was less distant than before, Hugo still wasn't sure what he wanted, or if he had a chance of a future with Brand. All he knew for sure was that he had to take this slow or he'd scare Brand off for good. "I had a lot of experiences that I'll always be grateful for, and I've made some amazing friends over the years. I'm not entirely sure what I do want other than to see my mother on a more regular basis. Rem's scooter ain't the best transportation, but it gets me places."

"Well, I'm glad it got you to see me today. I wish Frank was home to say hello."

That makes one of us, Mom. "Maybe the three of us can have dinner some night soon. Catch up."

"Before long, it'll be the four of us again."

Hugo's entire body went rigid, his stomach turning into a boiling cauldron of acid. "Four?"

Mom fiddled with her glass, caught between joyful and tentative, and Hugo didn't like that one bit. "Yes. Buck got parole yesterday. He's coming home soon."

"Oh." Only a lot of years of ignoring his feelings and demurring to others kept Hugo in his seat and not fleeing for the front door. His nightmare was on the loose again soon, and this was not what he'd expected to learn today.

Mom was oblivious to his distress, as usual. "Yes, there've been some overcrowding issues. It's earlier than anyone expected, but he'll be home by the end of the week. A free man."

"That's, um…" He swallowed hard but not even a sip of lemonade soothed his dry mouth. "A surprise."

"He's worked so hard to make up for his mistakes, honey."

"Beating up your girlfriend isn't a mistake, it's a deliberate action. So is attacking a sheriff's deputy."

Mom flinched. "We weren't there and have no place to judge what Buck did or didn't do."

Anger rippled through Hugo's chest. "Sure, just like no one else was there whenever Buck shoved me, kicked me, sat on me, threw something at me, or called me all kinds of horrible things. You didn't hear it so it didn't happen, right? Even though I showed you the bruises?"

"I thought you'd let all those things go, honey. It was a lifetime ago, if it happened at all."

If it happened at all. More than anything else, her inability to believe him after all these years broke something deep inside of Hugo. A part of himself he'd hoped to try and fix with his mother. But now he was pretty sure that was impossible. Just like creating something real with Brand was impossible. He should have stayed in California.

"It happened, Mom," Hugo said, his voice hoarse with a mix of anger and grief. "I never lied. All I wanted was for you to believe me. But you believed your husband instead, and I was left out in the cold. I stayed away for almost a decade. Now I'm back and nothing has changed. If you let Buck into this house once he's paroled, I won't be back. I will not allow that bastard back into my life."

"Hugo—"

"No, Mom. No. I respect your marriage, but I am your son. Your blood. Buck is neither. He isn't a victim. He's a product of his own choices. His own bad, violent choices. If you choose them over me... Mom, I don't see us coming back from this."

"Frank's my husband."

"And I'm your son."

"I made vows to him."

Darkness settled over Hugo's mind, and he put the glass of lemonade down hard enough he was surprised the cup didn't crack. "So you can make vows to have and to hold your husband, but you can't promise to love and protect your own kid? What kind of fucked-up society makes these rules?"

"There's no need to curse, honey."

"There's every need to curse. Every fucking need. This was a mistake. This whole, entire goddamn thing. I should have stayed in California. At least I was happy there."

"Hugo—"

"No. Thank you for the lemonade, but I won't be back. You have clearly chosen Frank and Buck over me." He stood and stalked toward the door, his anger so thick around him he had trouble breathing. "I love you, Mom, but I think this might be goodbye." He slammed the storm door behind him when he left.

Adrenaline and anger left him shaking by the time he reached the scooter, and he had trouble securing the chin strap. As he fumbled to get it on and the key into the ignition, the tiny little boy inside him kept hoping his mother would come after him, apologize, ask him to stay. Anything.

She didn't.

Hugo drove away from his childhood home for what was very likely the last time. Hell, if he hadn't committed to a full year working at Woods Ranch, he might have kept on driving straight to the airport in Amarillo. But Hugo kept his word, and he was no quitter. No way was he going to run back to Clean Slate with his tail between his legs like a beaten dog.

He'd stay and do his job. He'd try to pretend his tormentor wasn't going to be free soon. And he'd do his best to be Brand's friend, even if they never had anything more between them.

He was so focused on his own thoughts instead of the road that he didn't see the pickup heading right at him until it was almost too late to swerve. Then he was rolling and pain became his entire world for a while.

Chapter Nine

Thursday morning, Brand sat on the porch with Brutus and hand-fed his dog bits of cooked chicken, a treat Mom kept on hand for the poor wounded animal to supplement his kibble. Brutus was acting a bit more like himself as his body healed, wagging his tail whenever he saw Brand, and attempting to play a bit with Dog when she came around. Watching him drink water with that cone was kind of hilarious and he usually made a mess, but he was getting better.

Sitting on the porch was also a convenient excuse to wait for Hugo's arrival. Rem mentioned Hugo was going to visit his folks yesterday, and that they had a strained relationship, and Brand was curious how it had gone. And what kind of mood Hugo would be in today.

Hugo was supposed to report at eight, and by eight-fifteen, Brand began to worry. Except for the first day when he was figuring out the scooter, Hugo was always on time. Brand checked his phone but didn't have any texts or missed calls, and he hadn't heard the house line ring. Rem was off today, and Jackson had begun the feed/haying process, so there was no one around to distract him and his fears.

At eight-twenty, he very nearly called Hugo's cell.

Then he heard an engine in the distance. Not the buzz of the scooter, but a deeper rumbling. After a few moments, a classic 1955 Ford pickup appeared in the distance. Only one person in the county had a truck like that, and the instant Brand spotted the image of Elmer Fudd painted on the hood, his internal alarms went off. He stood and walked out to meet the truck near the barn.

Elmer was driving, and Brand's alarm calmed a fraction when he saw Hugo in the passenger seat, head down and a little slumped. Elmer rolled down his window as he pulled to a stop. Brand stepped up to the door but Hugo didn't look up.

"You're late," was all Brand could think to say.

"Seems the boy had a bit of a mishap yesterday," Elmer replied. "Scooter went off the road just outside of Daisy, and they both got pretty banged up." Brand spotted the scooter in the bed of the truck. "Gonna drop this off to Murphy's on my way out. Needed to go in town for some groceries anyway."

Brand didn't give a shit about the scooter. "Hugo, are you okay?"

He shrugged one shoulder. "Scraped my hands up good and banged my head off the ground, but no permanent damage. I can work."

"With scraped-up hands?"

Hugo looked up, and something in his eyes said to let this go. "I need to work. Sir."

"Okay." Brand knew when to back off. "Thanks for bringing him by, Mr. Pearce."

"Happy to do it," Elmer replied. "Just you make sure he keeps those bandages clean, hear?"

"I will. I'll find him a pair of clean work gloves."

Hugo grunted and climbed out of the truck, his lunch

bag in hand and a sour look on his face. No one liked being talked about as if they were a child, and the poor guy was probably still in some pain. He didn't limp, exactly, but he walked a bit stiffly. "Thanks for the ride, Elmer," Hugo said, then headed for the barn.

"Thanks again," Brand said to Elmer. He tipped his hat as the elderly man drove off, leaving a light cloud of dust in his tracks.

Brand followed Hugo to the break room, where Hugo was stuffing his lunch into the fridge. "You sure you're okay to work today? You said you hit your head."

Hugo turned, his expression fierce and determined in a brand-new way that was…kind of appealing. "Yes, Father, I can work. I'm not concussed, I've just got a little road rash."

"What happened?"

"Just what Elmer said. I wasn't paying attention, like a dumbass, and I went off the road. Hit the shoulder hard and rolled a few times. I'm damn lucky I didn't get tangled up in the scooter and break my leg or something."

"Yeah, damn lucky. You see a doctor?"

Hugo looked like he was barely resisting rolling his eyes, but Brand had to ask these questions. Hugo wasn't just an employee, he was also a friend. "Yes, a guy who saw me go off took me to a doctor in Daisy. She patched up my hands, shined a light in my eyes, and ordered me not to sleep for a few hours just in case. I called Elmer, and he came and got me. And the scooter." His expressive eyes flashed with fear. "I hope Rem's not too mad about the scooter. I'll pay for the repairs."

"I think Rem will be glad you're okay. Scooters are a lot easier to fix than people."

"Don't I fucking know it. So where do you want me today, boss?"

Brand took the hint that he was done talking about it. "Well, I don't think you should be up on a horse one day after banging your head off the road, so how about you stick to barn chores today? Me and Jackson can tend to the herds and check the fence lines."

"Fine."

"There should be a few new pairs of work gloves in the tack room cabinet. Mom can rewrap your hands after lunch."

"Yes, sir." Hugo headed out, still stiff, shoulders a bit hunched. Something about the way he walked and held himself hinted that more was bothering him than the pain and embarrassment of an accident. Maybe the visit with his folks hadn't gone well. Brand couldn't imagine being so estranged from his parents that he didn't see them for nine years, but Hugo obviously had his reasons. Reasons he didn't seem intent on sharing with Brand anytime soon.

Just as well. Brand had a ranch to run, and he couldn't go getting attached to one of his employees. That was why he'd broken things off with Jackson, to keep up that barrier between employer and employee. Right?

He quietly observed Hugo for a few moments while he gathered gloves and a feed bucket, before tacking up No Name. Jackson and Dog came in, and Brand instructed Jackson to saddle up so they could ride the fence lines. Sometimes a steer could wander off from the main herd during the night, so they always checked for stragglers. Especially after Brutus was attacked. The last thing they needed to do was lose a head to a wild dog or rabid coyote.

If Jackson noticed anything different about Hugo that morning, he didn't say a word. At lunch, though, Hugo couldn't hide his hands. Brand usually ate at the house with his parents, but today he brought his food out to the break room in time to hear Jackson question Hugo about the bandages. Hugo explained the accident in a frosty, clipped tone that baffled Jackson and Brand both. The younger man was always polite, if not downright cheerful at work.

This slightly pale, slow-moving man was not that guy today.

"How's your head feel?" Brand asked. "I can get some ibuprofen from the house if you've got a headache."

Hugo hesitated. "I'll get some later, if Rose is still okay to change my bandages." Despite wearing heavy-duty gloves, the white was now gray and even pinkish-red in a few spots where he'd probably rubbed his scabs off. Brand wanted to just send him home for the day, but instinct said Hugo would just double down and work harder if Brand tried to baby him.

Stubborn brat.

"I asked her when I got my lunch," Brand said. "Go up to the house whenever you're ready. She'll take care of it."

Hugo offered him a wan, not-quite-real smile, then ate a potato chip. He was the first to finish and leave the break room. Once he was gone, Jackson said, "He's not himself today."

"He face-planted on the pavement twenty-four hours ago," Brand replied.

"Nah, it's something else. Hugo strikes me as the guy

who gets up whenever life smacks him down. Maybe he's sore, sure, but there's something else bothering him."

Jackson didn't seem aware Hugo had seen his family yesterday, so Brand didn't bring it up. Wasn't his business to spread around. "His personal life is his to share or not. As long as he shows up and does his job, it's not on me to pry." Even though Brand wanted to pry right into Hugo's head and figure out what was bothering him. Maybe Brand couldn't fix it, but he could be there for his friend.

"Fair enough." Jackson gave the crust of his sandwich to Dog. "He and Rem seem to be pretty good friends again. Maybe Hugo will talk to him about whatever's bothering him."

"Hope so. See you out there, okay?"

"Sure." He cleaned up, then headed back out.

Brand finished his own pot roast sandwich and coleslaw—a lunch staple in the Woods household—then headed up to the house to deliver his plate and iced tea cup. Dad was still finishing up his food, but Mom was gone, her half-finished plate still on the kitchen table. She'd probably taken one look at Hugo's hands and gone into mother-hen mode. Brand lingered for a few minutes, idly chatting with Dad about which steer to show at the upcoming county fair.

Two sets of footsteps descended the old, creaky staircase, which made sense. The farmhouse only had one full bathroom upstairs, which was where Mom kept most of their first aid stuff. The downstairs half-bath had given them more toilets growing up, but sometimes one tub for seven people had been a pain in the ass. Now that it was just the three of them, shower times were much easier to manage.

Mom entered the kitchen first, followed by Hugo, who narrowed his eyes at Brand a split second before his face went neutral. His hands were neatly re-bandaged, though, and he seemed a little perkier. "You be gentle with Hugo this afternoon, Brand," Mom said. "Those hands are a mess and then some."

"If Hugo needs to take the afternoon off, I can drive him home," Brand replied, perfectly willing to do exactly that.

"I'm fine to keep working, ma'am," Hugo said to Mom. "Keeps my mind off things."

Mom huffed. "Yes, well, you just had an accident, so don't overdo yourself to try and prove anything. Don't want you to hurt yourself worse, hear me?"

"I hear you, I promise. If you'll excuse me?" Hugo nodded politely at Mom, then left the room. A few seconds later, the front screen door slammed shut.

"The boy's got a stubborn streak, I'll give him that," Dad said once it was just the three of them.

"He wants to work," Brand replied. "But I'll keep an eye on him. Make sure he doesn't overdo it and hurt himself worse."

"Good man. Sometimes people with something to prove can't see their own limitations."

Brand held Dad's gaze a beat, unsure if they were talking about Hugo or about Brand, then looked away. "Thanks for checking his hands, Mom. I've gotta get back to it."

"Never a bother," Mom said with a tender smile. "See you at supper."

Normally, Brand would spend part of his day in the

office, going over numbers or brainstorming new ways to bring money into the ranch. Today, he spent his afternoon out in the pastures with the herds, observing their grazing habits, especially with the organic steer. Their grass was getting a bit low in the current pasture, so they'd have to gather and move them soon to fresher land.

At quitting time, Jackson and Dog headed out pretty quick, and Brand didn't blame him. He'd been pulling a bit of overtime and was probably glad to get gone for a while. Brand found Hugo in the break room, sitting in a chair and staring at his hands. The bandages were bloody again, and Brand swore when he saw the heartbroken look on Hugo's face.

"Damn it, what did you do?" Brand asked as he approached. He grabbed the first aid box on top of the refrigerator.

Hugo looked up with big, unhappy eyes. "I worked. Did my job. Still hurts, though."

"Your hands? No shit. Jesus, man."

"Not my hands." Something else was haunting Hugo, and Brand didn't know how to ask about it. "Should've stayed in California."

That hurt like a punch to the kidney. "Why? You aren't happy with the work?"

"It's not that." Hugo flinched when Brand began unwrapping his left hand, which seemed bloodier than the right. "I came back to fix some things that I guess won't ever get fixed."

He went out on a limb. "Things with your folks?"

"My mom." Hugo grunted. "Frank's never been a father to me. I don't give a shit what he thinks. I guess the little boy inside hoped that just once my mother would believe me. Be on my side for a change."

Brand dabbed a peroxide-soaked cotton ball over Hugo's scraped-raw palm. "Believe you about what?"

"Bad stuff." His wounded expression hardened. "Don't worry about it. It's my shit to deal with, and I don't mean to bring it to work."

Those sparse sentences told Brand more about Hugo's past than he'd ever known before. The jumpy teenager he'd once been made a lot more sense if there was something bad going on that Hugo's own mother wouldn't acknowledge. And it piqued Brand's curiosity—as well as his protective instincts. No one got to hurt Hugo and get away with it.

"I'll listen if you ever need to talk, Hugo." He placed a non-stick pad over Hugo's palm, then began wrapping it with gauze. "About anything."

"Not today. Please?

"Okay. Backing off."

"Thank you. I just…can you be my friend? I could really use another one."

"Definitely." He taped the gauze down. "I'm your friend, but I'm also your boss, and I'm ordering you to take tomorrow off. Your hands need the rest."

Hugo grunted. "Fine. I need to call Elmer for a ride."

"Let me fix up your other hand and then I'll drive you home." Hugo opened his mouth. "No arguments."

He shut his mouth and nodded. Brand unwrapped his other hand, tossed the dirty bandages into the trash, and began to fix him up. They didn't speak. The simple brushes of skin on skin seemed to be enough to communicate something neither man could say. Brand was helping; Hugo was accepting the help. For as much as

Brand wanted to dig answers out of Hugo's head, he wouldn't risk alienating his friend at this delicate time.

They cleaned up the break room. Brand texted his father that he'd be home late for supper, then headed for his truck. Hugo stayed a few steps behind, seemingly unwilling to go with Brand, but he'd agreed. Until the scooter was fixed, Hugo would need rides, and Brand was not above helping out an employee. Or a friend.

No one spoke on the short drive to Elmer's place. There didn't seem to be a need to. Brand wanted to fix this for Hugo, but unless Hugo told him exactly what was going on, all Brand could do was be attentive. Supportive. For as much as Brand tried to tell himself he didn't feel something for Hugo, his whole body wanted to just lean over and hug him until he smiled again.

Hugo had a great smile.

He pulled into Elmer's driveway and idled behind Elmer's truck. "You want some company?" Brand asked before he could stop himself.

Hugo stared at him like he'd spoken in a foreign language. "What?"

"Company. We could go get dinner in town or something."

"I, uh…" He seemed to consider it for a moment. "Nah, thanks, though. I'd be terrible company tonight, anyway. Rain check?"

"Sure, right. And I meant what I said before. If you ever want to talk, I'm all ears."

Hugo held his gaze for a long moment, the sadness from before disappearing behind a glint of anger. "Nah. Can't change the past by talking about it, right?" With Brand's own words flung expertly back in his face, Hugo climbed out and slammed the truck door shut.

Brand sighed, waited until Hugo was inside the trailer, and then backed out. Headed home. He was surprised to see Shelby's car by the house. She, Rem, and little Susie were eating in the dining room with Mom and Dad. "Didn't know you guys were coming over," Brand said as he leaned down to kiss Shelby's cheek.

"Hi, Uncle Bran," Susie said. She rarely pronounced the d in his name, and he didn't mind.

"Hey there, sunshine." He dropped a kiss on the top of her curly head. She had her mother's golden-blond hair and great big smile. "Do anything fun in kindergarten?"

She shrugged, more interested in her mashed potatoes than talking. "Puzzles."

Okay, then. Brand sat at his place and accepted the platter of baked barbecue chicken pieces from Dad. As he ate, Brand occasionally eyeballed Rem, curious how much his brother knew about Hugo's past. The pair had been best friends for years, with Hugo spending a lot of his time here at the ranch instead of his own home. He'd get off the bus here after school, and stay for dinner most nights that Brand remembered.

Before that kiss scared Hugo away and he left town.

"Dude, you awake?" Rem snapped his fingers in front of Brand's face.

Brand jolted. "Yeah, sorry. What?"

"I asked how Hugo was today. Mom said he had an accident with the scooter."

"He was okay. Worked himself too hard, so I made him take tomorrow off so he can rest his hands." He was not bringing up anything about the visit with his mother, though. Even if Brand knew more than surface stuff, that wasn't for Brand to spread around.

"Probably a good idea." Rem stabbed a green bean with his fork. "He's the type that likes to work through his issues, not dwell on them. I'll call him later, make sure he knows I'm not mad about the scooter."

"Elmer dropped it off at the repair shop already."

"Cool."

Mom brought up something she'd heard on the radio while cooking supper, and Brand kind of tuned it out, his thoughts still full of Hugo. Of the absolute misery on his face when Brand had walked into the break room and seen him with his bloodied hands. He couldn't imagine what was so bad inside Hugo's head that he'd worked through that kind of physical agony without a second thought.

After Brand had put his plate in the dishwasher, he tugged Rem out the kitchen door and into the cool, late March night air. "I kinda downplayed Hugo's mental state," Brand said. "Apparently, he went to see his mother yesterday and it didn't go well. He's upset but he won't talk about it. He just works himself to exhaustion."

"That's Hugo, dude." Rem chewed on his lower lip. "Look, Hugo's private stuff isn't mine to share around, okay? You were in college half of the time we were friends, and even when you came back, you two didn't exactly buddy around because you were so busy helping Dad with the ranch."

"I know that, but I'm his boss now, and I'm trying to be his friend if he'll let me. He's upset after seeing his mother, and I can't get him to talk about it."

"Yeah, good luck with that. Hugo can rattle on and on about ranching, horses, and handyman work, but talking about himself? Shit, we were best buds for years, and I still don't know the whole story."

"The whole story about him and his mother?"

"And his stepbrother."

Brand squinted, as if that would help him remember what he knew about Hugo's family. Hugo's stepfather, Frank, worked at the Grove Point CSA, and his mother... Brand wasn't sure if she worked or not. He recalled Rem mentioning Hugo had a stepbrother but not much about the guy—wait. "Wait, you're talking about Buck Archer? The guy who got a couple of years for assaulting a sheriff's deputy?"

"Yeah, that's him. They hated each other growing up and for good reason. Buck's an asshole, always has been, and I'm betting he came up in conversation with his mom yesterday. Probably why Hugo was in a lousy mood today."

Hugo's big mood today seemed like more than that, but Rem had been his friend for far longer and knew Hugo better. Even this older, more confident Hugo. "That's why Hugo was here all the time before? To stay away from his stepbrother?"

"Pretty much. All he talked about that last year or so was turning eighteen so he could get out of there."

"Why? What did Buck do to him?"

Rem shook his head. "Not my place, brother. If Hugo wants his boss to know the details of his past, he'll tell you." Bro code for: back the hell off.

"Yeah, okay. Call him, please? Maybe he'll tell you what's eating him."

"I will. Thanks for looking out for him today."

"Sure." Brand winked to try and shave a bit of seriousness off their conversation. "Gotta look after my new star employee."

"Eh, fuck off."

Brand knuckled him in the shoulder, then went back inside. That night, he lay awake for a long time after the house settled. Moonlight cast a silver glow across the wood floorboards, but he found no comfort in its familiar sight. His mind was still haunted by Hugo's wide, devastated eyes and the reasons behind those emotions. Reasons he desperately wanted to know, but also feared.

He feared knowing what sort of ghosts could put that kind of pain back into a man who'd once stood so confidently. And he silently vowed to do everything he could to save Hugo any more of that pain in the future.

Chapter Ten

After making himself a ham sandwich for dinner—and not deli ham, but thick slices of real ham Elmer had cooked for his own supper the other night—Hugo stretched out on his bed and stared at the ceiling, while his hands throbbed. The pain kept him both firmly in the present, but it also tickled at his past. At other bruises and small injuries.

"Boys will be boys," was his mother's tired old song whenever Hugo had complained of Buck's actions.

"Some boys will be abusive fuckers who grow up to assault their girlfriends," he told the ceiling.

It didn't reply.

Tonight felt like a beer night for sure, but Hugo didn't have the energy to go out, even if he'd had a working scooter. Elmer might let him borrow his truck, but Elmer had already done so much for him since yesterday. After Hugo swerved to miss the truck head-on, the scooter had caught in the shoulder's gravel, spun out, and he'd been tossed into the ditch. He hadn't blacked out but the world had gotten really fuzzy for a while, until he registered the middle-aged man squatting next to him, asking if he was okay.

The gentleman had been genuinely worried—and

had probably wondered if Hugo was drunk in the middle of the day—but Hugo had assured him he had simply gotten lost in thought. The accident was completely his fault, but the man had been kind enough to put both Hugo and the scooter in his truck and take Hugo to a doctor.

Calling Elmer for help later had been humiliating. Elmer had shown up with a paternal smile and taken Hugo home. Straight into Elmer's home so Hugo could rest on the couch and Elmer could make sure he didn't fall asleep. The doctor didn't think Hugo had a concussion but it was better to be safe. Hugo had appreciated the kindness more than he'd been able to properly express. In some ways, Elmer reminded him a bit of Arthur Garrett and the paternal way he interacted with all of his Clean Slate employees.

Hugo really should have called out today and rested, but his mind had been a whirring mess, full of thoughts of Buck being free soon. Mom had, in all likelihood, told Frank about Hugo's visit yesterday, and Frank was going to inevitably tell Buck that Hugo was back in the area. He knew he'd run the risk of seeing Buck when he came back to Texas, but he'd relaxed a lot when Rem told him the asshole was in prison.

And now he was getting out.

His cell rang. Hugo glanced at the screen, half hoping it was Brand, and not surprised that it was Rem. "Hey, dude."

"Hey back," Rem said. "Brand told me about your accident. How you feeling?"

"Sore and tired, mostly. I am so sorry about the scooter, but it's getting fixed and I'll pay for it."

"Don't worry about that, I'm just glad you didn't get

creamed or something. Brand said you worked too hard today and he's making you take tomorrow off."

"Yeah."

"So what happened at your mom's house that had you so distracted you ran off the road?"

Leave it to Rem to get right to the point. He'd always been a blunt person, and it was nice to see some things never changed. "He's getting out, Rem."

A beat of silence. "Who's getting out of—Wait. Buck?" His voice rose on that single-syllable name. "Are you shitting me?"

"Nope, not shitting you. Overcrowding in the prison or some kind of bullshit excuse. He'll be out by the end of the week, and Mom didn't say it outright, but I'll bet you my entire year's salary he'll be allowed back into their house while he serves whatever parole they slap on him."

"Fuck, I can't believe it. No wonder you were a mess today."

Hugo grunted. "Brand said I was a mess?"

"Well, he didn't use that word, but he could tell something was bothering you and that it had to do with your mom. He asked about you and Buck, but I said it was your private business. The stuff you told me in confidence, man, I don't spread that around. Never have, never will."

"Thank you." His heart squeezed tight with affection for his old friend. "I'll be honest with you, pal, I've really questioned my decision to come back here since yesterday. I thought by being away my mother would realize she missed me. That maybe I was worth more to her than Frank and Buck. But I think the opposite happened. I think me staying away made her cling to them harder. And that's my fault."

"Hey, fuck that. You left because you weren't safe

in that fucking house, and that's as much on your mom as it is on Frank and Buck. But you do still have family here. My family. Mom adores you, and you've really impressed Dad and Brand with your work. Maybe we ain't blood, but we're your family, too."

Hugo closed his stinging eyes, unwilling to cry over Rem's kind words. "Thanks, brother. I needed to hear that."

"Anytime. Maybe we aren't as close as we once were, but I miss my friend. I hope we can be best friends again."

"Same."

"So what's your lazy ass gonna get up to tomorrow with an extra day off?"

Hugo snorted. "No idea. Probably sleep a lot. I might help Elmer out in the barn. He's been teaching me a little bit about welding, and I like watching him work. He's making some kind of weathervane or something out of a box of old silverware he picked up at a swap meet last weekend."

"That man and his mind. He really should set up a booth at the county fair and try to sell some of his crazy shit."

"I mentioned that last week, and he just laughed at me. Says he doesn't need the money, he just needs to keep busy. He mentions his son, Michael, once in a while, but I get the impression they don't have a good relationship."

"Yeah, that's always been the gossip. Elmer's good people, though."

"I know, he's been great helping me out. It's funny to think that way back when, we used to be scared of him. Like he was some kind of crazy recluse who'd capture and eat kids like the witch in Hansel and Gretel. Honestly, I think the poor guy is just lonely."

"You're probably right. And hey, if you need to really talk about Buck getting out and how that makes you feel, I'll listen. We can go get a beer or six. Dump it all on me, dude, I can take it."

"I'll think about it, Rem. Honestly, even though it hurts that my mother chose them over me, as long as Buck stays the fuck away from me I think I'll be okay."

"Cool. Listen, I gotta go. I think Shelby's ready to head home."

"Home?"

"Yeah, we had dinner at the house tonight. It's why Brand cornered me about you. And he does seem to care, so if you don't wanna talk to me, I bet he'd listen."

No fucking way was Hugo ever telling Brand about the shit Buck had once put him through. If he did, Brand would always see him as the helpless teenager he'd turned down all those years ago. "Thanks, but not gonna happen. I'll see you Friday, okay?"

"Yeah, see you then. Bye."

Hugo shut off his phone, uncaring about any future calls or texts from anyone that night. His head hurt, his hands ached, and his soul wanted to screech its discontent. For as much as he'd wanted to try and win over Brand as an adult, he could never do that if Brand knew the whole truth about Hugo's past. A past who'd be walking the streets again in less than two days.

A past Hugo had tried so hard to forget, especially after the most embarrassing moment of his life…

"This is seriously what you want for your graduation present?" Brand asks.

Hugo stands slightly behind Rem, who's just announced what he wants for his high school graduation present, and it kind of surprises Hugo, too, because it's pretty ordinary. But also very Texan. Rem graduated last night, around middle of his class, but his family is still crazy proud of him. He isn't as book smart as his older brother Brand, but Rem still glows with pride over the accomplishment.

"Yeah, this is what I want," Rem replies, beaming like he's won the state lottery. "You said anything within reason, and this is definitely within reason."

"A four-hour drive to a truck stop for their corn nuts."

"They aren't corn nuts, you heathen, they're Beaver Nuggets and they are so worth it. The entire experience is worth it. Where else but there are you gonna find a fifty-thousand-square-foot truck stop with everything you never knew you needed?"

"We've got one of those near Amarillo."

"Not as big and not the same. Dude, all you have to do is drive. And maybe pay for half the snacks."

Brand rolls his eyes. Twenty-four, two years out of college, and Hugo's living wet dream, Brand is the perfect blond-haired, brown-eyed cowboy, complete with leather boots and his first, newly purchased Stetson. Real Stetsons are pricier than most cowboys can afford, but Brand's is perfect for his height and face shape. Hugo only dreams of one day getting a genuine Stetson fitted for himself.

"So you want your graduation gift to be a road trip for junk food?" Brand asks. He's six years older than Rem, who has the darker hair of their mother, and eight years older than Hugo. But eight years is nothing when just looking at Brand makes Hugo's heart sing. Not that he's told anyone, not even his best friend, Rem, that he's gay and has the world's biggest crush on Brand.

Living in a small, homophobic town is a great reason to stay firmly in the closet, but damn. Brand gives Hugo thoughts. Dirty, dirty thoughts.

"Exactly," Rem replies, and for a split second, Hugo is confused. But Rem means the road trip for junk food. "It's a state establishment with the best junk food. I can stock up for months with all the right stuff. Don't tell me you don't miss their peppered beef jerky."

Brand grunts. "Fine, I'll take you guys out there. But if my car's engine dies for some reason, you're buying your own junk food."

"Deal." Rem elbows Hugo in the ribs. "Junk food paradise, here we come. You are coming, right, dude?"

"Yeah, of course," Hugo replies. He loves the idea of this trip, even though he doesn't have much extra cash to spend on service station snacks. Hanging with Rem and Brand is reward enough for his time. Especially with Brand, who's been back at Woods Ranch for two years since graduating college. Two long years of Hugo gradually realizing he doesn't care that SueEllen has boobs as big as cantaloupes, or that Jenny Lou has been flirting with him for weeks. Brand fascinates Hugo more than any other person in his life.

And it terrifies him for what it means.

They plan the trip for Thursday, two days after graduation. Brand has the day off from working his father's ranch, and Rem isn't scheduled to start working there for the summer for a few more days, giving the recent high school graduate time to enjoy his graduation week. Hugo adores his best friend, but he's crushing so freaking hard on Brand that nothing matters more than a long day spent in a car with the man.

They set out at seven in the morning, all three sharing the front bench seat of Brand's used pickup, Hugo in the middle. Rose sent them along with a bag of breakfast sandwiches and a thermos of coffee to share, which they nibble and sip for the first hour of the trip. Rem needs a pit stop halfway there because coffee goes through him like crazy, and it's a good excuse to stretch their legs. Being so close to Brand for two hours straight is fucking with Hugo's head a lot.

Despite the slightly cramped truck cab, it's a fun trip full of fart jokes, real farts, and basic bathroom humor between three guys. Brand and Rem, especially, have gotten closer since Brand came home from college, probably because of the way their oldest brother, Colt, disappeared eight years ago. Rem hadn't been friendly with the Woods family yet when that happened, but he heard about it.

Sometimes Hugo wishes his stepbrother, Buck, would disappear, too.

They sing along to country songs, none of them with a great voice, and the Texas countryside passes them by as they travel southeast toward the outskirts of Dallas and their destination. The service station appears like a beacon on the side of the highway, a sprawling plaza that advertises over a hundred gas pumps, the cleanest bathrooms in the state, and every snack food you could ever want. Hugo has only been to it once before, when he was a kid, and it's as grand as he remembers.

Brand needs gas for the trip home, so he pulls up to a pump and shoos Hugo and Rem into the massive store. "You've got an hour to play around in there, and then I'll meet you at the register."

Rem grabs Hugo by the wrist and drags him inside. Hugo picks up a shopping basket, fully aware it will be overflowing by the time Rem is finished treating himself to a bazillion goodies. It's fun seeing his best friend so alive over something so…ordinary. The first place Rem goes to is the display of Beaver Nuggets, and he tosses four bags of them into the basket. "These are why we came, pal," he says to Hugo. He adds a fifth. "One for you, too."

Hugo laughs. "Gee, thanks."

They make their way carefully around the food area, studying the wall of packaged gummies and other candies. The counter full of different kinds of dried sausages and jerky, of which Rem makes several selections. The place has all kinds of prepared foods, too, from fruit cups to sandwiches, which they'll probably come back to for their lunch before leaving. Rows of branded merchandise fill another section of the store, everything from T-shirts to stuffed animals to shot glasses. They aren't interested in any of it but it's fun to goof around.

Hugo spots Brand by the jerky counter once, but for the most part, Brand gives them space to enjoy themselves. He's just the chauffer, after all. But Hugo also wishes he could make some fun memories of this place with Brand. Try to make Brand see him as someone other than his little brother's sixteen-year-old best friend.

Rem's basket is loaded with junk food by the time their hour is finished. They meet up with Brand at the register line. Hugo tries to pull his few snacks out of the basket, but Brand insists he leave them in. He and Rem will split paying for the entire haul, and that sweet gesture makes Hugo's insides tingle in a wonderful way. Brand is treating him. Well, so is Rem, technically, if they split the purchase, but it means more coming from Brand.

The total is more than Hugo's entire allowance for two months, but Brand and Rem take turns swiping their debit cards like it's nothing. Hugo's family isn't poor, exactly, but assistant manager at a farmer's market doesn't bring in the same cash as a cattle ranch. Frank works hard, though; Hugo just wishes he paid more attention to the actions of his own spawn. Buck is a fucking menace.

Once they get back to the truck, they divide the snacks into four bags for Rem, and one each for Brand and Hugo. Brand's has a bunch of different beef jerky flavors and not much else, while Hugo's has a bit more variety. Rem's stomach gives a mighty growl, which makes Brand laugh. They go back into the store for sandwiches and fountain sodas, which they consume in the bed of the truck, with the June sun beating down on their shoulders.

It's one of the best days of Hugo's life, and it's all about the camaraderie and friendship.

Rem shares one of his bags of Beaver Nuggets on the drive home, and Hugo has to admit they're delicious. And addictive. He'll have to ration his single bag.

They arrive back to Woods Ranch around supper-time, and Rose invites Hugo to stay. He's more than willing. Rose is an amazing cook, and it means more time around Brand, and less time at his own house. The entire day has been spectacular, and after supper is over, he volunteers to head down to the barn with Brand for the horses' evening feed. They're short-staffed at the moment, so the family is stretched out over the various ranch chores, and Hugo doesn't mind. He loves the big

Woods barn. It reminds him of his earliest childhood when his mom and dad had a ranch of their own.

Before they lost everything and his parents split, leading to Mom marrying Frank and starting the worst period of Hugo's life so far.

"You know," Brand says as they put their work gloves away, "if you were older, I would totally hire you on as a hand. You're good with the horses."

Hugo tries not to smile too broadly. "I spent the first ten years of my life on a ranch. I miss it sometimes. Living in town isn't the same."

"I bet. I've only ever lived here, other than on-campus in college, and I can't imagine being anyplace else. A lot of my family has lived on this land, and I've got some big shoes to fill."

"You'll fill them, Brand. I know it."

Brand smiles so kindly Hugo isn't sure how to feel about it. "I just hope my dad has the same faith in me you do. I didn't grow up expecting to take over the ranch but life has a way of taking a random shit on your plans."

"Don't I know it."

"Dude, you're sixteen. You've still got the world at your feet."

Hugo's hand goes to the fading bruise on his lower back that hasn't bothered him all day. "I don't have as much at my feet as you think. Can't afford college and ain't smart enough for scholarships, so I'll probably never get out of this town."

A long, silent moment passes between them before Brand smiles. "Supposed to be a full moon tonight. Wanna sit up in the hayloft with me and watch it rise? We always get a great view from up there."

"Yes." Fuck yes, Hugo wants to sit in the hayloft with Brand. "That sounds great."

He loves the big barn's hayloft, which is only half filled with bales of hay. The big doors open to a beautiful view of the ranch and its sprawling lands to the southeast. It's a few minutes past dusk, and the moon has started to rise in the starry night sky. Hugo sits on the edge of the loft, feet dangling down, no fear of heights or accidentally falling to the hard ground below. No fear of Brand doing a single thing to hurt him, because Brand is a genuinely kind person. He's nothing like Buck.

Brand fiddles with a board nearby, and when he sits next to Hugo, he has a sealed sandwich bag in his hand. Hugo isn't sure what's in it until Brand produces a lighter and a joint. "I don't wanna be accused of contributing to the delinquency of a minor," Brand says, "but you want a hit?"

Hugo has never smoked pot in his life but he isn't about to chicken out in front of his crush. "I'm only a minor for a few more months."

"That's age of consent for Texas. Technically, you're a minor until you turn eighteen."

"And technically, this is illegal no matter what, so sure. I'll try it."

Brand studies him a moment, then pops the joint into his mouth and lights up. Inhales and holds the smoke for longer than Hugo expects, before exhaling slowly. He passes the joint over to Hugo. The acrid smell doesn't appeal at all, but he inhales anyway. And promptly starts coughing, unused to smoking anything, much less weed.

"That's kind of gross," Hugo says as he gives the joint back to Brand.

"Not everyone likes it. I usually only take a few drags and put it out. Just enough to relax me after a stressful day."

That piques Hugo's interest. "Today was stressful?"

"A little, and not because of you or Rem, specifically." He takes another drag, holds, releases. "It's just we were so far from home, at a big truck stop with hundreds of other cars and people, and I guess... I don't know."

"Hey, dude." He nudges Brand's shoulder with his own. "You can talk to me. I won't spread your shit around, swear to God."

Brand stares at the smoldering end of the joint a beat. "Ever since Colt disappeared, I've been protective of my other siblings. I'm the oldest now. I didn't like Rem wandering around in that place full of strangers, but he had you with him. I knew you'd protect my little brother."

"I would. He's the best friend I've ever had, Brand. He's older but he listens to me. Just listens and doesn't try to fix things. Especially the shit that can't be fixed."

"Shit like what?"

Hugo looks out at the stars and the bright moon shining her silver light down on them. "All kinds of shit. You're lucky to have him as a brother, and he's lucky to have you." The bond between the Woods siblings is clear as day to anyone who looks, especially Hugo. And Brand's words tonight only enforce that bond. Meanwhile, Hugo's own stepbrother doesn't give two shits about his welfare. Never has, never will.

He takes the joint and tries a second hit. Coughs less

this time but still doesn't see the appeal, so he gives it back to Brand. Brand takes another drag, then licks his fingers and pinches it out. Above them, the moon glimmers a bit more brightly, and Hugo wonders if the smoke is finally going to his head. Doing something. Making the world lighter, bigger than ever before.

"You ever want to turn into a bird and just fly away?" Hugo asks. His mouth is running away with him but he doesn't care. Not in this moment. "Find something totally new?"

"Sometimes. I guess that's a little bit what college was about. Getting away for a while, doing something different. Always knew I'd be back, though."

"If I go, I don't think I wanna come back." Hugo uses the side of the door to stand and stares out over the vast property. At the ground that seems much farther away than before. Maybe he can fly out of this hayloft and into a new life where his stepbrother doesn't beat on him, his mother actually loves him, and he isn't as attracted as he is to Brand. Where Hugo isn't gay and can lead a safe, normal life.

As if.

But maybe. He inches closer to the edge of the hayloft door. A warm breeze tickles his face and ruffles his hair. He closes his eyes. All he has to do is step forward. To fall into the wind and let it carry him away to a better place than this. To a—

"What the fuck, dude?" A heavy body slams Hugo to the wood floor, flat on his back, and Hugo's eyes fly open. Brand looms over him, face creased with worry, wavy hair falling down over his forehead and cheeks. "What was that?"

"Huh?" Hugo doesn't understand anything other than

the solid male body above him, pinning him down in a way that doesn't scare him in the least. Because it's Brand. His Brand.

"For a second, you looked like you were gonna jump."

"Thought about it."

The wounded look on Brand's face makes Hugo want to weep but he doesn't. He inhales Brand's light aftershave and studies the way the dim light glints off his coffee-brown eyes. Eyes that seem to really see him for the first time. Brand doesn't move away, doesn't get off Hugo. He simply looms there, a calming presence Hugo wants more of. Wants for always. "Why would you jump?" Brand asks. "Your home life can't be that bad. Is it?"

"It's not just what happens at home." Maybe the weed he smoked has loosened Hugo's tongue but he can't turn off his honesty button. "It's who I am. I don't wanna be me anymore but I don't know how to be anyone else."

"There's nothin' wrong with you. You're a great kid."

Kid. Hugo's temper snaps and before he realizes what he's done, he grabs Brand's hips and smashes his groin against Hugo's. Neither of them are hard, but Brand makes a soft, almost-moan deep in his throat, and Hugo's insides quiver with want. Need. "I'm not a kid anymore," Hugo snarls as he thrusts upward.

Brand gasps sharply, his expression going from concerned to fierce in the blink of an eye. "What are you doin'?"

"I have no fucking idea but it feels good." It feels too fucking good, and it takes the last of Hugo's restraint to keep still rather than buck up and get more pressure on his dick. This is too amazing, too right, with Brand's pot-scented breath fanning over his face. They were so close now, in each other's space with nowhere else to go.

Brand stares down at him, a war happening in his eyes and in the twitches of his mouth and cheeks. He wants this, Hugo can see it, but he's hesitating. So Hugo takes a chance and slides his right hand around the back of Brand's neck. Urges him forward, down. Parts his lips. Gives a gentle thrust up with his hips. Brand moans, and the sound only drives Hugo's need. He pulls Brand's head down until his mouth covers Hugo's.

For a moment, Brand doesn't move, his entire body frozen. Hugo chances moving his lips and that seems to wake Brand up. His lips quest over Hugo's, as if asking a silent question, and Hugo tries to say yes without words. The kiss is everything Hugo dreamed of, everything he wants and needs. Brand's broad body drops down heavily over his own, his groin flush to Hugo's. Hugo rocks his hips upward, gently rutting while their mouths move and explore. He's only kissed a girl once, and it was basically a quick peck on the lips, but this is so much more. It's intensity and need and perfection in one action. Brand plunders his mouth while hands play with the ends of Hugo's short hair, exploring without holding him down. Questing without taking. As the kiss goes on, Hugo wants to give him everything. Whatever he asks, for no matter what.

A little drunk from the kiss, Hugo wraps his calf around Brand's leg to keep their hardening dicks pressed close, the friction almost overwhelming, even through two pairs of jeans. This is the first true kiss of Hugo's life, and he never wants it to end. He reaches for the edge of Brand's shirt and tugs it from the waistband of his jeans. Tries to get it off.

Brand lurches away with a pained gasp and sort of crab-walks backward until he hits a bale of hay. Hugo sits up, panting, half hard, and unsure why everything stopped. The naked horror in Brand's expression stabs him right in the heart, and he nearly flings himself out the hayloft doors to avoid the humiliation of what he knows is coming next.

"I shouldn't have done that," Brand says, voice rough. "I'm sorry."

Hugo covers his flaming face with both hands, his erection dying a fast death as he realizes he's just lost his friendship with Brand. No way is the older man coming back from this, not considering the look on his face.

"Hugo, I didn't mean to take advantage."

He hazards a look at Brand, confused by the statement, because Hugo had been the one to initiate all this. To rub on Brand and then bring him in for the best—and now worst—kiss of his entire life. "You didn't." Hugo doesn't recognize his own fractured voice. "It was my fault. I shouldn't have."

Something flickers in Brand's eyes that seems to disagree with him. "No, I'm the adult here, and I should have known better. I'm twenty-four, and you're only sixteen."

"I'll be seventeen in a few months."

"That's not the point." Brand scrubs a hand over his face, then through his sun-kissed hair. "Even if I was gay, which I'm not, I couldn't. You're my brother's best friend and you're way too young for me."

Annoyance begins overtaking Hugo's humiliation, and he stands, no longer wanting to talk about this on the floor. Brand remains seated, though, staring up at him with a weird mix of regret and determination. "I may be sixteen, but I'm not a child, Brand. I had to grow up quick when my dad left us, and then Mom re-married and life became a new nightmare. Maybe kissing you was the wrong thing to do but I wanted to feel good for a change."

I've also had a crush on you since the first time we met, but no way am I admitting that now. Or ever.

"Thanks for, uh, whatever this was, but I'm going home now," Hugo says. "Can we just, you know, forget this happened?" As if.

He swears Brand's gaze drops to his lips once before he nods. "Yeah, of course. Um, do you need a ride?"

"Don't worry about it. I'll ask Rem." Hugo flees then, taking the ladder more quickly than is probably safe, but he needs to get away from Brand. To put distance between this awful failure and lick his wounds. Having a crush is one thing but to get stoned and then act on it? Stupid. Epically stupid.

Once he's on the ground, he texts Rem to come get him, then storms over to the truck Rem and Brand share. Leans against the passenger door and stews in his own mistakes. He glances up at the hayloft doors once. Brand stands there, one hand braced on the frame. They seem to hold eye contact for several seconds, and then Brand backs away and disappears into darkness.

Chapter Eleven

When Hugo reported for work on Friday morning, he seemed more like his old self. Less like the spooked teenager he'd once been and back to the more confident guy Brand knew now. But something had changed in Hugo and it bugged Brand. Hugo was completely professional around him, acting like any employee, rather than someone Brand had started to consider a friend.

Exactly how Hugo had acted around Brand after that ill-fated kiss in the hayloft. For a little while, Brand had allowed himself to have something he didn't even know he'd wanted until Hugo showed him what it was like to kiss a man. To press against another hard body and grind his dick against a thickening dick.

Thankfully, Brand had come to his senses before anything more had happened that night. He'd seen the hurt in Hugo's face and had wanted to make it better, but he'd also had to be the adult. To shut that down before they both got in trouble. Now Hugo was very much an adult, and his lingering feelings for Brand seemed to be gone, while Brand's were only growing stronger.

Since Hugo's hands were still healing, Brand sent him and Jackson off to ride the fences and check on the herds, while he took over the task of mucking the stalls. As the boss, he usually delegated that particular chore, but he didn't mind so much today. The physical labor kept him out of his own head for a while, away from his tangled thoughts about Hugo.

For a little while, anyway.

Those thoughts came rushing back at lunchtime. Brand was already in the break room with his sandwich and potato salad when Jackson and Hugo entered, chatting and laughing about something, Dog right on their heels. Hugo instantly sobered when he spotted Brand and that…kind of hurt.

"Hey, boss," Jackson said with a grin as he grabbed his brown bag lunch out of the fridge. "Have fun playing with horse shit this morning?"

"Loads," Brand replied. "Bet it's nice to see the boss can still get his hands dirty."

Hugo shot him a funny look, then retrieved his own lunch. Brand kind of hated that Hugo's lunch always seemed to be a plain roast beef sandwich and a cola. Then again, he didn't have much of a kitchen setup in the trailer. Not like the big, airy kitchen Mom cooked meals in every morning and evening. Sending her men into the field full of eggs and sausage, or pancakes and bacon. Or sending them to bed each night full of some home-cooked meal or other, often with leftovers ready for everyone's lunch the next day.

But Hugo was paid a fair wage, he wasn't starving, and it really wasn't Brand's job to critique the kid's food choices. He just…cared. Way more than he should.

Their trio didn't talk much as they ate, and Brand fed Dog a few bits of roasted chicken from his sandwich. Brutus was getting around the land a bit more easily now, but he tended to still prefer his bed on the big porch. A nice, soft spot for a healing—and aging—dog.

Dog came sniffing around Hugo for a snack, and Hugo gave her a bit of bread crust. "Hey, Jackson, how come you never gave her a name?" Hugo asked.

"I did," Jackson replied with a shrug. "Named her Dog."

Hearing her name, Dog looked over her shoulder at Jackson, clear blue eyes expecting something. Jackson tossed her a potato chip.

"Jackson's one of those minimalist-type people," Brand said. "Doesn't surprise me he'd name his dog Dog. He probably sleeps in a tent pitched on the side of the road." He honestly had no idea where Jackson lived, because the guy was intensely private—when he hadn't been busy fucking Brand senseless in the hayloft. Sometimes in the afterglow, Jackson talked a little bit about himself but never enough for Brand to get a clear picture of the man, despite his having worked at the ranch for several years now.

Jackson merely winked at Brand and continued eating. He was also the first to excuse himself from the break room for a pit stop. The original outhouse still stood, built way back in the nineteenth century along with the farmhouse, but it was obviously no longer used. And while the old bunkhouse had a working bathroom, now that they were operating with a skeleton staff and the bunkhouse was storage, Mom was fine with their few hands using the downstairs bathroom when nature called.

Brand had already contracted for a Port-o-Potty to be delivered to the ranch when calving season began, so Mom didn't have a bunch of strangers running in and out of her house. That would probably start in the next two weeks or so. Bring a couple of brand-new calves into the world right in time for the county fair. Last year, one of their heifers had given birth at the fair, and it had been delightful to see so many kids watch that particular miracle live for the first time.

Hugo folded up his brown bag to reuse tomorrow, and when he tried to leave, Brand got right in his path. "How do your hands feel?" he asked.

"Fine," Hugo said, a bit of snap in his voice. "Taking yesterday off was a good call, so thank you. But I've got work to do."

He took a step to the side but Brand countered him. "We aren't done talking."

Hugo crossed his arms and grunted. "What, then? I've been doing my job fine all day, just ask Jackson."

"I'm not gonna do that, because I believe you. I just have one question."

"Fine."

"You still think you should have stayed in California?"

Hugo's jaw twitched. "Not as much as I did two days ago. Sometimes distance from an event gives us better perspective on our own actions. Makes it easier to realize the mistake it was."

While he was probably referring to the visit with his mother, Brand couldn't help wondering if he also meant their one shared kiss. So much had changed between them after that, and now, after one day's worth of interactions, Brand and Hugo were right back where they'd been after that kiss. Distant, tense, awkward.

"Right," Brand said. "We best get back at it, then."

"Yeah."

The next few weeks passed in a similar way, with that same tension between himself and Hugo. So different from the first few weeks of Hugo's employment. Brand didn't push, though. As much as he wanted to be Hugo's friend and crack through the walls he'd built around himself for so many years, Brand didn't know how. And Rem was no help at all, the big jerk. Then again, he couldn't fault Rem's loyalty to Hugo. Much.

So he threw himself into planning for the county fair, held at a big park outside Daisy this year. The usual fairgrounds had been hit by a tornado last year, and the buildings weren't fully repaired yet because of money issues. So Rock Point State Park was the new location. Smaller and less equipped for livestock, but the organizers would have tents for the animals being shown, and the main clubhouse was being converted into showrooms for the fruit, vegetable, baked goods, and handmade goods being shown for ribbons.

Brand had hoped one of their heifers would be ready to give birth by the weekend of the fair, so the attendees could see the live birth like last year, but so far no luck. No one was late or in trouble, though, so he was also making plans to manage those births once the fair was over. He had so much to do he was nearly able to forget about his Hugo problem. Nearly.

He sent information to a printing company in Amarillo so their beef booth would have not only a gorgeous sign advertising their organic, grass-fed cattle, but also pamphlets that folks could take with them. He wanted to get the Woods name out there as one of the best organic beef providers in the state. Or at least in north Texas.

For now.

Mom was baking up a storm, and every other night

one of his sisters stopped by to pick up a pie or loaf of bread she'd made as a test. She sent Jackson and Hugo home with treats most days, because she really wanted those blue ribbons, and Dad indulged her every wish when it came to perfecting her peach pie.

The fair was set to begin Friday afternoon, and that Thursday it was all hands on deck with the Woods family. Colt and Avery had flown in from California the night before, and while Avery seemed way out of his element during the hustle of prep day, Colt eased right into helping. Leanna and Sage were there with the oldest of their kids. Sage's stepson, Stephen, was eleven, and he got to help out with wrangling the organic cattle they planned on showing, and herding them into the trailer. Dog helped, while Brutus seemed to supervise from the other side of the pasture fencing. The poor old dog's herding days might be behind him, but Brand would make sure Brutus lived a comfortable life from now on.

Hugo and Jackson were staying behind for the weekend to tend to the horses and remaining cattle, so the family could enjoy the fair together. Rose, Wayne, Colt, and Avery would come home every night, but Brand was staying over with the cattle at the fairgrounds. He'd done it for a lot of years and he wasn't about to give up the tradition just yet. Sleeping on a cot six feet from a couple of steer and their dung wasn't the most pleasant thing ever, but it was part of the lifestyle.

Other ranchers were settling in for the evening with their prize animals, and Brand chatted with a few familiar faces. While he'd miss his own bed for the next three nights—and he'd also miss seeing Hugo—this was for the future of the ranch. He'd do his damnedest to make sure Woods Cattle Ranch took home that blue ribbon.

* * *

Rose got up before dawn on Friday to make a final peach pie, apple pie, and her jalapeño corn bread. The chili cook-off wasn't until Saturday, and it had to be made on the spot, so that was one less thing to worry about. Hugo went about his daily routine with a bit of sadness in his heart, remembering his earliest childhood when his parents were prepping for the same things. Mom always made amazing cakes, and their cattle had won a ribbon or two when Hugo was very young.

Not so much when he was ten and their herd fell apart from mistreatment. For all Hugo had loved his dad, the man wasn't very good at business or tending to animals.

Around eleven, Rose and Wayne packed up her food in the bed of his pickup and they headed out to Daisy. Avery and Colt followed in their rental. In some ways, Hugo was glad to see them go. He loved the idea of the Woods family spending the weekend together, enjoying good food, entertainment, and all kinds of games and contests for their grandkids. Part of Hugo wanted to be there, too, but the rest of him was glad to avoid any possibility of running into Mom, Frank, or Buck. Mom hadn't tried calling him once since their conversation nearly a month ago, and that was fine. Hugo had said his piece, and that was it, apparently. She'd chosen her husband over her own son.

If Jackson clued into his melancholy mood that day, he didn't mention it. Then again, Jackson was insanely discreet. He knew how to joke and make someone feel at ease, but he also knew when to back off and leave it be—a trait Hugo adored in his friend. That evening, Wayne and Rose came home with bags of kettle corn for each of them. Hugo shared the treat with Elmer that night as they worked on their newest puzzle: a five-thousand-piece image of hundreds of different dogs.

Hugo was pretty sure they'd never finish it, but he didn't say that to Elmer. "Why on earth did you buy this one?" Hugo asked as he tried to find the border pieces. So freaking many of them.

"I didn't." Elmer snapped two pieces together. "Michael sent it to me for Christmas. Just didn't get to it until now."

"I didn't think you and Michael still talked."

"We don't much. He knows I like puzzles. Keeps up my eyesight and dexterity, so I can keep up with my welding. He even sent me one of those weird-ass 3-D puzzles, but that just don't seem right. Feels more like building with blocks than doing a real puzzle. I need to see it laid out flat, not going up."

"Makes sense." Hugo glanced around the dingy, almost dumpy farmhouse that Elmer had lived in for decades and, for the first time, felt a surge of anger toward Michael. A man he'd never met but who, according to Elmer, had a ton of money. And he let his father live in the middle of nowhere with practically nothing. "If you had a million dollars, where would you go?"

Elmer paused with two pieces in his fingers that did not connect. "Probably nowhere. Spent most of my life here, and here is where I'll live it out, I expect. Wouldn't mind a real good tomahawk steak once in a while, but I can't complain about what I've got. I do wish I saw Michael more but the boy left to create his own life. Can't fault him for that."

Hugo saw an interesting comparison between Elmer and Hugo's mother. Elmer had somehow driven Michael to leave for the big city and a new life. Hugo's mother had driven Hugo west, seeking safety and freedom and a new life. Only, Elmer occasionally seemed to regret whatever had happened between himself and his son. Hugo's mother did not. At least, not that she'd ever said or shown to him.

He didn't comment on it that night, though. He went to his trailer and tried to sleep but had nebulous dreams about puzzle pieces smothering him in the hayloft, while Buck just stood there and laughed. He woke up in a cold sweat around four and stayed awake, watching shows on his phone until dawn made it seem okay to get ready for the day. The scooter didn't run quite as smoothly as it had before the accident, but it got him to work and back, and Hugo arrived just as Wayne and the others were leaving for a long Saturday at the county fair.

A basket of fresh cinnamon rolls waited for him in the break room, so after he stowed his lunch, Hugo indulged. Rose mothered everyone on the ranch, even if they weren't her own kids, and he appreciated the kindness. Plus, cinnamon rolls!

He and Jackson both occasionally checked their phones for texts from anyone in the family, even though the first blue ribbons wouldn't be assigned until the afternoon. The animal ribbons would be assigned tomorrow, and Hugo couldn't imagine how nervous Brand was right now. This was his dream for the future of the ranch, and their steer needed to place well. Those blue ribbons would look amazing outside a stall at the state fair.

After lunchtime, Jackson went out to ride the fence lines, while Hugo hung back to do a few chores around the barn and exercise the horses that hadn't been out in a while. None of those majestic beasts deserved to stay locked up in a stall for days on end, and Hugo had done this dozens of times at his old job. He loved watching them run around the corral, muscles bunching, manes flying. Not as free as racing across the pastures and plains, but close enough for now.

He'd just put No Name back in his stall when the sound of an engine caught his attention. Not the regular engine of a pickup or even a car, but louder and more distinct. A motorcycle. Weird. In the two-ish months he'd worked there, Hugo had never seen anyone drive up on a motorcycle. But the guy who'd injured his hand back in February was supposed to come back shortly, so maybe it was him?

Hugo latched the stall door and ambled outside, curious who was there when the rest of the county was probably at the fair eating corn dogs, deep-fried butter, and candied apples. He wouldn't have minded a caramel apple with peanuts but wasn't about to ask his boss to bring one home for him. Maybe he'd manage the fair next year. If he was still here.

The roar of the motorcycle engine grew louder as it approached the barn and house, and it came to a stop not too far from where Hugo stood in the big barn doorway. A tall, muscled figure in a leather jacket put down the kickstand and climbed off. Alarms began clanging in Hugo's brain even before the man took off his helmet and placed it on the cycle's seat. Turned to face the barn.

Hugo's insides clenched into a tight ball that nearly had him revisiting his lunch.

Buck stared at him from less than twenty feet away, as menacing as Hugo remembered. His brown hair was cut short, and his nose had a new crook to it, but it was still the same man who'd tormented Hugo for years. The terrified teenager deep inside Hugo wanted to flee into the barn and find a place to hide. The adult who was furious at Buck for daring to step foot in his new life wasn't going to back down. Not this time.

"What are you doing here?" Hugo snapped. Up on the porch, Brutus gave a curious woof, as if stating he had Hugo's back.

"Came up to say hello," Buck replied, as bland as if he was ordering a burger and fries. "It's been a while, little brother."

"Not long enough. This is private property, so unless you've got business here, which I know you don't because the family is at the county fair, you need to leave before I call the sheriff about a trespasser. That wouldn't look great for your parole, would it?"

Buck's eyes narrowed in a familiar, threatening way. "The fuck do you know about my parole? You ain't gonna call the sheriff on me. Imagine how sad that would make your old lady. If I got tossed back in prison because of her own kid?"

Fear and anger continued to battle inside Hugo, and he didn't know what to do. What to say to his waking nightmare to make him leave.

"Thought so," Buck said when Hugo didn't— couldn't—speak. "You missed my welcome home party, little brother. That wasn't very polite."

"That's because you aren't welcome anywhere near me. You are not now, nor were you ever my family, Buck." Finally, words. Angry words, and Hugo held on to that anger. "Go away."

"You always were a disrespectful little shit."

"Like you ever gave me anything to respect. You were an asshole to me from the day we met."

Buck shrugged. "That's not how I remember it. I remember a whiny little brat who never stopped talking about missing his real dad. Like my dad wasn't good enough for you. Like you were somehow better than us, because you rented a house in town, and suddenly had to live in a trailer after our parents got married. Your mom wasn't going to discipline you so someone had to."

That was seriously how Buck justified all of the physical damage he'd done? Discipline? "So I guess that's why you beat up your girlfriend, too, huh? It was just discipline?"

"She had it coming."

"Oh, sure, that's what all abusers say. You need to leave. Right the fuck now." Hugo was proud of the strength he'd managed to put into those final four words, even while his belly was a mess and still threatening to upchuck his lunch.

Buck took three long strides toward Hugo. Hugo held his ground, unwilling to cower in front of this man ever again. A flash of black and brown fur moved in his peripheral vision, and then Brutus was between them. Hackles raised, head low in a protective stance. One growl had Buck retreating to the other side of his motorcycle.

"That is one ugly dog," Buck said.

"He had a run-in with a wild animal a few weeks ago. He's got more strength and loyalty in his front paw than you've got in your entire body. Now get the fuck out of here!"

Buck watched him, clearly not happy at being run off, rather than leaving by his own choice. Another low growl from Brutus had Buck reaching for his helmet. Hugo only vaguely registered the distant sound of hoof-beats—a sound quickly drowned out by Buck gunning his motorcycle's engine. He sped off in a cloud of dust, and Hugo leaned his back against the side of the barn, all of his anger deflating as the terrified boy he'd once been won the battle for dominance. His knees shook, and he was chilly all over, despite the warm afternoon. He clasped his arms around his middle, unable to move from that spot.

Jackson pulled his horse to a stop near Hugo and climbed off with perfect grace. "Hey, man, are you okay?" He stepped closer, his big body too much like Buck's, and Hugo flinched. Jackson looked over his shoulder at the dusty trail left by the departing motor-cycle. "Who was that? Did they hurt you?"

Hugo shook his head no. He hadn't been hurt, not physically. Not this time. "He was no one."

"Bullshit. You look like you're going to pass out." He took a single, small step toward Hugo. "Let's go sit in the break room for a minute. Sip some water."

"No, I, uh, need some time alone." Alone so he could collect himself and get his emotions under control. Yes, his brutal relationship with Buck was one of the things he'd come back to Texas to face, but without his mom's support, it didn't seem worth doing. Those particular demons could have stayed buried, but then Buck had decided to show up and harass Hugo for no good reason.

Jackson studied him with dark, uncertain eyes before nodding once. "Okay. I've got a handle on things here if you need to take the rest of the afternoon off."

Brutus loped over and rubbed his face against Hugo's

thigh. Hugo absently petted the dog's head, grateful for his loyalty. "I don't know, I just need...um."

"It's fine. Go, sit and collect yourself. But man, if you ever need to talk, I'm a pretty good listener."

"Thanks."

"And whoever that was, do you think he'll come around again?"

"Hope not. He's got no business here."

"Okay." Jackson still didn't look convinced but he was backing off graciously, rather than pressuring Hugo, and Hugo appreciated that more than he could verbalize.

He headed into the barn, blindly seeking something and unsure what until he found it. Then he climbed.

Chapter Twelve

By the middle of Saturday afternoon, Brand was exhausted in the best ways. While not sleeping well on a cot for the last two nights was definitely a contributor—thank God the food alley had a truck that served coffee—he'd also spoken to more people the last two days than probably in the last two months. While the fair was open, he, Dad, and Rem worked in shifts at their booth, so they all had a chance to wander around. Mom spent most of Saturday with Leann, Sage, and her grandkids, and Brand knew she was in heaven.

Mom loved nothing more than to spoil those kids, especially if fun things like cotton candy and kettle corn were involved.

Besides the animal showing, food and crafts shows, and food alley, the fair also had a small carnival set up, with a handful of rides and some games for cheap prizes. Brand had tried his hand at throwing darts and balloons, won, and then handed the stuffed cow off to a little girl he passed. She squealed and said she'd name it Goose.

Why? No idea, but she was adorable.

At three o'clock he'd just swapped out his booth shift with Rem again, and his stomach growled with hunger.

Brand had been eyeballing the jalapeño corn dog truck since yesterday, and with the chili cook-off not starting until four, he had time to grab something to eat before he cheered Mom on.

Halfway to food alley, his cell rang. Jackson. His stomach pitted. "Yeah, it's Brand."

"Hey, man, I hate to bother you, especially if you're at the booth," Jackson replied, his normally even tone a little strained.

"I'm on a break, actually. What's going on?"

"I'm not entirely sure, but something is up with Hugo. About an hour ago, I got back from a perimeter check, and some guy was leaving on a motorcycle, and Hugo looked spooked. Like, seriously spooked by something, and Brutus was being kind of protective of him. He wouldn't tell me who the guy was, though, so I told him to take a break. He's been up in the hayloft for the last hour, just sittin' there."

Fuck.

A deep, protective instinct rose up inside Brand at the idea of Hugo hurting over a stranger's visit. And then it hit him: Buck. From what little he knew between conversations with both Hugo and Rem, the only person who could have Hugo so withdrawn and scared had to be his stepbrother.

"I'm on my way back," Brand said before he'd properly thought it through. Maybe he should have sent Rem, but Brand needed to make sure Hugo was okay with his own two eyes. "I should be there in twenty, maybe twenty-five minutes."

"Okay, boss. I'll keep an eye on him until you get here."

"Thank you, Jackson, I mean it."

"Not a problem. Hugo's a good kid. See you in a bit."

"Yeah."

They all had keys to the various ranch pickups, and it took Brand a few minutes to find the one his parents had driven up in that morning. He shot Dad a text that he needed to take the truck, and if Brand wasn't back at six, to ask Colt for a ride home. Dad didn't question him; he sent back a thumbs-up emoji. Once the ranch had gotten good Wi-Fi, Dad's texting game had improved tremendously.

Brand tried not to speed too much, because the county sheriff's deputies liked to watch certain roads, and one was the stretch of highway between Daisy and Weston, especially on weekends. He also didn't let his mind spin out too hard on what had happened between Hugo and maybe-Buck this afternoon. He'd find out, well, maybe not soon enough because Brand wanted to know right the hell now, but soon.

He finally turned onto the gravel road leading to the ranch, and he sped up as fast as he dared. As soon as he parked, Jackson came out of the barn, wiping his hands on a rag. "He's still in the loft," Jackson said. "He's been quiet, but he definitely doesn't want to talk to me."

"I'll do what I can."

"I know you will." Jackson smiled. "He's lucky to have you."

Brand didn't know how to respond to that, so he went into the barn and climbed the vertical wood ladder to the hayloft. Hugo sat near the big open doors, knees drawn up to his chest, leaning against a bale of hay. He seemed to be staring outside, but his expression was so vacant Brand couldn't be sure if he saw anything beyond what was haunting him inside his own mind.

"Hugo?" He eased onto the rough wood floor, taking care to move slowly and butt-scoot his way closer, instead of standing up. The last thing he wanted to do was scare or intimidate Hugo. "Hey, pal, you've been up here a while."

Hugo looked his way but didn't seem to see Brand for a long time. He blinked slowly, twice, and then his eyes popped wide. "Shit, what are you doing here? You should be at the fair."

"Jackson called me."

"Why?"

"Because you've been sitting up here for almost two hours, and he's worried about you. So am I. The guy on the motorcycle...was it Buck?"

Hugo immediately reverted to that nervous teenager Brand had known once upon a time. So different from the strong man who'd walked back onto the ranch in February. Brand scooted a few feet closer, grateful when Hugo simply watched him and didn't try to escape. "What did Buck do?" Brand asked, an odd fire in his voice he didn't recognize.

"He showed up." Hugo's eyes glistened, and if he started to cry Brand was going to lose his cool completely. "He walked into my job like he owned the place, acted like I'd somehow done something wrong to him, and tried to justify everything he's done. From beating me up to beating his ex-girlfriend. He's a bastard."

"From beating me up."

Brand kind of wanted to hunt down this Buck character and show how it felt for one grown adult to get a proper beating from another, but Brand wasn't a violent person. And as much as he'd like to exact a bit of revenge on Hugo's behalf, comforting Hugo was more important right now. "If he comes near you again I'll have him arrested."

"You can't do that. He hasn't threatened me."

"This is private property, so if I see his ass around here, I'll call in a trespasser."

"Don't worry. Physically, I can take care of myself now. One of my friends from Clean Slate taught me some good self-defense moves. It's just the mental and emotional stuff I still haven't gotten a handle on. That's why I freaked out so bad seeing Buck again."

"I get it." Brand did understand on an intellectual level, but he had no personal experience with that sort of physical trauma. Sure, he'd been spanked a handful of times as a kid, but his parents had never been physical or verbally violent beyond that. He and his siblings— while they occasionally fought, as most siblings did— hadn't tormented each other like Buck had tormented Hugo. "You don't deserve this kind of grief."

Some of Hugo's fear downshifted into anger. "What do you care about my personal problems? I'm just an employee. You've made that very clear."

"I care. God help me, but I do care. I've cared for a long fucking time." He'd cared ever since their first time in this hayloft, but he'd been too scared of so many things, including both Hugo's age and Brand's own sexuality. Scared of acknowledging that Brand was attracted to men as strongly as he was to women, and their forbidden kiss had only cemented that fact for Brand. "You're important to me, Hugo, and not just because you were Rem's best friend once."

"Then why?"

The stark challenge in both Hugo's voice and stare dug under Brand's skin, and all he could do was react.

He rose and knee-walked the final few feet between himself and Hugo, hauled Hugo up into his arms, and kissed him. Different from their first kiss, which had been all about attraction and their libidos, this kiss was about comfort. These weren't surface emotions anymore. Brand wanted the man in his arms, and he tried to put all of that into this long, sensual kiss.

Hugo didn't react at first, allowing Brand to do all the work. Then his arms snaked around Brand's waist and held him closer, fingers splayed on Brand's back. He opened for Brand, and Brand allowed himself to be sucked inside. To rub his tongue against Hugo's, getting the sharp taste of the younger man. Exploring and teasing while his dick thickened. Hugo's own erection pressed into Brand's hip. Brand shifted position just enough so their groins pressed together.

The breathy moan Hugo released sent excited shivers up and down Brand's spine. God, he did want the man, but Hugo had been upset, and what if this wasn't what Hugo really wanted or needed. Brand pulled back, his own breaths unsteady, and stared into Hugo's wide, simmering eyes. "Are you sure this is what you want?" Brand asked.

"Fuck, yes." No hesitation. Only two softly growled words. "I've wanted you for a long time, Brand. Even though I was just a kid to you, you made me feel safe when you were around."

"I'm sorry I didn't realize how bad things were for you at home."

"No one did. Rem didn't even know all of it. But he knew a lot."

Brand gently dragged his thumb across Hugo's cheek. "No one should ever hurt you."

Hugo's smile gentled and he threaded his fingers in the back of Brand's hair. "Kiss me again?"

The sweet, earnest way Hugo asked pushed all of Brand's buttons, and he dove in for another taste. Hugo pulled him down, in a mirror of the last time they'd done this: Hugo on his back, Brand slotted between his spread legs, their erections thrusting together. Everything about it was both new and familiar, perfect and scary. It was everything Brand had been waiting for without realizing it. Sure, he'd had good chemistry with Jackson but this was different.

This was... Hugo.

His Hugo. Older and stronger, but still so fucking vulnerable. And arousing. Brand couldn't let his attraction to Hugo go to his head and ruin their working relationship, but goddamn, he wanted this. Needed this.

Hugo broke their kiss and nipped at Brand's chin. "Fuck, I've wanted to get off with you for the last eleven years. Please."

Brand ground his cock against Hugo's, which earned him a sharp gasp. "Gonna be hard to explain two wet spots on our jeans to Jackson if he catches us."

"Then let's not come in our jeans." He reached between them, the back of his hand pressing against Brand's erection as Hugo thumbed open his own fly. Hugo's expression was so open, so trusting, like nothing would make him happier than this one thing.

Brand sat up and shoved his own jeans and boxers down to mid-thigh, baring his straining cock. He barely had time to catch a glimpse of Hugo's as he did the same, shimmying clothes down his narrow hips, before Brand pressed his entire body against Hugo's. Hugo sighed in a "yes, please" kind of way, then adjusted them both, his touch hot and wonderful, so their cocks aligned better. Then Brand began to thrust.

He'd gotten off like this with other guys before, but this was unique. This was…something bigger than just a hookup. Hugo gazed up at him, dark eyes filled with tender emotions and arousal. His cheeks were stained red, and a light flush colored his neck and shoulders, too. Brand wanted to study his blissed-out face, but he needed to kiss Hugo more, so he did. Long licks and sips from that enticing, talented mouth. The world went away, and for a long time, nothing existed but them, their moving bodies, and finding their pleasure.

Brand shoved Hugo's shirt up and stroked the firm muscles of his abs and pecks. Pinched his nipple just to swallow Hugo's gasp. Hugo's entire body tensed as he came, his release slicking their bellies, smoothing the way for Brand to follow him over. He moaned into Hugo's mouth as he continued to rut, milking this for every last scrap of pleasure that swamped his body and left him boneless. He collapsed on top of Hugo, face pressed into the crook of his neck. All he could do now was breathe for a little while.

Hugo's hands smoothed up and down Brand's back in a soothing massage that made Brand want to roll over and take a nap. Except their bare asses were hanging out in the hayloft, the big loft doors wide open to the world. The chaff in the air made Brand sneeze hard, and that effectively broke the spell. Hugo chuckled, the sound rumbling from his chest into Brand's.

"Wow," Hugo said. "That was better than I imagined it would be."

Brand wasn't sure if he should preen over that or not, so he levered up and sat back on his heels. Hugo's shirt had been spared, but his own was a mess. He always wore a sleeveless undershirt, though, so Brand whipped his work shirt off and used it to clean his belly and pubes. Then he handed it to Hugo, who did the same while Brand tucked his business back into his clothes.

Hugo sat up, then yelped softly and flinched.

"What?" Brand asked. "Are you okay?"

"Yeah, I just. Ouch." He raised his hips off the floor, reached under his butt, and then threw a few bits of hay to the side. "Got some hay in an uncomfortable spot."

Brand laughed. "Ouch is right." Not used to sex being more than simply sex, an odd sense of shyness overcame Brand. He waited until Hugo was zipped back up before asking, "Any regrets?"

"Fuck no." His face went blank. "Do you?"

"No." Brand balled up his soiled shirt. Even though he did his own laundry, he'd still rinse it out before he stuck it in the hamper. "Didn't plan for it to happen, but I don't regret it. It was...really good."

Hugo quirked an eyebrow. "Just really good? I'm losing my touch."

He kind of hated the idea of Hugo having been with someone else, even though that was superhypocritical, considering Brand's own previous arrangements with Ramie and Jackson. They each came with a sexual history, and besides, it wasn't as if either of them had declared their love for each other, or that they were dating. Hugo's life and past weren't his to police, period. "It was fantastic. Is that better?"

"A little." Hugo's amused grin sobered. "Thank you. Not just for the sex, but for coming here to check on me. For caring."

"I do care. Probably more than I should, considering you're my employee. But you were hurting, and I needed to do something."

Even though Brand's statement had been genuine, something in Hugo's expression shuttered right away, and Brand wasn't sure what he'd said wrong. "Got it," Hugo said in a hollow tone Brand didn't recognize. "Well, I've been hiding up here long enough, so I should get back to work. Thanks, boss."

Brand sat there, completely stupefied, until Hugo had disappeared down the loft ladder. What the fuck had just happened? They'd gone from basking in the afterglow and sharing their feelings about what they'd done, to Hugo practically running away. Hurt and confused, Brand grabbed his shirt and climbed down the ladder. Hugo wasn't anywhere in the barn, damn it.

Brand stomped toward for the main barn doors, only for Jackson to step out of the break room and block his way.

Great. Just what I need right now.

"I'm not gonna ask because it's not my business," Jackson said, "but I'll admit I had a funny feeling he was why you broke things off with me. He's a good kid."

"He's not a kid." Maybe Hugo was younger than them both but he was a grown man. Very much a grown man. "And it's complicated."

"Always is. Good luck." Jackson tipped his hat, then went down the barn to one of the horse stalls.

Brand didn't know what else to say or do, so he went up to the house for a quick shower and to wash his shirt. Today had not been a mistake, but it had absolutely altered the dynamic between him and Hugo. Sex with Jackson had just been that: sex. Yes, sex with someone he considered a friend and respected a hell of a lot, but they lacked an emotional depth that could have ever led to more. Same with Ramie. Sex with Hugo had been... intense. They'd made a connection that Brand didn't want to give up, but he was also terrified of what it might mean going forward.

Terrified of accepting his feelings for Hugo and all the ways it would change Brand's life. All the ways they could both get hurt if they came out as a couple—not only from small-minded bigots in town, but Brand's own family. His parents loved Colt, but they quietly tolerated his marriage to Avery because the pair lived hundreds of miles away. How would they feel about their second son being with a man?

He had no idea.

And the fact that Hugo had fled the hayloft so quickly after they had sex still confused him. They needed to talk and do it soon, before one of them did something they'd both regret.

Chapter Thirteen

Hugo had the day off Sunday, the day after his confusing encounter with Brand in the hayloft, and he was glad for it. He absolutely needed space from Brand to think about both his physical actions, and also his words after having sex.

"I needed to do something."

"You're my employee."

Those two small statements had hurt more than Hugo wanted to admit, which was why he'd fled the hayloft as fast as possible. Fled from the truth that Brand's first priority would always be the ranch. Fled before Hugo's heart got any more invested in the man who'd made his body sing, and then who'd broken his heart in only a few brief sentences. Fled from the man who never answered Hugo's very simple question to Brand's statement that Hugo was important to him: Why?

Instead of saying anything, Brand had kissed him. Kissed him, seduced him, and then basically called Hugo an employee he was helping through a bad day, the asshole. As amazing as the sex had been, the ending left a bad taste in Hugo's mouth and a sliver of pain wedged in his heart.

He spent most of his day in bed, watching random

shit on his phone. Elmer knocked once and invited him inside for a puzzle and supper, but Hugo turned him down, citing a headache, and Elmer accepted that excuse. He hated lying to Elmer about anything, because the man had only ever been generous and kind, but Hugo wanted to wallow.

Rem texted him that night with great news all around: the ranch had gotten a blue ribbon for their organic cattle, Rose placed second in the chili cook-off, and her peach pie took the blue ribbon. Rem also mentioned the Grove Point CSA got a few blue ribbons for their produce, but Hugo didn't care about that. Good for the farmers, but fuck Frank and his spawn. Fuck his mother, too, to be honest. She'd made her choice.

Monday was all kinds of awkward when Hugo reported to work. He, Jackson, Rem, and Brand were all on the schedule, and their quartet had a quick meeting first thing. Brand kept tossing Hugo significant looks that irritated the shit out of him, Jackson's expression was way too neutral, and Rem was completely oblivious to the strange vibes bouncing back and forth.

Lucky him.

Fortunately, Hugo and Brand had separate assignments that day, so Hugo could avoid the man. Great sex did not make up for the embarrassment that it had all been to make Hugo feel better—make a fucking employee feel better—and not because Brand had the same strong feelings for Hugo that Hugo had for him. Having sex with his boss, ten-year crush aside, had been a stupid thing to do. Even if the sex had made Hugo feel wanted and safe—truly wanted and safe—for the first time in his entire adult life. The way Brand had looked him in the eye, kissed him, paid attention to what they were doing, instead of simply taking from someone willing to give—all of it made him feel safe.

Rem also seemed kind of distracted, because he didn't butt into Hugo's personal life, and Hugo counted that as a win, even while wondering what was up with his friend. Later in the week, the previously injured cowboy had returned to work. Alan Denning's hand was healed, and while he was definitely the oldest guy on the crew, he was pretty cool. Hugo liked him just fine. By the following weekend, three temps had been added to the team to help with calf season, as most of the heifers were due to give birth soon.

Fortunately, this put Hugo and Jackson out running the fence lines and pastures most of the day, watching the herd and keeping stragglers from going too far. Calving wasn't Hugo's best event, so he was glad to be out in the countryside with Dog and a much-healed Brutus. The dogs didn't talk, and Jackson was practically mute most days, and Hugo enjoyed the peace and quiet.

Woods Ranch welcomed thirteen new cows and bulls into the family over the next few days. The bulls would eventually join the organic, grass-fed herd, while the cows would grow until they were old enough for their AI technician to inseminate them with other organic bull semen. All part of the circle of life on a working cattle ranch.

Ultimately, every cow and bull on the ranch would end up on someone's dinner plate, but Hugo admired the fact that Brand worked hard to ensure those animals lived the freest, most comfortable life possible until then. Rather than penned into tiny areas and given the worst, most fattening kind of feed just to add more pounds.

The third weekend in May, Hugo stood in the back of the barn where the heifers fed their calves, and he admired the beauty of such a thing. Teats heavy with milk and young mouths eagerly seeking sustenance. Mothers doing nothing more than nourishing their children, and his heart ached with grief. Maybe Buck had stayed away these last few weeks, but he hadn't heard from his mother since that ill-fated meeting two months ago. And that hurt. More than he expected it to. He'd been tempted to reach out himself on Mother's Day, but he simply couldn't make himself do so. She'd chosen her side and it wasn't her son's.

The mothers in the barn stalls only knew instinct, and their instinct was to nourish their children. The lovely sight made his eyes sting with jealous tears. That a cow could love her child more than a human mother. Sure, Hugo's situation wasn't unique at all, but it still hurt.

"Hugo?" Brand's voice broke the silence like a gong of doom.

Hugo flinched but didn't turn around. "Just making sure they're all feeding."

Brand stepped up beside him, hands deep in his jeans pockets, Stetson casting shadows over his face in the dim barn light. "It's a pretty sight, isn't it? Miracle of life?"

"Yeah." He cleared his throat, hating how his body reacted so strongly to the older man's proximity. He wanted to reach out and touch Brand, but no way in hell was that happening. Hugo didn't need to be embarrassed twice. "I've gotta go."

Before Hugo could leave, Brand placed a hand on

his shoulder. "Please, man, you've been avoiding me for weeks. We need to talk about what happened."

So Brand only wanted to talk to him when Hugo was feeling emotional and vulnerable? Just like that Saturday in the loft? Fuck that, now and forever. He plastered on his best "innocent face" and said, "Something happened?"

Brand flinched. "You know something did."

"What I know is that my boss helped me feel better after a bad day, and that's all it was. I'd also like to get back to work now, if you don't mind."

Hurt flashed in Brand's eyes, but he put his hand down and stepped back. "Fine. But something did happen, and you know it as well as I do. I don't know why you're pissed at me, but I want a chance to fix it."

"You don't..." Was he fucking kidding right now? "Were we in the same hayloft that day?"

"Yeah, we were, so I don't understand what this cold shoulder is about. You've ignored me for almost a month, Hugo. I thought we connected but obviously not."

Connected? Brand had kissed him like a rock star, gotten off with him, and then basically said it was just to make Hugo feel better, boss to employee. Maybe Hugo thought they'd connected briefly, but that had been shot to hell with Brand's careless words. "Guess not," Hugo said. "Can I go? I've still got work to do before I clock out."

Brand's eyes narrowed briefly, before his entire face smoothed out. "You can go. I'll see you tomorrow."

Unfortunately.

Hugo turned and strode down to the other end of the barn, spine straight and head tall. So far, every reason he'd come back to Texas had ended up backfiring in his face. Reconnect with his mother? Nope. Maybe show Brand how he really felt about him? Huge miss. The only good things he had right now were his friendships with Elmer and Rem, a steady paycheck, and a roof over his head. For now, those things would have to do.

Beyond irritated by his non-conversation with Hugo that afternoon, Brand texted Ramie and asked if she was working that night. She wasn't and agreed to meet him at The Pointe, part of a long stretch of road that ended in a small cliff, over a dry riverbed that hadn't carried water in at least a decade. It was a favorite make-out spot for local teens, and also a quiet place for a private conversation.

Brand met her there at seven with a chilled six-pack of beer, no intention of getting drunk but he needed something to soothe his sizzling nerves. Being around Hugo drove him nuts. For all Brand thought they'd made a new, intimate connection the Saturday they had sex, Hugo was acting like they'd arm-wrestled and then walked away.

No one else was parked at The Pointe that evening, so they settled on a blanket in the bed of Brand's pickup and each cracked a beer. Brand took several long pulls before stopping and letting out an impressive belch.

Ramie snickered. "You're always so refined. What's up your ass this month? I've hardly seen you around the Roost."

"I'll give you four letters and none of them are in your nickname."

"Thought so. This has to do with Hugo?"

"Yup. We had sex about a month ago, and he's been ghosting me ever since."

Her eyes widened briefly, then she took a long drink of her beer. "Okay, I didn't see that coming. I thought he had some sort of long-term crush on you. Why would he ghost you after one lay? Did you suck or something?"

Brand snorted. "No. Not literally or figuratively. He was upset about something that happened with his mother, and I just...couldn't not do something. So I kissed him, and it was amazing, and I made sure he was into it before things went further, and we ended up rubbing off together. I thought it was great. More than great. But he just...shut down. He flirted with me like crazy when he first got here, and now that we've had sex, he's suddenly giving me the cold shoulder. I don't get it."

"So you had sex with him to make him feel better?"

"I mean, that was only part of it. I did want to sleep with him, I have for a while. I just...he was so upset. Something about it... I had to do something. Kissing him was the only thing that made sense."

"Okay." She drained the rest of her first beer and reached for a second. "So what exactly did you say to him after the sex was over? Word for word, if you can manage it, because it sounds like you put your foot in your mouth somehow."

Brand thought back to that moment so many weeks ago and pulled on what he could remember. "He said thank you, and not just for the sex, but for checking on him and caring."

"And you said?"

"That I do care, maybe more than I should because

he's my employee, but he was hurting, so I did something."

"Really, Brand? In that particular, delicate moment you had to remind Hugo that you're his boss?"

"But I am." Brand felt about as smart as a box of rusty horseshoes. "Why was that wrong?"

Ramie looked like she was a few seconds away from beating him with her beer can. "This guy has liked you for ten years. He came back partly to try and, I don't know, show you how he feels? Something like that. If you were upset and I had sex with you, and then I said 'I'm glad I made you feel better, bud' how would you feel? Like a pity fuck, that's how. And I bet you a month's salary that's how Hugo felt when he left the loft that day. Like what you'd given him was a pity fuck."

"But…" Brand stared at his own sweating can of beer, upside down and turned around by Ramie's statements, because they were true. And now it all made sense. He had absolutely not meant any part of that day to be a pity fuck, but he now saw how Hugo might have interpreted it. "Well, shit."

"Exactly. You're a great guy, Brand, but sometimes you can be really obtuse about other people's feelings."

He snorted. "I sure proved that the first time we slept together, didn't I?"

"Kinda, yeah." She smiled, though, holding no grudge about that night three years ago.

Brand had first noticed Ramie when she started bartending at the Roost, and he'd been instantly attracted to her. She was different from most of the girls in town. Sassy, blunt, and no-nonsense, Ramie wasn't afraid to tell off a rude customer, and he'd wanted to get to know her. Find out where she came from and why she'd chosen to settle in a small town like Weston.

Turned out she'd inherited a small house in town from a great-aunt with no other living heirs, so she'd left a corporate job in San Antonio to move here and live a quieter life. A quiet life that included weekend drunks and Monday night football crowds, but she was happy in Weston. After flirting hard for several weeks, Ramie finally invited him to her place. Just sex, she'd said, not interested in a relationship. Brand had been fine with that. The sex had been great, and during casual conversation afterward, Brand had commented on how much he enjoyed being single. No complications like Rem had with a wife and kid, and Ramie had gone stiff. Kicked him out.

When he finally got her to talk to him again a week later, she admitted that she did have a kid—one she'd given up for adoption a few months before moving here. He hadn't pressed her for details or reasons, because he understood the pain of giving up a child more than he'd been able to say. He hadn't told her his high school fuckup until about six months later, once their friends-with-benefits relationship was firmly established.

She was the only person outside the family he'd ever told about giving up all parental rights to his own baby before the kid was even born.

"Let me ask you a question," Ramie said.

Brand sipped his beer. "Go for it."

"Can you see yourself ever telling Hugo about the baby you gave up? Can you see yourself being that comfortable and trusting with him?"

"Maybe. I definitely need to get to know him more,

and every time it feels like we're making progress, he pulls away again. It's driving me nuts. It's almost like…"

"Like what?"

"Like he took a chance on his mother, but she threw that back in his face. Maybe he's gun-shy now, and he doesn't want to risk getting his heart bruised again. Especially after my major fuckup in the hayloft."

"Sounds reasonable. Also sounds like you gotta figure out a way to show him you care. And that you maybe want more than just friendship?"

Brand groaned and leaned his head back against the rear windshield of the truck. "That's the problem. I do want more, but I'm terrified of taking that step. It was easy with Jackson, because we were just fucking around, same as with you. But I could see myself dating Hugo. Being with him, and it scares me to death."

"Because of your parents?"

"Them and the ranch as a whole. We're taking a huge chance with transitioning to organic beef, and I don't want that to blow up in my face if a buyer decides they don't like dealing with a queer vendor."

Ramie tapped her finger against her beer can. "So you're gonna what? Stay single the rest of your life? Hope you meet a girl you're into and want to marry so you aren't alone?"

"I don't know. Life was so much simpler before Hugo came back."

"It might have been simple, but were you happy? Or were you just going through the motions?"

Brand let out a long, frustrated breath, grateful to have a friend who knew him as well as she did, and also annoyed by the same. She always had been able to read him easily, and he'd adored that about her. It was something he'd always wanted in a partner, but she had also been very clear from the start that they weren't dating. It had actually taken about six months and quite a few beers before Ramie admitted she was a sex-positive aromantic asexual. She loved sex and enjoyed having it, but in no way did she want or desire a romantic relationship with another person.

So they'd enjoyed three years of friendship and good sex. Until Hugo flipped Brand's life upside down.

"I don't know," Brand said. "I wasn't as happy as I could be, but at least things were simple. Now every decision I make feels like I could step on a land mine and blow everything up."

Ramie watched him steadily for several long moments. "Then let me ask you something else. How would you feel if Hugo went out tonight and hooked up with someone else? Maybe Jackson, or some rando he meets in a bar?"

Brand squeezed his fingers tight and crinkled his beer can, actively hating the idea—and a little scared of what his reaction meant.

"That's what I thought," she said. "So now you either need to get over this crush and move on with your life, or pull a Cowardly Lion, find your courage, and ask him out on a real date. Take a chance on maybe finding something real."

"You're right." He had no idea which choice he was going to make but this was why he'd wanted to talk to Ramie about the whole thing. She said what was on her mind, always had, and he appreciated that about her. "This is why you're my best friend."

"Damn right it is." She pressed her shoulder against

his. "No matter what happens, you've always got me, bud."

"I know. Don't know what I'd do without you."

"And hopefully you never have to find out."

They tapped the lips of their beers together in a silent salute. Brand took a long gulp, then gazed up at the blanket of stars above them. One of his favorite childhood memories was camping in their backyard with Colt. Rem had been too young and the girls weren't into it, but Brand and Colt had loved it. Looking at the stars, telling ghost stories and making spooky faces with a flashlight. Sharing fun times with his big brother.

A big brother who'd left one summer without a word. Brand had been heartbroken and furious, and he'd spent a lot of years hating Colt for putting their family through so much turmoil. But Brand grew up and into the role as eldest Woods son. And then Colt came back into their lives three years ago, and Brand finally understood why he'd disappeared. He'd gone away because he'd been afraid of never living an authentic life if he stayed.

Would Brand be able to live his own authentic life if he stayed and also chose to date Hugo? Maybe. Maybe not. Their parents loved their children unconditionally, even if they didn't always understand their choices. Mom and Dad might not like it at first, and Sage might be as cool to him as she was with Colt, but it wasn't like they'd kick him out of the house.

No, his biggest fear was any backlash against the ranch if folks found out. And they would. In a town the size of Weston, eventually people would talk.

He stared at the stars and silently wished for the answer to all his problems. The stars simply winked their thousands-year-old light at him and shined on.

Chapter Fourteen

Two days after Brand caught Hugo nearly weeping over baby cows and bulls in the barn, Hugo had managed to continue avoiding him while at work. Brand seemed preoccupied by something, likely to do with the business, so Hugo didn't bother wondering. He was just an employee.

Even though Alan Denning had been released by his doctor as fit for duty, Brand had him and Hugo assigned to riding with the herds, while Jackson got the fun duties of mucking stalls most days. Less stress on Alan's hand. The guy was almost old enough to be Hugo's dad, and sometimes while they rode together, Hugo got nostalgic for his early childhood at his family's ranch. Riding in the saddle with his dad, tending to their small herd. Playing horseshoes after supper and then snacking on kolaches.

Even though the man hadn't been part of Hugo's life in seventeen years, he still missed his dad.

He and Alan were heading back to the barn and the end of their workday when Hugo spotted a familiar motorcycle parked near the main house. His stomach plummeted to his feet. He pulled No Name to a stop by the barn doors and simply stared, chilled to the bone. What the actual fuck was Buck doing here again?

"Hey, Hugo, you okay?" Alan asked. He'd dismounted his horse and was waiting by the mouth of the barn.

Hugo couldn't look away from that motorcycle. "Can you, um, take No Name into the barn for me?" He dismounted slowly, careful never to take his eyes off the main house, and didn't stumble a step. No Name nudged his shoulder but he ignored him.

"Sure, no problem."

Alan probably thought he was some kind of idiot, but Hugo didn't care. He took several long steps toward the Woods house, furious at that motorcycle for being here and terrified by what it might mean, because he didn't see Buck anywhere in the main yard.

The front door opened and two men stepped out onto the porch: Wayne and Buck. Both men were smiling, and the sight made Hugo want to vomit. The feeling got worse when the pair shook hands. Hugo wanted to charge over there, rip the men apart, and demand Buck get the hell off the property. But it wasn't his place, and he couldn't make himself move.

Buck said something that made Wayne laugh, then headed for his motorcycle. As he picked up the helmet, he very deliberately met Hugo's gaze. The bastard winked. Hugo balled his hands into tight fists, silently daring him to make a move. Buck put the helmet on, started the machine, and drove away.

"Dude," Jackson said behind Hugo. "Wasn't that the guy from before? What's he doing back here?"

"I don't know." Hugo rolled his shoulders, determined to find out now that the bogeyman wasn't staring him down.

Wayne ambled toward them, hands in the pockets of his very worn jeans. "You boys having a good day?"

"It was great until I saw Buck." He hadn't meant to be so blunt with his boss, but the words were out now.

"You know Buck Archer?"

"Yeah, I do, and for all the worst reasons." A loud bark echoed from inside the barn, and it hit Hugo that he hadn't seen Brutus around since he got back. Brutus, who'd defended him the first time Buck showed here. "What did he want?"

"Came around looking for a job. He's gotta find one to meet the conditions of his parole."

"And he came here of all places?" Of course he did. The man was a menace and probably only showed up to fuck with Hugo, whether he landed a job or not. "You can't hire him, sir."

Wayne's eyebrows went up. "Hiring is my prerogative, young buck, not yours."

"I realize that, sir, and I apologize for being rude, but Buck is not a nice person. Do you know why he was in prison?"

"Yep, for assaulting a sheriff's deputy. He explained he was drunk at the time and shouldn't have resisted arrest."

Hugo bristled. "Did he forget to mention the deputy was there to arrest him for assaulting his girlfriend?"

"He didn't mention that, no. But I don't like to judge folks by their past mistakes. We've all made them, and we've all tried to atone for them."

"Sir, I know you don't like being told what to do with your business, but I know Buck. He's my stepbrother, he was abusive to me when I was younger, and I simply do not trust him to be around the cattle or your horses. He is not a nice person. He came here a few weeks ago to taunt me about being out of prison, and he probably would have attacked me if Brutus hadn't intervened."

Wayne's expression shifted from surprised to understanding. "That must be why Brutus wouldn't stop barking when Buck first showed up. I had to lock him up in a horse stall so Buck could come into the house for the interview. The man doesn't have any ranching experience, but I was considering him because we are short-handed." Before Hugo could object again, Wayne raised a hand. "But I also trust you, Hugo. Known you a lotta years, whereas this man's a stranger." He studied Hugo long enough for him to squirm. "Did your parents know what was going on back then?"

Hugo shrugged, not in the mood to dig around in his past right now. "Yes and no. But this ranch, sir? I always felt safe here. Still do." Even more so knowing Wayne was on his side.

"I'm glad, son. Gonna go let poor Brutus out. Probably doesn't understand why he was punished for protecting his family." With a tip of his hat, Wayne went into the barn.

"Do you need a break?" Jackson asked softly.

"No," Hugo replied, turning to face the older man, whose face was as serious as he'd ever seen. "I'm actually okay this time. Before, it had been years since I'd last seen him. I wasn't scared this time. Mostly pissed. And now grateful to work for such great people. People who believe me and who have my back."

"You didn't have that at your other jobs?"

"Some of them. Definitely at Clean Slate. I was the

newbie, but no one ever treated me like a dumb kid. I never really told anyone about Buck, though." And he kind of regretted it now. For all the nights he'd spent with Shawn, learning how to play chess, they'd never really opened up about their pasts. They each seemed to silently know the other had ghosts they didn't like to talk about. "Some people change, but I don't think Buck has. At all. If our last encounter says anything, then he just got meaner."

"We've got your back, Hugo, I promise." Something fierce hitched in Jackson's voice. "He comes after you, he's got me to deal with."

"Thanks." Brutus loped out of the barn and ran right up to Hugo. Nudged at his hand with his tawny head. Hugo scratched behind his ear. "Good boy. You knew."

Brutus woofed. Dogs always knew.

Hugo did go into the break room for some water, less upset about Buck infringing upon his safe space than he'd expected. But this time he hadn't been alone with a taller, bigger, older guy basically threatening him. Wayne had listened and believed him. Jackson totally had his back. Alan...well, Hugo didn't know him well but he seemed like a good guy.

Maybe things hadn't worked out with his mother or with Brand, but Hugo did have a safe place here. And that was everything.

Brand parked his pickup near the barn, its bed laden with sacks of feed for the horses. He'd decided to do the run himself today, just so he had the free time to think about his Hugo problem. Ever since his chat with Ramie, Brand was determined to make sure he and Hugo could have an in-depth, private conversation, but he hadn't figured out how yet. Hugo avoided him in any sort of social situation, and Hugo also refused to talk about personal stuff while they were both working.

Brand needed some sort of plan.

The main yard was surprisingly quiet for it being nearly quitting time. He whistled once, curious where Brutus was, but the dog must've been out in the pastures, because he didn't come. Huh. Brand lowered the tailgate and reached for the first sack of feed, prepared to haul them to the feed room by himself.

Dad came out of the barn and waved a hand so Brand let the sack rest on the back of the truck. "You get the whole order?" Dad asked.

"Yep, they had it all in stock. Always do when we order ahead." The odd question told Brand that Dad had something on his mind. "What's up?"

"Had an incident today that I wanted to let you know about in case it gets bigger than it already is."

Brand tensed. "Okay."

"Had someone show up today to interview in-person to work for us. No experience but he seemed eager to learn a new trade. Needed a second chance."

Dad was one of those folks who liked giving people a second chance so nothing about that was weird. "Okay...."

"The man admitted during the interview he'd been incarcerated and needed a job to fulfill his parole, and I was gonna have some sympathy for him, maybe give him a trial period, but I hadn't made up my mind when I walked him out."

Alarms began ringing in Brand's head like a tornado warning siren. "Was it Buck Archer?"

"Ayup. Didn't connect the name to Hugo's family

until Hugo saw the man drive off. He flat-out said that he wouldn't trust Buck around the horses or cattle, and he admitted that his relationship with Buck was...traumatic."

"I know it was."

Dad tilted his head to the side. "You do?"

"Yeah." Brand debated what all to say to his father against keeping Hugo's confidence. "When Hugo found out Buck was out of prison a few weeks ago, he was pretty upset. We talked for a while, and he didn't tell me anything specific that happened, only that he felt safe here when he was a teenager. And that his folks were both firmly on Buck's side."

"I understand supporting your kids." Dad grunted. "But sometimes you gotta take a stand against their actions or they'll never grow up. Never take responsibility for themselves and the things they've done to others. I hope I taught you kids to take responsibility."

"You did, Dad." His parents had only ever loved and nurtured their kids. And while Wayne Woods wasn't the father who comforted someone over a skinned knee, or sat by them with a cool washcloth while a fever broke, he showed his love in other ways. By always providing for the family, celebrating special occasions, and bringing home special treats after a trip into Amarillo.

"So I assume you aren't hiring Buck," Brand said, making it less of a question than a statement, because no way in hell would Brand agree to that even if he thought Dad was dumb enough to try.

"Of course not. Hugo's a good kid and practically family, so I'll take his word on this. I also don't want to see that man on this property again. Should've known something was off when Brutus barked and snarled at him."

Brand smiled, loving how protective his dog was when he sensed a bad person around. "I told Hugo the same thing, that this is private property, so if he comes around to call the sheriff and report a trespasser."

"Good man. So how about we get this feed unloaded?"

"Sure thing."

They were about halfway done moving the bags when Hugo appeared. He didn't look directly at Brand, but he also wasn't as upset as the last time he'd seen Buck. Hugo simply tossed a bag of feed over one shoulder and hauled it into the barn. By the time they finished, Brand had worked up a good sweat, so he grabbed a bottle of water from the break room fridge. Held the cold plastic to the back of his neck for a minute, then gulped a little too fast, because he got an instant headache right behind his eyes.

When he got himself under control, Hugo was standing in the doorway, arms folded, his expression perfectly neutral. But his eyes still flickered with... something.

"Even if you hadn't seen Buck and talked to Dad," Brand said, "as soon as I saw the name on the application, I'd have told Dad no way in hell."

"Thank you." Hugo let out a soft, adorable snort. "Alan probably thinks I'm crazy, because as soon as I saw Buck, I just sort of handed my reins over to him and said to take my horse."

"You don't have to tell Alan anything you don't want to. He's a decent guy."

"Yeah. Well, uh, I've still got some chores left before I clock out. See you."

"Sure."

Brand leaned against the fridge and sipped his water,

grateful for the simple exchange, which was as close to personal as they'd had in weeks. Somehow he had to find a way to get Hugo to talk to him. A foolproof way for them to be away from the main ranch, away from Elmer's place, in a quiet setting where they could just…talk. He needed to make it up to Hugo for pushing him away. Get them back on the same page. Maybe kiss more. And in a way that wouldn't arouse suspicion.

An idea popped into his head, one that would benefit them and also the herd. With a grin he couldn't hide, Brand left the barn and headed for the house, brain already sorting the puzzle pieces into place.

The evening following his second sighting of Buck on Woods property, Hugo was in the process of teaching Elmer how to play chess in lieu of their usual puzzle, when his cell rang. Unused to anyone calling him unless it was about changing his work schedule, he glanced at the screen. Brand.

He excused himself from the dining table and wandered into the kitchen. "Yeah, hello?"

"Hey, it's Brand. I wanted to let you know there's been a change in tomorrow's schedule."

Color Hugo (not) shocked. "Okay."

"We want to take the organic herd out to the far north pasture for a few days. The grass is high and plentiful, and we want to try and bulk them up before slaughter. But because it's so far from the house, you'll need to stay overnight. Camp for a couple of days with the herd in case any coyotes or bobcats get too close. After the incident with Brutus, we don't wanna take chances on a steer getting dragged off."

"I understand." Hugo loved camping. He'd adored

doing the overnights with guests back at Clean Slate. "Who am I going with?"

"Jackson and Dog. We'll have all the gear ready when you get here, plus food. You just need to bring clothes and your toothbrush."

"What about water?"

"There's a stream that crosses the pasture, and we had enough rain last week that there should be enough for you guys and the horses. We've got a purification kit so you don't have to worry about bacteria in the water."

Good to know. Maybe Hugo had drank from the garden hose as a kid, but sometimes freshwater sources could get people sick. "Okay, sounds good. Thanks."

"No problem. See you tomorrow."

Hugo ended the call, a little surprised Brand hadn't used it as an excuse to see how Hugo was feeling, as they were both technically off the clock. He was also glad Brand hadn't pried. While Hugo had been surprised to see Buck yesterday, he'd mostly been furious. Then grateful when Wayne said he wouldn't hire Buck, and for Brand's support in the matter.

And the idea of camping for a few days with Jackson held a lot of appeal. Nights under the stars, surrounded by nature, wildlife, and their herd. Cooking over a campfire and washing up in a stream. It was practically a paid vacation, and Hugo was all about it.

Elmer seemed delighted by the idea, too, when Hugo told him about it. "I used to love spending time out in the wilds," Elmer said. "But my old bones don't tolerate the hard ground anymore. You enjoy yourself for us both."

"I will." Hugo eyed the board, pretty sure Elmer had moved a piece while he was gone, but he wasn't about to call the old man out. Hugo wasn't exactly a pro himself, but he'd been taught by a friend, and this was all for fun anyway. "Guess you didn't get a card back from Michael, huh?"

"Nope, and I don't expect to." His son Michael's birthday had been four days ago, and Elmer had mailed him a card the previous week. No response so far, but at least the card hadn't come back marked *Return to Sender*. Elmer had tried to reach out, only to have seemingly been rebuffed. "Say, when's your birthday? If I can't celebrate my kid, I can celebrate my tenant."

"Not until August," Hugo hedged. He hated birthday parties with a passion since the first one he had after Mom married Frank. Right before the party with all of Hugo's classmates and friends, Buck had cut out a huge chunk of cake and eaten it. Mom didn't notice until she went to put candles on the cake. Hugo had been mortified, especially when Buck appeared to sing "Happy Birthday" with icing on his face.

Asshole.

"Besides," Hugo said, "your company is all the party I need."

Elmer laughed. "Yeah, well, you be careful out there camping, you hear? Can't have my best tenant getting hurt and not able to pay his rent on time."

"Gee, thanks."

The quiet camaraderie boosted Hugo's confidence a bit, though, and he coaxed Elmer through another hour of playing chess before calling it a night. In his trailer, Hugo packed a few things in a gym bag he could attach to his saddle: clean underwear, toothbrush and paste, sunscreen, bug spray, an extra pair of jeans, some beef jerky snacks, and socks. He took an extra-long shower the next morning, making sure he was as clean as he'd be for the next couple of days. Washing his face in the creek was fine, but he doubted he'd strip down for a full-on bath.

His scooter puttered down the road to the Woods Ranch, Hugo kind of looking forward to this trip. A few days away to clear his head sounded like pure heaven. Three horses were tethered to the rail outside the barn when Hugo parked, one burdened with most of their equipment, the other two saddled like normal. He didn't see Jackson's pickup yet, and Jackson usually beat him to work.

A figure emerged from the mouth of the open barn doors, and Hugo half expected Alan. Instead, Brand strode toward him, shoulders back and expression clear. Him around the barn this early in the day wasn't all that unusual, but something didn't sit right with Hugo. "Where's Jackson?" Hugo asked.

"Called out," Brand replied. He pointed to Mercutio, who had a pack attached to his saddle horn. "I'm going out camping with you instead."

Hugo's stomach twisted up tight. "You're what?"

"Taking Jackson's place for the three-day camp." He whistled and Brutus loped to his side. "We're running the herd together."

Well, shit.

Chapter Fifteen

Hugo's brain momentarily fuzzed out, because no way in hell had Brand just said they were going on a three-day camp together. Overnight. Just the two of them. No. Fucking. Way.

Except he had. "Jackson wouldn't call out unless he was in full-body traction in the ER," Hugo said. "What's wrong with him?"

"I didn't ask," Brand replied, way too calm and neutral. "But you're right, he rarely ever calls off or takes a personal day, so I'm giving him time off. Dad, Alan, and Rem can handle things while we're away. The more those steer eat, the more pounds we've got to sell. And we're gonna move them slow, so the muscles don't get too tight. I talked the whole thing over with Dad yesterday."

Hugo did his very best not to glare at Brand, unsure if he believed Jackson was truly sick, or if the entire thing was some elaborate ruse to get Hugo alone. Not that he thought Brand would do anything beyond verbally hound him to talk—which was bad enough in its own way. No, he'd be perfectly safe with Brand and Brutus, and he'd never been all the way out to the far north pasture. It was supposed to be good land with a lot of grass for the herd to graze on, and bringing them back each night was more exercise than the cattle needed. Meat was muscle, after all. Too-lean meat lacked fat and flavor.

"Fine," Hugo said, not happy with his plan at all, but he was a team player and this job meant everything to him. Maybe he'd failed in reconciling with his mother, and he'd failed at really connecting with Brand, but he'd be damned if he would fail at this job. "Are we ready to go?"

"I am. Mercutio is all packed up with the gear we'll need. We can start moving the herd at any time."

"Then let's get going."

Moving a herd of forty heads of cattle was a slow process, even with two men on horseback and a dog to nip at their heels. Cattle only ran when startled or in serious danger, and their slow plodding across the vast Woods land took most of the morning. They didn't stop for lunch, just ate jerky and sandwiches from their saddlebags and washed it down with water from their canteens. Brand took a short break to give Brutus some food and water in a collapsible silicone bowl, while Hugo kept driving the herd forward.

They didn't reach their destination until late afternoon, dipping close to evening. A good seven hours of riding and Hugo's ass felt every one of them. Once the herd seemed to settle into a group and begin grazing, Hugo and Brand only had halters on their horses, versus a full bridle and bit, so they could graze easily, too. They'd get oats later, but for now they were free to wander a bit. Brutus kept watch while his human companions began to set up camp near a burbling creek. A few weeks ago, it had probably been dry as a stone, but now it ran with clear water that Brand purified first thing so they each had something cold to drink.

Hugo took a moment to admire this particular bit of wild land. Vast green grass covered hilly terrain, marked here and there by clusters of bushes and scrub trees. Green as far as he could see, with some rockier hills to the west. It reminded him a bit of the ranch he'd grown up on and a sense of melancholy settled in his chest.

"Come on, man," Brand said. "Let's collect firewood before it gets too dark. Plus, I'm starving for a real dinner."

"Yeah, sure."

They split into different directions to gather wood and had a good fire going in no time. While Brand heated up two cans of beef stew, Hugo hunted through their equipment—and only found one tent. "What the fuck, dude?" Hugo asked.

"What the fuck what?" Brand didn't even look up, just kept stirring the skillet set on a rack over the fire.

"One tent?"

He shrugged. "Less weight. Plus, if it dips cold we can share body heat."

Yeah, that was not happening in any scenario. Frustrated and still melancholy, Hugo began to set up the tent. He was about halfway done when Brand presented him with a tin cup full of steaming stew, a spoon, and a piece of toasted bread. Brand's expression was…well, amused wasn't right but he was proud of himself for something. Probably the tent more than the stew. Any damned fool could heat up stew, but only a sneaky damned fool set them up to sleep in one tent for three nights.

Since they were out here now and making a fuss wouldn't help matters, Hugo took his food and settled on the ground near the fire. The evening air was still warm as the sun began to dip low, so he didn't sit too close. But the scent of grass and burning wood helped relax him as he ate. He loved campfires and bonfires and the way snapping wood created little embers that floated up into the air like fireflies.

Brutus sat nearby gnawing on a rawhide, perfectly content to be back out in the wilds again. The cattle grazed nearby, as did their horses. Hugo didn't speak and neither did Brand. There really wasn't much to talk about right then, and Hugo was not in the mood to bring up their roll in the hayloft (so to speak).

Brand finished eating first, washed his cup and the frying pan in the nearby creek, then went about finishing the tent. After Hugo cleaned up and added another log to the fire, he brought the pair of sleeping bags over. They probably wouldn't need them unless the wind kicked up and it got too chilly—as the wind was prone to do in this area in June.

After letting the horses drink again at the creek, Hugo tethered them to a nearby tree for the night. With the sun down, the cattle wandered less, some of them settling down for the night in clusters. Brutus sniffed the air a few times but didn't seem to sense any wild animals they should worry about. Brand sat with a shotgun near him, just in case, and they settled in to play cards for a while.

One of Hugo's favorite childhood games was War, because there was no real strategy. It was the luck of the cards that went down, and they played round after round, each getting more competitive than the next, until Hugo won the game.

"Since we're sitting here pretending to be ten-year-olds at camp," Brand drawled, "how about Go Fish next?"

"Sure. I'll kick your ass at that, too, old man."

Go Fish was somehow more fun at twenty-seven than it ever had been at ten, and Hugo allowed himself to enjoy the game. Brand grinned like a fool, clearly relishing the chance to do nothing more stressful than play a children's game for a few hours under the stars. No real responsibilities, no fear he was making a disastrous decision. Other than their brief dalliance in the hayloft, he'd never seen Brand so open and at ease with himself. As if the weight of the world—and his parents' ranch—wasn't precariously perched on both shoulders.

Hugo liked seeing this side of Brand, and it was the most relaxing evening he'd ever spent with the man. Fun like his nights with Elmer, but also different. More meaningful, because it made Hugo hope he and Brand could be real friends one day. That he could finally get to know the man Brand was now, not just the man Hugo remembered. Even if the romantic/attraction stuff didn't work out, Hugo would take all the friends he could get.

Hugo yawned first. Brand waved him off, so Hugo crawled into their tent, shucked his boots, and sprawled out on top of one sleeping bag. Sleep found him fast, and he woke sometime later to the much softer crackle of the fire, and also the quiet snuffle of Brand snoring beside him. He rolled to his other side, barely able to see in the gloom. Brand slept facing him, mouth slightly open, arms wrapped around the edge of his own sleeping bag. Peaceful and handsome, and all Hugo wanted to do was lean over and kiss him. Or maybe cuddle up closer.

Both were very, very bad ideas.

He had to pee, though, so he put his boots back on and crept out as quietly as he could. Found a bush to water and relieved himself. Brutus watched him from a spot in between the glowing campfire and the tent. Hugo stoked the fire a bit, mostly so the light could keep any stray animals at bay. He scratched behind Brutus's ears for a minute, so grateful for the loyal dog, and beyond happy he'd almost completely healed from his wounds. He still had missing patches of fur, but it would grow back over time.

"You're a good boy," Hugo whispered in the quiet night, broken only by the occasional moo from the herd. "Keep protecting your family, Brutus."

Brutus licked Hugo's hand, then settled his chin on his front paws.

"Night, boy."

Hugo went back to bed. Brand didn't move a muscle.

Brand woke to the wonderful scents of coffee and bacon, and for a split second, he wasn't sure why his bed was so hard. Then he clued into the sleeping bag and tent, and that it wasn't Mom cooking up a big breakfast for her, him, and Dad. He stretched, put on his boots, and crawled out of the tent. Hugo was warming corn bread and cooking up country ham in the skillet for breakfast, plus a tin pot of coffee.

He took a minute to water a bush, then sat near Hugo but not too close. Brutus was already out there, wandering with the cattle, who mostly ignored him in favor of the abundance of grass around them. "Sleep okay?" Brand asked as he accepted a mug of coffee.

"Not bad." Hugo sipped his own mug, perkier this morning than he had been when they'd first arrived at camp last night. "I got a lot of practice sleeping on the ground back at Clean Slate. Doing the overnight trips."

"I remember. The week Rem and I flew out to be real guests for the whole experience. It was fun. Great views."

"The best views. These are pretty special, too."

Brand didn't dare hope that was Hugo flirting, but there had been a subtle inflection in his voice.

"So there any fish in that stream?" Hugo asked, jacking his thumb.

"Doubt it. Runs dry most of the summer, but I packed a bit of line and tackle in with the other gear if you wanna try."

After they ate and cleaned up, Hugo seemed to take the fish question as a challenge, going out to the stream while Brand checked on the horses and herd. A few hours later, Hugo smugly brought six sunfish back to camp, which they carefully scaled and cleaned, then cooked up for lunch. Brand gave a few bites to Brutus, who seemed to enjoy the treat.

They chatted about nonsense for a while as they rode around, checking the perimeter of where the herd had gathered. No one had wandered off, which was always a danger, especially this far from home. A stuck or injured bull would be hard to get back home without assistance.

Brand radioed in with Dad late that afternoon, using their long-range walkies. All was well, no difficulties with the herd. Dad asked how Hugo was doing. "He's fine, plenty used to camping. I think he misses having that ghost town story to tell to tourists."

Dad chuckled. "Probably so. Check in tomorrow?"

"Of course. Out."

Hugo was out on No Name, running the far perimeter of the north pasture, checking for any stragglers, so Brand wandered among the herd on his horse. Weaving in and out, checking for any limps or signs of distress. They seemed to be eating well, and he spotted a few that would definitely be ready for butchering soon. Heavy and healthy with sets of horns that would likely adorn someone's man cave sooner or later.

Brand had never been a fan of hanging dead animals or their parts as decorations, but right now their ranch needed the income. Otherwise, it would just go to waste when the beast was slaughtered.

Hugo stayed away until around dusk, coming back to camp in time for heated canned chili and the last of the corn bread. They both ate with Brutus nearby, and it was the most natural thing in the world to Brand. Out here in Mother Nature's territory with his dog, a boy he liked, and animals all around them. Peaceful and right. He just wished Hugo would freaking *talk* to him.

After they'd cleaned up and were doing nothing more taxing than watching the fire shoot sparks into sky, Brand blurted out, "Have you ever been in love before?"

"No." Hugo didn't hesitate with his answer. "Had a lot of crushes over the years, but I've never been in love. You?"

"No. Been in lust a few times, I think, but never in love."

"Like with Ramie?"

Brand shrugged. "Ramie and I always had an understanding, but we're just best friends now. Same with Jackson."

"You had an *understanding* with Jackson, too?" He sounded more impressed than disgusted.

"Yeah. We all had itches to scratch in different combinations, and before you get any big ideas, no, there weren't any crazy threesomes between us. Far as I know, Jackson and Ramie haven't been together."

"So can I ask you something?"

"Do I really have a choice?"

Hugo smirked. "Not really. Do you like one better? Men or women?"

"Not really." Brand stared into the dregs of his coffee mug, glad to be talking about this with someone else for a change. Knowing without asking that Hugo would keep all this to himself. "Just depends on who I'm attracted to or not. It's about the person, not the parts." He tried to put *Like I'm attracted to you* into his eyes, but wasn't sure if he succeeded. "You ever been attracted to girls?"

"Nah. I tried for appearances' sake in high school, but the first time I saw you..." Hugo blushed and looked at his lap. "Yeah."

Now or never. "Hugo, I'm not sorry about what happened in the hayloft a few weeks ago. I know you've been avoiding me and the topic, but I really want to apologize for offending you. None of that, nothing I did, was out of pity or duty. It's because I'm attracted to you and I wanted to be with you. To kiss you and do everything we did. I hope you believe me."

"I want to." Hugo peeked up through a fan of dark eyelashes. "I guess I had a lot of stuff going on in my head that day, and I took my uncertainty out on you.

You aren't a nasty person, Brand, not like Buck. And you didn't take advantage of me. I gave freely. To you."

"But not to Buck?" He instantly regretted the question, because Hugo scrambled to stand. He didn't walk away, though, simply stood near the fire, arms crossed over his middle. "You can tell me anything, Hugo."

"I believe you." He stared down, firelight sparking in his eyes. "I disliked Buck the minute I met him. Frank was okay, but something about Buck was just...cold. The kind of person who'd kick a stray dog for fun, or cheer while another kid was being bullied. And in some ways, he seemed to resent our parents falling in love and getting married, even though he never acted out in front of my mom."

Hugo was finally talking about this, so Brand held tight with both hands and jumped. "When was the first time Buck"—*abused* was too strong a word right now—"did something that hurt you?"

"The day of the wedding was the first time he put his hands on me." Hugo took a few steps back, then sat, knees tight to his chest, eyes still on the fire. As if lost in the magic of those flames and the pain of his past. "We were both groomsmen, and he grabbed me hard by the biceps and said I'd better not fuck this up for his dad. Left some bruises."

Brand swallowed back the urgent need to growl.

"It wasn't every week, or even every month, but I was only twelve and he knew how to scare the shit out of me with just a look. Or a threat. He knew where to punch so it looked like I'd fallen off a swing or bumped into a door. Meeting Rem in high school was a godsend, I swear to Christ. He didn't care how many times I got off the bus with him, or how many hours I spent hanging around your ranch, so I didn't have to go home."

"I'm glad you had that safe place, I mean it. And your mother didn't have a clue?"

"I don't think she wanted to know or believe me. She did and does love Frank. After the ways my bio father failed her, I think she needed a hero to believe in, and since Frank believed Buck about everything, she believed her husband by default."

"I can't imagine how hard that was for you."

"It sucked beyond belief. And then after I made a fool of myself with you in the hayloft when I was sixteen, I just...all I could think about was getting out of that fucking town. The whole county. Away from Buck and you, and to just exist as a different person without all the guilt and baggage."

Brand studied Hugo's sad, pinched face, desperate to go over and hug him. To try and soothe this pain away, but a new question caught in the forefront of his mind. A question he needed to ask, even if Hugo told him to go to hell. "Hugo, did Buck ever...hurt you, uh, sexually?"

Hugo blinked at the fire a few times. "He never touched me sexually, no, but he also wasn't shy about walking around naked for no good reason, or whipping his dick out and jerking off in front of me. It was like he knew I was gay and was trying to torment me. Or make me do something to out myself. But I hated him so much that he could have pulled a full *Magic Mike* on me and I wouldn't have reacted."

"I'm sorry." New anger sizzled through Brand's bloodstream. He grabbed a slender piece of firewood, wishing he could break the thing over the back of Buck's head. Brand wasn't normally an impulsive or violent person, but he cared about Hugo, damn it. And he hated it when people he cared about were hurting. "But thank you for being honest with me tonight. I mean it."

Hugo met his gaze. "Maybe talking about the past doesn't change it, but I guess it can make the ghosts quiet down a little bit. Leech some of the poison out. Pick your metaphor."

"It can. You're right." He liked that Hugo was calling Brand on his own bullshit. Few people in his life ever did, except maybe Ramie and his old college girlfriend Sheryl. Sheryl had been sweet, sensual and blunt to a fault, and she hadn't let Brand get away with anything, especially hiding behind excuses or obfuscations. She'd been the first person in his life to openly ask if he was attracted to guys and suggest he was bisexual.

He owed Sheryl a lot for helping him figure that part of himself out. And to accept it, even if he'd only ever told a handful of other people until now.

"I hate Buck and I always will," Hugo said. "I don't owe him anything, least of all forgiveness. But I also don't want to spend more of my life actively being angry at him. I thought I could leave those feelings behind by leaving the state, but they followed me for a long time."

Curiosity overcame Brand then. "Can I ask where you've been since you left? Besides Clean Slate. I know it was a great place for you, because Colt talks about it all the time when we call each other or visit. What about in between here and there?"

"Did a lot of odd jobs. Fortunately, I knew a lot about ranching, horses, and cattle, so I could get seasonal work. Moved across the state heading west, no real destination in mind. I was young, alone, and I could be anyone I wanted to be. Made some friends over the years but nothing that really stuck. Think my longest job was working for a mechanic in Bakersfield, California. It was good work, a nice place to live, for the most part. Hard to find anyone to date so I just...didn't.

"Then I saw an ad in the paper for the Bentley Ghost Town opening, and it talked about Clean Slate. I looked into it, and they had a link for folks to apply to work there. I applied, did a phone interview, and got accepted. Worked there for a little over two years, before taking a huge risk in coming back here. Hasn't paid off much."

Brand refused to flinch. "I think it's paid off some. Maybe not in the ways you hoped, but now you know where your mother's loyalty is. You know you can face down your bogeyman when he's twenty feet away from you. You know you've always got friends in me and Rem and Jackson. Mom and Dad got your back, too."

"I didn't come back because I wanted to be your friend," Hugo snapped, his cheeks red, and not from the fire. "But I guess if that's all you're offering, I'll take it." He grabbed his own stick, scooted forward, and poked at the fire. "What scares you so hard about us, Brand?"

"Who says I'm scared?"

Hugo snorted long and hard, until it turned into choked laughter that annoyed Brand. "Please, I just told you some pretty personal stuff here, dude. You gonna share back, or is this conversation over for good?"

"What the fuck do you want me to say?"

"The truth." Hugo's eyes danced with both firelight and determination. "You felt something with me both times in the hayloft. More than just sex. We connected on a different level. We connected all those years ago and I've never shaken it. Have you?"

"No." He swallowed hard, mouth too dry. "But you're my little brother's best friend. I can't."

"Why not? Because I'm a boy?"

Brand couldn't find the words around the knot in his throat, so he only nodded.

Hugo scowled. "Why does that scare you so much? Why don't you think they'll accept you being attracted to a man? Your big brother is married to a man and your family accepts it."

"They tolerate it." Old fears resurfaced and tried to choke the air from Brand's lungs. "And it's different with me. Colt wasn't in charge of this whole ranch. He didn't hold the family's legacy in his hands anymore, because he got out before he could get trapped here. So I got trapped here instead. I don't care that Colt's gay, and I don't think Rem does much. My sisters are harder to read, because their husbands are homophobes, and they were raised in the whole 'honor thy husband' sort of family dynamic. But my dad wants a male heir to carry on the Woods name, and if I fall for a man, I can't give him that."

"Why not? Gay couples adopt or use surrogates to have children. It's just a name, not blood. Even if I wasn't your happily ever after, you could still fall in love with a man, have a kid, and pass on the Woods name. Hell, Colt and Avery could still do the same fucking thing, and then you're off the hook."

"Unless they give the kid Avery's last name."

Hugo blew out a frustrated, almost amusing breath. "Lord, you are stubborn about this. But I guess that's a Woods trait."

"Probably so. And it's not just me giving Dad an heir. It's the whole ranch. There are a lot of open-minded people out there, but there are also a lot of closed-minded bigots left to cause trouble. We are investing so much in both the wind farms and the organic beef, and I couldn't stand it if I sabotaged it because a buyer took offense at my personal life."

"So you'd give up your own potential happiness for this ranch? You do realize that with the acreage you've got, your parents could sell the whole operation and have a tidy profit to retire on, right? Do you ever think your dad is working so hard to keep it going because he believes running it is what *you* want?"

"I...no." He'd never looked at things from that perspective. The perspective that Brand expected to take over fully and inherit the ranch. That he and Rem would continue working on the land until they both retired and turned the whole operation over to someone else. Someone preferably related to them. "Huh."

Hugo inched closer to Brand until one of them could easily reach out and touch the other, and Brand's skin buzzed with his nearness. "Do you think maybe you should have that conversation with Wayne? There's still time to go back to school and be a teacher, if that's truly where your heart lies."

"It did once. But I lost that dream when Colt left, and the ranch has been my sole focus for nearly twenty years now. I don't know that I could change careers even if it was an option."

"You won't ever know if it's an option unless you talk to your dad." Hugo reached out and squeezed Brand's left shoulder, his touch hot even through Brand's shirt. Brand took a chance and bent his left arm up to cover Hugo's hand with his. Slowly, Hugo twisted their grips until they were holding hands in front of the fire. Under a canopy of twinkling stars.

"Honestly? Talking to Dad about leaving scares me."

"Why? Do you think he'll be upset and say no? Shame you for wanting to leave the ranch?"

"No." Brand's shoulders trembled once and he stopped trying to censor his insecurities and confusion. He reached for the part of himself he'd denied for so long, the part that had felt something for Hugo for a long damned time. The part that was attracted to men the same way he was attracted to women—a part of himself he was scared to share with his family. "I'm afraid he'll say yes, I can go. Reach for dreams I shelved a long time ago."

That I can finally reach for you.

Hugo rubbed his free hand up and down Brand's forearm. "Don't be afraid to be who you are, Brand. If you're a rancher, be the best damned rancher you can be. If you're really a teacher, go be the best damned teacher you can be. Stop letting the choice tear you in two."

They held eye contact for a long, intense moment, firelight glinting in Hugo's dark brown depths. "And if who I truly am is a man who is intensely attracted to you but has a hard time saying it?"

"Then don't say it." Hugo's gaze dropped briefly to Brand's lips. "Show me."

Brand barely breathed as he studied the barely contained longing in Hugo's eyes and the silent permission to act on their mutual desire. But Brand couldn't make himself move or reach for Hugo. He stared at Hugo's lips, needing to taste them again almost as much as he needed to breathe, and his chest ached with a confusing combination of lust and fear, but he couldn't seem to break free of either.

As if sensing the invisible barrier keeping Brand at arm's length, Hugo crushed it by scooting closer and pressing his hot mouth to Brand's.

Chapter Sixteen

Hugo had started this trip irritated as hell at Brand for what he knew had been a setup from the first phone call. But Brand had been all business until tonight. Tonight, when they'd both begun spilling long-held secrets. Telling Brand more about Buck had hurt but also felt good, like he'd finally unburdened some of those awful memories and the grip they'd long held on him.

Brand sharing his insecurities and fears? Priceless. And endearing as hell, because Brand rarely showed his vulnerable side. He was always the man in charge, with a solution for every problem. Right now, Brand had all kinds of problems and no real solutions to any of them, other than a potentially intense conversation with his father about the future of the ranch. In the best-case scenario, Rem would want to take over as foreman and give Brand the freedom to pursue a new career.

If that was what Brand wanted. He'd lived on the ranch his entire life, minus college, and he'd spent almost two decades focused on running it. Maybe leaving wasn't what Brand really wanted, but Hugo liked the idea of him realizing he had options, rather than simply living up to his father's expectations.

The look in Brand's eyes as they sat by the fire, the

intense need burning in them, matched by a tiny bit of fear, had Hugo moving closer and pressing their mouths together in the kind of kiss that was both a question and a demand. Brand's entire body relaxed, his lips softened, and that was all the cues Hugo needed.

He climbed onto Brand's lap, straddling the taller, broader man's hips. Their groins pressed together through tight denim and Brand moaned into his mouth. Hugo deepened the kiss, licking into Brand's mouth while thrusting his hips, waking his dick up with the friction. Need and arousal heated his skin, and he needed to get some clothes off before he burned up. He yanked Brand's shirt out of the waist of his jeans and rubbed over bare skin and flexing muscles. Brand made a snack of Hugo's neck, licking just under his ear in a way that sent shivers of arousal right down Hugo's spine.

"God, yes," Hugo whispered, then thrust his erection against Brand's. Hard. "Tent?"

"Tent." He squeezed Hugo's ass. "I brought stuff."

"Fuuuuuck." But of course he had. Brand had set this whole thing up, and in that moment, Hugo didn't give a shit. If this was his chance to finally get fucked by his childhood crush, even if only once, Hugo was going to take it.

He rose on unsteady feet, and they tugged at each other's shirts and jeans in a messy, desperate way as they walked to the tent. Went inside and shucked off boots, socks, and belts. Brand attacked Hugo's fly, and Hugo let him, taking the moment to yank his shirt completely off. The tent was cool, but not too cold, and things would heat up soon. Brand dragged his jeans down his legs, but left Hugo's briefs in place for now.

Hugo pulled Brand's shirt off, exposing that broad, tanned chest he hadn't gotten a good look at in a long damned time. A bit of dark hair littered his pecs and abdomen and disappeared in a dark trail toward his very tented jeans. Brand let Hugo wrestle him out of his own worn jeans, but when Hugo reached for his boxers, Brand grabbed his hand.

Brand watched him with an uncertain expression. "I've never, uh, been completely naked with a guy before."

That stunned him into sitting back on his heels. "Not even Jackson?"

"No. When we fucked around, it was usually a quickie in the hayloft, or sometimes we'd park his truck out of sight, but never, you know, naked in a bed. It wasn't that kind of relationship."

"Well, this isn't exactly a bed, but I'd love to see you naked, Brand. You're fucking gorgeous."

He couldn't be sure in the bad light, but he was pretty sure Brand blushed. "You're pretty fucking hot yourself. Can I suck you?"

"You'd fucking better." Hugo slipped out of his briefs, baring his straining erection, pleased by the way Brand's eyes brightened. "You have before, right? Given head?"

"Sure, me and Jacks—you know what? Never mind, I don't want him in this tent with us. This is you and me, Hugo, and I really wanna do this with you. Have for a while. It's why I ended my other arrangements. Didn't feel right anymore, not with you so close by."

As much as Hugo wanted to cheer over that, his imagination was exploding at the mental image of Brand's lips wrapped around his cock. He spread his legs and settled back on his elbows on top of his sleeping bag. "I'm all yours, Puck."

That got a startled bark of laughter from Brand. "Rem told you about that?"

"Sure did." His sophomore year in high school, Brand had auditioned for the high school's performance of *A Midsummer Night's Dream* and he'd landed the lead role of Puck, the magic fairy who manipulates the human lovers at Oberon's request. He'd been good, too, but then Colt disappeared, and it had taken too much of his free time away from the ranch, so Brand hadn't done any of the other school plays. "Your mom even showed me a home video of it once."

"Oh God, of course she did." Brand laughed again, though. "I did enjoy myself, though. Pretending to be someone else for a while. I think part of that is what drew me to the idea of being a teacher. Being in charge of an arts program like that to challenge a kid's imagination."

"I wish you'd been able to achieve that dream." A dream Brand could still potentially reach for, if that was where his heart truly lay.

"Can't change it now." He reached out and stroked Hugo's dick. "Besides, right now I've got more important things to focus on than untrodden career paths."

"Yeah, you do."

Brand knelt between Hugo's spread legs and kept stroking him, while he seemed to look everywhere at once, taking in Hugo's body. Hugo's face warmed at the intense way Brand studied him. Sure, he had his own muscles from tossing bales of hay and mucking stalls, but he was short and slender, while Brand was tall and broad with the kind of physique that belonged on a charity cowboy calendar or something. But Brand was looking at Hugo as if he was the most precious thing on earth, and that sent tender feelings right to Hugo's heart.

That heart sped up a thousand miles an hour when Brand bent at the waist and took half of Hugo's length right into his mouth. "Holy shit," Hugo panted. Brand knew exactly what he was doing, too, because after only a few bobs of his head, Hugo's arm gave out and he flopped onto his back. No longer able to see, only experience the ultimate wow that was Brand Woods sucking his cock.

Brand licked and nipped at his glans, rolled his sac, rubbed his taint, and did everything he could to drive Hugo out of his fucking mind. When Hugo began thrusting his hips, Brand stilled and allowed Hugo to shallowly fuck his mouth for a few moments. Until Hugo went a bit too deep and Brand gagged. Pulled back. His lips were spit-shiny, his eyes wide with lust and hunger. And tenderness.

Desperate to give Brand anything he wanted, Hugo said, "Get your stuff," then pulled his legs up and open more, displaying everything he had to offer.

Brand lurched for his backpack and produced several condoms and a few of those travel-sized packets of lube. He hesitated with both in his hands, and that just wouldn't do. Hugo sat up and shoved Brand onto his back. Brand released an adorable grunt of surprise, probably not expecting Hugo to overpower him so easily. With a smirk, Hugo climbed up his body to kiss Brand with long, sensual licks into his mouth, getting the faintest taste of himself. He kissed his way down Brand's neck to his chest, where he nibbled on Brand's nipples simply to hear the man gasp and pant. Licked his way into Brand's navel to experience the chuff of laughter and the way Brand's hands tightened in his hair.

Hugo pulled the waist of Brand's boxers down slowly, tasting each inch of skin as he bared it, loving the way Brand's abdomen quivered and his thigh muscles bunched, as if working to stay still and allow Hugo to lead this. To show Brand what it was like to be worshipped by Hugo—someone who truly desired him and wasn't just using him for a booty call.

When the elastic reached the top of Brand's pubes, Brand's hand snared Hugo's forearm and he paused. Remembered what Brand had said about never being totally naked with a guy before. He looked up the landscape of Brand's body and met his dark eyes. Smiled. Brand smiled back, then nodded, giving Hugo his trust.

Brand lifted his hips. Hugo only pulled the back of his boxers down below his ass, leaving his erection covered and straining against the thin cotton material. Determined to tease Brand out of his mind, Hugo mouthed at his cloth-covered cock, licking the fabric and trying to suck on the head. Brand whined in the sexiest way possible, so Hugo had half-mercy and revealed just the crown. Licked into the slit and tasted Brand's bitter precome.

"Mmm," Hugo purred. "Been dreaming about tasting you for so many years, Puck."

Brand snorted. "You keep calling me that, and I'll be laughing too hard to properly fuck you."

"Oh yeah? Should I call you Robin Goodfellow instead?"

His eyes gleamed with amusement. "'For if we shadows have offended, think but this and all is mended.'"

"I can't believe you still remember lines."

"It was my one and only starring performance. Until maybe five minutes from now when I'm balls deep in your ass."

Hugo shivered in the best way. "Fuck yes. But first." He yanked Brand's boxers the rest of the way down, then swallowed as much of Brand's cock as he could manage. Brand was average length but thicker than most of the guys Hugo had been with and dear God, he couldn't wait to feel it in his ass. Hugo hadn't had a lot of anal sex, just enough to know he enjoyed anal with the right top, and everything in him said that Brand was definitely the right top.

The right guy, period.

He worked Brand's cock until Brand was a swearing, bucking mess, then went to town on his balls, sucking each in turn. Putting the wonderful, musky scent of Brand in his nose and on his tongue. Dragging Brand closer and closer to orgasm. He glanced up once, his mouth full of cock, hoping to get a good look at Brand's face.

Brand's head was thrown back so, instead, he looked out the open tent and right into Brutus's eyes. The dog was sitting there watching, head tilted as if trying to figure out what the hell those two crazy humans were up to. Hugo started laughing so hard he fell over. Brand sat up, confused until he glanced outside the tent. "Git, Brutus," Brand snapped. "Go watch the herd or something."

"Guess we should have zipped up the flap," Hugo said between chuckles.

"Yeah, well." Brand untangled his ankles from his boxers, then did exactly that, giving them privacy from curious animals. "Not bad timing, though, you had me too damned close to blowing."

"Good thing we stopped, then." He clasped Brand's cock, loving that he was the only guy who'd ever seen Brand like this: fully exposed and intensely aroused. "I don't want you blowing until you're inside me."

"How much prep do you need?"

"Not a lot. Finger or two and lots of lube."

"Okay."

In a swift, sexy move, Brand reversed their previous positions, dumping Hugo onto his back. He bent to press a surprisingly tender kiss to Hugo's mouth before he wrangled Hugo onto his hands and knees. Massaged his ass cheeks a bit before reaching for the first lube packet. A single, wet finger rubbing around his hole made Hugo sigh with relief. Soon. Brand took his time, though, inching that finger slowly into Hugo's entrance, adding a bit more lube with every other stroke. Two fingers burned in the very best way, and Hugo moaned. Pushed back, needing more.

Brand's free hand stroked his cock and balls, and Hugo wanted to climb out of his own skin from the sensation overload. Too much and not enough, and he'd never been such a needy mess in his entire life. He dropped down to press his shoulders and upper chest to the sleeping bag, freeing his own hands. Reached around to pull his cheeks apart.

"Fuck me now," Hugo said, not recognizing his own strained voice. "Please."

Brand draped his body over Hugo's, chest to back, cock riding Hugo's crease, and he kissed the side of Hugo's neck. "You're absolutely sure?"

"Positive, please. Need you."

He continued to thrust against Hugo's crease, nowhere close to penetrating, just enough pressure for Hugo to whine and hump back against him. Needing to be filled and claimed by this man. This kind, generous, gorgeous, self-sacrificing man who put the needs of his family above his own. A man who'd once bought snacks for an awkward, skittish teenager with a secret crush. A man Hugo had wanted for over a decade and who was finally his—at least for tonight.

Right now, tomorrow didn't matter.

Brand sat up, leaving Hugo's bare skin too cool. Hugo listened to the sounds of a condom opening. The sticky sound of it being rolled down. More lube. Fingers trailed up and down Hugo's sides, waking his nerve endings, before sliding lower to massage his ass cheeks. Trace down his crease and over his hole one more time, somehow teasing and seducing at the same time.

Finally, the sensation he needed most: blunt pressure against Hugo's hole. Pressure that became an exquisite burn for one blinding instant, and then Brand was inside. Hugo moaned and pressed his face into the sleeping bag's sewn-in pillow, not caring if the cattle heard him. This thing he'd been craving for years was happening. "So good, Brand, please."

"Jesus fuck, you're tight," Brand panted. "So fucking perfect."

"Keep going. More."

Inch by inch, Brand worked his way deeper into Hugo's body, and Hugo did his best not to thrash. To simply hold himself open and give Brand more room to move, to fill him as much as he could. Brand's fingers raked lightly down Hugo's back from his shoulders to his ass, and Hugo keened into the pillow, overcome by the sensation of being so intimately connected to someone he had genuine feelings for.

Then Brand draped himself over Hugo again. The weight was too much; Hugo let go of his own cheeks and braced his hands on the hard ground. Brand wrapped his arms around Hugo's waist, pulled out, and then thrust back in on a long, sharp push of his hips. Hugo made a noise he didn't recognize, somehow both startled and perfectly at ease with whatever Brand wanted to do with his body. So much, so fast, but it was somehow perfect.

"Yes," Hugo drawled, unable to find any other words while Brand fucked him senseless. Never before had he so completely lost himself during sex. Nothing mattered except the thick slide of Brand's cock in his ass, the swelling pressure in his balls, and the urgent need to come very, very soon.

"Gonna make you come so hard, sweetheart," Brand panted into his ear. He licked the shell and Hugo moaned. Thrust his own hips back to meet Brand.

Somehow Brand managed to wrangle Hugo up onto his knees, still impaled by Brand's cock, and held him there, their chests heaving, both of them sweaty messes. Hugo didn't have words to express what he wanted other than to come, damn it. Brand thrust once, and Hugo nearly screamed, the pressure on his prostate almost too much. "Jerked off thinking about you sometimes," Brand whispered. "What it would be like with you. The real thing is more intense than I ever imagined."

Hugo whimpered, unashamed of the sound, because the compliment had him reeling with pride and joy. Brand wrapped a hand around his cock and jacked him hard, thumbnail rubbing over his slit, until Hugo shouted and came. He was vaguely aware of Brand's hips snapping a few times before burying deep.

They knelt together for a while, bodies connected, both of them breathing hard, coming down off their highs. Eventually, Hugo became aware of the ache in his knees and the thickness still spearing his tender ass, and he reached around to pinch Brand's hip. "Come on out, big guy."

Brand carefully eased out, then drew Hugo down so they were lying on their sides, Brand's front still plastered to Hugo's back. Brand kept his arms around Hugo, his fingers drawing nonsensical shapes across Hugo's quivering belly. Never in his life had sex made Hugo feel so alive. So wanted and seen by his partner.

So necessary.

"That was…amazing," Hugo said. "Fuck."

Brand nuzzled his neck. "You aren't sore?"

"Nah. Loved that. Especially the end. No regrets at all."

"Me, either. Wanna go clean up in the creek? We can give the cattle a show."

Hugo laughed. "Sure. Waking up covered in dried lube is bad enough in a bed, but I bet it's even worse in a sleeping bag."

"Probably so."

They snuggled for a few more minutes, until the urgent need to pee got Hugo moving. They unzipped the tent. Brutus sat a few feet away, chin on his paws, watching them in a way that suggested he was not impressed by all the noise. Hugo watered a bush, then joined Brand by the stream. The water was chilly, but not so awful that his balls wanted to hide inside his body. Brand helped him wash his ass clean of lube with the kind of tender care that sent gooey feelings right to Hugo's heart. Nothing about this right now was sexual. It was all aftercare. Making sure the other was okay with everything they'd done.

And Hugo was absolutely okay with it. He only hoped Brand was, too. He'd said no regrets, but Hugo couldn't help wondering.

They finished cleaning and dried off, then went back to the tent. Fortunately, Hugo's earlier release had hit the side of the tent, rather than either sleeping bag. Instead of going to separate bags, by some silent agreement they spread one out on the ground, and then used the other to cover themselves. Sharing their "bed" for the night, basking in the beauty they'd created. They kissed a bit more, until Brand cracked a loud yawn.

Hugo dozed, sated and exhausted and so fucking happy he couldn't think straight. He'd finally made love to his boyhood crush. He hoped to do it again and again and again, but that was ultimately up to Brand. If Brand couldn't step up and seize their future, then all Hugo had was right now.

And right now he had Brand: in his bed, in his arms, and in his heart. Until Brand made the next move, Hugo would treasure what he had while he had it.

It would have to be enough.

Chapter Seventeen

Over the next day and a half, Hugo and Brand made great use of the rest of Brand's condoms and lube— probably more use than was professional, considering why they were out there, but they also did not neglect their duties to the herd. They just happened to fuck every meal break, and again that night in the tent.

Hugo was pleasantly sore and a little unsure about more horseback riding on the morning of their third full day at camp when Wayne came over Brand's walkie. Brand checked in about the feeding habits of the herd and that they planned on bringing them back tomorrow.

"I think they should stay out longer," Wayne said, his voice a bit fuzzy over the walkie. "I've got Rem and Alan packing up and ready to relieve you two. Should be there around two with fresh supplies so you and Hugo can come on home."

Disappointment crushed Hugo's heart. He wouldn't have minded a few more days out here with Brand, but they both also understood the need to rotate the horsemen and supplies out. Plus, the herd would benefit from the additional grazing time.

"That sounds fine," Brand replied. "Creek's still running good, so they'll have water. We'll be waiting."

"Good boy. See you around supper."

"Yeah."

"Well, we knew we'd be leaving soon," Hugo said once the conversation was over. "We should probably air out the tent, huh?"

Brand laughed and pressed a kiss to his temple. "Good idea. They'll bring fresh sleeping bags, but I don't want to leave jizz stains on the tent walls if I can help it."

Even though their bit of paradise was about to disappear, they both found intense amusement in cleaning up their campsite before the new residents arrived. Brand had kept all their condom and lube trash carefully tucked into a re-sealable plastic baggie, so that was easy enough to tuck into his backpack. Hugo used a wet wipe to clean a spot on the side of the tent, not ashamed of these small bits of evidence of what he and Brand had done. But it was private.

Very private, since he and Brand hadn't talked about what—if anything—to tell people once they got home. Hugo didn't want to out Brand before he was ready, and fucking the boss wasn't exactly a great look for Hugo either, but he also didn't want them to go back to what they'd been before once they arrived back at the house and barn.

Hugo didn't know how he'd keep from reaching for Brand every time he saw the man. He *would* refrain, because Hugo was a fucking professional, but yeah, it would be hard. Really hard.

After lunch, Brand mounted his horse and did a quick perimeter check of the herd and surrounding pastureland while Hugo packed the last of their trash and personal items. Everything except the tent and cooking equipment, which Mercutio would bring back when Alan and Rem came home in a few more days.

For less than forty-eight hours, life out here on the plains had been some kind of dream for Hugo. A wonderful dream of freedom, open skies, and amazing sex with a man he was falling hard for—but Hugo wasn't always sure Brand was falling, too. Brand offered sweet kisses and nudges, and even a few random hugs, but some part of Hugo still hesitated. Probably the part that knew Brand had a huge decision to make—not only about Brand's own future at the ranch, but also his ability to openly embrace his relationship with Hugo.

Such as it was right now, but Hugo prayed it would become more. Brand made his body sing in ways no one else ever had, and without hearing the words, Hugo suspected Brand felt the same way about him. He saw it in the tender smiles and gentle touches. But Brand still had a lot of personal work to do.

Brand returned from his herd check around the same time that Rem and Alan arrived on their horses with fresh supplies and sleeping bags (thank God). Rem complained about the lack of fresh firewood to keep their campfire going, and Brand teased him about being lazy and to go gather his own. Neither Rem nor Alan seemed to notice anything different between Brand and Hugo, so after a brief chat about the herd, they mounted and headed out. Brutus followed them for a good ten yards before Brand ordered him back to Rem.

Hugo knew leaving Brutus out here would be hard for Brand, but it was safer for both the cowboys and the herd to have a capable dog around for the next few days.

The ride back was not comfortable for Hugo at all, but how could he complain? They rode at an easy canter, faster than with the herd but in no huge rush to get back so no need to push the horses at a gallop. About halfway back, Brand blurted out, "I'm not ready to be open about this. Us."

"I know." Hugo slowed to a walk so they could talk more easily and Brand did the same. "I didn't expect you to be, considering how new all this is for you. I don't like lying but I don't want to pressure you."

"Thank you. I don't like lying either, but right now this thing with us is private. Nobody's business. Also? We gotta go back to completely professional at work."

"Of course. I'm not gonna maul you in front of your dad, I promise. Even though I'll want to every time I see you."

"Trust me, the feeling's mutual. You make me lose my mind in all kinds of new ways, Hugo Turner. I just…"

He was quiet for so long as their horses continued plodding along that Hugo took a chance on filling in the unspoken words. "You just need time to make sure this thing between us will last before you risk imploding things with your parents?"

Brand ducked his head, hat brim hiding his face, and nodded.

"I get that," Hugo continued. "I do. And I'm not offended by it. I'm not exactly out here, either. Shit, I never even came out at Clean Slate, and at least half the hands there were queer, especially my closest friends. I just… I don't know. I could be me there, whoever that person was. Gay, straight, or other, I was just Hugo."

"You were lucky to have that."

"I believe you could have that, too. Here. You just gotta believe in yourself and in what you truly want." *Even if it's not me.* Losing Brand, after having him even for a short time, would hurt like hell, but Hugo would survive. If he got more invested in Brand, then Brand dragged his heels and dumped him after Hugo had fully given away his heart?

Hugo wasn't sure he could heal from that if he stayed in Weston.

No negative thoughts, not when everything between them was still so new—even if it had been simmering for weeks.

"I'll do my best," Brand said, offering him a crooked smile.

"That's all any of us can do. Everything else will sort itself out."

"Hope so."

They sped up a bit, and soon the barn rose up on the distant horizon. Wayne was tending to the heifers and calves, and he helped them un-tack and brush down their horses. Put their spare equipment away. Brand said he'd take both sleeping bags up to the house for laundering, and Hugo hid a smirk.

"You did good work, son," Wayne said to Hugo. "I appreciate the extra time you put in this week with the overnight."

"It wasn't a problem, sir," Hugo replied. "I love camping, and the herd seemed to enjoy having a new patch of land to explore."

"Good man. I expect you kept Brand grounded, then? He's never been fond of camping way out in the pastures, far from the house, so I was impressed he volunteered for the job."

Hugo resisted looking at Brand, whose back was to them both, a little surprised by that tidbit. And yet not. Brand had come up with a good way to get them away from the main ranch so they could talk (among other things). The fact that Brand wasn't much of a camper was both amusing and endearing as hell. "Brand did pretty good out there. Might have only been one other person, but being surrounded by dozens of steer makes it seem a lot less lonely."

"Not my fault I got bit by a snake the first time me and Rudy camped out with the herd for two nights," Brand said.

Hugo made a mental note to ask later if Brand was afraid of snakes, because that could be fun blackmail material.

Wayne laughed. "Come on, let's get up to the house and wash for supper. Hugo, you up for a home-cooked meal after three days of canned stew?"

"I appreciate it, sir," Hugo replied with a shake of his head. "But I am dog-tired and just want my bed for a long while. I appreciate the offer, though."

"No trouble. And you take tomorrow morning off if you need the extra rest."

"Thank you. I might take you up on that." If nothing else, a few more hours to let his ass rest before riding again sounded like a terrific idea. "Be back around lunch?"

"See you then."

Wayne headed down the length of the barn, leaving Hugo and Brand alone near the tack room. Once Wayne was nearly out of the barn, Hugo asked, "Snakes?"

Brand groaned. "I was thirteen, okay? And maybe it wasn't poisonous but the bite hurt like hell. The dogs and barn cats do a great job of keeping snakes and vermin away from the barn and house, but out on the plains...yeah."

"So you suffered your fear of snakes for me?"

"No." He tilted his head, unable to hide a shy smile. "For us. The us we could possibly be."

Hugo pulled back hard on his urge to kiss Brand. "Thank you. So I'll, uh, see you tomorrow?"

"Definitely. Rest up, Hugo." Brand winked, then went down the opposite end of the barn.

After taking a moment to admire Brand's departing backside, Hugo turned and headed for his scooter. Riding home on that thing was only slightly more comfortable than a saddle, but he managed. And he was surprised to see a sheriff's car parked behind Elmer's pickup. Hugo parked his scooter near the trailer and stood by it for a moment, torn between wanting to make sure Elmer was okay and not wanting to intrude on a private matter.

Before he could make a decision, the house's screen door opened, and Elmer and Sheriff McBride stepped outside. They must have heard the scooter's engine, because both men headed in his direction. Curious, Hugo met them in the yard about halfway. "Everything okay, Elmer?" Hugo asked.

"Something ain't quite right, no," Elmer replied, his voice thin and his face pinched. "My coin collection's gone missing. A couple thousand dollars' worth of gold and silver, a lot of them passed down from my own grandfather."

"Holy shit. Did someone break in?"

"No sign of forced entry," Sheriff McBride said in a stern tone. The man was tall and thick all over, and he had the kind of openly suspicious stare that made Hugo feel as if he'd committed a crime simply by existing. This was also the hard-ass who'd made sure Buck went to prison for assaulting a deputy, but this definitely wasn't the time to thank the man for that. "But Mr. Pearce also admits to not always locking up when he's running errands or out in his shop."

"Wow, that's a shitty thing for someone to do."

"How long have you been residing on the property, Mr. Turner?"

Hugo blinked dumbly for a few seconds. "Um, since late February. I work up at Woods Ranch."

"So Mr. Pearce tells me. Does the ranch pay well?"

"It pays fine, Sheriff, and I don't—Wait." He cast a helpless look at Elmer, who wouldn't meet his eyes. "You don't think I stole your coins, do you? I swear I have never been inside your house when you aren't home, too. Not even to do laundry."

"I'm simply covering my bases," Sheriff McBride said. "Can you account for your whereabouts these last three days?"

"Sure, I can. I've been camping out with the organic herd with Brand Woods, way out in the north pasture. You can verify that with Brand and Mr. Woods. Rem, too, when he gets back, because him and Alan Denning relieved us a few hours ago."

"I haven't seen the lights on in the trailer these last few nights," Elmer said.

"So you obviously weren't around to see if anyone suspicious was lurking about?" Sheriff McBride asked.

"No, I wasn't," Hugo replied. "I don't know when the coins went missing, but even before the camping trip, I don't recall seeing anyone lurking around the yard or the house. Elmer almost never has guests, just the mailman and occasional package delivery."

"All right. In the interest of putting the matter of your possible involvement to rest, do you mind if I search your trailer?"

Hugo refrained from bristling, because he was no fucking thief, but the sooner they got this over with, the sooner he could sleep. "Knock yourself out, Sheriff, I've got nothing to hide." He led both men over to the trailer and fished out his key. This lock was usually a little sticky and seemed loose when he turned it, as if he'd forgotten to lock it before he left, and the door swung open easily.

He stepped aside and allowed McBride to go inside first, his flashlight up and beam bright. Unsure of the protocol here, Hugo waited outside with Elmer, trying hard not to fidget. He had nothing salacious for the sheriff to find. Hardly any belongings at all, really, so the search shouldn't take very long.

"I'm sorry about this, son," Elmer said. "But he has to make sure."

"It's fine." It wasn't but Hugo could humor the man. His family heirlooms were missing and that wasn't cool. Hugo hoped McBride found the culprit and threw the book at them. "He's gotta do it by the book, right?"

"Sure."

"I'm really sorry this happened, though."

"Thank you, son."

"Mr. Turner!" McBride called. "Can you come inside for a moment?"

"Sure." Hugo went up the three short steps and into the trailer. McBride stood in front of one of the kitchen's open top cupboards, his flashlight shining at one of the shelves. Hugo didn't keep much in those cupboards except cereal, toaster pastries, and chips, so he didn't know what was so exciting.

"Can you tell me what that is?" McBride asked.

"Um." Hugo stepped over and followed the beam of light to some sort of small wooden box on the top shelf, partly obscured by half a bag of corn chips. "No. I didn't put it there."

"Does anyone else live here with you?"

"No, sir." He was officially confused now and aware of Elmer standing just inside the door of the trailer, watching.

McBride turned off the flashlight and tucked it back into his belt. Nudged the chips aside and pulled the wooden box down. Dark and definitely old, if the dovetail joints meant anything. But why was it—Oh no. McBride opened the hinged lid and showed off multiple coins, some in those little cardboard protectors and others loose in plastic baggies. All kinds of coins.

"What the hell?" Hugo blurted. "What is that doing there?"

"My question exactly," McBride said.

Everything stopped making sense for several horrifying moments. "But I didn't... I would never."

"Mr. Pearce," McBride said, "are these the items that are missing from your personal possession?"

Elmer shuffled past, his expression a confusing mix of surprised and hurt. He glanced into the box briefly. "Ayup, those are the coins."

"All right." McBride put the box on the counter, then pulled a pair of handcuffs off his belt. "Hugo Turner, you're under arrest for burglary and trespassing."

"What?" Hugo was so stunned he didn't fight it when

McBride turned him around and pulled his right hand behind his back. Snapped on a cuff.

"You have the right to remain silent."

The world grayed out briefly while McBride read him his rights. Elmer simply stood there, not saying a word. "I didn't steal anything, I swear," Hugo said to Elmer as McBride led him outside. "I'm no thief."

Hurt and confused, and already hungry and tired, Hugo didn't protest McBride putting him into the backseat of the sheriff's car. His face blazed with shame over being in the back of a cop car for the first time in his life, and worse, for something he absolutely had not done. Even if he hadn't been gone for the better part of three days, he would never steal from Elmer. Not for any reason. Someone had put those coins in his trailer.

But who? And why?

As soon as they arrived at the county municipal building and Hugo was processed, he demanded his fucking phone call.

Brand had just settled in the kitchen nook with his parents for a simple dinner of leftovers when his phone rang. Dad didn't like anyone to take calls during dinner if they could help it, so Brand gave his screen a quick glance. Sheriff's Office. He was pretty sure the sheriff had never called him before, so he couldn't imagine why anyone was calling now. Wrong number, maybe?

It didn't sit right with him, so Brand excused himself from the table. "Hello?"

"Brand?" Hugo's furious voice crackled over the line, and it was the last thing Brand expected to hear. "I need help."

"Hugo? What's going on? Why are you calling from the sheriff's station?"

"McBride arrested me for stealing from Elmer, but I did not and I would never, but I didn't know who else to call. Somebody put his coins in my trailer and I'm no thief, I swear to fucking God."

"Okay, dude, take a breath." Brand walked down the hall toward the front door, keenly aware of his parents' eyes on him. "So you're down at the county municipal building, right?"

"Yeah. I didn't do it, Brand, I swear to God."

"I believe you. What kind of evidence do they have?"

"Just that McBride found the box of coins in my cupboard but I've been gone for days, and I've never gone into Elmer's house when he isn't home."

That was slim to nothing. "Okay, I'll be down there as soon as I can. We'll figure this out."

"Thank you." Hugo coughed. "I didn't know who else to call."

"I'm glad you called me. I'll take care of it. You just sit tight."

"Like I have a choice."

The snark made Brand smile. "See you in a little while." He ended the call, then went back into the kitchen. "A friend needs my help so I have to go. I'm sorry, Mom."

"Don't worry, honey, you help your friend," Mom replied.

"Can we help?" Dad asked.

"Not at the moment, but thank you. I might be a few hours, I don't know.

"Well, you take care and call us if you need us."

"I will, thanks." Brand made sure he had his wallet and keys, then left the house. Before he even reached his pickup, he called the best lawyer he knew, who answered on the third ring. "Arnie? It's Brand. I need a favor."

Chapter Eighteen

Hugo didn't know how long he sat in a dreary holding cell with only a plastic bottle of water for company. The water did nothing to quench his hunger or his parched mouth. All he held on to was the knowledge that he wasn't a thief, and Brand was going to help. Somehow. Eventually.

He hoped.

At some point, a tall stranger Brand's age was allowed to speak with Hugo. He wore a smart suit and had that kind of arrogance that screamed *lawyer*. "I'm Arnie Patterson, an attorney and old friend of Brand's from high school."

"Brand got me a lawyer?"

"Yes, he did. I just wanted to speak with you and get some background information before I speak with Sheriff McBride."

"Okay." Hugo answered every question Arnie had honestly, because he had nothing to hide. Arnie took copious notes on a yellow legal pad, which he kept tucked under one arm when he asked for the guard outside to let him out.

"I'll take care of this for you, Hugo."

"Thank you."

With nothing to do now except stare, Hugo tried to entertain himself by looking for shapes in the water stains on the ceiling. He was pretty sure he spotted a giraffe but not much else. His brain was still stuck on the humiliation of being arrested, booked, finger-printed, photographed, and locked up for doing absolutely nothing wrong.

Buck, you son of a bitch.

He was the only person Hugo could think of with any sort of reason to set him up. Any ounce of revenge in his heart, despite Hugo having done nothing except tell the truth. Hugo had no proof, obviously. Then again, neither did the sheriff. Not against Hugo, anyway. He assumed they were still investigating Elmer's house and wherever the coin box had been hidden.

Hugo was ready to start gnawing on his boot, he was so hungry, when the door to the small holding area opened. Sheriff McBride came inside and unlocked the holding cell door. "You're free to go for now, Mr. Turner."

Relief punched Hugo right in the gut. "Thank you." He left without further prompting and followed Mc-Bride back through a reception area where Hugo collected his phone, keys, and wallet. In the small lobby, Brand waited with Arnie.

"You okay?" Brand asked. He seemed to be holding back the urge to pull Hugo into a hug, and Hugo was having the same problem.

"I've had better nights," Hugo drawled. "Am I really free to go?"

"Yes, you are," Arnie replied. "They let you go because they don't have any evidence to hold you."

"But they found the coin box in my trailer."

"They found it in Elmer's trailer." Arnie held open the door to the outside, and their trio went through. Daisy was the county seat, and Hugo hated being back here. But they were on a quiet street late at night, giving them quite a bit of privacy. "Yes, you rent it, but Elmer also still has a key. Your fingerprints were not found on the coin box, nor were they found anywhere upstairs in Elmer's house. They did, however, find a partial print of Elmer's on the box."

Hugo stared blankly at Arnie. "So you're saying Elmer set me up?"

"Not at all. I argued that their only circumstantial evidence was discovering the box in a trailer owned by Elmer himself, and that it would never hold up in court. All Sheriff McBride did tonight was hassle you and embarrass himself. This shouldn't go any further, but if it does, you call me." Arnie handed him a business card. "When McBride decides he doesn't like someone, he holds a grudge."

"Great. And thank you." Hugo tucked the card into his wallet, then shook Arnie's hand. "What do I owe you?"

"Don't worry about it. I owed Brand a favor."

The front doors to the municipal building slammed open, and Sheriff McBride strode out. He didn't even glance their way, just walked across the street to a car double-parked on the far sidewalk in front of someone's house. Hugo watched, curious about the man and what appeared to be a sort of hair-trigger temper. The car's driver rolled the window down and handed McBride a thermos of something. Hugo couldn't hear their conversation but McBride didn't seem happy if his wildly gesticulating arms were any indication.

Hopefully that wasn't the guy's poor wife delivering coffee at oh-dark-thirty.

McBride said something else that sounded like it ended with "Go home!" Then he turned and strode back into the building, still never giving their trio a second glance. The person in the car sat there a moment longer before starting the engine and driving off. Hugo got the briefest glimpse of a young male face but nothing else.

"That was weird," Hugo said.

"Looks like McBride's roommate," Arnie replied.

"Roommate?"

"Yeah. McBride used to work out in Randall County as a deputy, but he got promoted and transferred here after his divorce about three years ago. Eventually got himself elected sheriff. Bought a pretty big house and took in a roommate to help with expenses. Nice guy named Josiah. I met him at the Founders' Day picnic last year. Skittish guy but he's a CNA who does in-home care all over."

"CNA?"

"Certified nursing assistant."

"Got it." Hugo had no idea what to think about Mc-Bride, and right now he didn't care. All he really wanted to do was face-plant in his bed—maybe eat a sandwich first. He wasn't super picky at this point.

"Thanks again, Arnie," Brand said. "Hugo, I'll give you a lift home."

"Thank you." He was too fucking tired to care he was about to be alone in the cab of a truck with Brand for the twenty minutes or so it would take to get from Daisy back to Elmer's house. He was so tired that as soon as he was inside the truck, he leaned his head against the window, closed his eyes, and then Brand was shaking him awake.

"Dude, come on," Brand said. "You need a hand getting inside?"

"Mmm, love your hands." Hugo's brain was still a bit fuzzy but he blinked the outline of his trailer into focus. Then a big shape moved into his line of sight to stand by the trailer door. An Elmer-sized shape. He groaned, no energy to deal with Elmer tonight.

From the moment Brand met Arnie at the sheriff's station and first learned of the stupidly flimsy reason Mc-Bride had for arresting Hugo, Brand had been working off a low-simmering anger. McBride just…something about the man rubbed Brand the wrong way and he'd never been able to figure out why. Sure, he'd gotten Buck Archer sent away, but not for Buck beating up his girlfriend—for assaulting a deputy.

Arnie had calmed a lot of Brand's anger after he spoke with McBride and learned they basically had no case against Hugo that would hold up in court. Maybe Hugo was newish back in the county, Arnie had argued, but he had no prior records or arrests. And the fact that McBride had previously arrested Hugo's stepbrother could be seen as a conflict of interest—Brand wasn't so sure about that one, but it had worked.

Hugo had been released with no formal charges filed. He was still considered a person of interest, but Brand hadn't mentioned that part yet. When Hugo emerged from the station, all Brand wanted to do was hug the man. He was so defeated and exhausted, and Brand had chosen to protect him for a little while longer. Hugo dozing in the cab of his truck had been adorable and endearing.

Elmer stepping up to the trailer door like a sentinel sent all of Brand's protective instincts back to high alert. This wasn't going anywhere good. Brand and Hugo both climbed out of the cab and met in front of the truck, headlights still on. "Sheriff called and said you'd been let go," Elmer said, no real inflection in his tone.

"Because I didn't steal your coin collection," Hugo replied, exhaustion coloring his words. "I swear on my life, Elmer, I didn't do it."

"I wanna believe you, son, but those coins didn't walk into the trailer on their own."

Hugo's entire body wilted, and Brand saw it coming. "You want me to move out, don't you?"

"I'm sorry, son, but I do. I've never once felt unsafe or unable to leave my door unlocked on this property until tonight. I can't let you keep living here."

"Okay."

Brand didn't understand why Hugo was giving in so easily, rather than defending himself. Unfortunately, Hugo was living here under a handshake agreement, so he didn't have any real legal recourse that a proper lease might have offered him. "I'll help you pack," Brand said. "You can stay in our house tonight. My parents won't mind." He said that loud enough that Elmer could hear him; Brand knew Hugo wasn't a thief.

He followed Hugo into the trailer, and Hugo produced two suitcases. They emptied the small dresser and closet. Used a few shopping bags under the sink to gather up Hugo's meager supply of groceries and snacks. Once all that was stowed in the pickup's bed, they hauled Rem's scooter up and inside, too.

Hugo walked over to Elmer, who watched by his own truck, and handed over the key. "It's been a pleasure getting to know you, sir, and to play chess with you. I'm real sorry our friendship had to end like this, and I do hope they find the real thief."

"You take care, son," Elmer replied.

They didn't shake hands, and Brand did not miss the naked grief in Hugo's eyes as he got back into Brand's truck. Hugo had bonded with the elderly man, and this was hurting him. Badly. Brand wanted to fix it for him, but there was nothing he could do beyond support his friend. Boyfriend? They hadn't really talked about labels yet, and tonight it didn't matter. All that mattered was getting Hugo home safely and tucked into bed.

Hugo didn't sleep on this drive, but he also didn't talk. He stared blankly ahead, hands folded in his lap. When Brand made the right onto their ranch's road, Hugo abruptly said, "It's gonna get around town, you know. People will start thinking I'm a thief."

"No one with half a brain will believe it." Brand squeezed his shoulder. "Even if you'd known about the coins and been desperate enough to steal them, you aren't stupid enough to hide them in a kitchen cupboard for anyone to find. I honestly wouldn't put it past Buck to have done it just to fuck with you, and maybe also to fuck with us for not giving him a job."

"Fuck with you?" Hugo's entire body jolted. "Shit, will this hurt the reputation of the ranch? I don't wanna fuck up your business."

"Don't worry about the ranch's reputation, that's my job." He was a little nervous that this entire fiasco could somehow come back to bite them, but he wasn't going to let Hugo agonize over that. He hadn't done a single thing wrong. "I know you didn't steal the coins, and even if my parents had a reason to doubt you, which they don't, they'd take me at my word about it. Rem, too. We've got your back, pal."

"Thank you. After such a nice couple of days, this was a shitty thing to come home to."

"Yeah. Life knows how to kick you in the teeth sometimes. But we'll weather this and do our best to shut down any gossip before it gets going."

"I just feel sick thinking Buck could have done it. Broken into Elmer's house and then into my trailer. I swear when I put the key in the lock earlier tonight, it felt loose. Like maybe I'd forgotten to lock it before I left for our trip, because I usually have to put a little effort into turning it."

"Did you tell that to McBride?"

"I tried but he brushed it off. Said the lock didn't look tampered with from the outside, and you really can't get in through any of the windows." Hugo sighed heavily. "I just want to sleep for a while. Maybe everything will be more clear in the morning."

"Probably."

The outdoor security lights of the barn came into view before the structures themselves. Brand parked in his usual spot. Hugo didn't seem concerned with his luggage tonight, so Brand grabbed the perishable groceries and took those into the kitchen. A light had been left on but the house was quiet, so his parents had likely gone to bed. He fixed him and Hugo both half a roast beef sandwich so they had something in their stomachs, along with glasses of cold filtered water.

Hugo ate in a daze, already half asleep. When they were both done, Brand cleaned up, then led Hugo upstairs. Growing up, Brand and Colt had shared a bedroom, the girls had shared one, and Rem had lucked into the only single room (also the smallest). Brand still slept in his old room, and Rem's was now Brand's office, and the girls' room was their only guest room. He steered Hugo there and deposited him on the bed.

"We can get your clothes and stuff in the morning," Brand said. "And don't feel bad if you have to stay here a few days until we get new arrangements settled for you."

"No one will want to rent to a thief," Hugo mumbled as he yanked off his boots.

"You ain't a thief."

"Might as well be. Should've stayed in California."

Brand let that comment slide as part of Hugo's fatigue, but it still kind of hurt. Helped Hugo shuck his jeans and climb under the covers. The room was a little stuffy, so he cracked the window for some air. When he turned around, Hugo had pretty much passed out with his arms cinched around a pillow. So innocent and young like that. He wanted to reach out and brush a lock of hair off his forehead but refrained. For all the times he'd fucked Hugo these last few days, such a simple gesture felt too...intimate.

"We'll figure this out," he whispered to his slumbering friend. Unable to help himself, Brand stroked a single fingertip down Hugo's cheek. "Promise."

Hugo woke to sunlight on his face, in a strange room, and with the urgent need to pee. He sat up, a bit tangled up in the top sheet and a quilt, and when he spotted the framed photo of the Woods clan on a side table, it flooded back to him: Elmer, being arrested, and Brand bringing him home.

Both his suitcases stood against the wall near the door. He didn't remember bringing them upstairs last night, but so much of it was a blur, fuzzed out by his rioting emotions and shame over the entire incident. And also, oh so grateful Brand had his back the whole time. He tugged his toothbrush and paste, and a clean set of clothes out of one suitcase, then went across the hall to the upstairs bathroom.

Because of the age of the house, it only had one full bath upstairs, and Hugo kind of marveled that seven people had managed to use it and the half-bath downstairs for so many years. As much as he craved a hot shower—washing up in the creek had kept his body odor under control but he wanted to wash last night off him—he settled for washing his face in the sink, brushing his teeth, and putting on fresh clothes.

The man peering back at him in the mirror looked different this morning. Angry and exhausted and a lot older than his almost twenty-eight years. Like someone people would now look at and see as a criminal. And he hated it.

With no excuse to put this off any longer, Hugo grabbed his phone—it was only a few minutes after ten, so earlier than he expected—and went downstairs. The only person in the kitchen was Rose, and she greeted him with a warm hug and a mug of steaming coffee. "You look like you could use this, sweetheart," she said.

"Thank you, ma'am, I appreciate it." Hugo helped himself to sugar from the bowl on the nook's table.

"If you're hungry, I've got pancake batter in the fridge."

"I'd appreciate it, thank you."

Hugo settled with his coffee, and he was beyond grateful when Rose delivered a plate of three huge, hot pancakes and a bottle of real maple syrup. Being waited on still felt strange, after so many years of fixing his own meal plates, but he accepted the attention. God knew he'd miss it if Wayne decided to fire him over last night's fiasco.

"Everyone else at work?" he asked.

"I expect they will be soon. Wayne met Brand and Jackson out in the barn to call a meeting over the walkie with Rem and Alan, so everyone knows what's going on." She squeezed his shoulder. "Don't worry, I know my husband and sons, and your job is safe. Wayne just wants everyone on the same page."

"Okay." Hugo wasn't sure he'd believe that until he heard the words from Wayne's mouth himself, but he did believe Rose believed them. He ate his breakfast and drank a second cup of coffee, the caffeine doing wonders to unfog his brain. And he was grateful Rose didn't ask him about last night. Brand had probably filled his family in on all the details anyway.

It was after eleven by the time he finished eating, but then Hugo didn't know what to do or where to go. Because of the overnight trips, he wasn't supposed to start today until after lunch. He also felt weird simply puttering around the Woods house when he didn't live here; he was just a temporary guest. So he volunteered to help Rose hang a load of laundry on the long lines behind the house. Simple work, but something he'd done with his own mother once upon a time.

Back on another ranch just like this one. He'd been born into the cattle ranching life, but maybe this wasn't the future he thought it was. Except the idea of leaving, of losing Brand when he finally had him, hurt too much to consider yet. So he hung laundry in the sunshine and waited to be told what to do.

At noon, Rose had lunch ready and on the table when Wayne and Brand entered the kitchen. Brand seemed a bit distracted, but he also gave Hugo a friendly smile. Hugo had done his best to help prep lunch, but the only thing he really excelled at cooking-wise was assembling sandwiches. Wayne walked over to Hugo and held out his hand. Hugo shook, apprehension tightening his gut.

"I wanna reassure you right now, son, that I believe Brand's assessment of things," Wayne said. "I dunno how those coins got into your trailer, but you've proven yourself to be a hardworking, honest boy. Your job is safe."

"Thank you, sir." His gut loosened, and he took in a centering breath. "I appreciate you allowing me to stay last night, but I don't wanna impose on your family. I need to start looking for a new place."

"I admire that, but Brand here actually has a good idea."

"For once?"

Brand laughed. "The old bunkhouse. Half of it's just used for storage, but it's still got electricity, and the bathrooms should work if we turn the water back on. Just need to clean it out, and you've got a cheap place to stay. Plus, an easy commute to work."

"That's...wow." The solution was kind of perfect. He'd have a place to stay close to work, and he'd feel perfectly safe here on the Woods property. In some ways, being kicked out of Elmer's trailer had been a blessing. Suspecting Buck had broken into his place would have left Hugo sleeping with one eye open for the rest of his time there. To Wayne, he asked, "Are you sure you're okay with this?"

"Absolutely," Wayne replied. "I've always said I try not to judge people for their past mistakes, so I can't possibly judge you for something you didn't even do. You're part of the family, Hugo."

"Thank you. Truly, sir, thank you. And I'll do all the cleaning the bunkhouse needs, I don't mind."

"It definitely needs a good airing out. I've got Jackson and myself working this afternoon, so you can get started after we eat lunch."

Hugo kind of wanted to cheer, because boy howdy, the idea of a place where he and Brand could have some real privacy was amazing, but he nodded instead. "I hate to ask, sir, but how do Jackson and Alan feel about what I was accused of?"

"They're on your side, too. Jackson's had his own problems in the past, and Alan's never been fast to judge others."

"I appreciate that."

"Good, now let's sit and eat. I'm starving."

Hugo laughed and joined the men, plus Rose. He hadn't eaten pancakes all that long ago, so he kept his own portions small and sipped at his lemonade. No one really spoke much, and at the end of the meal Brand volunteered to take Hugo out to the bunkhouse so he could look around and see what repairs might need to be made so it was livable again.

How was Hugo supposed to say no to that?

The bunkhouse was a squat, single-story building that reminded Hugo of something out of *Little House on the Prairie* with its rough-hewn board walls and caulked seams. It had a small front porch and lots of windows. Brand opened the front door and a waft of hot, stale air greeted them. He went inside first, and Hugo followed, curious because he'd only ever seen the interior through the grimy windows.

It had a large front room that served as both a living space and a small kitchen, with a wood-burning stove, a wide industrial sink, and no other appliances. A small addition to the right housed the bathroom that, according to Brand, had been added on in the late fifties. Two other doors straight ahead led to two bedrooms. One of them was crammed full of stuff, be it usable or not, and the other was just dusty and dim, with three sets of bunked beds and a few stray trunks for storage.

"Wow," Hugo said. "Talk about a blast from the past."

"Yeah, it's been a long time since we've had enough workers on the land to need this place," Brand replied, one hand wiping dust off the side of a bunked bed. "All the mattresses probably need to be beaten. I'm sure Mom's got furniture polish and stuff up at the house you can borrow, but I'd definitely start with opening the windows first."

"Thank you."

Brand smiled. "Not a problem. I'm honestly not sure why we didn't think of this when you first moved back. I guess because Jackson and Alan have their own places, and we're such a small operation now it didn't seem like we'd ever need the bunkhouse again."

"I didn't just mean for this place, Brand. I mean for everything. For last night and all the days before that. For defending me to your parents and everyone else. Since coming home, I've been disappointed a lot, over and over, but not this time. You were really here for me, and I appreciate that more than I can say."

"Then you're very welcome." Brand's gaze flickered down briefly, right to Hugo's mouth. "I'm selfishly glad you'll be nearby now."

"Me, too. Plus, I know I've said it before but I do feel safe here. I don't think I'd have been able to stay at Elmer's even if he hadn't kicked me out. Not after what happened. Even if it wasn't Buck, someone invaded my privacy and my home. So I'm crazy grateful to be here."

"Well, if Buck tries to get anywhere near you while you're on this property, we will make it very clear he is not welcome. I'll keep you safe, Hugo. Promise."

That beautiful promise melted Hugo's insides to goo, and all he wanted to do was drag Brand into the bedroom and relive some of his fondest memories from their camping trip. Somehow he refrained from letting his baser instincts win. Instead, he leaned in and pressed a gentle kiss to Brand's lips, happy when Brand relaxed and returned the kiss. His hands rested on Hugo's hips, and Hugo grabbed the front of Brand's shirt. The kiss didn't go any deeper, only went on and on until Hugo was drunk with it.

Drunk and delirious and so happy he wanted to burst.

An odd creak nearby made him jump backward, but he and Brand were still alone in the bunkhouse's living area, less than a foot from the bedroom door. The very tempting bedroom door, but no, they were both still on the clock. It was too damned risky in broad daylight until Brand came to a decision about what to tell his father.

"I should stop distracting you," Brand said. "Plus, I've got my own chores to do. Mom will give you clean sheets for the bunk. They're all stored in the attic, I think."

"Attic sheets. That sounds super fresh."

Brand swiped at his head. "I'm sure she's already got a load of laundry going for you. Just clean this place up. Who knows? Maybe we'll have a booming slaughter of the organic beef and be able to hire you some roommates."

"Are you trying to persuade me or dissuade me? Because I just got used to the idea of us having some privacy in proximity to a real-ish bed, and now you're trying to give me roommates?"

"Just thinking ahead. Gotta stay positive about the future." A bit of apprehension flickered in Brand's eyes. "You never know what might happen."

Hugo squeezed Brand's wrist. "Too true. Now get out of here and stop bothering me, boss, I've got work to do."

"Have fun."

As much as Hugo would have loved for Brand to stick around and help him clean, Hugo actually enjoyed the task. After throwing open every window he could reach—the second bedroom was packed too full to get to those—Hugo collected a bucket of cleaning supplies and a bunch of rags Rose had ripped out of old shirts no one wore anymore. He dumped all six mattresses from his new room onto the porch so he could dust and sweep both the bedroom and the main room.

When nature called, he found the exterior water main and turned on the water so he could flush and wash his hands. It ran brown for a little while, until the stream went clear. The place didn't have air-conditioning, just the air moving through the windows, so he'd worked up a good sweat by the time the interior was clean and shiny. So he went outside, got an ax handle from the toolshed, and set to work beating the dust out of the mattresses. He obviously would only need one but no sense in letting the others sit around dirty.

He had no idea what time it was when he declared himself finished and went out to the break room to get something to drink. Kind of wanted to grab the garden hose and drench his head with it to cool off but he settled on rubbing the icy water bottle against the back of his neck. He stood in the mouth of the barn, enjoying the shade and proud of what he'd accomplished today. Even though he had no idea how to cook on a woodstove—start and keep a fire going, yes, but not cook—he had a nice little home of his own on a safe piece of land.

Despite last night's setback, Hugo was finally starting to believe that coming home had been the right call after all.

Brand's truck passed and headed straight for the bunkhouse. Curious, Hugo wandered over. Brand opened the tailgate to reveal a boxy white thing that took Hugo a moment to recognize. A mini-refrigerator. "Hey, where'd that come from?" Hugo asked as he approached.

Brand grinned over his shoulder. "I got it from Rem's house. I took it with me to college, and then so did Rem, so it ended up sitting in his basement. I figured he didn't need it anymore so I kidnapped it."

"Thanks, that's super helpful. I won't have to keep all my food in the break room."

"Figured as much. I'll also head out to the supercenter tomorrow and pick up a microwave. Maybe even a small window a/c unit for the bedroom."

"I can buy that."

"Nah, it's fine. I can write it off as a business expense."

Hugo chuckled. "Naturally. Want some help?"

"Definitely. I kinda strained my back a little hauling that sucker up the basement steps."

Together, they wrangled the fridge into the bunkhouse and picked a spot near an outlet. It hummed to life; Hugo set the temperature so the interior chilled quickly.

"Looks real good in here," Brand said. "You ever hire out your cleaning services, let me know."

"I charge fifty bucks an hour."

He let out a low whistle. "Damn, I think I'll dust my own office. Although…" Brand wiggled his eyebrows. "I might be persuaded to pay that much if you clean in just a maid's apron and nothing else."

Hugo grinned. "I might lower my rate if you just wear an apron, too."

"How would either of us get any work done if that happened?"

Boots scuffled on the porch a moment before Wayne walked in through the wide-open door. Hugo and Brand weren't standing all that close, but Hugo still took a single step to the side, putting more space between them. "Damn, son," Wayne said. "You work fast."

"I had motivation," Hugo replied. "Rose offered to help but this felt like something I needed to do by myself. For myself."

"Good man. I expect you'll be joining us for supper tonight."

"I'd appreciate the meal. A woodstove is great for winter, but not so much in the summer heat."

"We'll have to get you a microwave or a hot plate. Not that Rose minds cooking for multiple folks, after raising five kids. You're always welcome at the house for meals, Hugo."

"Thank you. After supper I'll move my stuff here."

"Sure, sure. See you…" He looked at the wristwatch he always wore. "In about thirty minutes."

"See you then."

Brand watched his father go and continued to stare at the open door for several seconds later, an odd twist to his lips.

"What?" Hugo asked.

"Nothing. Dad's just worried and trying hard not to show it."

"Worried about what? What happened last night?"

"Nah, about Rem." Brand shrugged, then slid his hands deep into his tight jeans pockets. "He always worries when me or Rem are out on overnights. He told me a story once about when he was in his early twenties, his older brother did a few days out in the fields with the herd. Came back bit by a snake he didn't think was poisonous, but it was. Ended up losing his hand."

"Fuck." For some reason it'd never occurred to him that Wayne had siblings. "Is his brother still around the area? I've never met him."

"No, he died when I was really small, maybe four. I only vaguely remember the funeral. Dad's protective of his family, blood, or otherwise. He'll worry until Rem's home."

"You have a great dad, Brand. I envy you."

"Thanks." His brown eyes flickered. "I just hope that doesn't change if he finds out we're, uh, together?"

If *he finds out, not when.*

Hugo didn't want to dwell on that. He was exhausted and sore from cleaning half the day, and his stomach rumbled to be fed. "We're whatever we want to be. Don't particularly see the need for labels right now." Not when there was still a small chance Brand could change his mind about telling his father and call the whole thing off. Hugo didn't want to believe he'd do that, but it wasn't completely impossible.

"How about after supper," Brand said, "we go out to the Roost for some beers? My treat."

"Are you sure that's a good idea?"

"We've been out together before."

"No, I meant because of the coins. Elmer. The arrest."

"I think it's the perfect idea, because it shows folks you aren't hiding away. You aren't ashamed because you did nothing wrong. But if you're uncomfortable, I get it."

"I'm not." Well, maybe a tiny bit but he'd never admit that to Brand. "Okay, fine. Let's go get some beer."

Please don't let this be an epic mistake. Please.

Chapter Nineteen

Four hours later, while Brand held a towel of ice against his split lip, he was starting to think that having a few beers at the Roost had been a bad idea on his part.

Dinner with his parents and Hugo had been a quiet affair, much like lunch, and then Brand had helped Hugo settle into the bunkhouse with his things, plus a basket of clean towels and sheets from Mom. They kept their hands to themselves because the sun was still up and the windows didn't have curtains; they didn't want to risk Brand's parents seeing them in a compromising position.

However, once they left in Brand's truck for the Roost, Brand pulled off the ranch road and they kissed for a long time in the front seat. He'd missed this simple intimacy with Hugo and the kissing left him half hard. He wanted to say fuck the beer and drive them up to The Pointe so they could fuck, but going to the Roost was to prove a point, damn it. That no matter the gossip, Hugo wasn't a thief, he wasn't ashamed or hiding, and that Brand had his back.

"Used to fantasize about this as a kid," Hugo said. "Making out with you in the cab of a pickup. After the first time Rem bragged about doing it with a girl, it was all I could think about for a long time."

"I guess if you wait long enough fantasies do come true." Brand nipped his chin. "You ever fantasize about us getting off together?"

"Hell yes."

"Then let's save that for a future dream come true."

Hugo grunted but pulled back. They collected themselves and headed into town. Ramie was working the bar, and she flashed him a bright smile that Brand returned. Hugo found them an empty table near the back, while Brand ordered a pitcher of beer from Ramie. He took it and two glass mugs to Hugo's table, mindful of the occasional glance tossed his way. But Brand was a regular and a local, and he walked with his shoulders back and spine straight. Maybe this wasn't as forward as holding Hugo's hand or bluntly saying they were together, but he was making his own kind of statement.

A statement that said Hugo was still his friend.

It was a Thursday night, so the bar wasn't too packed, and good music piped over the speakers. Some folks were dancing, most drinking, snacking on simple bar food, and chilling with their friends. Brand and Hugo sat in mostly silence as they drank, not really much to say between them. Twenty-four hours ago, Hugo had been in hell, accused of a crime he didn't commit, and now here he was, having a quiet drink and silently daring anyone to approach them.

Ramie popped over on her break with a basket of warm pretzels and beer cheese dip for their trio to share. She drank water, though, because the Roost owners frowned on their bartenders drinking on the job, even if patrons were willing to buy them shots. "I'd rather lose thirty bucks of income a night," Ramie had once told him her boss said, "than worry about my bartenders over-pouring, not noticing they're over-serving, or driving home drunk."

Good bosses.

After Ramie left, Brand scraped out the last of the beer cheese with his finger, because it was good fucking stuff. Hugo watched him with amusement in his eyes and a smirk, and Brand really wanted to lean over and kiss that smirk right off his face. Instead, he went up to the bar and ordered two single mugs of beer, because another pitcher would be way too much. Ramie handed his change back, and then her gaze went over his shoulder. Hardened.

Brand turned. Two guys loomed over Hugo at their table, and while Hugo didn't look afraid or even annoyed, Brand's hackles went up. He grabbed the beers and threaded his way back to Hugo, plunked them down on the table, and gave the men his steeliest stare. He vaguely recognized them from town, pretty sure they worked on another ranch.

"Evening, boys," Brand said. "Nice night for a quiet drink."

"For most of us it is," replied the blonder of the two. "Don't particularly like drinking near a thief. Might lose my wallet."

Brand's chest burned with annoyance but he plastered on his best "innocent" face. "A thief? Can't say as I know what you mean."

"Don't be stupid, Woods, you know that kid stole from Elmer Pearce last night." Blond's loud voice boomed over the momentary silence as one song changed to another, and it seemed like half the bar heard his words and looked at their quartet. Hugo still sat but his face blazed with anger.

"What I know," Brand said in a dangerous tone, "is that someone stole from Elmer recently, and that the sheriff had no grounds to arrest my friend and employee. Now, you are free to believe what your tiny mind wants, but the truth will come out. Now please leave us in peace to enjoy our beers."

"Tiny minds, huh?" Blond tossed his friend a sneer Brand didn't like. "Told you so. That kid is trash just like his stepbrother is trash. The whole family is trash."

Hugo stood so fast his chair fell over backward with a clatter. "Say it again, fuckwad," he snarled. "I don't give a shit about my stepbrother, but you did not just call my mama trash."

Several other pairs of eyes from different tables had zeroed in on their conversation. As much as Brand wouldn't mind a good fight, he didn't want to trash the place or cause Ramie any extra trouble. "Maybe you should walk away," Brand said to Blond. "We came here for a drink, but you're the ones stirring up trouble."

"Trouble tends to find trash," Blond retorted. "This really the hill you're gonna die on, Woods? Some troublemaking thief?"

"Yes." Brand didn't hesitate, his temper flaring to nuclear levels. He moved closer to Blond, pulling up to his full height, aware the other man was slightly taller and bulkier than him. "And seeing how you're dumber and drunker than me, I'll give you the first swing. But be sure now, because your first will be your last."

Half the bar was watching them now, and Brand was keenly aware that the music had gotten quieter. One of the bouncers inched his way closer, but he was taking his time, probably curious to see how this played out. Brand was curious himself. Antagonizing others into attacking him wasn't his default mode, but this asshat was insulting Hugo openly and deliberately. It had obviously been a risk in coming out tonight. Now that he was shoulders-deep in the shit, though, Brand wasn't backing down.

"Make it a good one, shit stain." Brand angled his head slightly, exposing his jaw to the drunk asshole. "Then maybe the rest won't laugh so hard when I kick your ass from here to next Sunday."

Someone behind Brand let out a soft cheer. For him or for Blond, he didn't know or care. He watched the subtle tics in Blond's face, the way his right arm tensed and drew back, preparing to punch. Brand knew how to fight, both careful and dirty. He half-expected Hugo to try and be the peacekeeper here, but he stayed quiet, his hostile glare saying everything he didn't need to with words.

Hugo's eyes said, *"Bring it, motherfuckers."*

Either Blond was too self-confident or too drunk to make a smarter choice, because he swung at Brand with his right fist. A wide swing Brand easily blocked with his left forearm, giving him plenty of space to jab Blond twice in the stomach. Blond doubled over but didn't go down. His buddy lunged at Brand in a very sloppy way, and Brand sent the idiot careening into the back wall.

Brand turned, surprised when Blond straightened so fast the top of his head connected with Brand's chin, and Brand stumbled backward. Then Hugo was there, and one solid punch had Blond flat on his ass, blood pouring from his nose. Brand caught a glimpse of the bouncer from the corner of his eye, but some other guy lunged at Hugo, and Brand reacted out of instinct. He tackled the newcomer to the floor and punched him twice in the face, splitting the skin on his knuckles. The guy got one solid punch to Brand's mouth before going limp. The bouncer hauled Brand up and off, then gave him a light shove to the side. Away.

"You startin' trouble, Joey?" the bouncer asked Blond. "You git your friends and you git outta here."

"I didn't do nothin'," Joey snapped back. But when the bouncer glared, Joey backed down. He collected his friends and headed for the door.

Brand turned and relaxed a fraction to find Hugo only an arm's reach away, his eyes blazing but his skin blood-free. Their gazes met, and something zinged between them. A silent promise that they had each other's back, no matter what.

The bouncer made a circling motion with his hand and the music went back up. Folks turned back to their drinks or the dance floor. Ramie came over with a towel of ice for Brand's busted lip, which stung like a mother-fucker now. "You really know how to liven up a Thursday night," she quipped.

"All we wanted was a quiet drink," Brand said. "Those assholes got on Hugo's case."

"I knew someone would," Hugo whispered, still clearly angry—but now Brand wasn't sure if he was angry at the assholes who'd interrupted their evening, or at Brand for insisting they come out tonight.

Brand didn't regret it one bit, even though his lip and chin did. "Yeah, well, you didn't steal shit, and I will defend you to anyone who comes at you."

"I learned some pretty good self-defense moves of

my own from a friend back at Clean Slate, but I appreciate the help."

Ramie glanced between them, seeing everything neither man had actually said out loud. "Yeah, well, maybe next time stick to brawling in the parking lot? You're lucky you didn't bust a table or chair."

"I'll do my best." He squeezed her wrist. "Thank you."

"Not a problem." She looked at Hugo. "And if it helps, I believe you. If Brand says you're innocent, then you're innocent. Besides, Sheriff McBride isn't the most popular guy in the county. Last election, he nearly lost sheriff to a challenger, but at the last minute a deputy found a bag of weed in the guy's car. Lost him a lot of votes, so McBride won."

Brand thought back to the moment last night when McBride had gotten coffee from his roommate. The man had a temper for sure, and Brand did not want himself or Hugo on the wrong side of it.

"If he's got a target on my family's back because of Buck," Hugo said, "then I'm not surprised the guy doesn't like me. Even if I haven't done anything wrong."

"Don't take it personal." Ramie squeezed his wrist, a gesture Brand wished he was brave enough to make in front of others. "There are folks who are on your side. Gotta get back to work."

After she left, Brand glanced around but no one else was openly staring at him or Hugo. The brawl was over, attentions elsewhere for now. Brand sipped his warming beer, not really sure he wanted it anymore but it was a good prop while the ice against his chin slowly melted into the towel. That cut and bruise would be fun to explain to Dad tomorrow morning.

"Thank you," Hugo whispered. "For defending me."

"I always will. You're my friend and my...you know. I've got your back."

"Yeah."

Neither of them finished their beers before leaving. Brand felt eyes on him as they threaded their way to the front doors and left. Warm June air had Brand sweating almost immediately, and he undid the first couple buttons on his shirt on the walk across the parking lot to his truck. Nearly there, three shapes came out of the shadows, and Brand went on instant alert.

Joey and his two buddies stood between Brand and Hugo and the truck, and all three were as menacing as vipers, ready to strike at any provocation. Brand stopped walking and subtly shifted to block Hugo from them, Hugo's self-defense training be damned. Anyone who wanted to touch him had to go through Brand first.

"You really wanna go another round?" Brand asked. "'Cause I'm tired and wanna go home."

"Ain't our fault you hang with the wrong people, Woods," Joey said. "My daddy knows a lot of folks at the slaughterhouse. You keep this up, you might find yourself with a little bit of trouble slaughtering your herd when the time comes."

Brand sensed more than saw Hugo bristle. "If your daddy is as smart as you, the folks he probably knows best are the dead cattle themselves."

Joey snarled and pounced. The second fight lasted longer than the first, and Brand took a few solid licks to his ribs and back before gaining the upper hand. Hugo hit the gravel parking lot once on his hands and knees, and the blood on his hands made Brand see red. Between them, though, they fought off Joey and his pals, knocking one guy nearly unconscious, while a small crowd of at least half a dozen gawkers gathered.

Thankfully, no one called security or the sheriff over this fight. Brand drove him and Hugo home, furious by the blood streaming from Hugo's nose and the raw scrapes on his hands. Brand's own mouth throbbed with a fresh cut, and his ribs ached, but he didn't regret any of it. Not really.

At home, he dragged Hugo into the dark house, illuminated only by the kitchen light and the moon outside. He got them both ice, and they sat together in silence for a while. Mom must have heard the commotion, because she came downstairs, took one look at them, and got the first aid kit. She didn't ask questions, just fixed them both up. Hugo's nose had stopped bleeding and it was slightly swollen. "I don't think it's broken," she said. "You'll probably have black eyes in the morning, though."

"Thank you, ma'am," Hugo said. "I'm sorry to be a bother."

"You're no bother. If I know my boy and you, the men who started this fight are the bother." She assessed Brand's slightly numb face, thanks to the ice. "You won't need stitches but that cut on your chin might leave a scar."

"Thanks, Mom."

"I take it you boys beat whoever it was that you fought with?"

"Sure did. Twice, actually. Some guys just don't know when to stay down."

Mom clucked her tongue. "Men and their pride. You'll carry it to your graves, the lot of you."

"Probably." He looked at Hugo, who was an odd mix

of contrite and sad. "You feel safe sleeping in the bunk-house alone tonight? I can take one of the other bunks. Especially after a night like this."

"I, um…" Hugo glanced at Mom but her expression was perfectly neutral. "I feel safe here on the land but it would, uh, be nice to have a friend nearby. Just for my first night."

"I think that's a fine idea," Mom said. "You boys go get some sleep. Breakfast will be ready at eight." She started tidying up the kitchen table and tossing away trash, so perfectly innocent about all this that Brand wanted to hug her. To tell her the truth about him and Hugo.

Not yet.

Brand went upstairs to get sleeping clothes and brush his teeth. Brutus met him at the bottom of the stairs and followed Brand out of the house. When they arrived at the guesthouse, only the bedroom light blazed. Hugo had done up the bottom bunk across from his and he lounged on his own bed, reading something on his phone. Hugo had even put his handmade "Live, Laugh, Fuck Off" latch hook rug on the floor by his bunk. Brand wanted to climb right into bed with Hugo and hold him all night long, but that obviously wasn't what Hugo wanted. So Brand went into the bunkhouse bath-room to change his clothes and take a whiz, and then climbed into his bed for the night. His face still hurt but it was a small price to pay for defending Hugo's honor.

"How do you feel?" Hugo asked.

Hugo had put his phone down and Brand met his gaze across the smallish room. "Sore but proud. We kicked their asses twice. How're your hands?"

"Sore, but I got worse road rash when I crashed the

scooter. I think I need to start wearing work gloves everywhere I go."

Brand snorted. "Probably. You are safe here, Hugo. Not just on the land, but Brutus is out in the front room. He's the best dog."

"Yeah, he is." Hugo looked at his lap briefly. "I don't wanna risk us getting caught by asking you to sleep with me tonight, but, um, can I kiss you goodnight?"

"For sure. I love kissing you."

Brand sat up, overjoyed when Hugo padded across the wood floor to sit on Brand's bunk. Hugo cupped both sides of his face in a gentle grip and gave Brand the softest, most sensual kiss of his life. Careful of Brand's cuts and bruises, Hugo made love to his mouth in the sweetest way possible, leaving Brand breathless and aching for more. But Hugo simply kissed the tip of his nose, then returned to his own bunk.

For as exhausted as he was, Brand didn't fall asleep for a long damned time. He stared at the random shapes on the walls and floor, cast by the bright moon and lack of curtains on the windows. Hugo snored softly, the lucky bastard finding rest that eluded Brand. Eventually, Brand drifted in and out of sleep, only to come awake with a start, heart pounding in his chest. Someone whined nearby, and it took him several seconds to realize Hugo was in distress.

He scrambled out of bed and crossed the room to sit on the edge of Hugo's bunk. Hugo's face was scrunched and sweaty, and he clung to his thin blanket. With no a/c, the room was uncomfortably warm, but Hugo clutched at the blanket like it was a shield from the rest of the world.

"Hey, come on, H, wake up," Brand said quietly. "It's just a bad dream."

Hugo jerked violently as he came awake, his upper half jackknifing into a vertical position. He held the blanket high against his chest for several long, agonizing moments before recognition smoothed his expression. "Brand. Sorry, did I wake you?"

"I wasn't really asleep." He unclenched one of Hugo's hands from the blanket and held it tight, trying to give some of his strength to Hugo. "Bad dream?"

"Yeah, happens sometimes."

"Do you remember what it was about?"

"No, I almost never do." Hugo let out a long breath, then covered Brand's hand with his. "Mostly it's just the fear. Being trapped. Suffocated. Scared. Only the second time I've had one since I've been back to Texas."

"When was the first?"

"The night after I saw Buck again for the first time in years. He made me feel like a helpless kid again, but not anymore. Tonight, I guess between being arrested and two fights, it just got to me."

"Hey, I'd be worried if all that shit in twenty-four hours didn't affect you somehow." Brand took a chance on brushing a kiss across Hugo's forehead, grateful when the younger guy seemed to relax even more. "It's been a crazy few days."

"No shit." Hugo surprised the hell out of him by dragging Brand down on top of him, the blanket and top sheet separating them. But Brand swore he still felt Hugo's enticing body heat between the layers of cotton. "I like this."

"Me, too." Brand pressed his forehead against the side of Hugo's neck and breathed in the familiar scent of the man. A man he was very much falling for. And falling fast. "I was scared tonight. For you."

He scowled. "I told you I can handle myself in a fight."

"It wasn't about you being able to defend yourself in a fight. It was just…" He bit back the instinctive urge to growl and kissed Hugo's jaw instead. "I need you safe, Hugo. I can't explain it, but I do."

"Climb under the covers and keep me safe tonight?"

How was a man to refuse such a request? It took a minute or two for them to get the covers situated. Then Brand was curled up close to Hugo from behind, draping his broader body over Hugo's slimmer one, loving the way Hugo fit there. Loving everything about this. Tucked close together, sharing body heat, despite the warm room. He nosed the back of Hugo's neck, enjoying the scents of sweat and something like aloe. His shaving soap, maybe.

Perfection.

Hugo angled his head backward just enough so they could kiss each other on the mouth. A claiming and a declaration of what they were going forward—even if what they were was a secret for a little while longer.

Chapter Twenty

Hugo woke with sunshine on his face, a hot body draped over his, and the unfamiliar sound of someone snoring near his ear. Brand. They'd spent the night together in the bunkhouse but why was Brand in—Oh yeah. Nightmare. He half expected a bit of embarrassment from the nightmare but none came. Brand had been supportive, concerned and kind, and Hugo adored him for that. For not teasing him like Buck used to, and for all of Brand's words the night before.

Getting into bar fights was out of character for Hugo, but he wasn't going to let himself be bullied anymore. Especially when he'd done nothing wrong. And watching Brand bristle and snarl like a protective bulldog? Hot as hell. Hugo didn't need a defender, but he loved knowing he had one anyway in his longtime crush.

A longtime crush sleeping right beside him, exactly where Hugo had wanted him for years. As much as he didn't want to move and ruin the moment, he really had to pee, so he gently extricated himself from Brand's arms. Brand snuffled once, then pressed his face into the pillow and kept snoring.

Hugo did his business, then fetched a bottle of water from the mini fridge. He'd had a few with his stash of food from the trailer, but he'd need to buy a new case soon. Maybe he could borrow Brand's truck and hit up the supercenter this evening, get a few things to make the bunkhouse a bit homier, like curtains for the big windows. Brand would probably insist on paying for anything specific to the bunkhouse, and not Hugo's personal needs, so he could get the tax write-off.

Brand was still sleeping when Hugo went back into the bedroom. He'd rolled onto his back, and despite the bruises on his face, he looked peaceful. And so fucking handsome Hugo's chest ached. So much had happened in the last four days, everything from having sex in the tent, to Hugo's arrest, to last night's bar fights. It was all so surreal, like he'd dreamed it rather than lived it.

But memories didn't lie, and Hugo had lived it all. He could also see himself living like this far into the future. Herding cattle with Brand, sleeping together every night, turning Woods Ranch back into the success it had always been. Loving each other and watching their family grow all around them. On this unique piece of land in north Texas.

He sat on the edge of the bunk. "You stole my heart a long time ago," Hugo whispered, so soft he barely heard his own words. "Please take care with it, and I'll take care with yours."

Brand snuffled once, as if hearing the quiet declaration. His eyes moved behind the lids several times before he blinked them open. Initial confusion shifted into a bright smile when he spotted Hugo hovering over him. "Morning. Sleep okay?"

"Yeah, I did. You?"

"Like a stone. Must have been the company."

Hugo leaned down and pressed a soft kiss to Brand's

mouth. "I enjoyed the company, too. And I'd offer to make you breakfast, but all I've got are protein bars."

Brand chuckled. "No worries, Mom invited us up to the house for breakfast, remember?"

"Right, sorry. So much has happened recently, I keep forgetting shit."

"No one's gonna blame you for that. What time is it?"

Hugo checked his phone. "Seven-thirty. Still time to shower and get dressed. Wanna save water and share?"

"Have you seen the shower in this place?"

He hadn't actually peeked behind the plain white— and likely to break apart if they moved it too fast—plastic curtain to inspect the shower. Standing shower, not a tub, but the size of it actually made Hugo laugh. It had two separate showerheads, probably to help speed things along back in the heyday when the bunkhouse had been full, with no real light other than the standard bulb over the sink. The thing seemed designed to get guys in and out as fast as possible.

It also gave them room to share and play a little. Hugo hadn't yet had the chance to admire Brand's fully naked body, standing in front of him in all its glory. Work-hardened muscles, dark-blond hair on his torso and upper thighs, a few scars here and there from accidents or injuries Hugo didn't know about. The kind of guy who'd be at home in any cowboy calendar lineup.

And he wanted Hugo.

They washed and played and both got hard, but since they didn't have a lot of time before breakfast, simply jerked each other off before rinsing a final time. It was such a simple thing but it ticked off another box in Hugo's long list of fantasies with Brand: shower sex. Sure, Hugo's hotter fantasies had involved Brand pushing him up against the tile wall while fucking him from behind, but they could save that for later.

Brand had forgotten to bring a clean shirt for this morning, so he wore his same jeans and went bare-chested, because yesterday's shirt had bloodstains on it. They walked up to the house together, and Brand sneaked upstairs for a shirt, while Hugo headed for the kitchen.

The enticing scents of cinnamon and coffee greeted him. Rose bustled about, Wayne nowhere in sight yet, and Hugo helped himself to a mug of coffee.

"Sleep well, hon?" Rose asked.

"I did, thank you. I appreciate the chance to stay close right now." He blew across the top of his coffee. "Being able to stay here is a very generous gesture by your family."

"Well, it's been far too long since we've had folks living out there. Hard times and all, so it's nice to see the building being used for more than just holding on to junk my husband can't seem to get rid of. I keep saying he needs to clear that mess out, maybe have an auction. Make space for when Brand turns us into the most popular organic beef supplier in six counties."

Hugo grinned at her absolute faith in Brand. "I'll drink to that, ma'am. Brand has an amazing mind. Your ranch is in good hands with him."

"Thank you, dear."

Rose had a pan of fresh cinnamon rolls plus a fruit salad on the table by the time Brand joined them. "Morning, Mom," he said as he poured himself coffee. "Where's Dad?"

"Went down to the barn early," she replied, "but he should be up soon. He knows when breakfast is."

Hugo's skin prickled with unease. Wayne had been out and about early this morning. But Wayne had never struck him as the prying sort, so the man had no reason to peek into one of the bunkhouse windows. Right?

They ate in near silence. The cinnamon rolls were heaven, the fruit nice and sweet. Hugo ate his fill and insisted on helping Rose fill the dishwasher. Wayne didn't come inside until Hugo and Brand were heading out to start their day, and he gave them both cursory nods. Hugo met Brand's gaze, and Brand simply shrugged. Hoping he was just being paranoid, Hugo headed out to the barn with Brand and they got to work.

Two mornings later, Brand was out checking the organic herd for slaughterhouse readiness—the steer needed the right amount of fat on the brisket and the tail rolls—when Rem found him. He and Jackson had brought the herd back last night, and Brand hadn't expected to see him today.

Rem rode up on Juno and pulled to a stop nearby. "I guess I don't have to ask if the rumors are true," Rem said, "judging by your busted face."

"Depends on the rumor." Brand ran his hand down one steer's flank. A good number he'd checked so far seemed ready, and he hoped they got a Prime rating for the meat at slaughter.

"The rumor that you and Hugo got into two fights at the Roost a few nights ago and you kicked ass both times."

"Those are very true." He looked up but the sun was right behind Rem, so he had to squint. "Wasn't about to let a couple of assholes give Hugo shit about something he didn't do. They didn't like getting their asses beat once, so they came at us for a second round."

"Man, I wish I'd been there to see it. Can't rightly picture Hugo in a bar brawl."

"He held his own. As long as the right rumors spread, I don't think he'll have much grief going forward over the burglary arrest." In some ways, that had been the entire point of last night's outing. While Brand hadn't intended for them to do battle, he couldn't argue with the results. Hugo was no one's fool, and Brand wouldn't allow others to insult or mistreat him.

"I doubt it, too. And putting him in the bunkhouse was a smart idea. He can stop wearing the life out of my scooter every day."

Brand snorted. "Like you ever drive that thing anywhere. It's a dust collector, just like everything sitting around the other bunkhouse bedroom. And the attic. And that spare stall in the barn. We could easily downsize and invest that money back into the ranch."

"Good luck with that one, bro. Dad's parents lived through the Great Depression and the dirty thirties. All that dust and devastation. He learned how to save everything in case he needed it again one day."

"Yeah, but old glass canning jars with no lids that fit? And it's not like Mom cans all that much anymore, especially since she stopped gardening. I get his experiences, but sometimes you gotta let shit go."

"Hey, I agree with you. Maybe the next time Colt's out to visit, the three of us can gang up on him? It's worth a shot."

"True." After losing him for sixteen years, Dad now had a soft spot for Colt, and if anyone could convince the man to let go of some stuff, it was likely their older brother. "Anyway, we've got some head ready for slaughter, I think. I'll call up to the slaughterhouse later and see when they can get us in."

"Great. Should see a tidy profit from that."

"Hope so. As long as the demand for organic, grass-fed beef stays high, we should do well over the next year or so. Plus, the regular herd is about ready to send, too, I think. Right age, right fat consistency. I just really wanna test out the organic market first."

"I get it. If that's the future of Woods Ranch, we need to see what's what. I trust you, brother. We all do."

"Thanks." Brand didn't hear those words often from his little brother and they meant the world to him. They rarely talked about anything serious, period, sticking to surface things and goofing around, and Brand took this opportunity to pick his brother's brain. "You ever think you might want a bigger part in the business than just as a rustler?"

Rem blinked down at him. "Like what? Your accountant? This is my job and my role in the family. Even before Colt left and you got the foreman job, I knew my place. Why? You thinking of leaving?"

"No, not really. I guess some nights I've been sitting up wondering what my life could have been if Colt stayed. Or if you were older than me and had my job, so I could've done something else. Not that I want a different life, I just…can't help wondering."

"Makes sense. I mean, I do sometimes wonder how different my life might have been if Shelby hadn't gotten pregnant when she did. If we'd waited longer to get married." His pensive expression brightened. "But I love Susie to bits and wouldn't give her up for the world. These are our lives, bro. All we can do is live them."

"Yeah." Brand didn't completely agree that all they could do was live them. They all had choices, forks in the road, roads less traveled they could attempt to take. Pick the metaphor. All they had to do was be brave enough to say, *"I want something else."*

Brand wanted something else, and he wanted it with Hugo. But he didn't know if he was brave enough to reach for it, much less fight for it.

Let me be brave enough when the time comes. I don't want to lose him.

By the end of June, Hugo's life had settled into something quite boring, and he loved it. He'd fixed up the bunkhouse with a microwave and two-burner hot plate, added curtains to the bedroom and some furniture in the living area he'd gotten from social media swap sites. The space had become his in its own way, and it was the first time he'd had his own living space in ages. Sure, the trailer at Elmer's had been private, but despite its proximity to the Woods house, Hugo felt at peace here.

He missed Elmer and their evenings spent together. Sheriff McBride had no new suspects in the burglary of Elmer's house, but he also had no more proof Hugo had done anything wrong, so Hugo tried to let the whole thing go. He focused on his job and on Brand. He focused on Brand as often as possible.

Their conflicting schedules didn't allow a lot of time for sex, but they worked in encounters whenever possible, usually in the bunkhouse. Every time Hugo welcomed Brand into his body, he felt a deepening connection between them. Every time Brand kissed him hard and needy during sex, Hugo adored the man even more. They moved together, sometimes without words, and each encounter was more amazing than the last.

This wasn't just two horny men getting off; this was something real. And completely different from anything Hugo had imagined between them when he first returned to Texas. But his expectations had been colored by his memory of the man he remembered from a decade ago. The Brand whose kindness toward Hugo had fueled a teenage crush. Back then Brand had been a flawless hero in his eyes, even after the incident in the hayloft. The Brand he knew today was a very flawed man making huge life decisions that would affect a lot of people. People they both cared about.

Brand was no longer his hero but an equal, and he truly hoped Brand saw Hugo the same way.

About half the organic herd went to slaughter. Brand had hoped for Prime but they rated Choice. Still a high rating for beef, though, so no one was disappointed. Especially for their first organic attempt. Dad even had one organic steer processed for their own family, stocking up the freezer in the basement. He planned on contributing to the barbecue at this year's July Fourth picnic in town and advertising their meat. Brand liked that idea.

On the second day of July, Brand spooned up close to Hugo from behind, loving the way his condom-covered spent cock rubbed against Hugo's crease. They'd fucked for what felt like hours, but had probably been twenty minutes, finding a brief respite from the summer heat in the air-conditioned bedroom of the bunkhouse during their lunch break. He loved these stolen moments with Hugo, when they didn't have to do anything except exist together. Love each other.

Not that Brand had said the words yet, but he had very strong feelings for Hugo. Stronger than anything he'd ever felt in his life. He just didn't know how to say it. Or when was the right time, while Brand was still hiding who he was from his family. Hiding his relationship with Hugo. Hugo hadn't pushed him to define it or come out, and Brand adored him for that. But Hugo deserved better than being a secret. He deserved Brand's open affection and honesty.

He deserved so much more than Brand was giving him.

They took turns rinsing off before returning to work. Hugo and Alan headed out to the pasture on horseback, while Brand went up to his office to do paperwork. His least favorite part of the week, but it needed to be done. The ranch had gotten a decent return on their first organic slaughter, but Brand had budgeted for more so he had to wiggle some numbers around. He vaguely heard the stairs creak, and he wasn't surprised when Dad appeared in the office doorway.

"Hey," Brand said. Dad seemed tense, which had been his standard operating emotion lately, but he refused to talk about why. "Something wrong?"

"Not sure exactly." Dad eased into the leather chair across from Brand's desk, his weight making the old wood creak. "I don't wanna accuse you of nothing, Brand, but you've been different these last few weeks. I'm curious about it."

"I'm not sure what you mean, Dad." He knew exactly what his father meant, but Brand wasn't about to voice it first, just in case he was wrong. "I'm happy with what we got for the slaughter and sale of the meat. We've got a handful of guys coming by in the next few weeks to buy steer for their families and to stock up their freezers. The wind farm is doing great."

"That's all business stuff. I'm curious about your personal life, son." Dad cleared his throat hard. "I, uh, was under the impression you were seeing that pretty girl from town. Rachel?"

"Rachel Marie, but we all call her Ramie. Dating didn't really work out." Oh God, were they doing this now? Brand tried hard not to squirm or give away how nervous he was over whatever his father might say next. "We're just really good friends now."

"Hmm. When did that happen?"

"A while ago. May, maybe? I don't exactly remember. We're better as friends than anything bigger. And before you ask, Dad, it was mutual."

"I see." Dad tapped his foot on the wood floor several times before stopping. "It's just you've been different since Hugo came back. Can't really put my finger on it."

Brand eyeballed his empty coffee mug, wishing he had something to both use as a prop to stall and to wet his now-dry mouth. Dad was poking around the edges of something Brand wasn't ready to talk about. "Hugo's a good friend."

"Another friend?"

"I can only have one good friend?" He tried to tamp down on his defensiveness because it wouldn't help him. "I never really got to know Hugo the first time because he was in high school. Now he's an adult and we get along. I can see why he and Rem were friends for so many years before Hugo left."

"Friends who spend the night in each other's bed?"

If Brand hadn't been sitting he might have lost his balance and hit the floor. "What are you talking about?"

Dad leaned forward, elbows on his knees, eyes blazing with something Brand couldn't name. "The first night Hugo spent in the bunkhouse. You stayed with him. I was up early that day and heard Brutus scratching at the door. Let him out. Peeked inside to see all the work Hugo had done to clean up the place. Saw you two."

His stomach twisted up tight, and he put down the pen he'd been making notes with, afraid of the way his fingers wanted to shake. "Saw us what, sir?"

"Sleeping together. Same blanket, same bed." Dad sounded less disgusted and more confused, but his face conveyed what his voice didn't: distrust of anything Brand had to say.

"He had a nightmare about Buck. I tried to help."

"And lunch break last week?"

A strange sense of dread fell over Brand like cold, oily sludge. This was it. The moment he'd dreaded for ages. All he could do now was straighten his spine and square his shoulders. Look his father in the eye. His fingers trembled. "That was unprofessional on my part."

Dad's eyes narrowed. "Which part?"

"Sleeping with him." Brand wanted to cry, scream, and throw up all at once, but he kept still. And as calm as humanly possible while he potentially broke his father's heart. "I'm his supervisor and it was unprofessional." Now or never, and never wasn't going to happen. "Dad, I'm bisexual. And I'm...with Hugo."

So many things flitted through Dad's face that Brand couldn't identify them all. He stared at Brand for a long time. So long Brand started to wonder if he'd imagined the entire conversation. Then Dad stood. His chair scraped backward so loudly that Brand flinched. Dad turned and walked out of the office, leaving Brand alone.

Shit. Shit, shit, shit, shit. What have I done?

Brand stared at his lap, allowing his hands to shake now that the confession was out there. He couldn't take it back, couldn't amend the statement. He'd said it. All he could do now was accept his words and deal with the consequences.

Chapter Twenty-One

After riding the fence line all afternoon looking for stragglers, Hugo's ass needed a break from the saddle, and he was glad when he and Alan returned to the barn. After untacking and settling their horses, he grabbed a bottle of water from the break room and wandered a bit, hoping to spot Brand. No dice.

Hugo hadn't been invited to the house for supper, so once it was quitting time, he headed for the bunkhouse. Tossed a frozen dinner into the microwave and ate it by himself at the small dinette set he'd purchased and set near one of the windows facing the main house. Warm air trickled in through the screenless window, and he never caught a glimpse of his target. He shot Brand a quick text, asking if he'd had a good afternoon. Short and simple.

When twenty minutes passed with no response, Hugo didn't let himself worry. He cleaned up and settled on the faded green couch he'd found via a "Free" ad online to play a game on his phone. At one point he dozed off, only to wake from the beep of his text notification.

Brand: Afternoon was fine. Can't talk tonight. Sorry.

A little odd but not concerning. Maybe they had some sort of private family thing going on tonight—which would make sense if Rem or their sisters had come over, but there weren't any extra cars by the house. Whatever. Hugo had had a great day, so after a quick shower he slid into bed. The twin bunk felt almost too big without Brand in it, crushing him to the mattress with his broader body.

He woke on July 3 with a weird pit in his stomach that a breakfast of microwaved oatmeal and coffee didn't fix. Today was a busy day for the family as they prepared for tomorrow's July Fourth celebration in town. Besides the town-wide barbecue, there'd be a local country band playing, plus folks setting up tables to sell locally made goods and food. Booths from local businesses, churches, and other organizations handing out free swag like paper fans on Popsicle sticks and pens. As a kid, Hugo used to love walking those tables and collecting as much stuff as he could, just so he could admire it all later when he got home.

Just like at the fair back in May, Woods Ranch would have a booth to hand out literature on their beef, and Wayne was going to barbecue up all cuts of meat for folks to sample. Plus, he'd donated a bunch of ribs to the Baptist church organizing the main portion of the barbecue. Hugo wasn't part of any of that, though, so he stuck to his regular duties, annoyed and unsettled at not seeing Brand almost all day.

Not until about three in the afternoon. Hugo had finished mucking the last horse stall, and he caught a glimpse of Brand walking past the barn's main entrance. He leaned his shovel against the nearest stall door and bolted. Brand was reaching for the door handle of his pickup when Hugo overtook him. "Dude, are you okay?" Hugo asked.

Brand looked at him with a spooked expression that made Hugo's insides sour. "Been busy. Lotta work to do before tomorrow."

"I'm sure you do, but…did I do something yesterday to piss you off? I feel like you're avoiding me."

"You didn't do anything. I did."

"What did you do?"

"I got involved with an employee, and it's hugely inappropriate. I am your boss and supervisor, and I never should have put you in that position."

Hugo stared at Brand, uncertain whom he was actually looking at. Brand was nothing like the confident man who'd left his bed twenty-four hours ago. Instead, he was pale and pinched, and Hugo didn't buy this whole "inappropriate" act for a second. "I put myself in that position, willingly and plenty of times. You didn't take advantage of me, Brand, not once. And I know you're not the type of guy to fire me if I broke things off. Not that I want to, because I really, really like what we have."

I'm falling in love with you, you jackass, so what is this?

Hugo couldn't bring himself to voice those thoughts, though.

"He knows, Hugo," Brand said in a soft, hesitant tone he'd never heard before.

"Who knows what?"

"Dad. He saw us in bed together. More than once." He pinched the bridge of his nose, and when he met Hugo's eyes again, Brand's were too shiny. "He confronted me yesterday afternoon. I couldn't lie to his face, so I came out as bi. Dad hasn't said a word to me since."

The bottom seemed to drop out from beneath Hugo's feet, even while he silently cheered for Brand finally coming out to his dad. For owning up to that truth, instead of explaining away seeing Hugo and Brand in bed together. No wonder Brand and Wayne had both been scarce these last twenty-four-odd hours. The elder Woods had to come to terms with a huge revelation, while the younger had to—he hoped—embrace who he was, fully and finally.

"So it's out there," Hugo said. "We don't have to hide."

Brand squinted. "Did you hear me? My dad won't talk to me. He won't even look at me."

"He came around with Colt being gay. He'll come around with this. You just gotta have faith in that, Brand."

"It was different with Colt."

"How? Your dad couldn't accept Colt was gay and he drove Colt away for years. Your dad regretted it, and he was thrilled when Colt came back into your lives. You really think he's gonna drive you off because you're bi and with a guy? That he'll risk losing another of his sons for God knows how long?"

"I don't know." Brand slammed his open palm against the side of his truck. "I just don't know. He's never acted like this with me before, and it terrifies me, okay? I just…need some space. Please."

"Space from me?" When Brand nodded, Hugo's heart shriveled a little bit. "So what I think and feel doesn't matter? Doesn't matter that I'm falling in love with you?" Brand flinched, and that made Hugo take a step backward, putting suffocating space between them. "You know, when I was accused of stealing from Elmer and you stood by me, I thought it meant you always would. Now I see I was wrong."

"Hugo, I'm sorry."

"Fuck that." He allowed his anger and hurt to wash over him and power his words. "I get this is complicated for you, but it's fucking complicated for me, too. I came back to Texas for two main reasons. One was to reconcile with my mother, maybe have a relationship again, but that didn't happen. She made her choice. The other was you. To stop hiding my feelings and take a chance. Well, we took that chance and I guess it costs too much for you."

"I just need time."

"Time for what? We've been circling each other since February and fucking for weeks. We've talked about this more than once. What do you still need time for? Huh? To decide the kid of a failed rancher isn't worth it in the long run? That you'd rather go back to your fuck buddies than take a harder road loving me? What do you need time for, Brand?"

"I'm sorry this is harder for me than for you," Brand snapped, his dark eyes blazing. "I blew up my life yesterday, and I need time to work through that. My family is all I've got."

Hugo did not let himself flinch or otherwise react to the hurtful statement. "Right. Then from now on you stay away from the bunkhouse and out of my bed. *Boss.*" He put every ounce of fury he had into that final, single word. With nothing left to say, Hugo turned neatly on his heel and stalked back to his place. But once he passed the threshold to the bunkhouse and locked the door shut, grief swamped him like a heavy, wet blanket he couldn't untangle himself from. He slid to his butt, back against the door, and shook for a while. He didn't cry or scream or do any of the things his body craved to dispel the negative emotions buffeting him.

All he could do was exist in them and wonder if his broken heart would ever beat right again.

Brand had been on his way to meet Ramie at The Pointe so he could vent about coming out to his dad, when Hugo ambushed him by his truck. He'd hoped to avoid Hugo until he could figure out how he felt about everything, but Hugo's tenacity had fucked that right up. And Hugo's challenging words had set Brand's back up in the worst way. Brand had responded out of self-preservation rather than emotion, and he'd managed to drive Hugo away.

Did we break up? Is that what happened?

He had no idea.

He also had no energy left to meet up with Ramie tonight, so he texted her, calling it off with no explanation. She responded, telling him to call her whenever. Instead, he called for Brutus and they walked. Brand didn't go in any particular direction, he just walked and absently stroked Brutus's head once in a while. Brutus loped along with him, happy to be with his human, while Brand's brain spun out in all kinds of directions without landing on any single thought.

All he knew for sure was that his father was ignoring him, Hugo was angry with him, and Brand didn't know what to do to make both men happy.

So he walked.

* * *

Hugo slept for shit that night, tossing and turning, alternating between too hot and too cold, and more than once he swore he heard Brand's gentle snores in his ear. But every time Hugo opened his eyes, he was alone. He was haunted by thoughts of Wayne Woods banging on the bunkhouse door and demanding Hugo pack his bags and leave. Also with thoughts of Brand storming into the room and declaring them done.

Both thoughts left Hugo unsettled and queasy. He gave up on sleep when the sun rose and was to work early. He'd been given half a day today, since their herds were less than half the size they'd previously been, and his initial plans had been to spend his afternoon at the July Fourth celebration in town. Maybe hang with Brand for a while and share some kettle corn with him.

Now he wasn't so sure.

He worked his half-day, aware of the quiet around the ranch with Wayne, Brand, Rose, and Rem all at the celebration, having fun and pushing their cattle. The isolation fucked with his head a little bit. His only saving grace was Brutus, who hung close to Hugo while he worked in the barn. He adored this dog, who was as loyal as they came. His fur was still a bit uneven in a few places where he'd had stitches all those months ago, but all in all, Brutus was thriving.

If only Hugo could say the same thing about himself. Right now, he was barely treading water. The only thing keeping him sane was that he hadn't been fired yet. Then again, Wayne could be scared of Hugo retaliating, considering Brand was his immediate supervisor and Hugo could scream coercion. Not that Hugo ever would. He'd walked into this thing with Brand with his eyes wide open. Hell, Hugo had instigated the entire relationship.

Were they waiting for Hugo to resign and run away with his tail between his legs? He'd never do that. Not again. He had run once but he'd come back. No more running. If he left again, it would be because he had no other choice in employment. Right now, he had a job he loved, a place of his own, and choices. Until something dramatic changed, Hugo wasn't going anywhere.

Except maybe into town.

Hugo drove the scooter to the Roost. The place was pretty empty, probably most folks busy at the festival happening at Westwood Park near the Baptist church. Someone had put up patriotic bunting around the bar, and only a few tables had customers. The Roost served regular food through six o'clock, then switched over to a few simple appetizers, plus bowls of peanuts and pretzels for the drinking crowd.

He sat at the bar, not surprised when Ramie came over with a menu and a curious smile. "Figured you'd be at the festival," she said. "Getcha a drink? We've got a Patriot Beer special."

"What's that?"

"Basically a Boilermaker but with a double shot."

"Sounds good." He looked at the simple menu of sandwiches, burgers, and apps while she made the drink. Boilermakers weren't usually his thing, because combining beer and hard liquor was a good way for Hugo to end up with a hangover, but he didn't care right now. His heart hurt, and he needed something to soothe it. When Ramie came back, he ordered their classic burger with all the fixings, plus extra bacon. If he was going to indulge in alcohol, might as well line his gut with greasy food first.

Since Ramie only had a handful of customers to attend to, she very deliberately began wiping down the clean counter in front of Hugo. "Are you and Brand okay?" she whispered. "We were supposed to get together last night to talk, but he blew me off. And now you're here alone, looking like someone kicked you in the balls."

Hugo sipped his drink and nearly gagged at the flavor. There was a reason he didn't order these things. "I don't know what we are, but I do know you can keep a secret. Right?"

"Of course. Brand told me about you two and I haven't told a soul. Swear."

"His dad found out and Brand came out as bi. But now his dad isn't talking to him, and Brand isn't talking to me, and I think we might have broken up last night." He briefly described their interaction by Brand's truck as he worked his way through his Patriot whatever drink.

"I'm sure his dad is just surprised," Ramie said. "I mean, who wouldn't be? Coming out at thirty-five like that. Give them time."

"I want to, but I hate that Brand is keeping his distance. I just want him to talk to me, that's all."

"So go talk to him."

"I can't. Not right now, he's busy with the family business at the festival, and I don't wanna make this into a public spectacle. I just…have to wait, I guess. Maybe catch him tonight after the fireworks."

"And do what all afternoon? Mope here at the bar?"

"Maybe."

She snickered. "How about a compromise? I get off in a little over an hour. You hang here, and then we can go walk around the festival together."

"Really?"

"Sure. Just don't drink too many of those in the meantime, or you'll be so drunk I'll be carrying you around."

Hugo chuckled. "Good advice. Thanks, Ramie, I mean it. I really do care about Brand and I want what's best for him. And the ranch."

"Well, it's not selfish to also want what's best for yourself. If Brand is who you want, then you gotta fight for him. Fight hard. He's a great guy, and you seem pretty cool yourself, Hugo."

"Thank you. You, too. I'm glad you're his friend."

"I am a pretty great friend." With a wink, she went off to fill a drink order from the place's lone server.

His burger came up a while later, so he took his time eating in between sips of his drink. He did end up ordering a second drink, because the very slight alcohol haze made it not taste quite as awful, and it went down a lot faster with the burger and fries. A decent burger, too, and he couldn't help wondering where the Roost got their beef.

He paid his tab and left with Ramie when her shift was over. The Roost was within walking distance of the festival, so they left their vehicles in the lot and strolled down a side street toward the sounds of music and laughter and so many voices that Hugo's skin crawled. He never used to dislike crowds of people, but after his arrest, he wasn't comfortable being out in public anymore.

Fuck that. Today, he was going to reclaim himself.

Even if Brand didn't want him anymore, Hugo knew who he was, damn it, and that person was going to try and enjoy himself today.

They browsed the freebie tables first. Ramie picked up a paper fan from someone running for Congress in their district, and it was wide enough to give them both a decent bit of air on their faces. Ramie carefully avoided the Woods Ranch table, and Hugo averted his gaze, pretending not to see who was there. They found the food booths and while Hugo was full, he treated Ramie to lemonade and a corn dog. They listened to music for a while, then watched a dance troupe perform.

Ramie found a tent selling ice-cold beer, so they each indulged. The entire afternoon was fun in its own way, and he understood why she was Brand's best friend. She was funny, supportive, and her dry wit impressed Hugo. They got along great and at suppertime they got in line for the barbecue. Everyone got a Styrofoam container with a roll, bag of chips, dill pickle, and their choice of a half-chicken or ribs. Sauce choices were at the end of the line just past the cash box.

Hugo indulged in the ribs, because they were from his ranch. No sauce; he wanted to taste the meat.

A few picnic tables were scattered around but they settled in a shady patch of grass to eat. The ribs were perfect, and he used the time to people watch the crowd. A few folks waved at Ramie but most ignored Hugo. Whatever, he didn't care if this town liked him or not.

As the sun got lower and the food cleared from the park, music started up and folks began dancing. Something to pass the time until dusk, when the fireworks would start. Hugo was hot and tired, but he also couldn't say no when Ramie asked him to dance. She was good, too, practically leading him through some of the faster numbers, and then relaxing for the slow ones.

At one point, the skin on the back of Hugo's neck prickled, and he looked up. Brand was watching them from the sidelines, arms crossed, face annoyingly blank.

Holy shit, is he jealous?

In that moment, Hugo didn't care. He pulled Ramie down into a gentle dip, then back up, grateful this was a country song he knew and could dance to without looking like a fool. She laughed and didn't seem to notice they were being watched. She was living in the moment, uncaring of the world around them, and Hugo wanted so much to be like her. To truly be her friend.

They listened to local bands, as well as a few church choirs, play and sing for a while longer as the sun continued to set. More folks began congregating in the open area of the park. Hugo wasn't sure exactly where the fireworks were being set off, but everyone seemed to be facing east, toward the darkest part of the sky.

The first to go off was small, a simple burst of red and white. Then larger fireworks turned the sky into a kaleidoscope of colors and bright lights. Sharp booms rent the air. Hugo hadn't seen fireworks like these in a long time, and the finale was breathtaking. He applauded along with everyone else, and the day's celebration was over.

Ramie generously offered him a ride home, but Hugo turned her down. The scooter would get him home just fine. His beers were wearing off, and since he had to work early and Ramie didn't, he headed back to the Roost alone to fetch his vehicle. The walk was quiet, most of the town's activity still in the park, and he'd just crossed into the Roost's parking lot when a big shape blocked his way.

Hugo took a step back out of habit, and then his stomach sank when he recognized Buck. A glassy-eyed, listing Buck, who had a beer bottle in one hand, while the other held the remains of a six-pack. Two pickups separated them from the dim light of the Roost's entrance, leaving them a bit too alone for Hugo's liking.

"The fuck are you doing out here, Buck?" Hugo asked. "You get caught walking around drunk, your parole officer is gonna shit kittens and send you back to lockup."

Buck tilted back his bottle and sucked the contents down. "Didn't know you gave a shit."

"Honestly? I don't, but the last thing I want is for you to embarrass my mother again with your fucked-up behavior. Go home and sleep it off." He tried to walk around Buck in the near-empty parking lot, but Buck got in his way. Instead of getting scared, though, Hugo's temper rose. "Let me by."

"You always were a little shit, weren't you? Never giving a good goddamn about the people around you."

"That would be you, Buck, not me. I gave a shit for a long time and about a lot of people, but I stopped giving any shits about you when you started terrorizing me. I honestly don't care if you go back to prison, I just don't want my mother to get hurt because of you. Maybe she doesn't care about me anymore, but I still fucking care about her."

Buck snorted, puffing beer-scented breath into his face. "You're a piece of work. I never wanted you in my life, but there you were. The golden boy, the great student, while I was always the fuckup. Then you finally left and I still couldn't get any fucking peace, because you were still there."

"What are you talking about?" Hugo was turned around by this entire conversation, and all he really wanted to do was get on the scooter and go home. Get away from this confusing mess. "All I ever wanted was for you to ignore me. Pretend I didn't exist. You're the one who kept coming after me."

"Because you were always fucking *there*." He dropped the remains of the six-pack; glass clinked in the gravel but nothing burst or broke. "Even after you left, it was *Hugo this*, and *Hugo that*. Couldn't never see what was so special about your queer ass, and now you've got Brand Woods sticking up for you? You take it up the ass for his protection, little brother?"

"Excuse me?" First Buck was mad because Hugo got better grades than him, and now he was accusing Hugo of buying Brand's protection with sex? What the fuck? Then again, he had no idea how much Buck had had to drink already tonight. "Buck, just leave it and go home before you get arrested for disorderly conduct or something. Go home."

"Not until I find out what makes you so fucking special."

Before Hugo could figure that out, Buck grabbed him by the shoulders and hauled Hugo against his chest. Hugo couldn't do anything to stop the wet mouth that slammed down on his, or to dislodge the bigger, more muscular man who clung to him like a life raft. Hugo struggled, hating the tongue licking around his lips, the taste of beer, and the sour smell of Buck himself. A familiar smell that sent him right back to his sixteen-year-old self, terrified of the next punch, slap, or kick. Only this time, Hugo was ready to fight.

He drove his knee up but had a bad angle, so he only skimmed the inside of Buck's thigh. "What?" Buck snarled. "You'll give it up for Woods but not me? We ain't related."

Close enough. Hugo tried to dodge, but Buck caught his shoulder and shoved him back-first against the side of the nearest pickup and tried to kiss him again. This time, Hugo bit Buck's lower lip. Buck yelled and pushed him so hard Hugo's head cracked off the truck's cab, and his ass hit the asphalt. Pain jolted up and down his spine from his head and his butt.

Surely someone had heard the fight by now. Where was everyone?

Buck grabbed a beer bottle from his six-pack and smashed it against the fender of the truck, letting glass and beer fly. He held the jagged edges of the bottle close to Hugo's face, and Hugo sucked in a terrified breath. One slice to his carotid and Hugo was dead. He'd seen Buck drunk and pissed before, but this was something brand-new, and it terrified him to his bones. "Please, don't," Hugo said.

"Don't what? Cut your fucking throat? You never should've come back to Texas, brother. Couldn't even get you sent to fucking jail to show your mom you aren't the golden boy, because here you are."

What the what? Is Buck admitting to stealing Elmer's coins and planting them in the trailer?

"Let me go, Buck," Hugo said, his voice steadier than he expected. "You're drunk and don't know what you're doing."

"Oh, I know exactly what I'm doing. And if you

know what's best for you, you'll get up and get your ass in my truck."

"Not a chance." If Hugo got into that truck, he'd be dead by sunrise, of that he had no doubt. Someone had to leave the Roost sometime soon. Someone had to see them like this, to take notice and give a damn. All Hugo had to do was stall for a little while longer. "I don't know why you hate me, but I never did anything to you. My own mother chose you over me."

"She chose my dad, and that motherfucker can rot in hell, too. He left me out to dry with that assault conviction."

"You did it, you idiot, and you deserved to serve your time, not just for assaulting that deputy but also your girlfriend."

Buck held that broken bottle closer to his neck, and okay, maybe goading the guy with the weapon was a stupid idea, but Hugo was inching beyond the border between reason and insanity. He was angry, scared, and close to panicked, and those were not a great combination. "You don't know shit," Buck snarled.

"I know I take responsibility for my fuckups. Do you?"

Buck's hand drew back and Hugo saw his own death in Buck's drunk, angry eyes. Light flashed off the jagged edges of that bottle. Then Buck went flying as another body slammed into him, and two men wrestled for control of the bottle. Hugo gaped at them long enough to recognize Brand as the person struggling with Buck. They flailed in the gravel parking lot, Buck attempting to attack while Brand kept that sharp bottle at bay with all the strength he had.

"We need help!" Hugo shouted, unsure what else to

do. He scrambled to his feet, still screaming for help. A car door slammed somewhere. Buck rolled so Brand was on his back, and Hugo cast about for a weapon. Anything to get Buck off Brand. Nothing except a fist full of gravel and that wouldn't help him.

Brand hollered. A spurt of red shot over the gravel and hit Hugo's shoes.

No.

Chapter Twenty-Two

The sight of Brand's blood on his shoes made something primal flare to life inside Hugo. The pained whimper Brand released lit the fuse and fury exploded deep inside Hugo. He flung himself at Buck and tackled the bigger man to the ground. They went rolling. Hugo waited for something sharp to slice his skin, but the only thing that hurt were rocks in tender places. Somehow, he ended up on top and swung with everything he had. His fist smashed into Buck's face. The blow jarred up Hugo's arm and shoulder but he'd never felt a sweeter pain in his life. To finally punch the son of a bitch.

He swung again, splitting at least one of his own knuckles on Buck's teeth, then Buck went limp beneath him. Hugo stared down, kneeling over Buck's still form. Blood poured from Buck's nose and his eyes were closed. Hands empty. No bottle.

"What the hell?" a stranger's voice yelled. Male. Nearby.

Hugo looked to his right and his heart skipped with terror. Brand lay flat on his back, staring up at the sky, both hands in a half-clutch near his abdomen without actually touching. And protruding from his gut was the neck of the beer bottle.

"No. No!" Hugo lunged for Brand, his brain spinning far beyond reasonable comprehension. He was vaguely aware of someone else there, someone not a threat, who was talking on his phone. Hopefully 911, because Hugo couldn't think to react. Couldn't do anything except grab one of Brand's flailing hands and squeeze it tight. "Hey, you're okay. Brand? Look at me, you're fine."

Brand stared up at him, his face too pale, eyes unfocused. He seemed uncertain of where he was or what had happened, and Hugo wasn't entirely sure, either. The only thing he knew was Brand was stabbed and bleeding, and Hugo needed to do something.

A man dropped to his knees across from Hugo and prodded Brand's abdomen. When Hugo shoved at his questing fingers, the man said, "It's okay, I'm a nurse. I can help him."

None of that made any real sense until Hugo got a better look at the man's face. The coffee delivery roommate from the night Hugo had been arrested. Jo-something, he didn't remember. The nurse yanked his own shirt off and wound it around the edges of the bottle, where Brand's belly oozed blood.

Someone else was nearby and talking on a cell phone, but Hugo didn't pay attention to who. All he could do was hold Brand's hand and stay present, willing Brand to be okay. To breathe and focus and be fucking okay.

"An ambulance is on the way," the other voice said. Hugo finally looked up. Right at Sheriff McBride. Had the pair been at the Roost together? Just passing by? Hugo honestly didn't care, he was simply grateful for the help. "What happened?"

"Buck attacked me first." Hugo couldn't properly explain the encounter with Brand watching him so helplessly he kind of wanted to cry. "He threatened me with that busted bottle. Brand got in the middle. Buck stabbed him."

"Are you wounded?" the nurse asked. "You've got blood on you."

"My hand." And his hand would heal just fine. "I'm okay, just help Brand, please."

"An ambulance is coming, you sit tight. Talk to your friend." The nurse checked Brand's pulse while keeping steady pressure around the stab wound.

Hugo couldn't look at it, terrified of what that jagged glass might have done to Brand's insides. And all for Hugo. "You saved me, you big hero," Hugo whispered. "You didn't have to do that."

"Sure did." Brand grimaced, the hand in Hugo's squeezing tight. "Never gonna let that bastard hurt you again. Promised."

"What are you even doing here?"

"Talked to Ramie after fireworks. Said you'd parked here. Took a chance. Missed you."

"Me, too. Right now, you just focus on getting better. The rest will sort itself out."

"Okay."

They'd amassed quite a few gawkers. McBride had rolled Buck onto his side and handcuffed him, and Buck seemed to be waking up. People whispered among themselves but Hugo didn't care. All he could do was sit there and hold Brand's hand, silently praying he was going to be all right.

The ambulance seemed to take forever to arrive. The nurse moved away, giving the paramedics room to do their thing. Then the nurse gently urged Hugo to the side. "They'll take care of him," he said. "Let them work."

"I want to go with him. To the hospital."

"Of course."

"I'll need an official statement from you, Mr. Turner," McBride said. "But I think it can wait until morning."

"Thank you, sir." Hugo hated being grateful to the man for anything, but he'd have had a fit if anyone tried to separate him from Brand right now. And the sheriff seemed to believe Hugo's version of the fight. "Buck attacked me with no provocation, assaulted me, and he practically admitted to planting Elmer's coins in my trailer to set me up."

McBride quirked an eyebrow. "Interesting. I'll be sure to ask Mr. Archer about that when he isn't quite so stunned stupid and drunk. He'll definitely be spending the night in my holding cell."

"Good." He was a fucking menace and needed to be off the street.

Hugo didn't even think to call Brand's dad until they were in the ambulance, tearing down the highway toward the county hospital. He called Wayne's cell first, unsure if the family would be home yet or not, and Wayne picked up after only a few rings. Hugo tried to explain what had happened, but he kept choking on the words, his eyes stinging and throat closing. Wayne seemed to get the gist of it, though, and promised to meet him in the emergency room.

The ER was quiet when they arrived and then Brand was lost to him. A kind nurse took Hugo to a sink so he could wash his bloody hands. She applied a bandage to his middle finger, which had the worst cut, and then gave him an ice pack for his bruised knuckles. He paced the waiting room, unable to settle. Someone came out and said they were taking Brand up to surgery to repair something, he wasn't entirely sure. His brain was a mess of static, but he did remember where they said to go to wait.

Wayne, Rose, Rem, Leann, and Sage all stormed the waiting room as a family—maybe they'd all been together for the fireworks?—and Hugo let Rose hug him. Sage looked like she'd been crying, but everyone else seemed ready to do battle on Brand's behalf. But there was no enemy to fight here, only a lot of time to wait.

He tried to explain the fight more fully as their unit moved to the surgical waiting room. His own part in goading Buck, Buck attacking him, then threatening him with the broken bottle. Brand coming to his rescue. The sheriff and the nurse helping.

"Josiah Sheridan," Wayne said. "He's one of those traveling caregivers. Helped nurse Mrs. Haggerty last fall when she busted her hip. He's good people."

"I'm just glad he was there tonight." Hugo needed to thank him personally at some point. After he found out Brand was okay. "I'm so sorry Brand was hurt. I never wanted him to get hurt because of me."

"He got hurt because he cares about you." Wayne's words were conversational, rather than accusatory, and it gave Hugo a sliver of hope that he might come around to the idea of Brand being bi. And with Hugo. Only a sliver, though, because the poor man might simply be in shock and not thinking clearly. Then Wayne shocked the hell out of him by adding, "You're part of the family, Hugo."

"Should someone call Colt?" Rem asked. "Shouldn't he know what's going on?"

"We'll call him when we know something about Brand," Wayne said. "No sense in him worrying when he's so far away."

"Okay."

They haunted the waiting room for what felt like an eternity of pacing and wondering, until a tall man in scrubs approached their group. "The bottle nicked part of his large intestine," the doctor said. "Which is why we had to operate. We repaired the damage and stitched up his other wounds. He's been given antibiotics to prevent any sort of infection. With a couple weeks' rest, he should be fine."

Hugo sank into the nearest chair and dropped his face into his palms. Brand would be okay. He'd hate the idea of taking a few weeks off to recover but Hugo would tie him to his bed to keep Brand from overexerting while he healed. Rem sat next to him and slung an arm across Hugo's shoulders. Hugo side-hugged his friend, both of them trembling slightly from relief and joy. The sisters were hugging their mom. Wayne spoke to the doctor for a few more minutes before the doctor left.

"Brand will be in Recovery for about an hour," Wayne said. "Once he's in a regular room, we can see him. But only briefly, since it's way past visiting hours."

"He is one lucky son of a bitch," Rem said.

"God was watching over my boy tonight." Wayne briefly met Hugo's eyes. "He was looking over all of us. If y'all can excuse me, I'll call Colt and let him know what's going on." He moved to the other side of the waiting room.

It took forever for a nurse to collect them and lead them to Brand's room. One at a time, first the parents, and then the siblings, went inside to see Brand for a minute or two, mostly to reassure themselves that Brand was alive and well. Hugo went last, his insides squirrely. They hadn't seen Brand bloody and broken, but he had.

Brand smiled so brightly at him that Hugo's entire body wanted to collapse into a grateful heap. Somehow he approached the bed and perched on the side. Brand reached out and Hugo took his hand. Squeezed it, then kissed the knuckles. "You could have gotten yourself killed tonight," he whispered.

"Worth it to save you." His smile was bright, but his voice was brittle and exhausted. "Buck?"

"In custody where he belongs. Don't worry about him tonight. You need to rest and get better."

"Do my best." He looked at Hugo's bruised knuckles. "You okay?"

"I am now. Your dad's been…kind to me all night. Not to say I'm glad you got stabbed or anything, but I think maybe he'll come around to us."

"I hope so. Also realized tonight I didn't care if he did. When I saw Buck threatening you…it wasn't even a choice. I love you, Hugo Turner, and I don't even care who knows."

Warmth spread through Hugo's chest, and he leaned down. Held eye contact. "I love you, too." He brushed his lips over Brand's, sealing their declarations with a gentle kiss. They'd have plenty of time for bigger kisses later. Right now, all that mattered was Brand would recover, they'd declared their love, and they had the strength to face whatever came next.

As long as they did it together.

* * *

Bed rest was the absolute worst thing in the world, and Brand was a terrible patient on his best day, never mind when he had a dozen stitches in his gut and orders to stay still for the first few days at home. While he could stomach peeing in a bottle, he refused to use a bedpan for other business, so he still managed getting up and moving around once a day.

Mom was a gem, bringing him cold drinks and food. His siblings all came by frequently, especially Sage. Rem and Hugo came by together once with beef jerky and Beaver Nuggets from their favorite service plaza, which filled Brand with all kinds of warm memories. He Skyped with Colt a few times, happy to see his big brother's face even over pixels. Dad checked in multiple times a day but they never brought up the bisexual thing, or his romantic relationship with Hugo.

Hugo visited as often as seemed appropriate, since they hadn't come out as a couple to anyone except Dad. Brand treasured the visits. They made his days seem less boring, less dreary. Hugo reminded him of sunshine and fresh air and all the things Brand loved about being outdoors. Sometimes they watched movies together on Brand's office laptop; sometimes all they did was exist together in comfortable silence, holding hands until someone else made the floorboards creak.

Ramie visited him a few times, and so did Jackson. Neither teased him about his hero complex, for which Brand was grateful. He simply enjoyed time with his two best friends (aside from Hugo, of course).

Buck was cooling his heels in county jail for various assault charges against both Brand and Hugo. When Hugo detailed the things Buck had said and done, Brand had wanted to storm down to the jail and beat Buck for daring to assault his boyfriend. Buck had serious issues to work through, but he'd also hurt someone Brand loved, so part of him still wanted the guy to rot. The empathetic part of Brand hoped that, after his next stint in prison, Buck got the help he needed.

Even though Buck never admitted to stealing Elmer's coins and planting them in the trailer, Hugo reported to Brand that Elmer had come by the ranch to apologize for what had happened that night. Hugo had graciously accepted the apology, but had yet to return to the man's house for puzzles or chess. Some hurts took longer to get over, Brand expected.

Josiah stopped by one afternoon to check on him, and Brand expressed his gratitude for Josiah being there that night. His help until the paramedics arrived. "I was in the right place at the right time," Josiah said. "I'm glad you're on the mend."

A kind of sadness seemed to lurk in the young nurse, but Brand didn't ask about it. They were barely acquaintances, much less friends. Josiah did, however, take a peek at his stitches and suggest Brand should be fine for light movements. That got Brand a spot on the couch the next day, so he was able to see and experience more. Mom still hovered, which was fine, and at lunchtime, they picnicked in the living room with Dad, Rem, Hugo, and Jackson.

Brutus was around for it all, too. His faithful, furry friend.

Roughly ten days after the attack, Brand was channel surfing midafternoon when Dad came in the house. Instead of going upstairs or into the kitchen, he sat in the chair next to the sofa Brand was stretched out on.

Dad took his hat off and worried it in his fingers for so long Brand muted the TV.

This is it. This is the conversation.

"I'm sorry it's taken me this long to talk to you," Dad said. "I wanted to be sure of my feelings and not just react from stress."

"Okay." Brand's mouth went dry but he couldn't seem to reach for his lemonade.

"I'd be lying if I said I understood you liking men and women, any more than I understand Colt liking men. I don't understand it, but I also don't have to in order to love my kids."

His heart swelled with relief. "I don't really understand it, either, Dad, it's just who I am. Who I've always been."

"I accept that. You are my son, Brand, and I love you. It kills me to think I could have lost you without us ever having said certain things. That you could have died thinking I hated you, or was disappointed in you. I don't and I'm not. I'm trying. And if you're with Hugo, then I'll try with that, too."

"Thank you." If they were being honest here, Brand might as well go all in. "You know, for a long time after Colt left, I worried I'd always be your second choice as foreman. I worked so hard to prove I was good enough, not only to you but to me, too."

Dad's eyes widened with surprise briefly, before gentling with something that looked a lot like understanding. And love. "You have always been good enough, son. You, Colt, Rem. I'd trust any one of you to run this place when I'm gone, and that's the truth. Because you all love your family and this land."

"I really do. I resented Colt leaving for a long time,

and sometimes I wanted to go back to school and be a teacher. But that's an old dream. My new dream is here. On this land. With Hugo. I love him, Dad. I don't know when I fell in love with him, but I did. I probably should have said something sooner, but I was worried my choices might hurt the ranch."

"Don't you worry about that. The ranch will sort itself out. All I want for my kids is a safe, happy life with a partner who treasures them for the amazing human being they are. If you believe Hugo is that partner for you, then you have my blessing."

"Yeah?" Brand reached out, and Dad squeezed his hand. "Thank you. I don't know if me and Hugo are soul mates, but he makes me happy right now. Happier than I've ever been. I'd jump in front of any jagged bottle for him."

"I feel that way about your mother. But maybe let's cut back on the thrilling heroics and try to live a less eventful life."

"Deal. So, uh, I guess I should tell Mom and the others, huh?"

"Your mother knows. I already told her."

Brand's lips parted. "You did?"

"We've been married nearly forty years, son. I can't keep a secret from her. She's fine about it all, and she's already got a few birthday presents squirreled away in the attic for him. You can tell your brothers and sisters when you're ready."

"Okay." Colt wouldn't care. Rem might be weirded out at first but he'd accepted Colt being gay pretty fast, so that didn't worry him. His sisters did a bit, because both their husbands were quietly homophobic. But he'd deal with it. He'd deal with whatever he had to so he could finally live an authentic life.

He did come out the next day, telling Rem in person and his sisters over the phone. Rem was less surprised than he expected, but he and Shelby were also dealing with a close encounter of the "not pregnant again" kind, so he might not have completely absorbed Brand's news yet. "Dude, Hugo was my friend first," Rem said. "You be good to him, or I'll have to kick your ass. Besides, he's family, right? Now even more officially."

"Yeah, he is."

His sisters were a bit more terse, which was fine. He loved them, and his nieces and nephews, but this was his life, damn it. Time to put himself first for once and really start living it.

As he got used to moving around the house more, he saw less and less of Rem and Dad, and more activity seemed to be happening outside. One of those removable storage pod things showed up near the bunkhouse. Stuff was moved around. No one in the family answered a direct question about it, and Brand could only hope that Dad had finally agreed to let go of some of the junk cluttering up the bunkhouse and barn.

Two weeks after the stabbing, Hugo came into the house with a bright smile on his face and asked if Brand wanted to join him in the bunkhouse for lunch. Eager to get out of the house for a while, Brand accepted the offer. His abdomen was tender but not painful, and they walked slowly. Brand let the warm sunshine bathe his face the entire way, Brutus loping around them like a puppy. Probably happy to see Brand outside the house.

Hugo had made them both simple ham and cheese sandwiches, plus store-bought coleslaw, and Brand loved everything about it. They ate at the small dinette set, and Brand couldn't help glancing at the closed door of the second bedroom, which had once been all storage. Was it finally empty? He didn't ask, though, and downed his lunch with big gulps of iced tea.

Once they were finished, Hugo placed both hands flat on the table. "So your dad and I have been talking. About us. You and me, not me and him."

"I figured that. What about us?"

"Space and privacy. I mean, I've got this whole bunkhouse, and you still live with your parents, but there's a good solution to that, so we've been working a bit."

"I noticed." Brand didn't know what to make of the smile threatening the corners of Hugo's mouth. "What'd you do?"

"Made space." Hugo rose and held out his hand. Brand allowed himself to be pulled up and led to the second-bedroom door. "You don't have to say yes or no right away, but this is an option for us. With your parents' blessing." He pushed open the door.

Three sets of bunked beds and three trunks were the only things left in the dust-free room. The ample space surprised Brand, because he remembered this room being full of random junk, collected over decades. It looked exactly the same as the other bedroom, which confused Brand. "I don't understand."

"Choices, Brand. If you wanna move out of your parents' house and be more independent, then this room can be your office. The other room? Our bedroom. We can swap the bunks out for a regular bed. Make this place our home."

Brand stared at Hugo, shocked to his core by the offer. While he hadn't expected to live with his parents forever, he'd never had an opportunity to move out that made sense—until now. Sure, he'd still be living within a hundred feet of his childhood home, but he'd have four walls of his own. A house for himself and his boyfriend to make theirs.

A fresh start for them as a couple.

"You wanna live with me?" Brand asked.

"I've wanted to do everything with you since I was sixteen. Maybe I'll never get my blood family back and that's fine. This is my family now. You are my family. Take a chance with me? See where this goes?"

"Okay." He didn't have to think too hard to know this was the right choice. Building a home with Hugo, declaring their love, and putting everything they had into making their relationship work. Brand had earned his father's complete trust in running things, and the ranch was on track for another successful slaughter in a few months, not to mention the wind turbine expansion. They could do this. He knew in his heart they could. "Okay, I'll move in with you."

"Good answer." Hugo draped his arms around Brand's shoulders and nuzzled their noses together. "I love you. But no more getting in front of broken bottles."

"I'll get in between you and anyone who ever tries to hurt you. Promise. Say it again?"

"I love you."

"I love you, too, Hugo."

They kissed, a slow, sensual action that cemented what Brand knew to be true about his life: he was in love and ready to create something completely new within these four walls. There would be challenges, sure, but Brand was prepared to face them. He owed himself, his boyfriend, and his family nothing less.

Brutus barked and chose that moment to barge in through the open front door. He head-butted Brand's thigh, and both men broke apart to laugh and pet the happy dog. "Looks like it's gonna be a threesome," Brand quipped.

Hugo grinned. "I wouldn't have it any other way."

* * * * *

Acknowledgments

This book may never have happened without the support of the Carina Press editorial team, and I am so grateful to be able to explore the world of Woods Ranch and a new cast of characters. So much love and thanks to my editor of many years, Alissa Davis. You are a gem to work with every single time. Thank you to the creative team who dreamed up this new series cover style; it is amazing. I can't wait to see where we go from here.

About the Author

A.M. Arthur has been creating stories in her head since she was a child and scribbling them down nearly as long, in a losing battle to make the fictional voices stop. She credits an early fascination with male friendships (bromance hadn't been coined yet back then) with her later discovery of and subsequent love affair with m/m romance stories. When not exorcising the voices in her head, she can be found in her kitchen, pretending she's an amateur chef and trying to not poison herself or others with her cuisine experiments. A.M. Arthur's work is available from Carina Press, SMP Swerve, and Briggs-King Books.

Contact her at am_arthur@yahoo.com with your cooking tips (or book comments).

Welcome to Clean Slate Ranch: Home of tight jeans, cowboy boots, and rough trails. For some men, it's a fantasy come true.

Keep reading for an excerpt from **Wild Trail** *by A.M. Arthur*

Chapter One

"How come you look like you stepped barefoot on a horse pie?"

"Dunno, how come you smell like one?" Mack Garrett replied to his best friend. He raised his head, not at all surprised to see Reyes Caldero standing in the open doorway of Mack's small office. Reyes wore heavy boots and stomped around in them in a way that told you the man was coming long before he appeared.

"Looking over the roster for this week's guests." Mack held up the tablet with said roster on it, then pulled a face. He opened his mouth, but Reyes cut him off.

"Oh no, you're not," Reyes said. He stalked over to the desk. "I know you've got more responsibilities now, but don't you dare say you aren't coming out tonight."

Mack sighed, unsurprised Reyes had read him so well. Mack and their other best friend, Colt, had a tradition of going clubbing in San Francisco on Saturday night, looking for fast and dirty hookups. Reyes accompanied them on occasion, usually to drink and dance and let off steam. "I really shouldn't go into the city."

"Yes, you should, especially since you're the one who convinced me to go with you and Colt this time."

He knuckled Mack hard in the shoulder. "You are not leaving me alone to go clubbing with that man."

Mack couldn't help chuckling at the mental image of the more reserved, introverted Reyes clubbing alone with their excitable, flirts-with-everyone friend Colt Woods. "I need to make sure everything is ready for the new guests tomorrow."

"You've got hours to do that, my friend. Besides, maybe you'll run into your last hookup, the guy you said had a cowboy fetish and knew how to deep throat."

"Not interested in repeats, you know that." As much as Mack had enjoyed that particular encounter, he wasn't looking to date. And he absolutely wasn't interested in a new relationship, not after his last one ended with Mack's heart shattered.

Reyes nodded with understanding. "No repeats, but at least come out to dance. Saturday night is the only time we're not on call for guests and are allowed off the ranch grounds for fun and thrills."

"Says the guy who'd rather spend his Saturday reading a book."

"I like books better than people."

True enough. Reyes only occasionally dated—both men and women—and he'd never been a big fan of random hookups. He'd never come out and identified as bi, but Reyes also wasn't a big fan of labels. He seemed content enough in his solitary lifestyle, and that was good enough for Mack.

"What if I help you finish your work?" Reyes asked. "Tell me about the new guests."

"We've got a bridal party."

Reyes let out an exaggerated groan as he leaned against the doorframe. He was one of the most easygoing cowboys on the ranch, and even he found them stressful. Bridal parties at the dude ranch were rare, but they often tended to be the neediest and most disruptive because of their size.

"You think I can still switch my week off with Slater?" Reyes asked.

Mack grunted. "Doubtful. Slater bolted the second it hit three o'clock, and he's had an hour to make his getaway. He's probably in San Jose by now."

"Damn it."

"Chill out, pal, it's not that bad. This one is only five people."

"Really? Seems small. Our last bridal party was eighteen people."

"Trust me, I haven't forgotten." While Mack had enjoyed the novelty of the couple being gay, their friends had been high-strung and extremely anti-dirt. And dirt was impossible to avoid on a ranch in Northern California. "Maybe it's going to be a small wedding."

Mack glanced at his tablet and the list of names. "One woman and four guys. The reservation was placed by the Best Person to the bride, a Wes Bentley."

Reyes frowned. "Like the actor Wes Bentley?"

"Who?"

"Seriously? *American Beauty.* How can you not remember his eyes?"

Mack thought back to the film in question, which he'd seen once, in the theater. "The daughter's creepy boyfriend who filmed plastic bags blowing in the wind?"

Reyes rolled his eyes. "You have absolutely no taste in movies."

"Yes, I know, you've been telling me that since we were fourteen."

"You said *Pulp Fiction* was terrible and overrated."

"It is." Mack had wanted to set fire to that VHS after Reyes forced him through the film.

Reyes grunted. "You were mad that *D2: The Mighty Ducks* didn't get an Oscar nomination. Your film taste carries no weight with me. Ever."

Mack laughed at the familiar rebuttal. At fourteen, he'd been too busy obsessing over the male cast of a teen hockey comedy to really care about art films or cinematic storytelling breakthroughs. He'd wanted to watch Joshua Jackson ice skate. He still kind of did. The actor had barely aged a day since *Dawson's Creek*.

"Anyway," Mack said, "no, I doubt the Wes Bentley who made the reservation is the actor, but I guess we'll find out in the morning."

"True. How many guests total?"

"Sixteen, so almost a full house, and one of them's a family."

Figuring out the rooming arrangements wasn't usually Mack's job, but he'd been taking more responsibilities to help his aging grandfather work less and enjoy his ranch a little bit more. Arthur Garrett was a proud man, and even though he'd never admit out loud that he was slowing down as he neared his seventy-eighth birthday, his age and newfound forgetfulness worried Mack. After all, Arthur was the only blood family Mack had left.

Reyes had been family ever since they were twelve years old and jointly put cherry bombs in the girl's bathroom toilets at school. Mack's other best friend, Colt, had been in his life far fewer years, but he was family, too. Within the same six-month time period, each man had quit his previous career and moved to the ranch to find…something. Something new.

And to start over, away from the pain in their pasts.

Mack was still getting used to figuring out the sleeping arrangements for guests. He was in charge of overseeing the horses, guest interaction with horses and the camping trips. Simple things. Putting warm bodies into rooms in a way that made sense didn't come naturally to him, so he waved Reyes over.

"Tell me how this looks," he said, handing him the tablet.

Reyes scanned the rooms and the names attached, which was linked to the guest registration information that asked: Are you comfortable sharing a room with a stranger of the same or opposite sex? Other variations of the question gave Mack enough information to guess. The second floor of the guesthouse had four four-bunk rooms, each with a private bathroom. Sometimes strangers ended up bunking together—which also meant every other week, someone had an issue on arrival day and bunks had to be switched around.

Arthur had always rolled his eyes and muttered about tourists being coddled.

"No, this looks good," Reyes replied. "The bride said she didn't mind sharing with strangers, so putting her into a four-bunk room with the three single ladies is good. It all looks good."

"Always looks good on paper."

"Or pixels."

"Whatever." Mack took the tablet back. "Food delivery here yet?"

"Truck pulled up a few minutes ago. It's actually what I came to tell you. Arthur, uh, put the order in wrong."

Mack groaned. "Shit, what are we missing?"

"We're light on flour, eggs and bacon."

All breakfast staples for the guesthouse kitchen. "Great."

Every week, Arthur placed a food order for the next week's guests, and the food was trucked over Saturday afternoon. Arthur had been placing the order for years, and it was another weekly ranch task he was hanging on to tightly with his wrinkled, arthritic fingers. But this was the third mistake in four months.

He followed Reyes out of the barn and into bright May sunshine that had him squinting the whole hundred yard walk to the guesthouse. Their usual delivery guy, Juno, was standing by his truck talking to their cook, Patrice, and they both went perfectly still at Mack's approach. Mack was well aware that his squint made him look perpetually pissed off, but there wasn't much he could do. It was the only face he had.

"I'm so sorry," Juno said as soon as he was within earshot.

"It's not your fault," Mack replied, trying to put the guy at ease. He looked like he was ready to jump out of his skin. "Give me your list."

Juno handed over a paper printout from the grocery store that handled their business. Arthur preferred dealing locally, so Mack had to be nice and fix this without accusing anyone—not his best act. Mack logged into the business records and found their copy of Arthur's order. They matched.

"Our mistake," Mack said, handing the list back. "Go

ahead and accept the delivery, Patrice. Figure out the difference. I'll run into town and buy what you need."

"Bless you," Patrice said. A genuinely sweet lady, Patrice had been on the ranch for decades. She prepared every meal, kept the rooms clean, and generally doted over the guests, especially the children.

Juno and Patrice went off to restock the kitchen pantry.

Mack pivoted one-eighty to stare at the main house. The last original building on the property, the hundred-and-fifty-year-old single-story ranch home looked pretty good under a new coat of paint. Its wide front porch no longer sagged, thanks to Colt's handiness with a hammer and nails.

"You gonna tell Arthur?" Reyes asked.

"I have to. He'll wonder about the in-town credit card purchase if I don't."

"How do you think he'll react?"

"He'll brush it off as a one-time problem, like he always does."

"You think Arthur would be more receptive to it coming from Judson?" Reyes asked, spookily following along on Mack's silent train of thought. Twenty-four years of friendship did that.

"I doubt it matters who tells him. Once is a mistake. Twice is something to watch. Three times is a pattern and potentially a problem."

"Yeah."

"You gonna come into town with me for the extra supplies?"

Reyes shrugged. "Why not? We'll get it done so you don't have an excuse not to come into San Francisco with me and Colt."

Patrice came outside with a handwritten list. "Here you go, hon."

"Thanks." Mack stuffed it in his pocket. "I'll text Judson about the grocery trip, and then we'll get going. I can talk to Arthur later."

"Good luck with that chat," Reyes said.

Mack felt kind of bad about buying out the store's entire stock of bacon, but it was a breakfast staple at Patrice's table—both the one she set in the main dining room for guests, and the smaller buffet she provided for the ranch hands in the back room. This was why they ordered ahead of time: so the store's owner could fill their needs without depriving his own customers.

Oh well.

One of the stock boys brought boxes out of the backroom to use for the groceries, instead of wasting a bunch of plastic bags. Reyes bought himself a bag of barbecue potato chips, which had been a favorite of his since forever. Mack studiously avoided the ice cream aisle. Ice cream always reminded him of Geoff, and he didn't need to get depressed on his Saturday night off.

He and Reyes packed up the bed of the ranch's pickup truck with their supplies, then puttered back through town. Garrett had a meager population of five thousand, give or take, and had been settled during the gold rush.

Mack hadn't even known the town existed until about ten years ago, and now he couldn't imagine leaving. He loved knowing more about his roots, and he loved this old, dilapidated town.

The truck ambled through the worn downtown, past town limits, to where Mack could safely press on the gas. Their police force was tiny, but they gave out tickets for anything they could in order to keep funding their own jobs. Their town barely kept afloat year after year, as the population continued to dwindle. Arthur had long lamented he couldn't do more to drive tourists into Garrett itself.

"Stop it," Reyes said.

"Stop what?" Mack retorted. "Driving? We don't want the bacon to cook in the sun."

"Jackass. It isn't your job to save this town, and you know it."

"Maybe, maybe not. There's a lot of my family history here, buried on this land."

"Even so, worry about the ranch first. You still gotta talk to Arthur about the supply order snafu."

Mack grunted. A small part of him hoped Judson had taken care of that chore, but he'd yet to get a text about it. Mack would probably end up confronting his grandfather himself, and that would suck. He wasn't afraid of confrontation. Hell, Mack had been Los Angeles County SWAT for four years. No, he was more afraid of the emotional damage this might do. Reminding an old man he was just getting older.

He parked in front of the guesthouse. Reyes and Patrice helped him unload the truck and store the supplies in the kitchen's industrial walk-in. When they finished, Reyes took the empty boxes over to the garbage shed—the place they hid their garbage and recycling containers so they didn't kill the feel of the ranch, or attract unwanted pests. Behind the shed was also a compost pile for food scraps. The ranch made extra cash for the horse rescue by turning the compost into a nice fertilizer to sell to town residents. The smell stayed downwind of the guesthouse, so it had never been an issue.

Not that it should be. It was a ranch. The place smelled like horses and dirt.

Mack would never forget the guest two summers ago who'd carried a bottle of air freshener with him everywhere the first day, until he tried spraying it around the horses. After that, Mack banned its use to the guesthouse.

He moved the pickup to its usual spot east of the main house, next to Judson's personal vehicle, and the garage that housed four ATVs that the staff had free range to use.

"Mack!" Arthur's voice dragged his attention to the front porch. He stood at the top step in his ever-present denim overalls, the purple undershirt making his white hair and beard stand out even more.

A widower from a young age, Arthur had served in the Army for a lot of years, before turning a struggling cattle ranch into a successful vacation spot and horse rescue. And while no one was getting rich working here, he took care of his staff. But he was also aging, and sooner or later, he'd have to retire from the business end of things and turn control over to his general manager and foreman, Judson Marvel.

"Yes, sir." Mack strode over to the porch, shoulders straight.

"You got the sleeping arrangements done for tomorrow?"

"A while ago. I posted it so you could take a peek, but Reyes double-checked me. It's good."

"Excellent. Food delivery come okay?"

Mack stifled a sigh; Judson hadn't talked to him. "It came, but we had a slight hiccup. You under-ordered again. Three staples."

"Well, shit." Arthur frowned. "You checked—"

"I checked your original order against the one Juno had on him. They matched. Reyes and I went into town a bit ago to get what extra Patrice needed. You'll see the charge on the business card."

"I'm sorry about that. Honest mistake."

"On flour, bacon and eggs that you've been ordering for ten years?"

Arthur's shoulders slumped. Mack loved his grandfather and hated seeing him upset, but this was about the business. Arthur's business, and they both had to protect it.

"We fixed it, but this is the third incident in four months," Mack said. "This coming week, just let me or Judson double-check you before you send the order over. We all need a second set of eyes sometimes. Just like I had Reyes double-check me today."

"Makes good sense. Better for business."

"And I think the store will appreciate it. I bought out all of their bacon."

Arthur's eyes lit up with silent laughter. "Hopefully no one in town wants a BLT for dinner tonight."

"They would be shit out of luck."

"How's our new batch of guests look?" Arthur descended the four wood steps to stand next to Mack. They had similar heights and builds, and some folks swore they saw Arthur in Mack, but Mack never could.

"Not too bad. Married couple, small family, two groups of friends and a bridal party. Sixteen total."

"Good, good. You and Colt going out tonight?"

The abrupt conversation shift startled Mack. He'd come out to Arthur years ago, right after Arthur came out to him—gay his entire life, but hiding it for decades until he said fuck it, I'm out. Hence his purple T-shirts and the rainbow flag proudly displayed on their flagpoles each day next to the American flag and the California state flag. The Clean Slate Ranch was gay-friendly and proud of it.

"Yeah," Mack replied. "Reyes is coming out for a change."

"You're never going to meet someone if all you ever do is visit bars and dance clubs."

Mack shrugged. "I don't want to meet anyone right now."

"Hmm. Maybe, maybe not. Why don't you try those dating apps on your phone?"

"What's with the sudden urge to marry me off?" That came out with more anger than necessary. "Sorry, I just… I'm not ready."

"It's been nearly five years, son."

"I know how long it's been, believe me." Long enough that he could think about Geoff without his heart breaking wide-open, but not long enough that he was ready to risk his heart a second time. Losing Geoff had hurt too damned much.

Arthur sighed. "Why don't you come have dinner at the house with me and Judson tonight? Reyes and Colt, too." Also a widower, Judson was the only person who lived in the main house with Arthur. A row of two-man cabins fifty yards north of the house was where the hands lived.

Mack could have had a cabin to himself, but he genuinely didn't mind sharing with Reyes. He was quiet, tidy, and he'd seemed to really need the companionship when he first moved to the ranch, only a few months after Mack. "Sure, why not?" he replied. "You cooking?" Silly question, because if Arthur loved anything more than his horses, it was cooking. Even if his recipes were pretty basic.

"Certainly. I've had a roast in the slow cooker all day."

Mack sniffed the air, but couldn't detect the scent of cooking meat over the rest of the odors of the ranch. "Mashed potatoes?"

"Of course. What kind of monster do you think I am?"

"Just checking." And teasing. Arthur was a tried-and-true meat and potatoes man. Where there was one, there was the other. "I'll see you around six, then?"

"Six it is."

"Cool. I have to get a few more things ready for tomorrow's check-in. See you in a while."

Mack strode toward the tourist barn and his office. Most of his work for tomorrow was finished, so he bypassed the office and walked down two stalls to his personal horse, Tude. A paint mare with several ugly scars on her flanks, thanks to a brutal previous owner, she'd come into Arthur's care around the same time as Mack. Mack had fallen in love with the high-strung horse, renamed her Attitude, Tude for short, and Arthur had helped him retrain her.

She nickered at his presence, her big head rising over the stall's gate. Mack held up a cube of sugar that she greedily picked up with her lips. He rubbed a hand over her smooth nose, up her long forehead. She had big brown eyes that simultaneously said "I like you" and "I dare you." Attitude.

"What do I need a boyfriend for when I've got you,

lady?" Mack asked softly, the only sounds in the barn the quiet movements of the other horses.

Tude didn't have an answer for him.

Don't miss Wild Trail, *available now wherever ebooks are sold*

www.CarinaPress.com